Please turn to the back of the
book for a conversation between
Mary Daheim and Emma Lord

Praise for Mary Daheim and her
Emma Lord mysteries

THE ALPINE ADVOCATE
"An intriguing mystery novel."
—M. K. WREN

THE ALPINE BETRAYAL
"Editor-publisher Emma Lord finds out that
running a small-town newspaper is worse than
nutty—it's downright dangerous. Readers will
take great pleasu____ ____ ____ Daheim's new
mystery."
—CA____

THE A____
"If you like cozy myst____ ____ ____ ____ry
Daheim's Alpine series. . . . Recommended."
—*The Snooper*

THE ALPINE DECOY
"[A] fabulous series ... Fine examples of the
traditional, domestic mystery."
—*Mystery Lovers Bookshop News*

*Please turn the page
for more reviews. . . .*

THE ALPINE FURY
"An excellent small-town background, a smoothly readable style, a sufficiently complex plot involving a local family bank, and some well-realized characters."
—*Ellery Queen's Mystery Magazine*

THE ALPINE GAMBLE
"Scintillating. If you haven't visited Alpine yet, it would be a good gamble to give this one a try."
—*The Armchair Detective*

THE ALPINE ICON
"Very funny."
—*The Seattle Times*

By Mary Daheim
Published by The Ballantine Publishing Group

THE
ALPINE
MENACE

Mary Daheim

FAWCETT BOOKS • NEW YORK

A Fawcett Book
Published by The Ballantine Publishing Group
Copyright © 2000 by Mary Daheim

All rights reserved under International and Pan-American Copyright Conventions. Published in the United States by The Ballantine Publishing Group, a division of Random House, Inc., New York, and simultaneously in Canada by Random House of Canada Limited, Toronto.

Fawcett is a registered trademark and the Fawcett colophon is a trademark of Random House, Inc.

www.randomhouse.com/BB/

Library of Congress Card Number: 00-103093

ISBN 0-345-42124-8

Manufactured in the United States of America

First Edition: October 2000

10 9 8 7 6 5 4 3 2 1

Chapter One

THE LAST TIME I saw my cousin Ronnie, he was half of a sack race at a family picnic. He was a clumsy kid, and the leg that was tied to my brother, Ben, managed to trip them both, so that they finished dead last. I never imagined that the next time I saw Ronnie he'd be in the King County Jail on a homicide charge.

The Ronnie Mallett I remembered from the gathering at Seattle's Woodland Park was nine or ten, an undersized, unremarkable boy except for his cheerful disposition. I'd been entering my junior year at the University of Washington and felt the natural superiority that comes from age and the use of good grammar. Maybe that's the thing I remembered best about Ronnie: He said *ain't* a lot.

"I ain't guilty, Emma," Ronnie said now, his thin face wearing an earnest expression that didn't quite suit him. "Hey, why would I kill Carol? I was nuts about her."

Carol Stokes was his girlfriend, a thirty-four-year-old woman who had been found strangled in the living room of her one-bedroom apartment in Seattle's Greenwood district. Obviously, I was supposed to say something reassuring, such as, "Of course you didn't, Ronnie."

But I couldn't and didn't. I hadn't seen my cousin in over twenty-five years. For all I knew, he could be a serial killer.

"I'm not sure I can be of much help," I said, substituting candor for comfort. "I'm not exactly sure why you asked me to come down from Alpine to see you here."

Ronnie's knuckles whitened as he gripped the edge of the table that separated us. We weren't more than three feet away from each other, yet I felt the distance might as well have been the eighty-plus miles between Alpine and Seattle. The visitors' area was painted a pale blue, about the color of Ronnie's eyes, and just about as lifeless. My chair was hard and uncomfortable; so was Ronnie's, I supposed. The difference was that after I stood up, I could leave the building.

"Like I said," Ronnie explained, "a coupla months ago Carol told me you were some kind of detective. See, she was raised in Alpine, but moved out when she was just a kid."

The original message I'd received from Ronnie's court-appointed lawyer two days earlier had asked me to visit my cousin in jail because I was an investigator. I was puzzled, since my job as editor and publisher of *The Alpine Advocate* didn't seem to qualify.

"I'm not a detective," I said firmly. "I do some investigative reporting for the weekly newspaper I own in Alpine."

"Carol said you caught a couple of killers," Ronnie said in an accusing tone.

"Not exactly." An editor, a publisher, a reporter in a small town can get caught up in a case when local law enforcement is hampered by size and budget. Certainly in the ten years since I'd bought the paper, I'd helped out with some homicide investigations. Digging for information was an occupational necessity. But I was no sleuth. "Carol must have misunderstood. My main job is to report the stories after they happen."

Ronnie's lean face fell. I knew he was in his mid-thirties, but he looked younger, if pinched and hollow-eyed. His dull blond hair fell over his high forehead, his upper lip disappeared when he smiled, and his eyebrows didn't quite match. Ronnie's overall appearance was that of a very old little boy.

I could see no family resemblance. Ronnie was fair, while I was dark-haired and dark-eyed. His narrow face with its ferretlike features was the flip side of my softer, more rounded contours. Maybe one of us had been a changeling.

"What'll I do?" Ronnie asked in a helpless voice.

"You've got a lawyer," I pointed out.

Ronnie shook his head. "He can't do me much good. Alvin's kinda young and real busy."

On the phone, Alvin Sternoff had sounded as if he was straight out of law school and maybe had finished in the bottom 10 percent of his class. He hadn't offered much advice on how I could help Ronnie.

"What do you want me to do?" I asked my cousin, and immediately cursed the soft heart that matched my even softer brain.

Ronnie leaned back in the plastic chair and gave me his guileless smile. "Find out who really killed Carol," he said, " 'cause I ain't guilty."

"Do you believe him?" Vida Runkel asked the following Monday morning as I stood in *The Advocate*'s newsroom drinking coffee.

"I don't know," I said with a shake of my head. "The problem is, I don't know Ronnie. The last time I saw him, he was just a kid, and I don't think our families had gotten together more than four or five times before that. My parents thought that his parents were—as my mother put it—'party people.' I translated that as 'too dumb to be hippies.' "

"My, my," Vida said, setting down her mug of hot water and adjusting the pinwheel straw hat that sat at a peculiar angle atop her unruly gray curls. "And you say his girlfriend—the victim—came from Alpine?"

The local angle intrigued Vida more than Ronnie or the murder. My House and Home editor is so thoroughly centered in the town of her birth that occasionally she has trouble accepting events that happen elsewhere as important or even real. Indeed, even World War II had been reduced in Vida's mind to how she had traipsed along with her father on his air-raid-warden duties and looked into the windows of those foolish enough to leave the lights on and their shades pulled up. Snooping into other people's homes was a habit that she had never outgrown.

"Yes. Carol Stokes. Don't tell me you know her?" I was aghast. Vida knew everybody in Alpine, going back to the generations before her birth some sixty-odd years ago.

She grimaced. "Honestly, I can't say that I do. Carol Stokes." She said the name as if it were an incantation. "She must have left town at an early age and married. Carol Stokes," she repeated. "Carol . . . Carol . . . Carol . . ." Obviously, Vida was reaching into the past, taking inventory of every Carol who had walked Alpine's steep streets on the face of Tonga Ridge. "Ah," she exclaimed at last, "Carol Nerstad! Now I remember!" Her broad face beamed in triumph.

"Nerstad?" The name was unfamiliar.

Vida nodded, the straw hat swaying dangerously. "Her parents died quite young, and Carol's brother, Charles, I think, is his name, moved to California. Burl, the father, was killed in the woods, and Marvela, the mother, had cancer. A shame, of course, though they were a bit odd."

I refrained from asking Vida how odd. In her critical mind, the word could have described a penchant for putting gravy on gingerbread or having a physical relationship with the family pet.

"Goodness," Vida mused, "that must have been almost twenty years ago. As I recall, Carol left town under a cloud, as we used to say."

My ad manager, Leo Walsh, turned away from his computer screen. "You mean she got knocked up?"

Vida scowled at Leo. "Mind your language. Yes, I believe she was pregnant. One of the Erickson boys. Or was it a Tolberg?" She stopped and stared at me through her red-framed glasses. "Carol Nerstad was murdered? Heavens, that's a page-one story! Why didn't you say so, Emma?"

My family problem had finally landed in Vida's lap. "Because I didn't know Carol was from here until I saw Ronnie when I was in Seattle over the weekend. Yes, it is a story for *The Advocate,* even though the actual murder happened a couple of weeks ago."

Vida was agog. "What about services? Where was Carol buried? Who handled the arrangements?" She slapped at her visitors' chair. "Do sit and stop prowling around like a cat on a griddle. Why didn't we get a notice from the funeral home in Seattle?"

With a sigh, I sat down next to Vida's desk. "I haven't any idea about the burial. You know perfectly well that we don't always get alerted when a former resident dies. If my cousin had anything to do with it, he probably didn't even mention where Carol was born. I'm not sure he knows where *he* was born."

"But you do," Vida said, looking as if she was about to pounce on me.

"Yes, he was born in Seattle." I stared at Vida. "So what?"

"Family. Kin. Ties. Really, Emma," she said in reproach, "except for your parents and your brother, Ben, you don't speak much about your relatives. Frankly, I've always found that odd."

Leo chuckled. "I find it a damned good thing. The

trouble with you, Duchess," he went on, using the nick-
name Vida despised, "is you've got so many relatives and
in-laws and shirttail relations that nobody can keep them
straight."

"I can," Vida snapped. "One of the things that's
wrong with this world is that families don't keep up with
each other. They move here, there, and everywhere like a
bunch of nomads. What are they looking for? Trouble,
mostly. If Carol Nerstad had stayed in Alpine, she
probably wouldn't have gotten herself murdered. Now,"
she continued, her voice quieting, "tell me what happened, Emma."

"I would if I could get a—"

" 'Morning, all," said a deep voice from the doorway
as Scott Chamoud arrived, late as usual. "What's up?"

"The Duchess's dander," Leo replied. "Thanks for
joining us, Scotty. We're having a staff meeting."

My young reporter's limpid brown eyes grew wide.
"We are? Did I forget?"

"No," I managed to get in, "you didn't. Leo's kidding.
But," I added with a meaningful glance at my watch,
"you're late. It's almost eight-thirty."

Scott waved a white paper bag he'd been hiding behind
his back. "I know. It was my turn to stop at the Upper
Crust Bakery. Anyone for fresh doughnuts and some cinnamon twists?"

It was hard to get mad at Scott. He was not only a good
writer, but handsome as hell. I didn't bother to remind
him that he would have been late with or without the
bakery stop.

"I'll take a twist," I said, holding out my hand. Vida,
who is always dieting to no perceptible effect, staunchly
shook her head. Leo snagged a couple of doughnuts before Scott sat down behind his desk.

"Okay," I said, taking a deep breath, then glancing at
Scott. "I'm filling everyone in—I guess—on the recent

murder in Seattle of a young woman who grew up in Alpine and 'left under a cloud.' "

"Pregnant?" Scott asked.

I deferred to Vida, who nodded solemnly. "Anyway," I went on, "she happened to be living with a cousin of mine who I hadn't seen in years. Ronnie Mallett is kind of a loser, and a week ago Friday, the girlfriend—Carol Nerstad Stokes—was found strangled in the apartment they shared. Ronnie doesn't have an alibi, a neighbor overheard them quarreling earlier, and when he was picked up by the cops a few hours later, he looked as if he'd been in a fight. I get the impression that he was a smartmouth when he was interrogated, and not very helpful. Ronnie probably annoyed the detectives, which no doubt made the situation look bad for him. He swears he didn't do it, and he asked me to help him prove it. Or something like that."

"Drink," Vida intoned. "So often at the source."

"Or drugs," Leo said, lighting a cigarette in spite of Vida's usual dagger-eyed look. "Does this Ronnie do drugs?"

"I don't know," I replied. "He seems like the type who'd smoke weed. From what little I saw of him at the jail Saturday, the verb *do* and Ronnie don't seem to have much in common."

"Did he do it?" Scott asked, with that dazzling grin.

"He says he didn't," I answered slowly. "Ronnie claims to have been in a neighborhood bar. Unfortunately, he can't recall which one."

"Drink," Vida repeated. "Didn't I say so?"

"How was the girlfriend strangled?" Leo asked, blowing smoke rings, though fortunately not in Vida's direction.

"With a drapery cord," I said after swallowing a bite of cinnamon twist. "Carol was found by her daughter, who called the police. They were still there when Ronnie staggered home. I guess the daughter has it in for him, at least according to Ronnie."

"A daughter," Vida echoed. "I wonder, now . . . Would she be the child that Carol was carrying when she left Alpine?"

I had no idea. Ronnie hadn't been good at details, and we hadn't been able to spend much time together.

"Why'd he call you," Leo asked, "when you just said you hadn't seen him in years?"

"Good question," I said as Ginny Erlandson, our office manager, came in to refill the coffeepot. "Somewhere along the line, Carol found out I was Ronnie's cousin. She must have had some fairly recent Alpine contact, because she told him—or so he claims—that I was some sort of super-sleuth. Ronnie remembered that, if not much else, and got his attorney to ask me to come see him."

"Lose the guy," Leo advised. "Why get involved with some long-lost cousin who's probably lying through his teeth?"

"Really, Leo," Vida said in disgust, "what a crass attitude. He's kin. Naturally, Emma wants to help."

I blinked at Vida. "I do?"

"Of course," she asserted, joining Ginny at the hot plate and pouring herself more hot water. "He's fighting for his life. How could you reject his plea?"

"I'm not a detective," I declared. "I don't really know the guy. I live in Alpine, not Seattle. Where would I find the time to investigate the case? Vida, you're nuts."

"Nonsense," Vida said calmly. "You'd feel guilty if you turned him down. If he's really innocent, and yet is convicted, you'll never forgive yourself. Besides," she added, her majestic bust thrust forward as she returned to her desk, "I'll help."

I didn't argue with Vida—then. We had a paper to put out. Our pub date is Wednesday, and this was the week before Easter, which meant the paper would double in size because of the extra advertising. That, in turn, meant that we had to have enough editorial copy to balance off the ads. Dutifully, I typed up the story on Carol's murder, relating the facts as I knew them. I left Ronnie's name out of it, referring to him only as Carol's boyfriend and the prime suspect. At least the six inches of copy would help fill the front page.

Not that I was ungrateful for the extra advertising revenue. Contrary to rumor, weekly newspapers aren't a cash cow, at least not *The Advocate*. This would be the first time in my ten-year career as editor and publisher that I'd face advertising competition, a subject that inevitably came up whenever Leo and I talked.

"This Fleetwood guy is supposed to go on air June first," my ad manager announced when he came into my cubbyhole of an office around nine o'clock. "I drove by his shack on the fish hatchery road last night. It looks like they're getting ready to install the hardware. You still good for next Tuesday?"

I glanced at my wall calendar, a promo for Harvey's Hardware and Sporting Goods. Harvey Adcock only used one color photo for the year, almost always a different view of Mount Baldy, looming over Alpine.

"As far as I know," I said. "I suppose I should have met this Spencer Fleetwood sooner."

Leo shrugged. "Why? You've covered the story. One feature interview's enough for a guy who's trying to steal our customer base."

"I don't see how he's going to survive," I remarked. "Heck, I don't see how we're going to survive. There are seven thousand people in this county, and I'm not sure we can support a newspaper and a radio station. How's he going to pay staff?"

"He isn't," Leo replied, lighting another cigarette. "KSKY will be on the air from five until midnight, at least for starters. He'll handle most of the work, maybe use some kids from the community college as interns, and then buy those canned music programs, with a generic host."

"The locals won't like it if they find out their favorite announcer is from Philadelphia," I noted.

Leo shook his head. "There are shows produced in Seattle and Tacoma. Spence, or whatever he calls himself, can get people who know a mountain from a molehill."

I grimaced. "You aren't making me feel better."

Leo's green eyes crinkled at the corners. He was from Southern California, in his mid-fifties, divorced with grown kids, had overcome a problem with the bottle, and found a home at *The Advocate*. In other words, he was a middle-aged cliché, another loser who'd cut his losses.

"I thought," Leo said, his expression droll, "being a journalist, you searched for truth. The truth is, Spencer Fleetwood is a pain in the ass as far as we're concerned. Hell, he asked me if we wanted to exchange ads. You know, quid pro quo."

"Do we?"

"Sure, unless you want to start a blood feud."

"No. There're enough feuds in Alpine as it is," I said, watching Leo exhale and wondering how long I could stay off cigarettes this time. "Tuesday, noon, the ski lodge, right?"

Leo stood up. "Right."

So why did I feel it was wrong?

There were many things wrong with my life, though my car wasn't one of them. But that night, around five-thirty, as I walked out to the two-year-old champagne-colored Lexus parked at the curb, I suffered mixed emotions. The car was a semi-gift from my longtime lover and the father of my only son. Tom Cavanaugh had been in Alpine last December when a crank destroyed my darling Jaguar with a sledgehammer. Since Tom had been staying with me and his middle name is Guilt, he had offered to replace the Jag. I'd resisted. My finely honed independence wouldn't permit such a gift. I'd told Tom it made me feel like a kept woman. Tom had laughed and agreed to a loan arrangement, the terms of which I set down: I'd pay him fifty bucks a month until he married me. Considering how much even a used Lexus costs and Tom's ability to stall, I figured the car would be paid off about the time I was confined to a nursing home.

Thus I wasn't entirely happy with our little agreement. I resented Tom's easy extravagance and my not-so-easy acquiescence. On the other hand, the Jag had been wrecked just before Christmas, and I was broke. The meager insurance money had made me feel a little better, because I'd turned the check over to Tom. But while he guided his daughter through the first stages of single motherhood in San Francisco, I fumed in Alpine. Tom had been a widower for over a year, and we had no definite plans for the future.

The immediate future, however, was another matter and even more vexing. I eased the Lexus along the driveway to my little log house at the edge of the forest and just sat there. In the past few months I'd begun to dread going home. As I drummed my fingers on the pearl-gray steering wheel and watched a pair of crows flap their wings in one of the tall firs that stood behind my house, I found it ironic that I couldn't kill time by listening to the radio. Apparently, I was in some sort of dead zone. The signals from Everett and Seattle got through only on an irregular basis. I was as likely to pick up San Mateo or Spokane as to tune into a regional station. Because of the mountains, reception from out of town was unreliable for most Alpine residents. Which, I had to concede, made an ideal situation for Spencer Fleetwood and KSKY.

Finally, I got out of the car, gritted my teeth, and went into the house. As usual, the living room was strewn with toys, baby clothes, dirty plastic dishes, and tabloid newspapers. Two Siamese cats batted a dirty disposable diaper between them. Amber Ramsey and her baby, Danny, were nowhere to be seen, but I could hear the TV blaring in my son Adam's old room.

The cats, Rheims and Rouen, abandoned the diaper and rushed to rub up against my ankles. Then they each let out that eerie cry that is the breed's call to dinner, among other things. No doubt they hadn't been fed all day. Grimly, I marched into the kitchen—another mess—and opened a fresh can of Friskies Mariner's Catch.

"Poor babies," I murmured, giving each a passing stroke before they got down to business at their dishes by the back door. I'd inherited the cats from a friend, and they were considerably cleaner than my so-called houseguest.

"Amber!" I shouted, going into the little hall that leads to the two bedrooms and the bath, "can you turn that thing down and come out here?"

The sound was lowered slightly, then Amber, carrying five-month-old Danny, wandered into the living room. "Hi," she said without much enthusiasm. "You okay?"

"No," I declared, waving a hand at the debris. "Amber, how many times have I asked you to pick up after yourself and the baby?" Nag, nag. "This place is a wreck." Nagging wasn't my style. "I really don't like coming home to more work after a day at the office." Double and triple nag. I was turning into a battle-ax.

"I was just going to do it," she said, pouting a little. "Danny's been fussy today."

I regarded Danny with a skeptical eye. He looked perfectly happy to me, cheeks ruddy and fists waving mightily. He even laughed when I got closer. Danny was definitely a charmer.

But his mother was not. With no place to stay, Amber and son had landed on my doorstep during a Christmas Eve snowstorm. A runaway at seventeen, Amber had been in search of her father, who had recently moved to Alpine. Dean Ramsey was the new county extension agent and had been in the midst of moving his second family from Oregon. He had promised to take Amber and the grandson in as soon as they were settled.

Then, after New Year's, Amber's stepmother had decided to stay in Salem until the end of school in June. She and Dean didn't want to uproot their two adolescents until it was absolutely necessary. Consequently, Dean still hadn't bought a house, and I was stuck with Amber and Danny.

"Here," Amber said, thrusting Danny at me. "I'll pick up."

I took Danny and backed my way to the sofa. There was barely room to sit, but I was damned if I'd volunteer to clean up after Amber one more time. It had become a ritual—I'd come home, the house would be a mess, I'd chastise Amber, she'd repent, I'd feel sorry for her, then I'd do the work for her. Danny had been sleeping through the night since early March, he took at least one long nap a day, and since Amber obviously wasn't looking for a job, the least she could do was shoulder some of the responsibility in exchange for her free lodging. I wanted to be kind, I wanted to be charitable, but Amber Ramsey was driving me nuts.

"Here's what we'll do," I said, bouncing Danny on my knee. "You keep the house clean every day. I'll go on providing the food." My gorge rose as I said the words. Amber qualified for food stamps, but I'd never benefited. I didn't know what she used them for, and I didn't ask. At least she wasn't trading them for drugs. As far as I could tell.

"Okay," Amber said, giving in so easily that my heart sank. "Does that include dishes?"

"I have a dishwasher," I retorted. "What's so hard?"

Amber paused in putting the collection of tabloids in the basket on the hearth and pushed the dark blonde hair out of her eyes. "You said once you didn't like the way I loaded it."

"You have to have a system," I said. "Just figure out where the plates go, the bowls, the glassware. It's not that difficult."

Amber gave me a truculent look. "You said I did something that made the blades or whatever stop turning."

"You put a two-foot vase in the damned thing, Amber. The blades can't turn with anything that high in the way."

"Oh." She returned to her tasks. "Shall I make your bed, too?"

I looked askance. I didn't know that Amber had ever made the bed that had once belonged to my son. "No. I'll do that. Amber, don't put that dirty diaper in the fireplace."

She regarded me with wide blue eyes. "It's disposable."

"Not by fire. Where's the diaper pail?"

"The cats got in it. I took it outside."

That didn't make much sense, but I didn't ask for an explanation. Danny went on bouncing.

"Do cats really suck the breath?" Amber asked, her expression now worried.

"What?"

"You know—I heard they smell the milk on a baby's breath and then they try to get at it by sucking the breath out of the baby and killing him."

"I don't think that's true," I replied as Danny seemed to rise on my knee and began emitting unpleasant odors. "I think your son needs changing."

"Go ahead," Amber said blithely. "I trust you."

I was saved by the bell, which rang on my phone. Wedging Danny between my hip and the back of the sofa, I turned to grab the receiver.

"Hi, Emma," said a vaguely familiar voice. "It's me. Your cousin Ronnie."

Great. Why not the Green River Killer, asking me out for drinks?

"They let me call you, 'cause you're my next of kin."

Great. Really, really great. "What's happened?" I felt compelled to ask.

"I remembered where I was when Carol got killed."

Great, great, great. "Good," I said. "Did you tell your attorney?"

"Yeah, and he said you should come down as soon as you can to help me out. See, he needs a witness."

"A witness to . . . what?" Danny was trying to escape. Rheims and Rouen had finished dinner and were sitting at my feet. Amber was studying each toy in turn before she put it away in a big plastic basket.

"To where I was," Ronnie replied, sounding as if I were the one being unreasonable.

"You mean . . . I'm supposed to find this witness?"

"Right. You got it. When can you get here?"

Never? "I don't know, Ronnie. Tomorrow is our dead-line for the Wednesday edition. This is Holy Week, and I sort of lie low . . ." I stopped. Ronnie probably didn't know Holy Week from Hell Week. "Really, I've no—"

Ronnie was laughing. "My dance card's open. How about Friday? Hey, got to go." His voice suddenly grew strained. "There's a very big, very . . . nice dude who wants to use the phone. See you soon."

I picked up Danny just before he squirmed off the sofa. I held him at arm's length. I wished I could keep my cousin much farther away.

Chapter Two

SHERIFF MILO DODGE was in love, and it galled me. On this mild Tuesday morning in April, his smile was as bright as the daffodils that bloomed in the concrete planters along Front Street. There was spring in the air and spring in his step. I wanted to avoid him, but I couldn't.

"Emma!" he called, arms outstretched even though he knew damned well I wouldn't hug him. "What's new?"

"Whatever it is, you'll read all about it in tomorrow's *Advocate*," I responded, hoping I didn't sound as sour as I felt.

"I hear Dean Ramsey's finally found a house," the sheriff said, hands now stuffed in the pockets of his regulation jacket. "He made an offer on the McNamara place across the street from me. The McNamaras are moving to Tacoma."

I barely knew the McNamaras, who hadn't stayed long in Alpine, but the news was too good to be true. "Are you sure? Amber hasn't said anything about it."

"I just heard it this morning, before I went to work." Milo was looking over my head, apparently drinking in the soft April air and loving life. "Man, it feels like spring, doesn't it?" He actually sniffed.

"It feels like rain," I said, resorting to my usual perverseness. It's the seventh of April. Unpredictable weather. Thunder-and-lightning weather. Earthquake weather."

Milo chuckled and regarded me with his hazel eyes. "You don't seem very cheerful this morning. How come?"

Dense. The man wasn't stupid, but he sure was dense. Had it occurred to him that since he'd found a new love, I might feel at least a little irked by his uncharacteristically buoyant mood? I had been the one to call a halt to our relationship, hoping we could still be friends. It hadn't worked, not until Milo fell head over heels for Jeannie Clay, Dr. Starr's dental assistant. Maybe I would've been happier for him if Jeannie hadn't been young enough to be his daughter.

"I'm not very cheerful," I admitted, waving at a couple of fellow parishioners from St. Mildred's as they honked and passed on by. I glanced at the courthouse clock down the street. It was almost noon. "You want to eat?"

Milo shook his head. "I can't." Something close to regret passed across his long, homely face. "I've got to meet Jeannie at Harvey's Hardware. She wants to show me the new ten-speed she's looking at."

And a Barbie doll and a Muffy VanderBear, I thought nastily. My reaction was not only mean, but unfair. Jeannie Clay was a very nice young woman, probably not that far from thirty. The trouble was, I wasn't that far from fifty.

"Then I'll catch you later," I said, starting to turn away.

Milo put out a big hand. "Emma—are you pissed?"

"No," I lied. "Why should I be? After we broke up, I always hoped you'd find somebody else." But not a bouncy blond with a twenty-four-inch waist who could be my daughter.

"Good," Milo said, taking the easy, masculine way out. "One of these days, we'll have lunch or drinks, okay?"

"Sure." I forced a smile. "Next week, maybe. After Easter."

The sheriff's lighthearted mood was restored. I crossed the street, headed for the Burger Barn. Carla Steinmetz Talliaferro was coming from the opposite direction, wheeling her four-month-old son, Omar, in a dark blue pram that looked as if it should have had an English nanny at the helm.

I greeted my ex-reporter with a warmth I hadn't always felt when she was working for me. Carla had been diligent, but disorganized and not always accurate. In fact, she had been a bit of a ditz. Now, as a wife and mother as well as the adviser to the student newspaper at the community college, she seemed to have acquired some sense of maturity. Or at least some sense, as Vida would say.

"Omar's crabby today," she announced, the April breeze blowing her long black hair around her shoulders. "I think he's getting his first tooth."

I looked down at Omar Talliaferro, who was as dark as Danny Ramsey was fair. "He seems happy now," I noted.

"That's because I'm wheeling him all over town," Carla said with a martyred air. "He likes to be driven in the car, too. Ryan and I are afraid he's getting spoiled."

"That happens," I said, recalling how I'd doted on Adam, some twenty-six years earlier. Unlike Omar, Adam hadn't had a father in the vicinity. I felt I had to make it up to him because Tom Cavanaugh was still married to his neurotic wife, Sandra. "Are you and Ryan and the baby still coming for Easter dinner at my house?"

Carla's hand flew to her cheek. "Gosh! I forgot to tell you, Emma. We can't. Ryan's folks are driving over from Spokane. They can't get enough of Omar."

"That's okay, Carla. Leo and Vida will be there. Scott's having dinner with Kip," I said, referring to Kip Mac-Duff, who kept our plant operations running smoothly.

"I think Kip has a young lady he wants to introduce to Scott."

"One of Kip's castoffs?" Carla said skeptically. "Scott's an incredible hunk. He can do better than that."

I agreed. Scott might not be able to tell time, but his good looks and writing ability were a welcome addition to the newsroom. I parted with Carla and little Omar, heading for the Burger Barn. In recent months, babies seemed to be a new part of my life. It was a bittersweet thought. Adam was in St. Paul, studying to be a priest. My dreams of becoming a grandmother were dead. Maybe that was just as well. Having Danny Ramsey around the house had undermined my maternal longings.

The rest of the day was hectic, as Tuesdays always were. We sent the paper to Kip in the back shop at five-ten. As usual, Scott was late with his front-page story, which called for a special election in June on the location of the new bridge over the Skykomish River. The original choice had been at the east end of town, near Icicle Creek, but after the college was built, there'd been a push to move the site to the west end, by Burl Creek and the campus. The county commissioners had dithered so long that unless the citizenry acted, the bridge wouldn't be needed because we'd all be whizzing around in space capsules.

That night, I asked Amber—who had exerted some effort at housework—if she knew that her father had made an offer on the McNamara house. She was vague about it, adding that she'd probably hear more when she accompanied Dean to Salem for the Easter weekend.

Wednesday was always our brief lull, which was broken after *The Advocate* hit the streets and the mailboxes. The phone calls would start after three-thirty, when our readership had had time to digest my editorials and call in to tell me that I was a two-headed Nazi/Communist/atheist/pope-kissing moron.

Around nine-thirty that evening, after returning from Holy Thursday liturgy at St. Mildred's, I was planning my Easter menu when the phone rang. I froze, wondering if Ronnie Mallett was on my trail again. Then, with a sigh of resignation, I picked up the receiver.

It was Leo Walsh, sending his regrets for Sunday. "I'm leaving for Seattle in just a few minutes," he explained. "My son Brian and his wife are in town for the weekend. Instead of Monday, I'll take tomorrow off for my Easter break, okay?"

Unlike Scott, Leo never missed a deadline. Besides, I was happy for him that he and his three grown children had finally reconciled after his divorce.

"That's great, Leo," I enthused. "I'll tie up any loose ends that come along for you. I'm taking tomorrow afternoon off, and I'll be in late on Monday. See you then."

Despite the cheer in my voice, I felt glum as I replaced the receiver in its cradle. My festive Easter dinner was now down to two, Vida and me. Ordinarily, she would spend the holiday with one of her three daughters, but somehow this year they had all gotten caught in the in-law trap and were celebrating with their husbands' families.

"Dad's picking us up at noon," Amber announced from the doorway into the hall. "Are you sure you won't get lonesome?"

"Huh?" My head snapped up. "No, I'll be fine. Honest." I tried to put some warmth in my smile. "I think it's nice that you're going to get to know your step-mother better."

"She's never been real friendly," Amber said as Danny wiggled in his mother's arms. "I used to spend weekends and holidays with her and Dad after they got married. I didn't know which was worse, my stepmother being so stuck-up, or Mom's creepy husband, Aaron."

I'd heard the complaint many times, and it always

elicited a pang of sympathy. Amber hadn't had it easy. Her parents had split when she was four. They'd both remarried, and had shared custody. But if Dean's second wife had been cold, her mother's new husband had put the make on Amber. She'd run away and ended up in Las Vegas, where she'd been raped and gotten pregnant.

"You're a grown woman now and a mother," I said, not for the first time. "You may never have a mother-daughter relationship with your dad's wife, but you can be friends."

"I hope so," Amber said, trying to hold on to Danny, who was now beginning to cry. "Sometimes I forget what it's like to have a real mom."

I didn't doubt it. I'd only met Amber's mother, Crystal Bird Ramsey Conley, once. It was enough. She'd gotten herself murdered, and for a time I was the prime suspect. Crystal's name could still leave a sour taste in my mouth.

Amber wandered off to put Danny to bed. My glum mood brightened. I'd have the weekend to myself. It would only be the second time since Amber and the baby arrived. They'd gone to Salem in February for a family visit with Dean and the rest of the Ramsey clan.

The next morning, I informed Vida that she and I would be alone for Easter dinner.

"What do you mean?" she demanded, whipping off her glasses. "I thought you were going to Seattle. I assumed dinner was canceled."

I stared. "No. You and I have to eat. Why would I cancel?"

Vida stared back. "But aren't you going to Seattle to help your cousin?"

"No," I said, annoyed. "I never promised any such thing."

Vida put her glasses back on and clucked her tongue. "You can't refuse. I'll go with you."

"Vida . . ."

"Now, now. Isn't there a big Presbyterian church downtown? I can go there Sunday while you attend your services at the cathedral. St. James, isn't it? Where shall we stay? I imagine the city is crowded for the holiday. Nothing too expensive, of course. A motel. We'll share expenses. What time do you want to leave? I can be ready by one o'clock."

My head was spinning. "What about Buck? I thought he was going to be back from Palm Springs Sunday night."

Vida shrugged at the mention of Buck Bardeen, her sometime escort for the past few years. "That was my understanding. But he'll be worn-out, what with Easter brunch with his children and grandchildren and then the flight home and the drive from Sea-Tac. I'll catch up with him Monday night."

Buck, a retired air force colonel, had spent the past month in a time-share condo, soaking up the desert sun and playing golf. Every so often Vida dropped a hint about the romance's progress, but so far the couple had no plans. I think Vida preferred things the way they were. Like me, she is a very independent woman.

I sank into her visitors' chair. "I was trying to ignore Ronnie. What can I do to help him? Assuming he's not guilty."

Vida picked up a No. 2 yellow pencil and twiddled it between her fingers. "He needs an alibi, correct? He says he was—what? In a neighborhood café?"

"A bar," I said dryly, knowing how Vida regarded such lowlife activities.

"A bar." She wrinkled her nose. "Well, we can't change that. He undoubtedly wasn't alone. I wouldn't think it should be too difficult to find someone who remembers seeing him there at the time the murder was committed. The police have an estimated time of death, I take it?"

"Sort of," I replied, trying to remember all that Ronnie had told me during our one and only visit. "I recall that it occurred between nine and ten at night. Apparently, Ronnie came home to the apartment just before closing time at two A.M. The daughter had found Carol shortly after ten-thirty."

Vida gave me her bright-eyed stare. "Well. That's not so difficult, is it? The time frame is very narrow. Do you know the name of this bar?"

I shook my head. "There are about five of them within a two-block strip near the apartment house. Ronnie wasn't entirely sure which one he was in."

"Oh." The brightness faded. "Still, it's a start."

"Vida, don't tell me you're willing to hang out in bars until we find somebody who was drinking with Ronnie at the fateful hour?"

Vida winced. "I don't relish the idea. But needs must. I can drink tea. They do serve tea in those places, don't they?"

"Probably." I watched her closely. "You're serious, aren't you?"

"Of course!"

"You're bored," I remarked.

"What?"

I shrugged. "It's been quiet around here lately. The women's shelter is under way, the bridge is coming up to a vote, we've finally got a new MD to back up Doc Dewey—Alpine's going through a calm phase. You're bored."

Vida gave me her gimlet eye. "Aren't you?"

"No. I was looking forward to a quiet weekend without Amber and Son. I could use some boredom around here."

Vida's wide shoulders slumped. "I certainly understand that part. But really, Emma, Ronnie is your cousin.

I can't imagine stepping aside and seeing kin being rail-roaded on a murder charge. Don't you have some fond memories of him?"

"Not particularly," I admitted. "Ronnie was some-thing of a cipher. We didn't see much of his parents or their kids. Let's face it, my mother was kind of snooty." Like you, Vida, I wanted to say, but didn't. "She didn't care much for people—even kin—who drank and couldn't hold down a job."

"Yes, I can understand her point of view," Vida con-ceded. "But it's only for a short time, and it might do some good. Haven't we managed in the past to help solve a crime or two?"

"It comes with the job," I allowed.

"Of course it does." Vida adjusted her glasses. "You go ahead and make the arrangements. You know the city." She gave an almost imperceptible shudder. "A nice, clean motel. Perhaps with cooking facilities. That will cut down on our expenses."

The truth was that if I were going to spend a weekend in Seattle, I would have preferred a four-star hotel with room service and an honor bar. But that was out of my price range. Dutifully, stupidly, resignedly, I went into my office and got out the Yellow Pages for Seattle. It took seven phone calls before I found a vacancy at the bottom of Queen Anne Hill. It was close to downtown, and not that far from the neighborhood north of the ship canal where Ronnie had lived with Carol.

"I'll pick you up at four," I told Vida. "I'm leaving here at two to pack, then I'm going to St. Mildred's for Good Friday services at three."

Vida, looking satisfied, smiled. "I'll be ready."

I wasn't so sure I'd be.

Traffic was heavy all the way into Seattle. The Friday commute was worsened by the holiday weekend, which prevented us from getting to our motel until after six. It was too late to visit Ronnie, so I called the jail to leave a message that I'd see him in the morning.

"Maybe," the detached voice at the other end of the line said, "Mallett will be out of the infirmary by then."

"Why's he in the infirmary?" I asked, unexpected concern surfacing.

"I can't tell you that," responded the voice, which could have belonged to either sex.

"I'm a . . . close relative." I gulped on the phrase. "A first cousin. At least tell me if he's sick or if he got injured."

"It's not serious. He'll heal."

That was all I could get out of the voice, so I hung up and told Vida, who'd been hanging over my shoulder. "Somebody may have punched him out," I said. "Or worse. Poor Ronnie."

"Indeed," Vida replied. "Jail can be a nasty place, especially in big cities. I don't imagine Ronnie's cellmates are particularly civilized."

"Damn," I swore, ignoring Vida's disapproving glance. "Now I actually feel sorry for the poor twerp."

"Of course you do," Vida responded. "He's family. Tsk, tsk."

"Vida—" I began, but stopped. She was right. I must have felt some kind of connection or I wouldn't have felt the surge of guilt.

"Where's an inexpensive restaurant close by?" Vida asked, glancing out the window at the Space Needle.

I considered. "There's a place out on Phinney Ridge that's quite good and reasonable. We could swing by Ronnie's apartment house. I got the address from him the other day. It isn't far from the restaurant."

Not wanting to lose the daylight, we headed for the apartment first. It was about three blocks from the neighborhood's business district, an unprepossessing two-story brick-faced building with eight units.

Half of the uncovered parking places in back were empty. A large, overflowing Dumpster stood next to the building, along with several garbage cans. There was no yard as such, just overgrown blackberry bushes, ferns, and weeds. Vida shook her head in disapproval.

"No pride," she declared. "Wouldn't you think they'd band together and have a work party? Some nice perennials, a few bulbs. What's wrong with city people?"

Since many Alpine residents considered a rusted-out pickup as garden statuary, I didn't comment. We walked around to the front, where stairs led up both sides to the second-floor balcony.

"Ronnie is downstairs, in 1-B," I said, studying the mailboxes. "Here, only Carol's name is on the box."

Vida was already at the picture window next to the door marked 1-B. The drapes were pulled, but didn't quite meet. "I don't see anyone," she murmured. "No lights are on." She tried the knob, but it was locked.

"They've taken away the crime-scene tape," I noted. "That's not a good sign as far as Ronnie's concerned. They must figure the case is closed."

"Mmm," Vida responded, still trying to peer inside. "It looks as if there are some cartons on the floor."

I joined Vida at the window, but before I could get a good look, the door to 1-C opened.

"It's not for rent yet," a rumpled redhead in her early thirties said. "Next week, maybe. You got the landlord's number?"

I started to deny that we were in search of an apartment, but Vida moved in front of me. "Why the delay?" she asked.

"The place has to be cleaned out first," the redhead answered, flicking cigarette ash onto the concrete floor. A TV was making disjointed noises from inside her unit. "It's only a one-bedroom. You sure you and your daughter are interested?"

"It's not for me," Vida replied, not exactly lying. "We understand that a murder occurred here."

A tiny twitch at the corners of the redhead's full lips indicated that the fact somehow pleased her. "Yeah. A couple of weeks ago." She shrugged. "Mr. Chan, the landlord, told me that you have to tell people when somebody gets killed. You know—future tenants and all that."

I decided it was time to step out from behind Vida's shadow. "That's sort of gruesome, though," I said, trying to sound chummy. "Who got killed?"

The full lips twitched again. "Her name was Carol Stokes. Her boyfriend did it. I ought to know—I heard them fighting just before it happened."

"Really," Vida said, sounding impressed. "Did the police interview you?"

"Yeah, a couple of times." The redhead tossed her cigarette into an empty planter, which had obviously served as an ashtray on previous occasions. "It's tough on him, but I had to tell the truth, didn't I?" Her blue eyes widened in an attempt at playing the innocent bystander.

"Of course," Vida said, tipping her head to one side. "You knew the couple, I take it?"

The redhead nodded emphatically. "Yeah. They were always fighting. Carol was the kind who liked to argue and all that."

"You must be Ms. Swafford," I said, remembering the name on the mailbox for 1-C.

"Right," Ms. Swafford replied, holding out a hand that sported two long acrylic nails and three short, natural ones. "Maybeth, to you. Hi."

"I'm Mrs. Runkel," Vida said, "and this is Emma." She tugged me forward. "How nice to meet you."

"You want to come in?" Maybeth asked, gesturing at the living room.

"Why, thank you," Vida said. "Just for a minute. We're on our way to supper."

The lack of neatness in Maybeth Swafford's apartment obviously disturbed Vida. She sniffed the air, which smelled of cigarettes, burned food, and acetone. She frowned at the furnishings, which appeared to have been sold as discount floor samples. She used her toe to push aside a *TV Guide* that was lying on the littered floor. She grimaced at the television screen, which was showing a sitcom I didn't recognize.

Maybeth must have followed Vida's gaze, because she turned off the TV and indicated we should sit on the lime-green couch. We did, and it sagged beneath our weight. Our hostess, who was dressed in tight slacks and a T-shirt proclaiming MY OTHER BUST WAS FOR DRUGS, curled up in a plaid recliner.

"It must have been frightening to realize you'd probably heard your next-door neighbor being murdered," Vida said with a shudder that may or may not have been feigned.

"Well, I didn't know she was being murdered then," Maybeth replied, picking up an acrylic nail from a small plastic tray. "I just thought they were having another fight."

"That was . . ." Vida gazed up at the ceiling. "When?"

"Umm . . ." Maybeth also gazed at the ceiling. Maybe there was something there I'd missed; all I could see were a few dangling cobwebs. "Three weeks ago tonight. I remember because it was a Friday and I was supposed to go salsa dancing, but my allergies were acting up. They always do this time of year. Pollen and trees and all that."

"Yes," Vida said in a sympathetic tone, "spring is such a difficult season for people with allergies. Was it very late? Did it wake you up?"

Maybeth shook her head. "It was around nine. I forget what I was watching on TV. *Nash Bridges* comes on at ten, and it was too soon for that. Don Johnson's a hunk, don't you think?" The question was aimed at me.

"Yes," I said, though I hadn't seen the actor since his days on *Miami Vice*. For my lonely Friday nights, I'd preferred *Homicide*, which seemed appropriate under the circumstances. "Was there a lot of screaming?"

"Yelling, mostly," Carol replied, making a face as she tried to apply a third nail. "Ronnie was still yelling when he slammed the door."

Vida's eyes slid in my direction. "Really," she breathed. "Most interesting. Did you tell the police that?"

Maybeth looked up. "What?"

"That this Ronnie was still yelling?"

"I suppose." Maybeth shrugged. "Hey, you want a beer or something?"

This time Vida's shudder was real. "Heavens, no! We're fine. As I mentioned, we're going to supper. Tell me, Maybeth, why do you think this Ronnie and Carol stayed together if they didn't get along?"

Maybeth examined her new nail. "Don't ask me. Carol was a real bitch."

"You weren't friends, I gather?" Vida said.

"Not exactly." Maybeth's mouth puckered up. "We used to hang together, way back. When she first moved in, she seemed okay. Then—" She stopped and stared at us. "Hey—how come you're asking all these questions about Ronnie and Carol and me? What's that got to do with renting Carol's apartment?"

Vida placed a hand at her bosom and laughed merrily, a very uncharacteristic sound. "Do forgive an old lady her rampant curiosity. People are so interesting, don't you think? Especially when one of them gets murdered."

The explanation didn't quite erase Maybeth's skepticism. "I probably shouldn't be blabbing all this. I mean, I don't know you two, do I?"

"No, you don't," Vida agreed, standing up. "But perhaps you soon will." With a Cheshire cat smile, she headed for the door.

Naturally, I trailed along behind her, feeling like a small dinghy behind a large yacht.

"Very unreliable," Vida remarked as we headed for the parking lot. "Why would Ronnie still be yelling when he left if Carol was already dead?"

"Good point," I replied. "How long do you intend that we should keep up this farce that I'm looking for an apartment?"

"As long as it works," Vida replied, waiting for me to unlock the passenger door. "I'm glad I thought of it. Now you know."

"Know what?" I asked as we both got into the Lexus.

"That Ronnie's innocent." Vida looked very smug. "Isn't that what we came for?"

Chapter Three

VIDA CONFESSED THAT she hadn't been to the Woodland Park Zoo since she was eight.

"Monkey Island," she said as we finished our meal at Val's just two blocks from the zoo. "That was my favorite, such busy little creatures, so like us. As a child, I found them fascinating, rather like watching neighbors through a window." Vida smiled in reminiscence; I smiled at Vida's early proclivity for voyeurism. "Shortly before the war," she continued, "we drove to Seattle to see the floating bridge over Lake Washington. My father refused to believe it wouldn't fall down. Of course, eventually it did."

"They all do—eventually," I said, thinking of the Hood Canal floating bridge between the Kitsap and Olympic peninsulas that had collapsed twice.

"I should think so," Vida said, then grew pensive. "It's not yet eight o'clock. There's no point in wasting time. Who's next on your list?"

"I don't have a list," I admitted.

Vida scowled. "Really, Emma, that's not very organized of you."

"Look," I said, taking out the hand-tooled Navajo leather wallet Ben had given me for Christmas, "until we talked to Maybeth, I wasn't convinced that Ronnie was innocent."

"And you are now?" Vida queried.

31

"No," I said, leaving a tip on the table and getting up, "it takes more than an unintentional slip from somebody we don't know to ensure Ronnie's innocence. In fact, Maybeth thinks he did it. The only reason I'm giving him the benefit of the doubt is because I don't think he'd go to all this trouble to run me down and ask my help unless he really didn't kill Carol Stokes. Besides, it bothers me that some goon is using Ronnie for a punching bag at the jail."

"If Ronnie did commit the murder, he'd still be desperate," Vida pointed out. "More so."

"I suppose," I admitted, then looked at Vida sideways. "Whose side are you on?"

"Yours, of course," Vida declared, her navy blue duster flapping at her calves as we left the café. "Where's the daughter?"

"Carol's daughter, the one who found the body?" I shrugged. "I've no idea. Maybe she's the one who's cleaning out the apartment."

The Lexus was parked two doors away, just out of a bus zone. Vida didn't say anything until we reached the car. Then she stood at the passenger side, staring up Phinney Avenue. "What's that?" she finally asked, pointing across the street and down a couple of blocks. "Is that the Norse Home?"

"Yes," I replied, following Vida's gaze in the direction of the Lutheran retirement residence. "Why?"

"Olive Nerstad," Vida said. "She married Burl Nerstad's older brother Burt and moved to Seattle. Burt committed suicide by jumping off the Bainbridge Island ferry a few years ago. I can't think why. Nobody heard he was sick, so what excuse could he possibly have for killing himself? Anyway, I heard that Olive moved into the Norse Home sometime after Burt died."

I gritted my teeth. Even though she disdained my

hometown as a vast and faceless metropolis, Vida still managed to find connections to people she knew. For all I knew, Olive Nerstad was a shirttail relation. Vida's extended family seemed to surface everywhere. If I should ever climb the Himalayas, I wouldn't be surprised to find a Runkel or a Blatt or a Gustavson pumping some hapless sherpa for the local gossip. "You want me to make a U-turn in the middle of Phinney and drive down there?"

"Why not?" Vida said, now getting into the car. "There's not a great deal of traffic. I'm rather surprised."

Dutifully, I turned the Lexus around, headed south, and found a place in the parking lot that was reserved for visitors. I had no idea what Vida expected to find out from Olive.

"Do you keep in touch?" I asked warily as we approached the front desk.

"Not recently," Vida admitted. "She stopped sending me Christmas cards after Burt jumped. They never found him, you know. I think that upset Olive. She may be a little . . . queer."

The pert young blond who welcomed us looked like she was about sixty years away from becoming a permanent resident. I wondered if it ever occurred to her that someday her eyes would fail, her joints would stiffen, and her hair would turn to gray. I'd thought about it on nursing-home visits, and my reaction was to run away as fast as I could, while I still could. But I knew I couldn't ever run far enough or fast enough.

The atmosphere at the Norse Home wasn't gloomy, however. A handsome couple in their seventies nodded and smiled at the receptionist as they headed out for the evening. Notices on a big bulletin board called attention to choral practice, square dancing, and travel. Considering that Norwegians in particular seem to live to be about a hundred and ten, I supposed that many residents looked forward to a long and happy life. At least I liked to think so.

Olive Nerstad was in Apartment 205. Apparently, she was accepting visitors, so we took the elevator to the second floor. The door to her unit was covered with a floral wreath and a wooden cutout of a duck. Vida rang the bell, then tapped her foot as we waited.

The woman who opened the door had bleached-blond hair and a suspicious expression. "Vida Blatt?" she said, glowering with sharp blue eyes. "What are you doing here? I never liked you."

"I can't think why not," Vida retorted, unruffled by the remark. I, however, was taken aback, with visions of ancient, simmering Alpine feuds spinning through my brain. "What did I ever do to you, Olive?" Vida asked.

"You said I was a beanpole," Olive replied, still not opening the door more than six inches. "That's because you were always fat."

"I never was fat," Vida asserted with a lift of her chin. "I was big for my age."

"You still are," Olive shot back. "Why are you here? And who's that hiding behind your fat frame?"

Vida rustled the duster. "It's this coat. It makes me look . . . large. Oh." She glanced over her shoulder. "This is Emma Lord. Her cousin may have killed your niece."

The shock tactic worked. Olive stepped back from the door and stared. "What? Carol?"

Vida took advantage of catching Olive off guard and marched into the apartment. It was a tidy, if crowded room with solid furnishings, probably as many as Olive had been allowed to bring from her family home.

"Well, well," Vida noted, taking in every upholstered chair, beribboned lamp shade, and mahogany table. "You certainly crammed your belongings into this place. How long have you been here, Olive? I forget when Burt jumped."

"I don't," Olive snapped. "It was June fourteenth, 1992. Burt never liked you, either."

"I never cared much for him," Vida replied, seating herself on a sofa that was covered in a bright yellow, pink, and green floral print. "Goodness, how ever do you get around with all this furniture?"

"Easily," Olive said, still standing. "I'm slim, remember?"

Olive was indeed slim, and tall, too. She looked like someone who had dieted all her life, but maybe it came naturally. Except for a few wrinkles, she could have passed for sixty-five, but I guessed her to be five to ten years older. Her features were sharp and plain, but carefully made up, as if Olive expected a steady stream of visitors.

"So what's this about Carol?" Olive demanded. "I heard she was dead. It doesn't surprise me."

"Really," Vida murmured. "And why is that?"

Slowly, Olive moved to an armchair that matched the couch. "Carol liked trouble. Don't pretend you don't know why she left Alpine. You always liked knowing everything, Vida Blatt."

"I've been Vida Runkel for going on fifty years," Vida asserted. "Yes, of course I know why Carol moved away. Did you see much of her? She lived only a mile or so from here."

Olive's head jerked around in my direction, where I'd settled in next to Vida on the couch. "Who did you say you were? What's this about a cousin who killed Carol?"

"Actually, I didn't say—" I began, but Vida interrupted. "We'll get to that, Olive. Tell us about Carol."

Olive scowled at Vida. "You never let anybody get a word in edgewise, do you, Vida? Why should I tell you anything? You've brought a stranger, a killer's cousin, in here, and you expect me to reveal all the family secrets. Go on with you!" She waved a thin hand at Vida, then folded her arms across her flat breast and sat back in the armchair.

I could sense the convoluted thought processes going on in Vida's busy brain. "Emma and I believe that her cousin is innocent. That's why we're here. We'd like to talk to Carol's daughter. Do you know where she is?"

Olive's eyes narrowed, then her face relaxed. "Innocent, huh? I'll bet. Is he the moocher who was living off of Carol?" She paused, then looked at me. "I have to admit, I can't see much of a family resemblance to that cousin of yours. You don't talk much, do you?"

"Sometimes," I said dryly.

"I can't say as I blame you, with her around." Olive paused again, then turned back to Vida. "I'm not sure where Kendra—the daughter, such a crazy name—lives. With her parents, I suppose."

"Her parents?" I echoed, proving that I really could come up with something on my own.

Olive nodded, seemingly pleased at the surprise she'd created. "That's right. Carol gave her baby up for adoption. She never seemed interested in what happened to her kiddy until she heard from Kendra a few months ago. Then Carol started asking me questions, but what did I know after the arrangements were made? Then Carol and Kendra got together, and Carol brought her over to meet me and show her off. Believe me, it was a rare visit. Carol usually paid no attention to her widowed aunt."

"Was Ronnie with them?" Vida asked.

Olive shook her head. "No, but Kendra complained about him, always hanging around and being a pest."

"When was this?" I asked.

"Oh—a month or so ago," Olive replied. "The next thing I knew, Carol had gotten herself killed. It was in the paper, so was the obituary. I didn't go to the funeral, though. I had stomach flu." Olive's annoyed expression indicated she was sorry to have missed such a dramatic event.

"Do you know who handled the funeral arrangements?" Vida inquired.

Again, Olive shook her head. "It wouldn't be that Ronnie. He wouldn't have enough sense. Maybe Kendra, along with her parents. Their name is Addison. I think they live near Green Lake."

"Do you have an address?" Vida asked.

Another shake of the head from Olive. "If Kendra is like the rest of the young people nowadays, I wouldn't expect to hear from her again. Especially not now, with Carol dead."

Grudgingly, Vida admitted that was so. "Did you keep the news story about Carol's murder?" she asked.

"As a matter of fact," Olive said, picking up what looked like a daybook stuffed full of clippings and letters, "I did." A glance showed lengthy obits with names like Skylstad and Nygaard and Lundquist. I suspected that Olive kept a record of her world in that dog-eared book. "You want to see it?" she asked.

Vida said she did. When she had finished the two-inch article, she handed it to me. It contained the bare facts, that Carol Stokes, thirty-four, had been found dead in her Greenwood-area apartment, and that her alleged boyfriend, Ronnie Mallett, thirty-five, was being held for questioning.

"Here," Olive said, giving Vida another clipping. "You might as well read this, too."

We both did. The second story was equally brief, relating that Ronnie had been charged with second-degree homicide and was being held in jail, awaiting a trial date.

Vida returned the article to Olive, then stood up. "Thank you. You've been somewhat helpful."

"Hunh," said Olive, also rising from her chair. "That's

my middle name. You'd have thought Carol'd be more grateful after all these years."

"Yes?" Vida said.

"She came here when she was expecting," Olive said, her face suddenly showing its age. "By here, I mean to Burt and me in Seattle when we lived in Crown Hill. Carol stayed with us until she had the baby. We were the ones who helped her arrange the adoption through my doctor. I had some fibroids in my uterus that had to be taken out. Then, after all we'd done, she took off and never came 'round again until she was getting married to that Marty Stokes. I figured she wanted a big present out of us. The next thing we knew, she divorced him. Carol shows up again, broke and with no job. We helped her some more. Real saps, Burt and I were. But then we never had kids of our own. Probably because of those fibroids. Six, seven years went by, not a peep out of her until Burt died. She did come to the memorial service, I'll say that. Maybe she thought he left her money. He didn't. The next thing I know, she comes around, asking about the adoption and what I remembered about it. Then she shows up with Kendra, and two weeks later Carol gets herself killed. Didn't I say she liked trouble?"

"So you did," Vida remarked, now at the door.

"You always liked other people's trouble, as Burt used to tell me," Olive said, one hand on her hip, the other on the doorknob. "It's no wonder he didn't like you."

"Actually," Vida said in a deceptively mild tone, "he did. Burt asked me to go steady when I was a junior in high school." With a rustle of her duster, she departed.

"Is that true?" I asked when we reached the elevator. "About Burt?"

Vida gave a single nod. "Certainly. I turned him down. Sour grapes, on his part, saying he didn't like me. If, in fact, he really said that."

At the desk, Vida asked the pert blond for a Seattle directory. "There's a Sam Addison, on Ashworth," she murmured. "Is that close to Green Lake?"

"Very," I replied. "It's about a block or two off Green Lake Way. I grew up nearby."

"You did?" Vida seemed intrigued. "You must show me your family home."

"And swing by the Addison place?" I asked slyly.

"Well . . . perhaps."

We were less than five minutes away from the far side of Green Lake. I drove the old familiar route with a sudden surge of memories flooding my brain. Woodland Park, the tennis courts, the picnic tables, the playing field, and the modest but well-kept neighborhood that faced Green Lake Way. We drove up Fifty-fifth to Meridian, which had been a sleepy little two-block business district in my youth. The grocery stores were gone, replaced by trendy restaurants and an organic produce market. The building that had housed a design school and the Texaco service station had been razed for what looked like the start of condominiums. Only a revamped Briggs Pharmacy, the Jehovah's Witness Hall, and Leny's Tavern remained.

"It's too bad it's dark," Vida remarked as I slowed down by the huge maple that stood in front of my old home. The tree was in bud, its gnarled trunk taking up most of the parking strip, its old roots raising parts of the sidewalk. "This was your house?" Vida asked, leaning forward to look past me. "It's rather nice."

The Craftsman bungalow dating from the World War I era had received a coat of paint and a new roof since I'd last seen it ten years ago. Ben and I had made a sentimental journey before I moved to Alpine and he was transferred to the mission church in Tuba City, Arizona. After our parents had been killed in a car wreck eighteen years earlier, we'd sold the house to a newly married couple who were expecting. I had no idea who lived there now, but the lights were on and a small station wagon was pulled into the garage out back.

"Did Ronnie ever visit here?" Vida asked.

It was the furthest thing from my mind. "Ronnie?" I thought back, peeling the years away. "Yes, once or twice when he and his sisters were very young. They tore the place up. My parents were furious, but Aunt Marlene and Uncle Gary didn't do a thing to stop them."

"Memories," Vida murmured. "Family. How sweet."

I ignored the remark. My recollections were very different from Vida's fixation. Ben and me, plundering our presents under the tree on Christmas morning, our mother's Thanksgiving turkey roasting in the gas oven, our father loading us into the secondhand sedan on Sunday mornings to attend Mass at St. Benedict's. The irony that one of the altar boys was Tom Cavanaugh, who lived in a neighborhood two miles away in Fremont, but belonged to the same parish. He and I hadn't realized that until many years later when we were in bed.

"We didn't do a lot of things with the rest of the relatives," I said. "Dad had only the one sister, Marlene, and Mom had a brother who lived in Olympia and another in California. There wasn't much of an extended family to mingle with."

"A pity," Vida said, still gawking at the house and what she could make out of the garden, which was fairly large but well kept up. "Youngsters need aunts and uncles and cousins. It makes life so much richer."

"We had us," I said, feeling defensive. "Our own little quartet. It was enough."

Vida didn't respond, even though I knew she disagreed. Reversing down to the intersection, I took a left to head for Ashworth, just a few blocks away.

"You didn't plan on visiting the Addisons tonight, did you?" I asked Vida.

"Nooo," Vida replied, peering at her watch. She refused to read the time from the digital clock on the dashboard, having often expressed her disapproval of "unnecessary gadgets" in the newer automobiles. "It's after nine. We might be imposing."

The Addison house was a larger version of my old home, with stone pillars on the front porch. The lights were on there, too, and the front door was open. I was halfway into the curb when a man carrying two cardboard boxes came rushing down the front steps. A plump woman followed, screaming and waving her arms.

"Goodness!" Vida exclaimed. "What's this?"

The man, who was big and balding, dumped the boxes on the parking strip, opened the trunk of a Honda sedan, and was about to pick up the boxes again when the woman kicked him in the rear end. He whirled around and made as if to grab her, but swore instead. She swore back. Then, apparently noticing my headlights, they both stopped and stared.

To my dismay, Vida rolled down her window and leaned out. "Yoo-hoo! Is this the way to the zoo?"

"The zoo's closed!" the man shouted.

"No!" Vida cried. "That can't be! Are you sure?"

He took a step closer and lowered his voice. "Yeah, it's after dark. You'll have to come back tomorrow. It's right over that way." His arm shot out to his left. "Just follow Fiftieth Street."

"You don't have a map, do you?" Vida asked.

"Not handy," the man replied, impatient. " 'Scuse me, I'm busy here."

The woman, meanwhile, had picked up the boxes and was scurrying back into the house. He didn't notice until she reached the door, which slammed shut behind her.

"Damn!" The man pounded a fist into his palm. "Damn, damn, damn!"

"Dear me," Vida said. "Is there a problem?"

"You bet," he said, already rushing back to the house. We watched as he beat both hands against the door and yelled, "Kathy!" several times.

"What do you think?" Vida asked in a musing tone.

"I think we'd better get out of here," I said, pulling back into the street. "If we call on the Addisons again, how are we going to explain our nocturnal desire to visit the damned zoo?"

"Please, Emma, just because you're in the city doesn't mean you have to swear like the rest of these people."

"Sorry." I sighed, maneuvering the car down the narrow street, which allowed parking on both sides. "But haven't we blown our cover?"

Before Vida could respond, a small sports car came tearing around the corner. We both put on our brakes and must have missed a collision by inches. I let out a little cry, Vida emitted a gasp, and the sports car didn't budge.

"You have the right-of-way," Vida said in annoyance. "Why doesn't this silly fool back up so you can get by?"

The "silly fool" appeared to be a young woman. I could see the outline of a curly head of hair and a pair of hands held up in a do-something gesture. I did something—I honked four times. My adversary put her hands back on the wheel and emphatically shook her head.

"Idiot," I spat out. "She's just being stubborn. I'd have to back all the way to the Addisons' to pull over. Which I refuse to do. We'll sit it out."

"Good for you," Vida said, glaring at The Enemy. "Don't give in. She looks young and is probably spoiled. We'll teach her a lesson."

I folded my arms across my chest. There was no reason—at least that I could see from my boxed-in position—that the girl couldn't back around the corner. Vida and I were in no hurry; we could afford to wait.

Or could have, until a car honked behind us. I looked

in the rearview mirror and saw the Honda with the bald man driving.

"Great," I said, gritting my teeth. "Now she's going to have to move or we'll spend the night on Ashworth."

To my surprise, the girl got out of the car. I braced for a tirade, but she squeezed between the Lexus and a van parked beside me. Quickly, I also rolled down my window. She had reached the Honda.

"Dad?" the girl said. "Where do you think you're going?"

We couldn't hear the answer.

"Kendra?" Vida mouthed, her gray eyes wide behind the big glasses.

"Maybe," I said, craning my neck to get a better look at the argument that was going on behind us. I caught the words *leaving her* and *end of my rope* from the man I assumed to be Sam Addison.

"This isn't a good time," the girl said, her high-pitched voice carrying on the night air. "Calm down, Dad. Let's go inside and talk."

"I'm through talking," Sam retorted. "Move your car, Kendra. Let these two nuts in front of me get by."

"Dad . . . Hey, Dad, open the damned window! Don't be such an ass!" Kendra was all but hopping up and down next to the Honda.

"We're the nuts?" Vida breathed. "Really, now."

Kendra stomped past us without so much as a glance. She got into the sports car, which I'd finally identified as a Mazda Miata, and backed up. I offered her a halfhearted wave, then took a right to Green Lake Way, leaving the Addisons to their peril.

"Most interesting," Vida murmured as we headed for the Aurora Bridge. "What do you make of it?"

"Something has brought things to a crisis in the Addison household," I said. "I wonder if it has something to do with Carol's murder."

"A catalyst, perhaps," Vida said. "Drat. I shouldn't have asked about the zoo. Sam Addison will remember me."

I didn't mention that Vida was unforgettable, especially wearing a feathered hat that looked like it might have been one of Montezuma's ceremonial headdresses.

It seemed too late to start pub crawling in search of witnesses. In fact, it was probably too early, but Good Friday didn't strike me as an appropriate time for hitting the bars. Still, neither Vida nor I go to bed early, so I gave her a quick tour of the two major neighborhoods that flanked the city center, Queen Anne Hill and Capitol Hill. Then we drove around downtown, through the canyons between skyscrapers, and finally returned to our motel around eleven.

"So big." She sighed, sitting on one of the twin beds and removing her shoes. "So many cars. So many people. How do they stand it?"

"I like it," I declared. "I miss it. Seattle energizes me."

"Twaddle. How can you stand driving around and not knowing who lives in all the houses? How can you possibly feel connected to half a million people?"

"I don't need to," I said. "When you grow up here, you know your neighbors. At least most of them. Being anonymous is what many people like about a big city."

"Twaddle," Vida repeated. "It doesn't make sense."

It wouldn't to Vida, but it did to me.

We had breakfast at a café in the lower Queen Anne district, then headed downtown to the jail. Vida complained about the traffic, which was unusually heavy for a Saturday morning.

"It's the day before Easter," I explained. "Everyone's out doing last-minute shopping. We'll be lucky to find a parking place close to the jail."

"Parking!" Vida exclaimed. "I cannot think when I

haven't been able to find a parking space at the Alpine Mall."

There was no point in arguing. The mall was a collection of two dozen shops, none of them bigger than my modest log house. We were in luck, however. The city and county buildings are south of the larger stores, and since most office workers had the day off, we were able to find a meter a half block away.

Vida griped all the way to the visitors' area. People weren't friendly, the walls needed paint, the place didn't smell quite right. With her nose in the air she marched along beside me to the visitors' area, where I asked the guard if we could both see Ronnie at the same time.

We couldn't, so I went first, and was shocked to see my cousin. He wore a big bandage across his forehead, one eye was blackened, and his lower lip had been cut. He must have seen the sympathy in my expression because he insisted he was fine.

"I can handle myself," he asserted with a bravery I was sure he didn't feel.

"It doesn't look like it," I said. "Or is the other guy in worse shape?"

Ronnie avoided the question. "I guess I said the wrong thing to Bubba," he said with a pitiful smile. "Bubba rules."

"With his fists," I retorted. "How do you really feel?"

Ronnie's narrow shoulders went slack. "Crappy." He took a cigarette from the pack I'd brought him—against Vida's advice—and lit up. "How's Budweiser?"

"What?" I didn't think I'd heard him right.

"Budweiser. My dog. Buddy, I call him. Or Bud." Ronnie's beat-up face softened. "He's a mutt, but a real pal. I take him for walks around Green Lake sometimes. How is he?"

"I don't know anything about him," I confessed. "Where did you last see him?"

"At the apartment." Ronnie's face fell. "I took him outside before I hit the bars. Are you sure you ain't seen him?"

I shook my head. "I'll ask around, though. I promise."

Ronnie brightened a bit. "Good. I can't lose Buddy. Not after losing Carol." He paused, flicking his cigarette at a plastic ashtray. "What have you found out? Can I get out of here?"

"Not yet," I said with a feeble smile of my own. "We're just getting started." I explained what we'd done so far, which didn't seem like much, especially to Ronnie.

"What about my alibi?" he asked with a whine in his voice.

"We'll check that tonight," I replied, wincing at the thought of dragging Vida along to bars and taverns. "It'd help if you could remember where you were."

"It had to be one of four places," Ronnie said. "Five, maybe, 'cept I don't go to Top's that often. You shoulda gone last night, 'cause it was a Friday."

Feeling guilty for sightseeing instead of sleuthing, I grimaced. "You mean the same crew hangs out on the same nights?"

Ronnie yawned, then nodded. "Sure. Tonight might be different, though sometimes weekends draw all the regulars."

"We'll do it," I promised. "Look, is there anything else you can tell us? Something you remember or thought wasn't important? What about suspects? Who might want to kill Carol?"

Ronnie yawned so wide that I could see his tonsils. "Huh?"

"Motive," I persisted. "Had Carol quarreled with somebody? How did she get along with Kendra?"

"Carol and I argued a lot," Ronnie said, his eyelids drooping.

I leaned forward in the uncomfortable chair. "Ronnie, are you all right?"

He nodded twice, his chin almost touching his chest. "I'm just tired. I don't sleep so good in here."

I didn't want to think why Ronnie couldn't get a decent night's rest in his cell. "Is it better during the day?"

This time he nodded only once. "Sometimes." The words were muffled, his eyes were almost closed.

"Ronnie, try to tell me—" I stopped. His breathing had become shallow, he was slumped in his chair, and I heard what sounded like a snore.

Ronnie was sound asleep.

Chapter Four

I CALLED FOR the guard and went back into the waiting room. Vida rose as soon as she saw me. "Shall I see him now?" She looked particularly imposing, no doubt an attempt at rising above her sordid surroundings.

"No," I said, irked. "Ronnie went to sleep on me. I guess I bore him."

"Whatever do you mean?" Vida demanded.

"What I said. Ronnie fell asleep. Nighttime in jail isn't easy for the Ronnies of this world. He needs a nap."

"Heaven helps those who help themselves," Vida intoned, then made a face. "Unless they can't."

"Which is why we're here?" I remarked with a wry expression.

"Your cousin's resources are limited in prison," Vida replied.

As we made our way to the elevator, I tried not to look at the arriving visitors. No matter what sex, color, age, or size, there was something forlorn about them. A little black girl about four was stumbling along beside her mother, who carried an infant. The mother's eyes were empty, devoid of hope. The little girl clung to a stuffed Curious George, with a yarn monkey's bright-eyed smile. The child stopped and looked up at me. She, too, smiled, more shyly than her toy. Maybe there was still hope for one so young. I smiled back. But there was nothing I could do for her. I walked on.

Forlorn and forsaken, both the innocent and the guilty. I wondered if there was really anything I could do for Ronnie.

Before leaving the motel, I'd called his lawyer at home. Alvin Sternoff lived in a condo in Belltown, a couple of miles away. His offices were in the Public Safety Building adjacent to the jail. Alvin was coming into work for a few hours, and had agreed to meet us at ten-thirty. We were early, but I didn't want to waste my good parking place.

Alvin, however, was already struggling through a tall pile of beige folders. He looked harried, anxious, and incredibly young.

"Excuse the mess," he said, pulling out an extra chair and hitting his shin in the process. "My office isn't exactly fancy."

Alvin was right. It was austere, even drab, and the only personal, nonfunctional items were a figurine of Snoopy wearing a mortarboard and Alvin's law-school degree from the University of Washington.

"I hope you don't think I'm not giving your cousin my full attention," Alvin said after I'd made the introductions. "I'm not, but I want to. It's just that . . ." He waved a pudgy hand at the stacks of papers and folders on his desk, accidentally knocking a legal pad on the floor. "Sorry," he said, ducking down to retrieve the pad.

"You're overloaded," I said.

"Boy, am I," Alvin replied, his dark eyes wide. He was a chunky young man with black hair and a dimple in his chin. His heavy black eyebrows grew upward, like little bird wings. "I've only been doing public-defender work for six months. I figure it'll help me decide what kind of practice I want to get into if I go off on my own or join a firm." He jumped up, hands gripping the arms of his chair. "I forgot. Coffee? Tea?"

"We're fine," I said for both of us. "Can you go over the statement Ronnie made when he was arrested?"

"Statement," Alvin murmured, shuffling papers, some of which appeared to have food stains on them. "Statement, statement . . . Here it is. It's not very helpful."

Alvin was right. I shared the account with Vida, who leaned to one side and frowned.

I came home about one or so, Ronnie had written in a clumsy hand, *and there were the cops, with Carol dead. I'd been out drinking since nine or so. I think I was at Top's and the Satellite Room and maybe Freddy's, but I don't know where when. Carol and I had kind of a shouting match before I went out, but she was okay when I left and watching TV. I didn't hurt her, not at all. I ain't done nothing wrong, least of all kill Carol who I really loved.*

"The police didn't believe him," I said, handing the statement back to Alvin.

"Ronnie was drunk," Alvin said, fiddling with a ball-point pen. "He had some fresh bruises and scratches, as if he'd been in a fight. Carol was bruised, too, her shoulders, her face, and her chest. Whether or not Ronnie killed Carol, it's hard to believe that the two of them didn't come to blows."

"Do you think he strangled her?" Vida asked.

Alvin grimaced. "I don't know. If she'd been beaten to death, I'd have to believe he did it. But this strangling business puts a different spin on it. Whoops!" He dropped the pen. "Sorry," he said, making another dive under his desk. "Anyway, he swears he didn't, and that's all I need to know as a public defender."

"It was a drapery cord that was used?" I asked.

Alvin nodded. "About two feet long. I can probably plea-bargain the homicide charge down to man two, but your cousin wants me to get him off because he insists he didn't kill Carol. Maybe you could help talk him into a plea."

I was dubious about that, and said so. "I tried to find out this morning if there were any other suspects," I went on, "but Ronnie nodded off and I didn't get an answer. Do you know of anyone else who might have wanted to kill Carol?"

Alvin let out a big sigh, his shoulders slumping. "There's the daughter, Kendra, who found her. Do you know anything about her?"

Vida nodded. "Yes. She was illegitimate. Her adoptive parents seem to be involved in some domestic dispute. Not with her, but with each other."

"Really?" Alvin seemed interested. "How did you find that out?"

The reaction further eroded my confidence in Alvin Sternoff. Vida, however, explained about the disturbance at the Addison home the previous night. "We just happened to drive by. It was most fortuitous."

"I guess," Alvin said, regarding Vida with a trace of awe. "Anything else you've learned?"

"Not yet," Vida said smugly, "but we will."

"We met the neighbor, Maybeth Swafford," I said. "She's convinced Ronnie did it, but her story doesn't ring quite true."

"Really?" Again, Alvin seemed surprised. "In what way?"

"Have you interviewed her?" I asked, wondering exactly what Alvin had done on Ronnie's behalf.

"Yes. Of course," Alvin said hastily, giving his knuckles a painful whack on the desk. "Ouch. Excuse me. Maybeth said she heard them fighting and then Ronnie left and there wasn't another sound out of the apartment until Kendra arrived and found the body."

"Is Maybeth a credible witness?" I queried, wondering if Alvin would survive our meeting, let alone the trial.

He shook his head. "She won't hold up very well under my cross-examination."

"That's good," I said. "Who have you got for character witnesses?"

"Um . . ." Alvin riffled some more papers, losing a few in the process. "A couple of Ronnie's drinking buddies."

"But not able to give him alibis?" I asked.

With regret, Alvin shook his head. "One of them, Bobby Markovich, was out of town the night of the murder. The other, Rick Dietz, was home with his girlfriend. Ronnie's boss will testify for him under duress."

"So Ronnie was employed," Vida put in. "What did he do?"

"He drives truck for a roofer named Garvey Lang out in Lynnwood," Alvin replied. "Lang has a wood yard, too. Ronnie mostly makes deliveries."

"Why is Mr. Lang reluctant to be a character witness?" Vida inquired.

Alvin looked apologetic. "I guess Ronnie isn't the most reliable employee. He actually works part-time, but Lang said that he didn't always show up when he was supposed to. He would have let him go, but he said he felt sorry for Ronnie. He seemed like such a . . . loser."

"That," I said, "is my impression."

"Sorry," Alvin said. "I mean, he's your cousin. I don't want to disrespect him."

"Don't worry about it," I said. "As I explained to you on the phone when I was still in Alpine, Ronnie's side of the family and my side weren't close. If he weren't so pathetic—and such a loser—I wouldn't be here."

"Right." Alvin grabbed a pencil and jiggled it up and down. "I see plenty of losers in this job, and I've only just begun. It's kind of discouraging. Yikes!"

Somehow, he'd managed to impale his left hand with the pencil. Alvin checked to see if he'd drawn blood, then apologized once more. I asked him about priors, having gotten the impression from Ronnie that this wasn't his first arrest.

"Little stuff," Alvin replied, sucking on his hand.

"One assault, five years ago. He and some guy got into it in a tavern. Then he got picked up last year for smoking."

"For smoking?" I asked.

Alvin nodded. "It was in a bar down by the old *Post-Intelligencer* building. They had a big sign outside saying 'Smoke-Free Lounge.' Ronnie thought it meant he could go in and smoke free cigarettes. He lit up his own and they tried to throw him out. He put up a big fuss, and they called the cops. Oops!" Alvin knocked over Snoopy.

I was beginning to wonder if Ronnie was the only loser in this scenario.

For the first time since leaving Alpine, I remembered to check the voice messaging on my cell phone. Finally surrendering to the modern age in December, I'd bought the cell phone and spent the first month trying to figure out how it worked. Three months later I still hadn't gotten in the groove of checking it out on a regular basis.

"They *are* handy," Vida remarked as I poked various buttons while we sat in the Lexus outside the county-city buildings. "Do you think I ought to get one?"

The question surprised me. Vida was still a computer holdout, relying on an ancient typewriter and lightning two-finger accuracy on the keys. Despite the fact that Kip had to enter all her copy in the back shop, she refused to give in. But a telephone was different: Vida could communicate directly with her many sources. Maybe if she got a cell phone, she'd eventually come around to a word processor.

"I think of this as a safety device," I said, hearing the unctuous recorded voice of a woman who might be dead by now for all I knew. "You have one new message . . ." I poked two more buttons. "Milo nagged me until I realized it was only stubbornness that prevented me from . . . Oh, shoot. It's Ed."

The call was from my former ad manager who had in-herited wealth and, with it, a sense of superiority. Ed Bronsky was calling not from his so-called villa in Alpine, but from the Hyatt Regency in Bellevue.

"Shirley and I are taking a meeting with Irv and Skip today," Ed said, sounding all puffed up even in a recorded message. "I heard you were in Seattle, so I thought you'd want to sit in on it. It's big, Emma, really huge." Like Ed, I thought. "We've got a producer lined up for *Mr. Ed*."

Mr. Ed was Ed's rags-to-riches autobiography, pub-lished by a vanity press on the Eastside. The publishers, Irving Blomberg and Skip O'Shea, were representing Ed in an attempt to sell the book to a movie or TV producer. Frankly, I thought they were stringing him along.

"The meeting's at one," Ed's message continued, "in the restaurant at the hotel. Talk about breaking news! You can be here in person to get the lowdown. By the way," he added slyly, "I'm buying."

"That *is* news," I said after repeating the message to Vida. "I'm almost tempted to go so we can see Ed pick up the check."

"We don't have time for such foolishness," Vida de-clared. "We must figure out a way to get into Carol's apartment."

The idea seemed useless to me. The police had undoubt-edly removed any sign of evidence. Still, Vida wouldn't be satisfied until we got inside so she could snoop around.

But first I had to call Ed back at the hotel. In their room—a suite, no doubt—Ed answered on the first ring. "Bronsky," he said in that pseudo-gruff voice he'd adopted since becoming rich. While he was my ad manager, he never picked up the phone until it was ready to trunk over to Ginny, and when he did, he uttered a beleaguered "Ed here, what can I do for you?" He always sounded as if he expected the worst, like having to dig our advertisers out of a rock quarry or save them from a raging bull at the Overholt farm.

Forcing regret into my voice, I explained that Vida and I were on a mission to help one of my relatives who'd gotten into trouble. I didn't want to be explicit, lest all Alpine learn that I had a cousin who was a jailbird. Worse yet, I didn't want Ed incorporating my problem into his life story.

"Darn," Ed said in a heartfelt tone. "This would be a big break for you, Emma. The producer, Manny Malone, has got the contract with him. It's going to be a series, for gosh sakes!"

"It is?" I gave Vida a startled look. "What happened to the cable-TV movie?"

"It didn't pan out," Ed replied. "Anyway, this is a much better deal. It's going to be animated."

"Oh." I'd maneuvered the phone so Vida could also hear. "You mean a cartoon, like *The Simpsons* or *King of the Hill*?"

"Kind of," Ed responded, his voice dropping a notch. "Only with animals. I'll be Chester White."

"They're changing your name to Chester White? How come?"

"It's not exactly my name," Ed replied, sounding impatient. "I'll probably still be Ed. Chester White is my breed. I'm a pig."

Surprise.

Maybeth Swafford wasn't home, but the resident of 1-A was. Henrietta Altdorf was a big woman of sixty, short of breath, with a florid face, graying auburn hair, and shrewd blue eyes.

"Maybeth told me you'd be coming by," Henrietta said with a wink. "Mr. Chan, the landlord, left the key with me this morning. He's anxious to rent the place. You know what landlords are." She winked again.

By the time Henrietta found the key to 1-B, we'd heard the story of her life. She'd been widowed once, divorced twice, and didn't have much time for men. Four years and eight months to go before she could retire from her job as an RN at Northwest Hospital. Her only son lived in Puyallup, which you'd think was four hundred miles away instead of forty. His two boys had no discipline, and his wife was a scatterbrain. Not that it mattered, since she was lucky if she saw any of them more than once a year.

"The younger generation." She laughed in a disgusted manner. "I don't understand them. They only think of the big I."

"So true," Vida murmured, mildly fascinated by Henrietta's recital. "Sometimes my three daughters and I are at odds."

Not for long, I thought as we entered Carol's apartment. Beth, Amy, and Meg hadn't inherited enough of their mother's spunk to stand up to her. But then few people could.

"Daughters must be easier to raise," Henrietta said, stepping aside to let us cross the threshold. "More thoughtful, too." She uttered a wistful sigh, then waved a hand. "Imagine," she went on, shaking her head. "Two weeks ago Carol was alive and happy. Now she's gone. Life's hard, isn't it?"

"You say she was happy?" Vida commented, her gaze taking in the desolate remnants of Carol's life. A half-dozen cardboard boxes, clothes on hangers draped over the back of a chair, furniture that mingled cheap with used, and a big-screen TV that probably cost more than everything else put together. The apartment itself seemed to lie between life and death, half its contents already removed, the other half in transition.

"Happy?" Henrietta repeated. "Yes, I think so, especially after she finally got together with her daughter. I've lived here six years, and after Carol moved next door about a year ago, she'd come over and have a couple of beers with me after we both got home from work. Once in a while she'd have one too many and start to get . . . maudlin, I guess you'd call it. She'd talk about the baby she gave away and how she wished she knew what had happened to the child. Then, just a few months ago, who shows up but the daughter? Carol was so excited."

"So Kendra was the one who sought her mother out?" I asked.

Henrietta nodded. "That's the way it works. Kendra turned eighteen, which meant she could learn who her birth parents were, at least her mother."

"Did Kendra spend much time with Carol?" Vida asked, pausing in her perusal of the cardboard boxes.

"Some," Henrietta said. "The truth is, Carol had a boyfriend, Ronnie. He's the one who killed her. Anyway, he was a lazy sort, drank too much, if you ask me, and worked only when he felt like it. I don't think he and Kendra got along. I wouldn't be surprised if he pulled some fast stuff on her." She winked.

Vida was opening and closing the drapes. The light of midday didn't do much to brighten the small living room. "Men," she said lightly. "Tsk, tsk."

"Was Carol a pretty woman?" I inquired, noticing a photo album in one of the cartons.

"Sort of," Henrietta replied, "at least when she got all fixed up." The album also caught her eye. "Let's have a look. There must be pictures of her in this. I'll point her out."

Only the first four pages of the album contained photographs, all apparently taken with the same camera. As it turned out, Carol was in almost all of them.

"See, that's her," Henrietta said, pointing to a laughing young woman standing by an artificial Christmas tree. "She looks rather pretty there, don't you think?"

The happy face that looked out at me was more piquant than pretty. Carol Nerstad Stokes had big brown eyes, a wide, generous mouth, and an upturned nose. Her hair was short and spiky, the tips dyed a golden blond. She was wearing a tight red sweater and tight black pants that showed off her curvaceous figure. Silver sandals adorned her feet, and I noticed that her toenails were painted a bright red.

"She's very nice looking, really," I said, and couldn't help but think that Carol must have been the girl who was an answer to Ronnie's prayers. I couldn't think of any other way he'd been able to get such a prize when it came to looks.

"Were you at home the night Carol was killed?" I inquired as we went into the kitchen.

"No," Henrietta replied with apparent regret. "I was at the hospital. I pulled a sixteen-hour shift that Friday. Somebody didn't show up—these young nurses, you can't rely on them. I used to work in private practice, but doctors are skinflints. Hospital work may have long hours, but the pay and the benefits are better. Imagine— working for a doctor who doesn't offer medical coverage!" She shook her head in a disgusted manner.

The kitchen was small, and apparently had been cleaned up and cleared out. Cupboards stood open and bare; the refrigerator, which Vida inspected, was all but empty.

"The daughter," Henrietta said, waving a hand at the boxes, which appeared to be filled with dishes, pots and pans, and canned goods. "She was here yesterday, after the police took down that nasty yellow tape. Mr. Chan wants everything out by Wednesday. Come see the bedroom and bath."

We trooped after Henrietta. The bathroom, like the rest of the rooms in the unit, was small and cramped.

Kendra had cleared it out, too, though the tiles and tub needed a good scouring.

"Did you talk to Kendra?" I asked.

"Just to say hello," Henrietta replied, leading us into the bedroom. "She seemed in a big rush. Not that she's the chatty type. You know these young people—they think you're nosy just because you show some interest."

"Indeed," Vida murmured. "So touchy. By the way, did you attend Carol's funeral?"

Henrietta made a face. "Such as it was, out at the cemetery. I felt an obligation, and as it turned out, I was right. Very few of her friends showed up, but no family except for her brother, who came up from California to make the arrangements. Of course it was during the day, so I suppose some of those people who used to hang out around here had to work. *If* they work," she added.

"Did you know any of them?" I asked.

Henrietta shook her head. "It was a young crowd," she replied. "Late twenties, early thirties. They weren't interested in an old coot like me."

"The brother," Vida breathed, snapping her fingers. "In California. What was his name?"

"Charles," Henrietta put in. "Chuck, they called him. He was in a big hurry to get back to San Jose or San Mateo or one of those Sans down there. Typical Californian, full of himself." She stopped to stare at Vida. "You know him?"

"Ah . . . No," Vida fibbed. "Not really."

I remembered to ask about the dog, but I had to be cagey since I wasn't supposed to know he existed. I brought up the subject by noting that the carpet and some of the upholstery had been chewed.

"That darned dog," Henrietta said as we finally moved out of the tiny hallway and into the bedroom. "He drove me crazy when they left him tied up outside. Sometimes he'd bark half the night, especially if they forgot to let him in. I haven't seen him since the night of the murder."

The double bed had been stripped, the closet had been cleaned out except for some shoes, and it looked as if Kendra had been working on the bureau when she quit. One drawer was bare except for a sachet, but the others were still full. The white wicker dressing table was also partially emptied.

"Does Kendra have an apartment?" I inquired as we headed back into the living room.

"I don't think so," Henrietta replied. "She graduated from high school last June, but she still lives at home as far as I know."

"Where did Carol work?" I asked, realizing that Vida hadn't joined us.

"At a seafood packing place in Ballard," Henrietta told me. "Carol mentioned she was trying to get Kendra a job up in Alaska for the summer at a cannery. The pay's so good, you know."

"Carol seems to have taken a real interest in her daughter's life," I remarked as Vida entered in her splay-footed manner.

Henrietta nodded. "She did for a fact. I suppose she was trying to make up for all those lost years."

"Where was the body found?" Vida asked, surveying the room as if she could make a corpse materialize before her eyes.

"There," Henrietta said, pointing to the floor in front of the bar that separated the living room from the kitchen. "I peeked in when the door was open and saw the outline. It must have been chalk, because it's gone now." She turned to look at the big-screen TV. "You'd think Kendra would get that out of here before somebody steals it."

"Is there a problem with burglars?" I asked.

"Oh—no, not really," Henrietta said, obviously embarrassed lest I be frightened off. "It's like anyplace else, especially when there's a vacancy. You know, Kendra mentions the big TV to her friends and one of them is into drugs and the next thing you know, they break in and steal what's not nailed down. Generally, I mean. We haven't had much of a problem. Not at all."

"What exactly is the rent?" Vida asked.

Henrietta looked relieved by the change of subject. "Six seventy-five, plus the usual damage deposit, first and last month's rent. You know the drill, I imagine."

"Oh yes," Vida said breezily. "But we don't want Emma feeling rushed."

"Of course not," Henrietta agreed, letting us out and locking the door. "Maybe you could come by Wednesday, after Kendra's finished."

"What a good idea," Vida enthused. "You've been very helpful."

"Could I get your number?" Henrietta asked. "So I can tell Mr. Chan."

Vida started to say something, but I interrupted, offering my cell-phone number. Henrietta thanked us, complained about the unkempt landscaping, thought better of it, and allowed that the landlord probably had someone coming in as soon as the weather turned nice.

"I gave her the cell number in case she thinks of something about Carol that we ought to know," I explained after we got into the car. "What were you going to do?"

"Tell the truth," Vida said, looking affronted. "That we were down from Alpine. That you're moving here to start a new job."

"Vida," I said, amazed, "that's not the truth."

"Part of it is," Vida retorted. "Though your answer may have been better. Less complicated."

"It'd be better if we'd been up-front with all these people," I grumbled. "Now we have to pretend, not to mention lie through our teeth. I don't like it."

"They wouldn't speak so freely if we didn't," Vida responded.

"Not that we learned much, except that Ronnie's reputation is in the drain as far as most of them are concerned," I pointed out, turning off onto Greenwood Avenue. "In fact, this was a waste of time."

"No, it wasn't," Vida said, looking smug.

"What do you mean?"

"While you were checking the furniture and the boxes," she began, "I was studying the windows."

I was puzzled. "The windows? What for? To see if someone could look in?"

"No, no," Vida replied. "I don't think Carol was one to open the drapes. Did you notice how faded they were in the living room? The short ones in the bedroom were, too. But you miss my point. I was looking at the drapery cords."

My brain finally clicked. "For the murder weapon?"

"Exactly," Vida said, still smug. "They were all intact, and very worn." She turned to look at me as we stopped for the traffic light at Eighty-fifth and Greenwood, the neighborhood's major arterial. "Which means, of course, that Carol was killed with a cord that did not come from her apartment. What do you think of that?"

Chapter Five

As USUAL, VIDA had a point. If Ronnie had wanted to kill Carol, he would have used whatever was at hand. Indeed, since she was strangled, he could have used his bare hands. For the first time, I saw a small light at the end of the tunnel.

"We've got to talk to the investigating officers," I said. "I'll call and see if they're in on a Saturday."

Tony Rojas was the primary on the Stokes case. He was gone until Monday, having taken a three-day weekend for Easter. I relayed the news upon returning to our table at the Twin Teepees, a stone's throw from Green Lake. The sixty-year-old eatery was a landmark, with its colorful wigwams enclosing the dining room and bar. In my youth, it had been a hangout for motorcycle cops, though I didn't see any in evidence that afternoon.

"I feel stymied," I told Vida. "We have to be back in Alpine Monday."

"Not first thing, though," she pointed out. "Haven't you taken the morning off?"

"Yes," I hedged, "but—"

"Then so shall I," said Vida, finishing her lunch of liver and onions. "My section is in good shape. I have that long feature on Dolph and Mamie Swecker's trip to Miami. The part about how they got mugged by a twelve-year-old takes up at least six inches by itself. It took some doing to explain—discreetly—that the mugger was their nephew and they didn't file charges despite the fact that Dolph never got his watch back. I realize the Sweckers hadn't seen their relatives in several years, but wouldn't you have thought they'd send pictures?"

"So what do we do in the meantime?" I asked, still feeling frustrated.

Vida was studying the dessert menu. "They have pie," she said. "I know I shouldn't go off my diet, but it *is* Easter. And I rarely bake at home."

Which, I thought idly, was a good thing. The only time I'd eaten a pie baked by Vida was when I first came to Alpine and she invited me over for dinner. She told me it was a rhubarb pie, but I didn't believe her. It tasted like broom straw, and the crust could have been used to resole a pair of caulking boots. For all the recipes she ran on her page, for all the kitchen hints and menu plans, Vida could not bake, broil, braise, or cook.

"Go ahead," I urged. "Try the pie."

"I think I will," she said with a decisive nod. "And you?"

"I'm good," I replied, never having been much of a dessert lover. Besides, my appetite was waning. Despite Vida's discovery, we didn't seem to be making much progress in clearing Ronnie's name.

"Why," Vida asked in a musing tone, "would anyone carry a length of drapery cord with them?"

"To tie something up?" I suggested.

"Yes, that's possible." Vida stopped to give the waitress her pie order. "Or to give drapes away. Let's say that Kendra—this is just an example, mind you, I'm not saying this is what happened—Kendra is moving into an apartment. Her mother—her adoptive mother, Mrs. Addison—gives her a set of old drapes. They're in her car when she calls on her birth mother, Carol. Are you following this?"

"Yes, go on."

"Carol gets into a row with Kendra, who becomes furious, and . . ." Vida frowned and bit her lip. "No, she'd hardly dash out to the car to fetch a drapery cord, would she?"

"Not likely."

"But what if someone brought it in with them?" Vida said, brightening. "That would make it premeditated murder."

"True," I allowed, "but why not use a stocking, a rope, a scarf?"

"Too identifiable," Vida responded. "A drapery cord could be taken out of a Dumpster or a garbage can. It might be traced to the owner, but not to the killer."

Vida had another point. In fact, it was a rather good one. But it still didn't ease my frustration. "So what do we do now?" I inquired dryly. "Find out how many people in the vicinity have thrown out old drapes in the past month?"

"Certainly not," she said. "You must call on the Addisons."

I was skeptical. "I must?"

Vida nodded. "Yes. I doubt very much if either of them will recognize you. In fact, Mrs. Addison wouldn't know me, but there's no point in taking chances. Nice as it is, your new car looks very much like many of the other cars these days. Even that shiny beige color seems popular."

Admittedly, that was true. At first glance, the Lexus looked like a Toyota, a Honda, and various other makes and models. I'd already tried to get into the wrong car four times since I'd got it.

"Where will you be while I visit the Addisons?" I asked with some reluctance.

Vida gave me an ingenuous smile. "At the zoo. Drop me off on your way."

*   *   *

The Addison house on Ashworth looked rather attractive in the daylight. Planter boxes held colorful displays of primroses, the rhododendrons that flanked the front porch were coming into bloom, and a giant forsythia bush at the side of the house was in the final stages of its golden glory. I admired bright daffodils and budding tulips as I went up the walk that led to six wide concrete steps.

The mailman, a smiling Asian fellow brave enough to wear U.S. postal regulation shorts on a fifty-five-degree day, was just leaving. By chance, a woman I assumed was Mrs. Addison came out onto the porch to collect the mail.

"Kathy?" I said, remembering the name that an agitated Sam Addison had called out the previous night.

Although I was at the bottom of the stairs, she hadn't noticed me and gave a start. "Yes? What is it?"

"My name's Emma Lord," I said, offering a friendly smile. "May I talk to you for a few minutes? It's about my cousin Ronnie Mallett." How much more up-front could I be?

Kathy frowned at the name. "You mean that awful man who killed Carol Stokes? He's your cousin?" She seemed incredulous. Maybe, in my chic clearance Anne Klein pantsuit from Francine's Fine Apparel, I didn't look like someone who'd be related to a man charged with murder.

"Yes," I replied, still smiling. "I'm from out of town, and I'm trying to figure out exactly what happened. Ronnie isn't much help." My expression turned pitiable.

"I don't doubt that," she said, looking harried and holding the mail close to her bosom. Then she sighed and gazed off in the distance. "I don't know . . . I probably shouldn't talk to you."

"I don't know where else to go," I said, growing more pitiful by the second.

"Oh . . ." She opened the screen door and motioned for me to join her. "Come in, but only for a couple of minutes," Kathy said, placing the mail on a small inlaid table near the door. "This isn't a good time."

I could guess why not. There was no sign of the Honda or Sam Addison. Maybe he'd actually left his wife. I hadn't seen the Miata, either. I felt lucky to have found Kathy Addison home alone.

The Addison living room and adjoining dining room were a far cry from the tawdry apartments I'd visited so far. Someone with taste had furnished the house in an eclectic, if unimaginative, style. There were Oriental rugs on the floor, tables and chairs made of solid oak and mahogany, a breakfront filled with English bone china, and matching leather-covered love seats. Bouquets of daffodils stood at each end of the fireplace mantel and camellias floated in a bowl on the polished dining-room table. It was as handsome a setting as you could find in an upscale furniture store—and just as cold.

Kathy added to the image by not asking me to sit down. She stood next to one of the love seats, her still-pretty face frozen. "I can't imagine what I can tell you about Carol's murder," she said, her voice stilted. "I hardly knew her, and I didn't know this Ronnie at all."

"What did you think of Carol?" I asked. "Was she a decent person?"

Kathy looked surprised at the question, her green eyes clearly puzzled. "Decent? What do you mean?"

"Did she drink? Use drugs? Sleep around?"

"All of those things, as far as I know," Kathy replied, faintly malicious. "People who get themselves killed in situations like that—women, I should say—aren't leading decent lives. Take my word for it. They're asking for trouble. It wouldn't surprise me if she was some sort of addict and a drunk as well."

My gaze had settled on a framed studio portrait on a teak end table. The smiling young woman with the curly red-gold hair and the wide-set blue eyes was very pretty. I assumed it was Kendra's senior picture. "What did Kendra say about Carol?"

Kathy's plump face froze up again. "She didn't talk much about Carol."

"I understood they hit it off rather well," I said, deliberately hoping to rile Kathy.

She gave a shrug. "They were cordial, I understand. It had to be awkward. And Kendra didn't think much of that Ronnie. I realize he's your cousin, but Carol called him a creep."

"Ronnie has his faults," I admitted. "Did Kendra spend much time with . . . Carol?" I was cautious about referring to the murder victim as Kendra's mother. I didn't think it would go down very well with Kathy Addison.

"Not really," she said. "They only became acquainted a few months ago. I suppose you could say they were making an attempt at bonding in some sort of way."

"But Kendra was the one who found Carol's body," I pointed out.

"So?" There was belligerence in Kathy's tone. "Kendra happened to stop by there that night to pick up something she'd left at the apartment a few days earlier, that's all."

"Then Kendra had a key?"

Briefly, Kathy looked rattled. "I guess so. I don't know. Maybe Ronnie left the door open after he killed Carol." She made a dismissive gesture with her hands. "Look here, if you're trying to find some patsy to pin the murder on instead of your cousin, go talk to Carol's ex. Kendra mentioned that he'd been hanging around lately. I can't imagine that he's much good, either."

"Marty Stokes?" I said, recalling the name that Olive Nerstad had given Carol's ex-husband.

Kathy frowned. "No. That's not him. It wasn't the same as hers. It was Roy Something-or-Other. Now leave me alone. I never wanted to get mixed up in this awful thing." She waved her hands again, as if shooing off a chicken.

I took umbrage. "But you *are* mixed up in it, Kathy. Your daughter—your adopted daughter has had her birth mother killed by someone, and I don't think it was my cousin. Doesn't that affect you?"

Her belligerence was obvious. "Why should it? I met Carol once. Twice, but that was only in passing when she picked Kendra up here at the house. Carol Stokes meant nothing to me. Your cousin means even less. Goodbye."

I couldn't resist. "Give my love to Sam," I called over my shoulder. "If he ever comes home."

I hadn't spent ten minutes in the Addison house, which meant Vida needed at least another half hour at the zoo. She was determined to see the monkeys, though I knew they no longer resided on Monkey Island.

To kill time, I drove past St. Benedict's Church, where Ben and I had attended parochial school. I'd started kindergarten the year that the new church was completed. Until then, Mass had been celebrated in the school auditorium. Parking across the street, I decided to go inside. I hadn't been in St. Benedict's since my parents' funeral almost thirty years ago.

Somewhat to my surprise, the doors were unlocked. But as I entered the church itself, I saw why: a half-dozen women and two men were decorating for the Easter Vigil Mass. Sprays of white lilac and snowball stood at the rear of the altar. There were yellow and white gladioli sitting in vases, waiting to be put in their proper place. Two women were twining garlands of baby's breath and small stephanotis along the aisles. I slipped into a pew at the back and said a quick prayer, for me, for Adam and Ben, for the repose of my parents' souls. At the last minute I remembered to pray for Ronnie. Then I added a Hail

Mary for Vida, though she'd probably scoff at such a papist offering.

The church wasn't quite as I remembered it. The altar rail had been removed and the pews had been placed at an angle. The changes weren't much of an enhancement to the uninspired architecture. Built in the mid fifties, St. Benedict's had followed a basic design that was in vogue for several of the Archdiocese's newer churches. It was austere and unlovely, the carved wooden statues with blank faces and graceless stance. I hated to admit it, but I preferred the old-fashioned plaster saints of St. Mildred's in Alpine.

Still, certain memories came back to me. My First Communion, my Confirmation, Ben's first Mass in his old parish, even though he was a secular priest and not a member of the Oblate fathers who had run St. Benedict's ever since I could remember.

We had always sat toward the back, on the epistle side of the church. I could see us, the tight-knit little group of four, with Ben giving me a kick and me punching Ben in retaliation before Dad separated us. We never lingered much in the vestibule. My parents weren't active in the church or the school, and seldom socialized with the other parishioners. It had never really occurred to me before, but we Lords were isolated, our own little island, watching the rest of the world from our private beach.

The sun was still flirting with the clouds when I came outside. The neighborhood around the church was much the same as I remembered, though I'd heard that the convent across the street no longer housed nuns but was the parish activity center. Perhaps the changes at St. Benedict's were small, but the basics remained the same. Had I changed so much from the pigtailed little girl in the blue-and-red-plaid uniform? Probably not. But until now I had never stopped in my former parish to pray for a relative who had been accused of murder.

* * *

I took the long route to the zoo, south through the Freemont district. As a small child, I could not only hear the boats toot their signals to raise the Freemont bridge, but the whistle of freight trains as they passed the small depot at the north end of Lake Union. The railroad tracks were still there, but they were no longer used; the depot had been converted into a takeout restaurant. But not far from the bridge itself was a life-size sculpture of men, women, and children called *Waiting for the Interurban*. The interurban train between Everett and Seattle had passed into history long before I was born, a victim of the auto industry. But the stone statues who waited were a reminder of another era, and tribute to their eternal patience was made by neighborhood residents who regularly decorated the sculpture for holidays, birthdays, anniversaries, and just for fun. Fremont had a reputation as a funky part of town, which helped explain the heroic statue of Lenin located off the main drag, and the monster-size troll that lurked under the Aurora Bridge, cuddling a real Volkswagen.

I found Vida waiting by the rose garden outside the zoo. She was agog over the changes that had been made in the past fifty years.

"Really, all this natural habitat!" she said as we drove down North Fiftieth Street. "It must have cost the world. How do cities find the money to do these things? Property taxes must be outrageous."

I admitted that they were considerably higher than in Alpine.

"I must bring Roger someday," she said, referring to her odious fifteen-year-old grandson, who, in my opinion, belonged in a zoo. "He'd so enjoy the tropical birds."

As in roasting them on a spit, I thought, but instead told Vida about my visit to Kathy Addison.

"Very defensive," Vida commented. "And no sign of Mr. Addison?"

"Nor of Kendra," I replied. "But I found out where she is."

"You did? Was Kathy helpful in that regard?"

"No, but the mail had just come," I said, feeling rather clever. "She set it down next to a couple of other items, and the envelope on top was addressed to Kendra. Kathy had crossed out the Ashworth address and written in a request for forwarding to someplace on Roosevelt Way."

"Which is where?" Vida demanded, as if I were keeping the area a secret.

"It's a long north-south street between the north end and Lake Union," I explained. "I couldn't quite catch the whole address, but it was near the city limits. We can call Directory Assistance to find out."

We stopped for lunch on Aurora, the main drag through the city, also known as Highway 99. I used a pay phone to inquire about Kendra Addison, somehow wheedling the address along with the phone number. I called to see if she was home, but there was no answer, no machine, no voice messaging.

"We'll have to take our chances," I told Vida as we headed north.

"Certainly," Vida responded, rubbernecking out the window. "Goodness, so many ugly businesses. I never cease to be amazed by how hideous this stretch of Seattle is. You won't find this sort of thing at home."

Aurora Avenue is one long stretch of car lots, fast-food restaurants, strip malls, motels, and gas stations. Even in my youth, it had not been an attractive part of town. The changes here were neither of style nor substance, but of density and development.

"Is that a prostitute?" Vida gasped, staring at a young woman who was thumbing a ride next to a bus stop.

"Probably," I said, amused. "I've been told that during

the week, before lunchtime, Aurora gets jammed up between the guys looking for a nooner and the senior citizens heading for the early-bird lunch specials."

"Heavens." Vida kept staring, no doubt in search of more hookers. "There's another one. So thin, so shabby, so young. How very sad. What brings them to such a pass? I really hadn't noticed before. I don't come this way into town. I always take the freeway."

We turned off to reach Roosevelt. Vida was playing navigator. "The next block," she said, checking house numbers. "It'll be on the right."

For a recent high-school graduate, Kendra Addison had done well for herself. The apartment building where she lived was almost new, with a shake roof and a shingle exterior. It sat snugly among tall evergreens, and every unit appeared to have a small deck.

Kendra's name looked as if it had been freshly hand-lettered in the space next to the brass mailboxes. Her unit was on the second floor. An elevator in the breezeway carried us upstairs.

"Nice," I commented, noting the almost new carpeting and wall covering. "It can't come cheap."

"No nicer than the Pines Village Apartments where Carla lived before she was married," Vida countered.

Since the Pines Village was the only apartment house in Alpine that was reasonably attractive and less than thirty years old, I halfheartedly agreed.

"How much?" Vida asked as the car came to a smooth stop.

"That depends," I said. "A one-bedroom in the north end of the city probably runs around eight hundred dollars a month."

"Eight hundred!" Vida cried. "A month! Why, that's outrageous. Pines Village doesn't have a single unit that's more than five-fifty."

"It's expensive to live in Seattle," I admitted. "Real-estate prices are out of sight."

"How could Kendra afford such a place?" Vida huffed as we approached the young woman's door.

As I pressed the buzzer, I was wondering the same thing. I was still wondering when there was no response after three tries.

"Did you notice her car?" Vida asked.

"The Miata?" I shook my head. "There were a couple of cars parked outside, but I saw an entrance to an underground garage. I couldn't see into it."

Nudging me aside, Vida jiggled the doorknob. "Drat. It's locked."

"Of course it is," I said, amused.

Vida looked a trifle sheepish. "Well—you never know. The young are so irresponsible."

"Now what?" I said, heading back for the elevator.

"Carol's ex-boyfriend? Her ex-husband?" She paused, leaning against a wooden rail and rummaging around in her purse. "I've got the names in here somewhere. . . . Ah! Look down there."

A white Miata was pulling into the drive, headed for the underground parking. From our vantage point, we couldn't see who was inside, but Kendra Addison was a good guess.

"Come," Vida commanded. "Let's duck around the corner."

Kendra's unit was the last one at this end of the building. It had a wraparound deck, closed off by a gate with a simple latch.

"Perfect," Vida murmured. "Look, there's a window. I can see the bedroom quite clearly."

So could I, and had a momentary urge to mention that window peeking wasn't legal. Except, of course, to Vida, who scoffed at such restrictive regulations.

"She'll come into the living room," I pointed out.

"Of course. Then we'll call on her." Vida pressed against the exterior wall, her sharp gaze glued to the window, one hand pushing back the cartwheel hat with its profusion of butterflies on the brim. I swear I could see her nostrils twitch.

Almost five minutes passed before we heard footsteps. Then, somewhat to our surprise, we heard voices, a male and a female.

"Not alone," Vida whispered, wiggling her eyebrows.

". . . for the kitchen," the female voice was saying.

"Why?" the male responded. "You don't cook."

"I will some—" The door closed on the young woman we presumed was Kendra.

"How long do we wait?" I inquired of Vida.

She looked at her watch. "Two minutes. I'll time it."

We remained silent as the seconds ticked down. Vida was giving me a nod when something moved in the bedroom. I flattened myself against the wall, looking straight ahead through the trees. Vida, however, remained at her post.

"It's them. Oh, my!"

"What?" I whispered.

"They're . . . My, my!" She gave a faint shake of her head, but kept looking.

I was about to ask her what was going on, but she was riveted to her small sliver of window. At last, Vida, now bug-eyed, ducked under the sill and crept toward me.

"I don't think we should call on them after all," she said under her breath. "I didn't know you could do it that way. Oh my!"

Chapter Six

"So KENDRA HAS a boyfriend," Vida said, adjusting the cartwheel hat as we returned to the car. "Goodness, she's certainly promiscuous. Just like her mother. Her real mother, that is."

"We don't know that for a fact," I countered. "The guy in that bedroom may be Kendra's one and only. How old did he look?"

Vida expelled an impatient sigh. "Young. Early twenties, no more. I really didn't get a very good look."

I couldn't resist. "Old enough not to be wearing Bugs Bunny underwear?"

Vida took offense. "Really, Emma. How do you think of such things?"

I laughed, but Vida continued in a musing tone. "It's not natural. It's . . . acrobatic."

I ignored the comment. "Let's not come down too hard on Kendra just yet," I said, heading south on Roosevelt Way. "What do we know about her? Apparently, she was happy to have met her birth mother, which indicates family ties are important to her. We saw her try to reason with her father last night. That means she believes in keeping the peace. She's moved out and gone on her own, which shows she has initiative. The only negative is that she accused Ronnie of hitting on her, which may be true. From what little I've seen of her, mainly a graduation picture, Kendra is very good-looking."

"Carol was good-looking as a teenager," Vida said in a musing tone. "Very fair. She was a Lucia Bride one year at the Lutheran church."

"So where did Carol go wrong?"

"That boy . . . If only I could remember . . ." Vida snapped her fingers. "Darryl Lindholm. That's who got Carol pregnant. Quite tall. He played basketball and football for the Buckers."

The Buckers was the nickname for Alpine high-school teams. "What happened to him?"

"The Lindholms were would-bes," Vida said, using her term for people who would be of a better social standing than they actually were. "They moved to Mount Vernon, where they became active in the bulb business. Darryl went to Pacific Lutheran University in Tacoma. Which, I believe, is why his parents put pressure on him not to marry Carol. It would have interfered with his upward mobility."

"So the Lindholms are long gone from Alpine?" I asked.

"Yes," Vida replied. "Very sad."

Vida always finds cause for grief when someone moves away. Typical of small-towners, she considers such defections a personal betrayal.

"Where are we going?" she asked abruptly.

"I don't know," I said. "It's almost three. We've got hours to kill before we bar-hop."

Vida shuddered. "Really . . . Will it be worse than Mugs Ahoy?"

Mugs Ahoy is Alpine's most popular tavern, a gritty watering hole on Front Street run by Abe Loomis, whose last name should be Gloomis. Abe is one of the most morose men I've ever met. At first, I couldn't understand how he could tend bar and offer sympathy to his customers as they poured out their troubles. Then it occurred to me that after a few beers, most people want to be told that the misfortunes visited upon them are unique, unparalleled, and couldn't happen to a more pitiful person. Then, by the final call, Abe can actually lift their spirits by revealing the horrible things that have happened to him since they last warmed his bar stools.

"Worse?" I echoed. "No. All taverns are the same. The tonier ones have become pubs in Seattle."

"That sounds much nicer," Vida said, looking fretful. "Why couldn't your cousin have aspired to higher things?"

I had no answer for that, but suddenly said, "Lynnwood," then signaled for a right turn onto Northgate Way. "We're going to see Garvey Lang."

"The roofer that Ronnie worked for? A splendid idea. Will he be there?"

"Somebody will," I said, heading for the freeway. "He also has a wood yard. Garvey can't be the only one who knows Ronnie."

Vida agreed. I noticed that she had grown pensive again. "I've never read those racy romances."

"What?"

"Nothing." She shrugged. "Still, one wonders . . ." Vida lapsed into silence, so I let the subject drop.

The suburbs change and spread so fast around Seattle that I always get lost. We stopped at a gas station to get directions, but the young man who came out to the car had never heard of Garvey Lang, a roofing company, or a wood yard. He only worked in Lynnwood and lived in Bothell.

We stopped next at a 7-Eleven, where the Pakistani behind the counter had barely heard of Lynnwood. The phone book had been stolen from the booth outside, so we went on to a Plaid Pantry. The spike-haired girl at the register had gone to high school with somebody named Garvey—or maybe it was Carvey—but couldn't help us. I finally found a directory at a pay phone by a Safeway store. The address for Lang's Roofing meant nothing. Thankfully, a checker with a Bob Marley hairstyle in the express lane told me how to get there.

We drove through the maze of malls, bucking heavy traffic and interminable stoplights. Vida complained constantly, a staccato accompaniment to the overhead street signs, the merging lanes, the bored expressions on the other drivers.

"The city indeed! We must be miles from Seattle. Where's Everett? Where are we?"

"Still in Lynnwood," I said. "I hope."

Lang's Roofing was located in an unpretentious house that had been converted into a commercial enterprise. Garvey's Firewood was next door, behind a chain-link fence. There was a sign in the window of the house: OPEN.

Two men, one young, the other late-middle-aged, stood staring up at roof samples that wrapped around the display room. Behind the counter, a burly, bald man of fifty was calculating what were probably roof dimensions.

"Garvey Lang?" I asked.

The man took off his glasses and smiled, revealing either perfect teeth or excellent dentures. "Can I put a roof over your head, young lady?"

I pretended to be flattered, then had to disappoint Garvey Lang. As Vida tapped her foot, I lowered my voice and explained my connection to Garvey's erstwhile employee.

"Ronnie's cousin, huh?" Sadly, Garvey shook his head. "Hang on. Let me get Hank out front."

Hank was probably Garvey's son. Same build, same smile, signs of early male-pattern balding. He took over as Garvey led us behind the counter and into a crowded office that featured a flowering cactus.

"You the aunt or the mom?" Garvey asked Vida.

Vida bridled in the armchair our host had provided.

"My word, no. I'm no relation to either of them." Her glance in my direction eloquently dismissed me as kin.

Tactfully, I explained that we worked together, but didn't say what we did. The word *newspaper* can close as many doors as it opens.

"I have to be honest," Garvey said. "Your cousin wasn't real reliable. He was often late, some days he didn't show up, he'd get the delivery addresses fouled up. I wish I could say better."

"But you kept him on," I said. "Why, if he was such a screwup?"

Garvey let out a heavy sigh. "I felt sorry for the guy. I had a kid brother like him. Maynard. He dropped out of high school, got into all kinds of trouble—nothing really serious—but it upset our folks. So I brought him into the business. It just didn't work out. Maynard was always screwing up, even got into a fistfight with a customer. I had to let him go. Two weeks later he got drunk, crossed the center line in his pickup, and killed himself and two other people out on 99. That was fifteen years ago. I never forgave myself. I see a lot of Maynard in Ronnie Mallett. I guess I kept thinking maybe this time I could make a difference. It looks like I was wrong, huh?"

"No," Vida declared. "We're not certain that Ronnie killed Carol Stokes. And you were right to fire your brother. He could have caused you to lose your business."

Garvey smiled at Vida. "But I'd still have my brother."

"Not necessarily," Vida said. "He sounds self-destructive. Like Ronnie."

Thanks Vida, I thought. He's not one of your squirrelly relatives, so butt out. Of course, I had to be fair. Without Vida's prodding—for the sake of "family"—I might not be here in the office of Lang Roofing, listening to the owner pour out his soul.

"Do you feel that Ronnie is capable of murder?" I asked.

Garvey sighed again. "Who isn't? I mean, I wonder about that. Under certain circumstances, I figure just about anybody could kill somebody else. I'll admit, though, I never thought of Ronnie as a violent guy."

"Did you ever see him drunk?" I inquired, silently agreeing with Garvey's assessment.

"A couple of times. He came in late—real late—and had a snootful. Sometimes he looked like he'd been in a barroom brawl. But he wasn't a belligerent drunk. He got even more mellow."

That didn't surprise me. "Did you ever meet Carol Stokes?"

"No," Garvey replied, "but Ronnie talked about her a lot. He seemed nuts about her. I never heard him say anything seriously critical."

"Nothing?" Vida put in. "Not even the usual masculine complaints?"

"You mean 'She can't cook,' 'She spends too much money,' 'She always has a headache' sort of thing?" Garvey shook his head. "Not really. I got the impression he wanted to marry her. It was Carol who wasn't interested. He moved in with her not long after I hired him."

"Which was when?" I asked.

"A year ago last month," Garvey answered. "March is the usual time for me to add a couple of people because business picks up when the weather is good. Not the firewood part of it—that's just the opposite—but the roofing jobs. Anyway, Ronnie mostly made deliveries. Not always to the right places, though. He had trouble with numbers. I wondered if he was dyslexic."

Ronnie might be a number of things, but *killer* didn't seem to be one of them. "If this comes to trial, would you act as a character witness for him?"

Garvey scratched his bald head. "I told his attorney I wasn't sure that I could. I mean, I'd have to be candid. It'd be hard to give Ronnie an outstanding report card."

"As an employee, yes," Vida noted. "But as a person?"

Garvey regarded Vida with a serious expression. "I see what you mean. Maybe I could at that. Basically, I always thought he was a decent guy. Maybe that's another reason why I was willing to go the extra mile. Say, who's taking care of his dog, Budweiser?"

"I don't know," I admitted. "The neighbor didn't seem to know, either."

"That Maybeth?" Garvey said with a frown. "She wouldn't tell you if she did. I figure the dog was one of the reasons they broke up."

"Maybeth?" I said with a little gasp. "I meant the nurse, Henrietta Something-or-Other."

"Altdorf," Vida put in. "What's this about Maybeth and Ronnie?"

"Sorry," Garvey said with a grimace. "I assumed you knew they used to go together until Maybeth and Ronnie moved into the same apartment building next door to Carol."

We didn't know that. But it was certainly interesting.

Vida insisted we head straight for Maybeth Swafford. "No more deception," Vida asserted. "We're going to tell her exactly who we are. Henrietta as well. If we have to."

It was almost five o'clock by the time we reached the apartment house off Greenwood. The afternoon had turned warm, and Maybeth had her door open. She also had a guest. The man who sprawled on the sofa was close to forty, with long, blond hair, a goatee, and a tattoo on each upper arm. In his wife-beater T-shirt, he looked like the perfect companion to go bar-hopping with Ronnie Mallett.

"What is it?" Maybeth called over the noise of the TV, which sounded as if it were broadcasting a car race or the end of the world. She was sitting on the floor, curled up next to the sofa.

"It's us again," Vida shouted. "We lied."

"What?" Maybeth's face screwed up in puzzlement. "Oh—hang on."

She didn't turn down the TV, but came to the door and stepped outside. "What did you say? I couldn't hear from in here."

Vida folded her arms across her jutting bosom and took a deep breath. "We lied to you. We're not looking for an apartment for my daughter. Indeed, she's not my daughter, she's a friend. My name is—"

"Hold it." Maybeth held her hands up as the TV continued to blare. "Slow down. If she's not your daughter," she went on, nodding at me, "who is she? Why can't she look for herself? Is she crippled or something?"

"We're not apartment hunting," Vida declared, an impatient note in her voice. "That's not our purpose."

"You want a house? A rental?"

Taking Maybeth firmly by the arm, Vida led the younger woman farther out onto the walkway. "Emma," she said slowly as she nudged me with her elbow, "is Ronnie Mallett's cousin. She's come to Seattle to help prove Ronnie's innocence. I'm here to help her."

Maybeth's blue eyes widened, then narrowed. "Innocent, my butt. Ronnie did it, and that's that. Hey, I don't much appreciate you two nosing around here and asking me a bunch of stupid questions. If you want to lie to people, go pick on somebody else before I call the cops."

Vida started to dispute the charges, but the blond man had gotten up from the sofa and was coming toward us with a bowlegged walk.

"What's going down, Beth?" he asked, glaring at Vida and me. "Who're these two broads?"

Maybeth pointed at me. "She's Ronnie Mallett's cousin. The other one's a big snoop."

"Get lost," the man ordered. "We don't hang with killers."

"Maybe you should," Vida snapped, oblivious to contemporary slang. "For all we know, you *are* the killer. Ronnie didn't do it."

"Where's Budweiser?" I demanded, finally getting a word in edgewise.

The man had started to pull Maybeth back inside, but he stopped. "The dog?" He glanced at his supposed girlfriend. "Where is he, Beth?"

"Dead, I hope. That stupid mutt nearly drove me crazy when Ronnie left him tied up out back. He'd bark and bark and bark, sometimes all night. Between the barking and fighting, it's a wonder I can hear the TV. Thank God that animal shut up after Ronnie left that night. I get a killer headache with my allergies."

The phrase seemed apt. I pressed Maybeth about Budweiser's whereabouts.

"I think Mr. Chan took him away," she said, shooting us another hostile look.

"Jeez, I hope not," the man said. "I liked that dog. I'll take him. Call Chan."

"Come on, Roy, you don't really want to—" Maybeth's words were cut off as Roy slammed the door in our faces.

"Roy?" Vida looked like a dog herself, a bloodhound on the scent. Her nose actually twitched. "Didn't you tell me that Kathy Addison said that Roy was the name of Carol's ex-beau?"

"I did," I said, marveling anew at Vida's mind for detail. "If Carol stole Ronnie from Maybeth, did she offer Roy as a consolation prize?"

"That's what it seems like," Vida said as we walked away from the building. "Of course, it could be a different Roy."

Vida had stopped just short of the Lexus. "We forgot about Henrietta. Shall we go back and ask her what she knows about Roy and Maybeth and Carol?"

"We might as well," I agreed. "We still have time to kill. Maybe I can call Mr. Chan about the dog. I'd like to give Ronnie some good news."

Vida looked askance. "You aren't thinking of taking him home with you? What about those dreadful cats you acquired?"

"First things first," I said as we returned to the apartment walkway. "Let's hope Henrietta isn't on duty."

She wasn't. "Five days off," she said, ushering us inside. "That's what I get after a long shift. It's nice. How about some coffee?"

We declined. Then Vida launched into her tell-all tale about who we really were and what we wanted. Luckily, Henrietta's reaction was different from Maybeth's. She laughed her head off.

"I never!" she exclaimed, her face turning red from laughter. "That's a hoot. You two sure had me fooled."

"I feel bad about the deception," I said. "It wasn't fair to you."

"Don't be silly," Henrietta asserted, waving a hand. "Let's face it, I lead a dull life. Work in the OR, listen to the doctors talk about their golf game and their stock investments, come home to an empty apartment, watch TV—why, nothing exciting has happened to me in years until lately." She paused and grew serious. "That sounds terrible, like Carol's death was some kind of entertainment. Sorry. Anyway, the cops talked to me, a nice detective was here, and now you folks. It makes my day."

"Tell us about Maybeth and Ronnie," Vida urged.

"Well." Henrietta settled back in the easy chair, which was like its owner—solid, comfortable, and showing traces of wear. At her side, a cup of coffee stood next to a family portrait, presumably of her son, his wife, and child. "I don't know much about it," she went on. "One day about a year ago Maybeth moved in. I guess Ronnie moved in with her, though I didn't see much of him. The

next thing I know, about a month later he was with
Carol. She'd dumped Roy Sprague, which was no big
loss, if you ask me. They were always fighting, and I
think he beat her up. A couple of times I saw him with
long scratches on his face and once with a black eye.
Carol had probably tried to defend herself. She and
Ronnie fought, too. Frankly, Carol was kind of hard to
get along with when it came to men."

"Men can be difficult," Vida noted.

"Can't they?" Henrietta made a face. "I've had three
husbands, and only the first one was worth a damn, even
if he did up and die on me at the age of thirty. Still," she
added wistfully, "it's not much fun to live alone." Her
quick glance took in the room, which was full of memo-
rabilia, knickknacks, and a trio of bowling trophies.
There were photos of a Hawaiian beach, the Inner Har-
bour at Victoria, BC, Hurricane Ridge on the Olympic
Peninsula, and Mount Rainier with the wildflowers in
bloom. The ceramic figurines that sat on end tables and
shelves looked as if Henrietta had made them herself, all
kinds of colorful creatures to keep her company during
long, lonely days.

"I live alone," Vida said quietly. "It suits me fine. For
the most part."

"Divorced?" Henrietta asked.

Vida looked faintly shocked. "Widowed. For almost
twenty years."

"Oh." Henrietta wore a sympathetic smile. "Sounds
like you were one of the lucky ones. I guess you still miss
him."

"I do indeed," Vida replied.

"Anyway," Henrietta went on, "Roy'd show up now
and then at Carol's and there'd be a big row. Then,
around Christmastime, he and Maybeth started seeing
each other. It seemed kind of natural. Two people who'd

been unlucky in love finding each other. To be honest, I thought it was sweet." She winked.

"Do Maybeth and Roy fight?" I asked.

Taking a sip of coffee, Henrietta shrugged. "I can't really say, with Carol's apartment between me and Maybeth. I wouldn't call her—what's the word?—docile, I guess, but she's not as ornery as Carol could be."

"Do you know if Roy had had any contact with Carol before she was killed?" I inquired.

Henrietta frowned. "Let me think—I did see him at her door one night when I came home late from work. That was probably a week or so before the murder. Carol wouldn't let him in. At least not while I was outside."

"In other words," I suggested, "Roy may have still had the hots for Carol?"

"Or just wanted to cause trouble," Henrietta said. "He strikes me as a bully." She drummed her fingernails next to her coffee cup on the end table. "I didn't speak very well of your cousin, Emma. May I call you that?" She saw me nod and went on. "Sometimes I tend to sum up people kind of fast. He was lazy and he drank and all that, but the only reason I thought he killed Carol was because the police said so."

"You don't agree?" I asked.

Henrietta's expression was uncertain. "Let's say that if you have doubts, then I shouldn't be so hasty. Ronnie seems like the most likely suspect, but I'd never think of him as having what you call a killer instinct. Does that make sense?"

I didn't say that *killer instinct* wasn't always necessary when it came to murder. Sometimes people killed out of frustration, stupidity, blind rage. They murdered almost by accident, and grieved as much as any loved one's survivor. Instead, I agreed with Henrietta. "He's much too easygoing." It seemed to be true, but in fact, she probably knew Ronnie better than I did.

She nodded. "He seemed too laid-back. The few times I saw him and Carol together, he treated her real nice. Of course they did fight, but I figure it was Carol who started things."

Once again, I inquired about the dog, and asked if I could get Mr. Chan's number. Henrietta knew it by heart and told me to use the phone in her bedroom. "Ronnie was real fond of that dog," she said. "He taught it to do tricks. Last Christmas he got Budweiser one of those red-and-green hats with bells on it. It was real cute, even if the dog was a pest."

I left Vida to continue the conversation and made my way into the bedroom. It took some explaining to make Mr. Chan understand who I was and what I wanted. His English wasn't proficient. At last he told me that the dog was at his son's place in Lake City. It was unclear whether or not they intended to keep the animal, but I got Peter Chan's number and called his home in the city's north end.

Peter, who sounded as if he'd been born in this country, was in, but hedged about Budweiser. The younger Chans had two boys, five and seven, who liked the dog. He told me to call back in a week or so.

Vida and Henrietta were discussing Kendra when I returned. Apparently, Vida had told our hostess about the new apartment and the boyfriend.

"Shenanigans," Henrietta said with a wink.

"Of a most peculiar sort," Vida asserted. "Whatever happened to classic lovemaking?"

Henrietta let out a gusty laugh. "Variety's the spice of life. A little innovation can perk things up. If you know what I mean." She winked again.

Vida apparently didn't know. But instead of showing disapproval, she moved uneasily on the sofa. "Perhaps," she allowed, then changed the subject. "You never saw Kendra with the boyfriend?"

"I hardly saw Kendra," Henrietta replied, looking

pained. "She seemed pleasant enough, but not one to visit with the likes of me. You know how these young folks are. If you've got a few wrinkles and a couple of gray hairs, they think you should be put to sleep."

"So true," Vida sighed, feeding into Henrietta's opinion of The Young, even though I knew of no one in Alpine, regardless of age, who would dare ignore my House and Home editor.

"Look here," Henrietta said as she showed us to the door, "if you have any more questions or if I can help you in any other way, feel free to stop by. I don't go back to work until Thursday."

We assured her we'd be in touch. She was smiling as we headed for the parking lot, but when I glanced over my shoulder a moment later, Henrietta's shoulders were slumped, and her expression was sad.

We were getting into the Lexus when we saw the white Mazda Miata pull in. It was Kendra, and she was alone. The sports car stopped halfway into the parking area, where Kendra whipped out a flip phone and dialed frantically.

"What's she doing?" Vida asked, craning her neck.

I hadn't yet started the car. "She's calling somebody."

"I see that now," Vida replied, still gawking.

The phone disappeared, but Kendra didn't move the car. The Miata blocked our exit. After a few moments she rolled down her window and leaned out.

"I don't know who you are," she shouted, "but you're stalking me. I just called the cops."

Chapter Seven

KENDRA IMMEDIATELY ROLLED the window back up and sat with her arms folded. She looked furious. I compared her with the graduation photo I'd seen at the Addison house. Kendra's face had changed, matured, the cheekbones more prominent. Her curly golden hair with its reddish highlights was pulled back into what appeared to be a ponytail.

"I guess postcoital bliss doesn't agree with her," I muttered.

"Emma . . ." Vida's tone was heavy with reproach.

"Let's try to explain," I said, but Vida was already getting out of the car.

"See here, young woman," she began as I dutifully followed on the parking lot's gravel surface, "we're not stalking you. We're trying to help Ronnie Mallett."

It was the wrong thing to say. Kendra thrust out her chin and bared her teeth. They were excellent teeth, white and even, and had no doubt set the Addisons back a few grand, courtesy of the orthodontist.

Vida was undaunted. She bent far down to bang on the window. The gravel's uneven footing threw her off balance; she staggered and fell against the car, the cartwheel hat sailing off to land on the Miata's hood.

Kendra not only stopped making faces, but burst out laughing as she finally rolled down the window.

"That's . . . too . . . funny," she gasped between peals

of laughter. "How much would you take for that hat? It's wonderful!"

As she righted herself, Vida looked furious. "That's not funny. Look what's happened to my butterflies. One fell off."

Kendra stopped laughing, but she still seemed amused. As Vida retrieved her hat and tried to stick the blue butterfly in with its red, yellow, and orange mates, I approached the car window.

"I'm Ronnie's cousin," I said. "I'm trying to help him. Could we ask you a couple of questions?"

Kendra rolled her eyes. "Oh, brother!" She paused, palms pressing against the steering wheel, gaze now fixed on Vida, who was putting her hat back on. "Okay, I'll give you five minutes. I'm still cleaning out my mother's apartment."

Vida and I walked slowly back toward Carol's unit. I half expected to see Henrietta in the doorway, or at least peeking out between the drapes. There was no sign of her, however. Perhaps she was making more coffee.

"Okay," Kendra said as she joined us, her step and speech brisk. "Let's get this over with."

She unlocked the door and went in ahead of us. The apartment looked exactly as we had left it when Henrietta gave us the tour. Like her adoptive mother, Kendra didn't offer us chairs. She merely stood in the middle of the room, fists on hips, her trim figure clad in blue jeans and a black knit top.

Vida formally introduced us. Kendra didn't put out a hand. "So why do you think I can help you and your dorky cousin?" she demanded.

I tried to phrase my words carefully. "You must have been happy to meet your birth mother. I'm sure that experience answered many questions for you. But I'll bet it also opened up some new ones. Such as, why she had a rather poor track record with men. You knew that your birth father hadn't married her, that she'd been divorced, that her other boyfriends seemed to be unsatisfactory. When you finally met her, she was going with my cousin Ronnie, who—I'll admit—is no prize. Tell me—did you bad-mouth him to the police simply because he was there?"

I thought I'd exhibited tact and self-control. Kendra didn't agree. She burst out laughing. "What a bunch of crap. My real mother's problem was low self-esteem. Her brother was the family favorite, a son, Pop's pride and joy. She told me all about that. He doted on Chuckie, and ignored my mother. Grandma Nerstad was a real cipher. She did everything that her jerk of a husband wanted."

I glanced at Vida. I could tell from her expression that she didn't disagree with Kendra's assessment of the Nerstads.

"As for Ronnie Mallett," Kendra went on, a faintly vicious note in her voice, "he was a real loser. So were the other men in her life, but what would you expect? All she needed was a good therapist to show her how special she was. Right after we met, I tried to get her into therapy, but she put it off."

Simple solutions for a simple teenage girl, I thought. "Someone who's a loser isn't necessarily a killer," I pointed out.

"Ronnie didn't like being bossed," Kendra said, her tone turning bitter. "He drank too much. He lost it and strangled my real mother. End of story." The girl's face was now frozen, and there was sadness in her blue eyes.

I shook my head. "That's not evidence, Kendra. I got the impression you had it in for Ronnie because he made a pass at you."

"So? Lots of guys do that. Besides, it wasn't real hard to discourage Ronnie. All I had to do was tell him that Gavin would beat the crap out of him if he ever touched me again."

"Gavin?" Vida said. "Is that your beau?"

"My what?" Kendra laughed some more. "How quaint. It goes with the hat. Let's say that Gavin Odell is my main squeeze."

"He's rather good-looking," Vida remarked, feigned innocence accompanied by an uncharacteristically sweet expression.

"How do you know?" Kendra shouted.

Vida smirked. "We're stalkers, remember?"

For the first time I saw a hint of alarm in Kendra's face. We were two and she was one. Maybe she was thinking we could actually be dangerous.

"Is that it?" she asked, slightly surly.

"No," I responded, taking advantage of her weak moment. "Please tell me what happened the night your . . . mother was killed."

"I wasn't here." She swung her head, the ponytail sailing at her back.

"You found her," I persisted.

Kendra bit her lip. "I did. Why do you want to know about that? I don't like talking about it."

I softened, for her emotion seemed genuine. "I don't blame you. I lost my parents in a car crash when I was just a little older than you. The hardest thing I ever did was go to the morgue with my brother and identify them."

Kendra winced. "I guess." The bravado seemed to have deserted her. "I'd been out with Gavin. We stopped by around ten-thirty so I could pick up a sweater I'd left here. We were coming from a movie at the Oak Tree on Aurora and going on to a bonfire picnic with some friends on the beach at Golden Gardens. It was kind of cold when we got out of the movie, and it was closer to stop by the apartment than to go all the way to my folks' house by Green Lake."

"You hadn't yet moved?" I asked.

Kendra shook her head. "I moved in the first of April. This was March twenty-seventh. I can't forget the date." She paused and sat down on the arm of a recliner. "I had a key—my mother made one for me—so when she didn't come to the door, I let myself in. Gavin was waiting in the car." Again, she paused and swallowed hard. "She was lying there"—Kendra waved at the area where Vida and I stood—"and at first, I thought she'd passed out. Then, when I bent down, I saw that awful cord around her neck. Her face was all purple and her eyes—" Covering her face with her hands, she stopped and didn't go on.

"That's okay," I soothed, wishing it were possible to pat her shoulder. "What did you do next?"

"I ran out and got Gavin. Then we called 911." Kendra rubbed at her mouth, as if she were trying to rid herself of death's foul taste. "We waited in the car. I couldn't stand being inside with . . . the body."

"Naturally," Vida said. "Did they arrive soon?"

For the first time in several minutes Kendra looked at Vida. "I honestly don't know. It seemed like hours. We had to go to the station out there by Northgate. I called my folks, and they came out, too. It was like two in the morning before we could go home. I was completely drained."

I gave Kendra a moment to compose herself. "Had you been at the apartment earlier in the day?"

"Yes," she replied. "That's when I forgot my sweater. Gavin and I stopped by on the way to the Oak Tree. My real mother wanted to tell me about jobs up in Alaska."

"Was Ronnie there?" I inquired, hoping that the mention of his name wouldn't set Kendra off again. We were approaching cordiality, and I didn't need any roadblocks.

But my cousin hadn't been on the scene. "He might actually have been working," Kendra said sarcastically. "In Friday-night traffic, it takes him a long time to come in from Lynnwood. Gavin and I had gotten there about six. I got off work at QFC at five-thirty and he picked me up after I changed out of my courtesy clerk outfit. We left around seven because we wanted to eat before the movie started. Ronnie still wasn't home. He'd probably stopped off for a few dozen beers on his way."

"Did Carol say anything about him while you were there?" I asked, thinking it'd be nice to sit down.

Kendra shrugged. "I don't remember. If she did, it was probably the usual."

"Which was?" I prodded.

"Oh—'Ronnie's late. I wonder why? Ha-ha.' Or 'I hope he didn't have too many beers and get into a wreck.' Nothing important."

"Nothing to indicate that they were on the outs?" Vida asked.

"No." Kendra didn't seem much interested in the question.

I wasn't giving up on my initial query. "So why do you think he killed her?"

"I told you," Kendra scowled. "They had a fight. Probably over money. Ronnie wasn't paying his share. He spent more on his dumb dog than he did on helping pay the rent."

Money, I knew, was the number one reason why couples fought. Not sex, not religion, not even infidelity, but who was cheap, who was extravagant, who didn't earn enough, why the bills didn't get paid. Yet it still didn't sound like a motive for my cousin. The more I heard about Carol, the more I could see her picking up Ronnie and shaking him by the ankles until his wallet fell out of his pocket.

Vida gestured toward the apartment next door. "What about this Roy? Was he still pestering Carol?"

"Roy?" Kendra looked puzzled. "Oh, him. Talk about

a creep—that's Roy's middle name. Yes, my mother complained about him a couple of times. He came over once
when I was here, a couple of months ago, and started
bragging about what great sex he and Whatshername
were having. My mother told him to get lost."

"Did he?" Vida asked.

"Yes," Kendra replied, a touch of pride in her expression. "He went off like a whipped puppy."

A pounding at the door startled all of us. Kendra's blue
eyes grew wide, then she slapped a hand to her forehead.
"The cops. I forgot about them."

Two young men, one white, one black, and both very
good-looking, stood on the threshold. They tipped their
caps as the black officer, whose name tag read BILLINGS,
politely asked Kendra what was going on.

Kendra was already blushing prettily; I sensed she
knew how to deal with handsome young men. "I feel terrible. I made a huge mistake. I wasn't being stalked.
These two women were trying to track me down to ask
some questions about my mother's murder."

"Oh?" The white officer, whose name tag identified
him as PLANCICH, eyed Vida and me with curiosity.
"How's that?"

I stepped forward and explained. Billings nodded
gravely. "We weren't on duty the night of the homicide,
but of course we got in on the case later." His chest
seemed to puff up a bit as he looked at Kendra.

"Well, now." Vida had edged her way between Kendra
and me. "You certainly solved it quickly. Back home in
Alpine, our sheriff takes forever to bring a murderer to
justice. Of course he's shorthanded and of a most delib-
erate nature. Not to mention that we don't have many
violent crimes. So safe in Alpine."

I tried not to wince at the exaggeration. Billings and
Plancich, however, didn't seem impressed.

"Small-town law-enforcement types don't have the

training or experience we've got here," Plancich said with a swagger that was undoubtedly aimed at Kendra. "We can't afford to take too much time solving cases. Our detectives are overloaded as it is. We all are. It's a tough job. Dangerous, too."

"So," Vida said, now smiling her Cheshire cat grin, "you must all be relieved when the solution to a homicide is so easy."

"This kind of killing usually is," Billings said, making a gesture that took in the entire apartment. "Domestic homicides are the simplest of all."

"Yes, yes," Vida agreed. "How convenient. For you, that is. Let me think—Rojas, that's the name of the detective who was in charge, correct?"

Both officers nodded. "Good man," Plancich said. "He doesn't have very many open cases."

"How nice for him," said Vida. "Of course," she added somewhat slyly, "you can't blame us for having our own doubts. Family, you know. So hard to believe that one of your own can be a killer." She put an arm around me. I wondered if I should burst into tears.

Next to Vida, Kendra was showing signs of impatience. Apparently, the officers were no match for Gavin Odell. "Hey, everybody, I've got to get to work on this place." She gave the policemen a big smile. "Thanks for everything. I'm sorry I put you to so much trouble just now."

"No problem," Billings said, again tipping his hat. "It's kind of nice to come around here when everything's calm for a change."

"Oh?" Vida's nose seemed to twitch. "Were you often called to Carol's apartment?"

"Ah . . ." Billings grimaced. "Two, three times maybe. Domestic violence. No arrests. They always seemed to have calmed down by the time we got here."

"That's often the case," Vida said. "Kiss and make

up. So tiresome for you, though. Was Carol ever badly injured?"

"Carol?" The officers exchanged quick glances. "No," Billings said. "But he was."

Billings and Plancich left after that. I sensed some tension between them as they headed back to their patrol car. Billings apparently had spoken out of turn.

We waited for the patrol car to pull out, which took a few minutes, since it looked as if the partners were checking in with their squad. Before we parted with Kendra, she asked if she could have the hat. Vida refused.

"Why, I've had this hat for over twenty years," she declared. "It would be like losing a family member. Look in the Sears catalogue. I'm sure you'll find some similar items."

Kendra hadn't looked enthusiastic.

Finally, when we got into the Lexus, Vida was agog. "Don't you see what that slipup by the police means? Carol was beating on Ronnie, not the other way around. I have to wonder if Roy's scratches and his black eye weren't defense measures by Carol, but attacks on him. And the whole case against your cousin is flimsy indeed, based on a common history, not solid evidence."

"That's what it sounds like," I admitted. "I wonder if they'd let me talk to Ronnie over the phone. I'd like to give him some encouragement."

"By all means," Vida urged. "It's suppertime. Where shall we go? You can call from there."

I remembered that there was a rather good grill over on Aurora that also had a full-service bar. Vida might scold, but I could use a drink. It had been a very long day, and the worst was yet to come.

While Vida mulled over the menu, I phoned from the restaurant. It took what seemed like forever to have the jailers put Ronnie on the phone, and when I heard his voice, there was no life in it.

"Tell me something," I said, knowing that there was a time limit to our conversation. "Did Carol beat you?"

"Huh? What do you mean?" Ronnie sounded confused.

"Did she hit you, throw things, try to punch you out?"

A long pause. "She could get real mad." Another pause. "Sometimes, yeah, she'd whale on me. It was no big deal. I can take care of myself."

"Did you ever call the cops?"

"Huh? The cops?" This time I could hear Ronnie suck in his breath. "Well . . . maybe we called once. Somebody else upstairs might've called, too. We were kinda loud."

I decided not to pursue that line of questioning. I figured I already had the answer. "We're making progress," I said, putting enthusiasm into my voice. "We think the police investigation was a knee-jerk reaction. There's no real evidence against you, Ronnie."

"Then why am I in the slammer?"

"Because you got railroaded," I replied. "Oh, I found out where Budweiser is. He's with Mr. Chan's son and grandchildren."

"They'll eat him," Ronnie said in a dismal voice. "That's what those Chinamen do. They eat cats and dogs."

"Not Peter Chan," I declared. "He's as American as you are."

"I'll bet. They're all alike."

"I'll try to get Budweiser back as soon as I can," I promised.

"Hunh. I'll bet. I mean," he added hastily, "they won't let him go. Buddy's probably already in the soup pot."

"Stop that, Ronnie," I ordered. "We've learned a lot of things in the last twenty-four hours, all to your benefit. Tonight we're going to check with the bars to find you an alibi."

"Yeah, sure." He paused again, then sighed. "Wish I was there. Damn."

Either Ronnie's telephone time was up, or he had hung up on me.

"Really," Vida said after I'd ordered a vodka gimlet, "if you plan on drinking this evening, why on earth are you ordering an alcoholic beverage now?"

"I don't have to drink in a tavern," I said. "I can order a soda or coffee, just like you will. Besides, we aren't going bar-hopping for a couple of hours. Vodka goes through your system much faster than any other kind of liquor."

"What an appalling piece of knowledge!" Vida exclaimed. "You've researched drinking? Emma, I'm shocked."

"No, you're not." I grinned. "It goes back to my college days, when it was very important to know how much you could drink without puking all over your date."

"Aargh!" Vida looked as if she might become ill from listening to me.

While we waited for our orders I checked to see if I had any messages on my voice mail. Somewhat to my surprise, there was one from Milo.

"Just thought you'd want to know," he said in his familiar drawl, "the O'Neills and the Harquists got into it last night at the Icicle Creek Tavern. Stubby O'Neill is in the hospital with two broken arms. Ozzie and Rudy Harquist are in jail. The tavern's damned near wrecked. Hope you're having fun in the city." He ended the conversation with an upbeat note to his voice, which indicated that he was probably looking forward to a romantic evening with his new love.

I relayed the information to Vida, who was aghast, but not for the reason I might have anticipated. "Is that what we're in for tonight? I thought people in the city merely shot each other or used knives."

"Not all the time," I replied with a straight face. "Blood feuds aren't as common here. Aren't you a little bit surprised about the O'Neills and Harquists? I thought things had calmed down between them."

"Apparently not," Vida said. "Cap Harquist and his boys have been logging over in Idaho off and on for the past few years, but I guess they came back to stay this winter. I suppose it was only a matter of time before the feud broke out again."

Fifty years ago, when logging was king in Skykomish County, Paddy O'Neill and Cap Harquist had worked together for one of the now-defunct logging companies. They had been best friends who'd had a falling-out—not over a woman or money or who was going to buy the next beer—but over a billy goat named Ted. The goat was Cap's pride and joy. He'd put a bell around the animal's neck and a straw hat on its head. One night Ted got loose out on the Burl Creek Road. Paddy, who was drunk, ran his truck over Ted. The only thing that didn't get flattened was the hat. Cap never forgave Paddy, and the feud was on.

Paddy was now in his eighties and confined to a wheelchair. Cap, however, was still robust at seventy-seven. There were three O'Neill sons and two Harquist scions. They had all gone through school together, fighting every inch of the way until the high-school principal expelled all of them. Now in middle age, the five men still picked fights with each other. Sometimes Cap joined in. Fortunately, there were only daughters in the third generation. They were mostly teenagers, and contented themselves with making cruel remarks about their enemies' weight, complexions, and wardrobes. I had to wonder whether the physical or the emotional abuse was more damaging.

"So silly," Vida remarked after our orders had arrived.

"It was always a relief when either one or the other of the families left Alpine to work somewhere else. Of course," she added, more softly, "it wasn't a good sign for the local economy."

I agreed. Only one mill remained in Alpine. For those whose vocation was logging, it meant working elsewhere, either in another forest or driving their trucks between far-flung destinations. Hard times had hit Alpine in the early eighties, as the last of the great harvests were completed and the environmentalists got their way. The song of the mill whistle and the rumble of the rigs had all but faded into history.

"The women in those families are as bad as the men," Vida said between mouthfuls of lamb chop. "Vicious. Mean-spirited. Very few brains between them."

"I hope Scott Chamoud knows about all this," I said. "He certainly wouldn't have the background."

"Of course not," Vida agreed. "I've never sat him down to give it. Luckily, we'll be back on Monday."

I sipped my gimlet and fretted. My youthful reporter was a city boy, from Portland, Oregon. He was unwise in the ways of small towns. Knocking on an O'Neill or a Harquist door could prove dangerous. I took the cell phone out of my handbag and dialed Scott's number.

He wasn't in, so I left a message. Then I remembered that he was going home for Easter to be with his family.

"Damn!" I struck myself on the forehead. "Scott's out of town. What was I thinking of?"

"So he is." Vida frowned. "Well, we have until Tuesday to cover the story. Unless," she added with a tilt of her head, "you want to go home now."

"No. We can't." The half-finished filet on my plate suddenly didn't look so appetizing. "I'm negligent. We shouldn't have left *The Advocate* so stripped of manpower. Here we are, running around on what may be a wild-goose chase, and—"

"You know it's not." Vida gave me a hard stare from under the cartwheel's brim. "We've made considerable progress."

"Ronnie doesn't think so," I pointed out.

"But we have." Vida put her fork down and rested her chin on her hands. "See here, Emma, I'm the last person to slight *The Advocate*. Not to be overly dramatic, but we may be saving your cousin's life. If you feel so strongly about this ridiculous brawl, then I can return to Alpine immediately on the bus. There's one that gets into town at ten-twelve, as you well know. What do you think?"

I was torn. It was true that we had most of Monday and Tuesday to cover the story. But it was a big one by Alpine standards, and we'd have to be very careful so that none of the feuding participants got mad and sued us. Milo would have the basic facts, but none of the details. Only Vida knew the full background.

"I'd prefer not going it alone here," I said slowly. "Hard news isn't your usual beat." Indeed, Vida's rare front-page stories always contained the flavor of her House and Home section. If I let her write up this one, I'd have to edit it closely to make sure we didn't get descriptions of what the brawlers were wearing, where they'd gone on their last vacation, and what kind of peanuts had been served at the Icicle Creek Tavern.

"Let me call the bus depot," I said, getting up to use the pay phone. I was wary of mounting charges on the cell. "I think the bus makes at least one stop out here on Aurora."

I was right. The local that went over Stevens Pass was due some ten blocks south in twenty minutes. We hurriedly finished our meal, paid the bill, and drove off in the Lexus.

"I really hate to see you go," I said. "What will you do for Easter tomorrow?"

Vida chortled. "Inflict myself on one of my relatives

whom I was trying to avoid. It'll be fine. I don't like leaving Cupcake alone this long anyway."

Cupcake was Vida's canary. "Edith Holmgren's feeding the cats," I said. Edith was a widow who lived across the street and one door down. We had never been particularly friendly until I acquired Rheims and Rouen. Then I discovered that she owned seven cats, and apparently didn't become chatty with anyone who wasn't a cat lover.

"Edith." Vida sneered. "She enters those silly cats in the county fair every year. They've never won so much as an honorable mention. Scruffy animals, if you ask me. One of them is cross-eyed."

We were five minutes early at the bus stop. I pulled into a passenger loading zone. "I'll wait until you get safely on the bus."

Vida started to say something, interrupted herself, and murmured, "Of course. The hookers. And their pimps."

"Right. Not to mention the drug deals going down on a Saturday night."

"Goodness. The city. I'll be glad to get home. So reassuring."

Since Vida's early return was triggered by mayhem, violence, and her desire to be in the thick of things, I had to suppress a smile. "Alpine. So quiet. So harmonious."

"Emma!" Vida turned sharply. "At least the O'Neills and the Harquists are still alive!"

"I know." I laughed, then saw what looked like the outline of an approaching bus. "Here you go. I won't forget your luggage."

Halfway out of the car, Vida glanced at me over her shoulder. "You be careful. I mean it."

"I will. Hurry, the bus has a green light."

I could see a couple of hookers near the bus stop, looking tired and bored. A few yards away, a homeless man was propped up against a low concrete wall. Three teenagers carrying a very large and very loud ghetto blaster boogied down the street. This was not Vida's turf; I wasn't even sure it was mine anymore.

Just as Vida moved closer to the curb, a man approached her from the other direction. He appeared to be middle-aged, with a beard and wearing jeans and what looked like a gold 49ers jacket. He spoke to Vida, who rebuffed him with a swing of her purse. The man slunk away in the same direction he had come. He must have been panhandling. I let out a sigh of relief.

The big silver vehicle pulled in ahead of me. I couldn't see Vida get on, but a moment later the bus edged into traffic, and she was gone. To a far, far better place—at least I knew that's what Vida was thinking.

Now I had to go it alone.

Chapter Eight

AFTER VIDA LEFT, I felt lost. I sat in the passenger loading zone for a couple of minutes, vaguely watching the motley crew that plied Aurora. A patrol car slowed down as it came by, and I assumed the officers were going to check out the pimps and hookers. Instead, they all but stopped to stare at me. Then they picked up speed and drove on. Apparently, a well-dressed middle-aged woman in a new Lexus wasn't considered a threat to the justice system.

At last I headed off to cruise the bars of Greenwood. Ronnie had mentioned Freddy's, which was on a corner at a major intersection. There was parking in back, but I decided to find a spot on the street. The Lexus might be a magnet for rowdy drunks staggering out of the bar.

Freddy's was also a restaurant, the kind where you could get a tough steak and a shriveled baked potato after you'd managed not to pass out in the bar. They served hard liquor as well as beer and wine. I sat down at a table slightly larger than a silver dollar and ordered the first brand I could think of. Which was, naturally, Budweiser. This was no place for Seattle's famous microbrews or exotic foreign imports. If I'd asked for a Harp's, they would have probably brought me a ukulele.

Naturally, I felt conspicuous. And nervous. To give my hands a task, I went to the cigarette machine and bought a pack of Winston Ultra-Lights. If Vida had been with me, *depraved* would have been the least of the adjectives she'd have used to describe me.

At going on nine o'clock, the large, utilitarian bar was about half-full. Twenty years ago Freddy's had been some kind of Masonic hall. I didn't know how many metamorphoses it had gone through since, but I doubted that any of the subsequent owners had spent much on decorating. Except for the usual neon beer signs and a couple of scenic paintings that looked as if they'd been done by the numbers—but not necessarily in order—the bar was strictly minimalist. I was already depressed, and I hadn't yet been served.

My waitress came toward me, walking as if her feet hurt. She was a dishwater blond on the plump side, probably about my age. The lines in her pale face showed the usual road marks of a life lived hard and unhappily. I took advantage of her mild expression of curiosity.

"Do you know Ronnie Mallett?" I asked, hoping I looked friendly.

She frowned. "Is he the guy who offed his girlfriend?"

"Allegedly," I replied. "I'm his cousin Emma. Who did he hang out with around here?"

The waitress glanced around the room. "See that guy with the long red hair sitting with the older bald guy? That's Morrie. He and Ronnie bowled together sometimes."

"Good," I said, spotting Morrie at a table near the jukebox. "Anybody else?"

"Mmm . . . I don't think so. Wait—there's a guy at the bar—I can't think of his name. He's the one with the ob- vious butt crack."

Great. "Great," I said, trying to sound enthusiastic. "You've been a real help. I think I'll mingle, okay?"

"Sure. You running a tab?"

I shook my head and went for my wallet. Leaving a

hefty tip, I decided to start with Butt Crack. Fortunately—
I guess—the bar stool on his left had just been vacated.

He had an extra chin and no neck, but his face was
pleasant enough when he turned to stare. "Got enough
room there, little lady?" he inquired.

It wasn't a great opening line, but given the circumstances, it sufficed. "I'm good," I said. "How would you
like to be interviewed?"

"Huh?" Butt Crack's broad face looked startled. "Like
on TV?"

"Not quite," I replied. "I'm a newspaper reporter."

Butt Crack chuckled richly, then motioned at the bartender, a tall, reedy man with half glasses. "Hey, Jack.
This little lady wants to put me in the paper. What do you
think of that?"

"I think she's crazy," Jack shot back. "Humor her."

"I sure will." With effort, Butt Crack turned to sit sideways on the bar stool. "What do you need? My opinion
of the war in wherever it is? What I think of Clinton and
those broads in the White House? Who's going to win the
pennant?"

"Let's start with a name," I said, dutifully taking a pen
and notepad from my handbag.

Butt Crack grinned, revealing a chipped front tooth.
"Avery. Rhymes with savory. Avery McMillan." He
reached out a big paw, clutched my hand, and almost
sent me to an orthopedic surgeon.

I tried not to flinch. "I'm Emma," I said again, putting
the mangled hand behind my back and wiggling my fingers to make sure they were still functioning. "I heard
you're a friend of Ronnie Mallet's."

"Damn," Avery said with a shake of his head. Up
close, he looked as if he was in his early forties. There was
a small scar etched in one eyebrow and another on his
chin. Avery would have fit in nicely at the Icicle Creek
Tavern. "Poor bastard," he muttered. "Whatever he did

to that Carol broad, she probably asked for it. She was one mean bitch. Excuse my language. I meant witch. They rhyme, see?"

"Yes, I do," I replied with a straight face. "Did Ronnie and Carol come here often?"

"Quite a bit," Avery replied as some of the other patrons began to edge closer. I figured the notebook was the drawing card. Most of the writing at Freddy's was probably done on cocktail napkins. "The last time they were here, about a month ago, Carol and that redheaded gal who used to go with Ronnie really got into it." He turned to the bartender. "Hey, Jack, you had to throw those two broads out, right?"

"You bet," Jack said with a solemn nod. "They were busting up the glassware."

"Do you mean Maybeth?" I asked, beginning to think that the Icicle Creek Tavern had nothing on Freddy's.

"Beth," Avery said with emphasis. "Rhymes with . . ." He stopped and scratched his head. "Never mind."

"Were they fighting over Ronnie?" I asked, remembering to scribble a note or two.

Avery glanced at Jack. "Was that what started it? Or was it something Beth's boyfriend said to Carol?"

"Roy?" Jack responded. "I don't know. It was a real mess."

"Roy," Avery repeated brightly. "Beth's Roy friend. Get it?"

"Yes," I said, and forced a smile.

"I think that's right," Avery went on. "It was Roy, only maybe he said something nasty to Ronnie. Anyway, the two girls got into it. Carol had a real bad temper, and you know what redheads are like. Va-va-vroom!" One hand shot up toward the ceiling, apparently in imitation of a rocket launch.

The man called Morrie had gravitated to the bar.

"Hey, Ave," he said in a good-natured tone, "did I hear you bad-mouth redheads?" Morrie shook his own long carrot-colored locks.

Avery laughed, the hearty chuckle that almost made him endearing. "How come nobody calls you 'Red'? You know—rhymes with bed." He leered and chuckled some more.

"Because my two older brothers were both called Red," Morrie answered with a smile. "Our mom never knew who'd come when she called."

Avery nodded as if this was one of the wisest statements he'd ever heard. "Can't blame her. Hey, the little lady's interviewing me about Ronnie and Carol. You jealous?" He nudged Morrie, who almost spilled some of the beer in the schooner he was holding.

"I might be," Morrie replied pleasantly. "What gives?"

I decided to get to the point and looked at Jack to include him in the conversation. "I'm trying to find out if Ronnie has an alibi for the night of the murder. Did any of you see him two weeks ago Friday late in the evening?"

Avery shook his head. "I came in early after I got off work. I went home around eight."

Jack gave the bar a swipe with a damp towel. "Ronnie was here, though. He came in before nine, had a couple of beers, and said he was going on to the Satellite Room down the block."

"Do you think he'd been drinking before he got here?" I asked.

Jack shrugged. "Could be. He wasn't drunk, though."

"I remember," Morrie said. "He was alone. He seemed kind of down."

"That's right," Jack agreed. "He was upset because his dog, Buddy, had gotten into a fight and come out the worse for wear. He'd had to take him to the vet's."

I remembered that when Ronnie had been arrested, he, too, had been suffering some wear and tear. "How were his spirits?" I inquired. "Did he look as if he'd had some kind of row?"

The men all exchanged glances that bordered on smirks. "You bet," Jack said with one of his solemn nods. "Poor Ronnie was all banged up. He didn't say anything, but my guess is that Carol went after him again."

"Again?" I feigned innocence.

Avery chuckled, but there was no mirth in the sound. "I said she was one mean . . . witch. She was always beating on Ronnie. Hell, she beat up Roy, too."

"Yeah," Morrie put in. "I heard once that was what broke up her marriage to some guy a long time ago. She'd whale on him while he was asleep. Jeez, you hear all this crap about men beating women, but there's two sides to that story. Women can be ornery as hell. Ornerier, maybe. They don't need to be drunk to get mean."

A sudden silence fell over the little group. Jack smiled for the first time. "Present company excluded, naturally."

"No offense," Avery hurriedly added.

"None taken," I said, smiling.

I, however, was more reasonable than some members of my sex. A raven-haired Hispanic woman and a frosted blond begged to differ.

"If men weren't such assholes, women wouldn't have to defend themselves," the blond asserted.

"That's not defending yourself," Morrie retorted, "that's going on the offensive. It's different, Terri."

"It's bullshit," the Hispanic woman snapped. "You men got to be so damned macho all the time. You think hitting women proves you got cojones. I spit on all of you." She spat not on them, but on the floor, only an inch from my Joan & David suede shoes.

"Knock it off, Nita," said Morrie, still trying to be

good-natured. "You're just pissed because that last loser of yours punched out a couple of teeth."

"Why shouldn't she be pissed?" demanded a tall black woman with imposing dreadlocks. "That's her whole point. You bastards always start it."

"Bullshit!" roared the older bald man who had been sitting with Morrie. "The only way you can get through to a woman is—"

"Men are scum! Listen to what Larry did—"

"Larry was on crack. He's okay the rest of the—"

"I had one old lady who—"

The argument was underway. I finished my beer, grabbed my cigarettes from the bar, and slipped away. Nobody seemed to notice.

I could see the sign for the Satellite Room from Freddy's entrance. It was midway down the block, across the street. I was waiting for the light to change when Terri, the frosted blond, came running up to me.

"You were asking about Ronnie?" she said, out of breath.

"Right. Do you know him?"

"Sure. Ronnie's a sweetheart. He didn't kill Carol." She glanced over her shoulder, as if she expected someone to follow her outside. "The night Carol was murdered, I sat with him for a while. She'd knocked him around, and he was really down."

"Do you remember when he got to Freddy's and when he left?"

Terri nodded. "I showed up around eight-thirty. Ronnie was already there. He left a little before ten. He was going to the Satellite." She pointed across the street. "He was meeting someone. It wasn't a date, it was sort of like business."

"Did he say who?"

"No. I got the impression it was a man. But not a buddy."

"Did you tell the police about this?"

Terri shook her head. "They never talked to me. I think they only talked to Jack, because he's the bartender. But Jack gets busy with his drink orders and doesn't always see what's going on. Unless there's trouble. He's good at spotting that."

Some noises were erupting from the vicinity of the bar. Terri whirled around. "I've got to go."

She dashed inside. I wondered if a full-fledged brawl was under way. Seattle and Alpine weren't so different after all.

The Satellite Room was in a restaurant that was a cut above Freddy's. Most of the diners seemed to be sober. I could almost imagine that the menu featured more than rib-eye steak.

The bar had been around in its present incarnation for a long time. The neon satellites looked like they came from the space-race era. There were plenty of customers, however, and I had to adjust my eyes to the dimness before I could find an empty table. Then, just as I was about to sit down, I decided to go straight to the bar itself.

A buxom woman about my age was on duty, her dyed platinum hair pulled back in a not-so-tidy chignon and her face heavily made up to cover old acne scars.

"What'll it be, honey?" she asked in a husky voice.

Wisdom dictated that I should stick to beer, so this time I got exotic and ordered a Heineken. Then I introduced myself, explaining what I wanted to know about Ronnie's presence in the Satellite Room on the night of the murder.

"Ronnie." The name slipped like Jell-O from the bartender's red lips. "I'm Honey, by the way." She put out a hand. "Nice to meet you. You don't look like Ronnie's cousin. Is he the family black sheep?"

"Sort of," I admitted. "At least he's the only one who's been charged with homicide."

Honey smiled. "Well, he was here that night. He came in a little after ten, I think. He had a shot of bourbon here at the bar"—she nodded toward the end where the cash register sat—"and then some guy came in to join him and they sat at a table over there by the Sputnik. They got into something really deep—I've never seen Ronnie so serious. He only had one more drink before the other guy left about eleven-thirty. I served Ronnie one more, then he took off a little after midnight."

"Did the police question you?" I asked.

Honey shook her head. "They came in on a Tuesday when I was off. They never came back. Walt—he's the other bartender—couldn't tell them anything."

I did some calculations in my head. Ronnie's alibi was solid from eight-thirty on. According to Terri, he'd arrived at Freddy's even earlier, which was well before Maybeth said she'd heard him slam out of the apartment. Either Maybeth was wrong about the time, or someone else had been with Carol after Ronnie left, but possibly before she was killed. Kendra had found the body around ten-thirty, while Ronnie was drinking in the Satellite Room.

"What about the other guy?" I asked after Honey had filled several orders from the cocktail waitress. "Did you recognize him?"

"No, he wasn't a regular." Honey paused to re-pin some of the platinum strands that had fallen into her eyes. "He was a big guy around forty, bald, broad-shouldered. He didn't look like a drinker, though he had a Scotch and soda. He paid for his own, by the way. I remember, because he didn't leave a tip." She made a comical face.

My brain did some more quick work. The man's description fit Sam Addison. But then it probably fit several thousand men in Seattle.

"Did Ronnie and Mr. Cheap argue? Or were they friendly?"

Honey nodded at someone across the room, presumably a thirsty customer. "Serious. They were both serious." She picked up a glass, filled it with ice, then squirted what looked like bourbon from the drink dispenser. "Excuse me, Mel needs a refill."

I'd learned what I was seeking, and maybe a little bit more. Leaving a five-dollar tip and a half-empty glass, I exited the Satellite Room. If Sam Addison—or anybody else—had met Ronnie in the bar, why hadn't my dim-bulb cousin mentioned it? And if it was Sam Addison, why had they engaged in an earnest conversation?

As I got into the Lexus, it dawned on me that there could be another suspect in the case. If Sam Addison had been with Ronnie around ten-thirty or eleven, he'd also been near the murder scene. But off the top of my head, I couldn't think why Sam would kill Carol.

I decided to sleep on it.

Easter Mass at St. James Cathedral was standing room only. I ended up near one of the exits, craning to see the altar, which had been repositioned in the middle of the church. At five-foot-four, I couldn't see much more than the occasional bobbing of heads. The music was lovely, however, a far cry from Annie Jeanne Dupré torturing the ancient organ at St. Mildred's.

The weather, however, was another matter. Clouds had rolled in and the wind was blowing from the west as I drove the short distance to the city jail. At a stoplight, I checked my messages on the cell phone. I thought Vida might have called, but there was no word from her. Instead, a terse male voice informed me that there had been an emergency regarding my cousin, one Ronald Mallett. Could I contact the jail as soon as possible?

With gloom to match the skies, I parked the car and hurried to the reception area. A plump black woman with very short hair was on duty. She checked my ID, then became less officious.

"Your cousin Ronnie tried to kill himself last night," she said in a low voice. "He's in the infirmary."

My knees sagged. I scarcely knew my cousin, but the news had the power to unsettle me. "How? By hanging?"

"No," the woman replied. "He stabbed himself through the ear with a fork."

"A fork?" My voice was incredulous.

"Yes." The woman remained very serious, though I suspected it took some effort. "The forks here have three tines. Apparently, he broke off the ones on each side and rammed the rest of the fork into his ear."

In almost thirty years of journalism, I'd never heard of anyone using a fork to commit suicide. There had been a surgeon in Portland who had tried to drown himself in the Willamette River, but had waded back to shore when he discovered the water was extremely cold and he was afraid he'd catch pneumonia. One of the Gustavsons in Alpine had eaten chokecherries, but they were so bitter that before he poisoned himself, he threw up all over his suicide note. And then there was Milo's ex-brother-in-law who had hit himself over the head with a ball-peen hammer, but had fallen unconscious long before he was dead.

A fork, however, seemed like a means of destruction suited to Ronnie. So did his failure to do himself in.

"How is he?" I asked, my nerves beginning to steady.

"He punctured an eardrum," the woman replied, allowing herself a small smile. "He may suffer some hearing loss. Would you like to see him?"

"Of course."

She gave me directions to the infirmary, which was on another floor. Ronnie was in a large ward with perhaps another half-dozen patients. He had a big bandage on his head, an IV in his hand, and appeared to be asleep.

There was no visitors' chair, though a stone-faced

guard stood at the end of the bed. I nodded at the man; he acknowledged me with a flicker of his eyelids.

"Ronnie?" I said softly.

No answer. I tried again.

Ronnie's eyes fluttered open. "Huh?" He grimaced as he tried to focus on me. "Emma?"

"Yes. How do you feel?"

"Crappy." He closed his eyes.

"Why did you pull such a stunt?" I asked, unable to keep the anger out of my voice.

"Why not?"

"Because I know you didn't kill Carol. I've got your alibi virtually established."

"Big deal." He moved awkwardly in the bed, one hand at the bandage by his right ear. The guard scarcely blinked. Maybe he wasn't real, just a cardboard cutout with battery-operated features.

"Don't you care?" I demanded. "Isn't that what you asked me to do? Why else am I here?"

He groaned a bit, then opened his eyes again and made a feeble effort to sit up. "My head sounds like there's a Harley in it. Can I have some water?"

I held the plastic carafe for him while he drank through the straw in fits and starts. "Tomorrow morning," I said, "I'm going to see Detective Rojas and tell him what I've found out. We'll see if they can drop the charges. Wouldn't you like to get out of here?"

Ronnie took one last sip, then pushed the carafe away. "Did you get Buddy from those Chinamen?" he asked, ignoring my question.

"Not yet," I admitted. "Buddy's fine. Mr. Chan's grandchildren love him."

Ronnie looked dubious. "You sure?"

"Yes," I said, not telling him that the children's affection could be an obstacle to Buddy's return. "Buddy's safe and sound in Lake City."

"Know what we did last year?" Ronnie's voice brightened slightly. "Me 'n' Buddy went to one of those Easter egg hunts for little kids. I let Buddy help the kids find eggs. They were all blind, see, so Buddy'd sniff out the eggs before the beeper things could go off so the kids'd hear where they were. Buddy was great. The kids loved him."

"Buddy sounds like a wonderful dog," I said. "Ronnie, you have to tell me something. Who did you meet at the Satellite Room the night of the murder?"

What little color there was in Ronnie's face drained away. "How'd you know about that?"

"I've been investigating, remember? Isn't that what you wanted me to do?"

Ronnie winced. "Yeah, yeah, but . . . Does it matter?"

"Does what matter?" I was getting impatient.

"Who I met?"

"Yes," I said emphatically. "It matters a great deal. Who was it?"

Ronnie expelled a big sigh, then another groan. "It was Darryl Lindholm, Carol's ex from way back. He finally wanted to marry her."

Chapter Nine

DARRYL LINDHOLM WAS certainly a name from out of the past, the young man who had abandoned Carol Nerstad and her unborn baby. I was so surprised that I actually stumbled against the bed, causing Ronnie to wince and groan one more time.

"When did he come back into the picture?" I asked in astonishment.

Ronnie gave what appeared to be a shrug. "I dunno. I'm not sure he was ever out of it."

"What do you mean?" Gingerly, I perched on the edge of the bed. These stand-up interviews were wearing me down.

"Carol'd been seeing him off and on for years," Ronnie explained. "At least, that's what I figured when this Darryl character showed up one night about two months ago."

"Why?" I asked, wondering what Vida would make of this revelation.

"I guess he still liked her." Ronnie's mouth turned down. "He'd been married and divorced a couple of times. Carol laughed it off, but I think she got a kick outta him hangin' around. 'Specially since she had their kid with her."

I tried not to get distracted by the sobbing family that had gathered around the last bed in the row. The little drama didn't seem to disturb the stone-faced guard. If I poked him with a safety pin, would he react? "Does Darryl live in Seattle?" I asked.

"I guess," Ronnie said, his voice still lifeless. "Carol didn't tell me nothin' about him."

"But you knew Darryl was Kendra's birth father, right?"

"He told me that," Ronnie said, "not Carol."

"Had Kendra met him?"

"Maybe. I guess." Ronnie was losing interest in the subject.

"Why did Darryl want to see you?" I persisted.

Ronnie grimaced. "He's a jerk."

"That's the wrong answer."

My cousin—oddly enough, I was beginning to think of him as an actual relative—wriggled awkwardly in the bed. "Like I told you, he wanted to marry her. He was tellin' me to butt out."

The sobbing at the last bed was growing louder and more intense. Unlike a hospital, there was no curtain to pull for privacy. "So why didn't you tell the police where you were while Carol was getting herself killed?"

"Say what?" Ronnie put a hand to his injured ear.

I repeated the question more loudly. Ronnie turned away. "It was none of their damned business."

"Ronnie . . ." I was getting exasperated. "If you'd told them about meeting Darryl Lindholm, you wouldn't be here. What's the big secret?"

Ronnie didn't answer. The sobbing subsided as a doctor hurried to the bed.

"If you don't tell me, I'm leaving," I declared. "Leaving, as in going back to Alpine."

He finally looked at me again. "You won't tell?"

"Of course not," I lied. The group by the last bed had withdrawn into a small cluster of bowed heads and slumped shoulders. A nurse had joined the doctor.

"Darryl wanted to buy me off," Ronnie said, showing

a spark of anger. Or maybe it was indignation. "Like I was some kinda boy toy."

"That's what upset you so?" Ronnie was full of surprises, few of them good.

"Yeah, sure. Why shouldn't it? A grand, like I was some cheap whore. You'da thought he'd offer me five figures, right?"

I sighed. The doctor was now speaking to the circle of visitors. They sighed. Or so it appeared.

"You think I'm gonna tell anybody that?" Ronnie said with anger in his voice. "A stinkin' grand. I told him to fuck off."

Though I was appalled at Ronnie's unconcern in the face of serving an unjust prison term, I took his wrath as a good sign. Near the last bed, the family members clung to each other and began moving away. The nurse was pulling a sheet over the patient's face.

I took that as a bad sign.

The guard kept looking straight ahead.

I tried to convince Ronnie that he had to tell his attorney about the meeting with Darryl Lindholm. Ronnie refused to agree, but by the time I left he seemed to be weakening. Naturally, I would tell Alvin Sternoff myself. But first, I had to track down Darryl Lindholm.

There was only one listing under that name in the Seattle directory. Darryl G. Lindholm lived in Magnolia, just south of Ballard and the Lake Washington Ship Canal. I dialed his number from the lobby, but wasn't surprised when he didn't answer. It was Easter Sunday, after all.

Certainly, it was the strangest Easter in my experience. On the surface, the Resurrection didn't mesh with barhopping, Ronnie's self-destructiveness, and a corpse hauled off before my eyes. Except, of course, that it did. In life there was death, and in death there was life. My spiritual side, slim as it may be, was being buried under my cousin's sea of troubles. But Ronnie was all about Easter, too.

I didn't leave a message on Darryl's machine. His announcement had been terse and to the point: "I'm out or on the phone. Leave your name and number."

Next I tried Alvin Sternoff. I assumed he was Jewish; therefore, maybe he'd be home.

He was, and sounded harried. "An alibi?" he said after I related all that I'd learned on my recent adventures. "Darn, why didn't he say so? This Darryl is Carol's ex-husband?"

"No," I corrected him. "The husband's out of the picture. So far, anyway. Darryl's the ex-boyfriend, originally from Alpine. He's the father of Carol's daughter. There's also Roy, a recent ex-boyfriend who's now dating Maybeth, the next-door neighbor."

"Boy, this is confusing," Alvin said. "Carol must have had something going for her."

"You realize that Maybeth's lying—or maybe just mistaken—about when Ronnie left the apartment," I pointed out.

"She is? Wow." Alvin paused, apparently trying to sift through my information. "But after Ronnie left, whoever came next got into it with Carol and then left her still alive?"

"We don't know that for sure," I said. "I'll be confronting Maybeth again this afternoon."

"Maybe I should come," Alvin said, though he sounded dubious.

"No need," I assured him. "I'll let you know what I find out."

"Would you?" Relief was evident in his tone. "I'm having dinner with my folks over in Bellevue. On Sundays, they always eat around three. They hate it when I'm late."

"That's fine," I said with a smile. Alvin might be disorganized, but he seemed like a very sweet young man. I wished I knew a suitable young woman. But then he probably already had a girlfriend. "We'll be in touch."

It was noon, but I wasn't hungry yet. On my way out to Maybeth's, I took a detour and drove to my old neighborhood. Sentimentality doesn't run strong with me, but I was curious. How did the present occupants of my old family home spend a cloudy Easter Sunday?

Just as I turned the corner, the rain started, small, harmless drops dotting the windshield. A boy about seven and a girl not more than three were searching the garden for eggs. Two women, both in their thirties, stood on the porch. By the old hydrangea bush, a bearded man with rimless glasses cheered on the children. An older woman in an apron held open the screen door and spoke to one of the younger women. I kept going, not just trying to avoid attracting their attention, but because an SUV was pulling up behind me. It parked under the maple tree, and in my rearview mirror, I saw two more children jump out onto the parking strip while a man and a woman emerged carrying covered dishes. It was a cozy, charming scene, but faintly foreign to me. We Lords had enjoyed a private celebration, usually feasting on ham or roast beef. There were always plenty of leftovers. That had seemed like a good thing at the time. In retrospect, maybe it wasn't. If family and friends had been allowed into our little circle, we wouldn't have had so much food to spare. Maybe that would have been a better thing.

Increasing my speed, I turned at the corner to head north and west to the Greenwood district. Skirting Green Lake, I wondered about the Addisons. Were they celebrating Easter together? Or was Sam holed up in a drab motel while Kathy sat proud and alone in their immaculate house? Was Kendra making mad, passionate love with Gavin Odell at her new apartment?

A block from my destination, I pulled over to call Vida. She'd be back from church, but probably not yet en route to whichever relatives were hosting Easter dinner.

"My, my!" she exclaimed. "You certainly have garnered some interesting information. Especially regarding Darryl Lindholm. I wonder what he's been up to all these years. It's dreadful when people move away and lose touch. Divorced, you say? Twice? What does that tell you?"

"He's a pain in the butt?"

"Emma, your language is deteriorating in the city," Vida scolded. "Perhaps the divorces indicate that Darryl never got over his first love."

"Carol?" I was doubtful. "She sounds like a real bit . . . of goods," I added hastily. "Women who beat up on men aren't any better than men who beat women."

"Frustration. Thwarted love. Perhaps they were meant to be together." Vida's voice had taken on a lilting note. Clearly, she had slipped into one of her pearls-and-lace romantic moods. "You, of all people, should know what I mean."

In such moods, Vida always rhapsodizes on my love affair with Tom Cavanaugh. No matter how many times Tom keeps postponing our long-desired union, his excuses make perfect sense to Vida. Indeed, whatever reason he gives is, in her opinion, evidence of his sterling character. Sometimes, I want to strangle both of them.

Which brought me back to Carol's murder. "I'm on my way to see Maybeth again," I said. "I know she's lying, or at the very least, she made a mistake about when Ronnie left the apartment."

"An unreliable sort of person," Vida agreed. "Are you certain Ronnie won't try to kill himself again?"

"He'll be watched," I replied, "and no, I'm not certain. The man is utterly spineless. If he does manage to get out of jail, what will become of him?"

"He needs a good woman," Vida declared, still on her pink cloud. "Someone who can straighten him out. Oh, I know the fallacy of trying to change people—but occasionally, it's a matter of not having had an opportunity. Have you spoken with his parents?"

"No," I replied. "They're in a retirement community in Arizona. I don't think Ronnie hears from them much. And from what I remember, they'd be no help."

"Which is why Ronnie never had an opportunity," Vida said. "Tsk, tsk." She paused for a moment. "A fork. Really, now. That brings to mind my husband's cousin Elmo. Years ago he tried to strangle himself by winding the suspenders on his overalls around his neck and jumping up and down. So futile. So silly."

I inquired about the Harquist-O'Neill feud. Vida hadn't had time to learn much, though she'd found out that Stubby O'Neill would be released from the hospital Monday, and that Milo was going to let the two Harquists out of jail in time for Easter dinner.

"So where are you headed?" I asked as the wireless connection started to break up.

"Ah . . ." The hesitation was unusual for Vida. "Buck is cooking dinner for me."

"I thought he wasn't getting in until late," I said.

"His plans changed," Vida replied. "One of the grandchildren came down with chicken pox. Whatever's wrong with your phone?"

"Technical difficulties," I said as the noise grew louder and more frequent. "I'll check in later. Happy Easter, Vida."

The rain was coming down harder when I approached Maybeth's door. Roy Sprague, attired only in boxer shorts and a T-shirt, answered my buzz.

"Do I know you?" he asked with a frown.

"Sure. I'm the Easter Bunny. May I hop in?"

My attempt at humor didn't make Roy laugh, but it

befuddled him. He stepped aside, then asked if I was a friend of Maybeth's. Having gained access to the apartment, I became candid.

"I was here yesterday," I confessed, "with my friend. I'm Ronnie's cousin."

"Oh." Recognition dawned on Roy, and it didn't seem to please him. "Hey, what is this? Why're you bugging us? Ronnie's toast."

"I don't think so," I said, and sat down in an armchair before Roy told me I couldn't. "I know what Carol did to you, Roy, and what she did to Ronnie. But I doubt that either of you would kill her for it. You're both . . . gentlemen." It wasn't true, but it sounded better than *weasels*.

The bit of flattery seemed to have some effect on Roy. "Hey, it wasn't all that bad. What can women do except scratch and claw and slap? It's no big deal."

"What's this?" Maybeth stood in the hallway door, her red hair wet and her thin flowered robe clinging to her curves. "You again?"

Not wanting to get off on the wrong foot, I smiled widely. "Maybeth, I must apologize for misleading you. I'm in a real pickle."

"So?" She reached behind the door and grabbed a bath towel, which she wrapped around her head. "Why should I care?" On bare feet, she padded into the living room and flopped down on the sofa next to Roy.

"You should care about the truth," I said, my smile disappearing. "You must know that by lying, you can be charged with obstructing justice. I don't want to see you get into trouble."

"What am I lying about?" Maybeth demanded with a pugnacious expression. "Why should I?"

"It may be a mistake," I said reasonably. "Look, we can probably clear this up in two minutes. Tell me again what you remember about the night Carol was killed."

Maybeth uttered an obscenity under her breath, then poked Roy. "If it hadn't been for you, I wouldn't have been around when all this crap went down. But oh, no, instead of going dancing, you played poker with your lame friends out on 99 until four in the morning. You lost, too."

"Not much," Roy said. "Hell, I raked in two large the week before."

"Which you didn't spend on me," Maybeth noted, and poked Roy again, only harder.

"How about it?" I said, wondering if Maybeth beat up Roy, too.

"About what?" Maybeth's blue eyes narrowed.

"What you heard the night of the murder." Once again, my patience was being tested.

"Oh, that." Maybeth lighted a cigarette from a pack lying on the floor. "It was around nine, maybe a little after. Ronnie and Carol were fighting—I could hear her yelling at him through the wall. Then he slammed out and she kept on yelling. That's it."

I nodded slowly. "That matches what you told us earlier. But Maybeth, if Carol was still yelling when Ronnie left, how could he have already killed her?"

Maybeth paused with the cigarette halfway to her full lips. "He came back, obviously. I didn't hear him, but that's what he must have done."

I shook my head. "You don't know that for certain. Look, Ronnie has an alibi for nine o'clock. He was at Freddy's. Terri saw him there at eight-thirty. You must have been mistaken about when he left. Would you swear in court that it was Ronnie you heard fighting with Carol around nine?"

Maybeth rubbed at her hair with the towel. Her phony nails had been painted a deep purple and curved slightly at the tips. "Ronnie's kind of a low talker," she admitted. "Sometimes when they argued, it was hard to hear him."

I didn't point out the obvious: If Ronnie and Carol hadn't quarreled, Maybeth probably didn't hear Ronnie leave before eight-thirty. "Did you hear anyone—anything—to indicate Carol had another visitor?"

"Well, I heard somebody," she asserted, the full lips pouting. "Even Carol wasn't bitchy enough to argue with herself."

"Maybe it was the bald guy," Roy said, getting up to go out to the kitchen.

"Which one?" Maybeth called after him.

"The one with the bike," Roy replied, returning with a can of beer. "It's a black Honda, early eighties model."

"I'd have heard him," Maybeth responded. "That bike is loud. It must have been the other guy."

From what little I'd seen of Sam Addison, he didn't strike me as the biker type. Of course, you never knew. "Is the biker's name Darryl?" I asked.

Maybeth shrugged. "I never met the guy. But I think he and Carol had something going on the side."

That sounded more like Darryl. Then again, you never knew. "Did the biker come around often?" I inquired.

"Not really." Maybeth poked Roy. "Hey, where's mine?" She pointed to the beer can. Obediently, Roy got up and went back to the kitchen. "Two, three times. You could always hear him coming. I only saw the other bald guy once. He knocked on my door by mistake."

"Was he a little older?" I asked as Roy came back with Maybeth's beer and one for me. I couldn't refuse his unexpected hospitality, so I thanked him and boldly lighted a cigarette. I was beginning to feel like one of the gang. Maybe I should get some acrylic nails from Stella's Styling Salon when I got back to Alpine.

"You mean older than the biker dude?" Roy said. "Yeah, a few years. The guy with the Honda was late thirties, maybe forty. It's hard to tell when guys are bald, 'cause you don't know if they really are or they just shaved their heads. Unless you get real close, that is."

"When was the last time you saw either of them?" I asked.

The couple exchanged glances. "Biker dude was here on a Saturday, maybe a month ago," Roy said.

Maybeth nodded. "He stayed about an hour."

"I assume he was calling on Carol," I noted. "Was Ronnie home?"

"No," Roy answered. "Ronnie was shooting pool. I ran into him at Goldie's down on Forty-fifth."

"Did Carol and the biker quarrel?" I asked, taking a sip of beer.

Maybeth giggled. "Heck, no. They were real quiet. I figured they were doing something else."

"And the older bald man?" I said. "Has he been here lately?"

Maybeth nodded. "He was here the day Carol got killed."

I'd taken a drag on my cigarette and was so startled that I choked. "He was?" I said in a strained voice. "When?"

Maybeth removed the towel from her damp hair and tipped her head to one side. "I'd just come home from work at the salon. It was six, six-fifteen. I didn't see him leave. Who are all these guys anyway?" She asked the question as if she'd only become curious about Carol's male visitors in the last two minutes.

"I'm not sure," I admitted. "One of them may be Kendra's adoptive father." I decided not to mention that the other man could be Kendra's birth father. But I did ask if Maybeth or Roy had ever seen the bald biker when Kendra was there.

"I don't think so," Maybeth replied. "But then I'm not nosy like some of the neighbors."

I assumed she meant Henrietta. But perhaps there were

other inquisitive tenants I hadn't met. After all, the remaining units might house some snoopy residents, too.

I put the question to my hosts. Again, they exchanged glances. "The people in the upstairs units are all kind of standoffish," Maybeth finally said. "The couple above us are real grouches. If we're partying and it gets noisy, they stomp on the floor and yell at us."

"The ones above Carol's are college students," Roy put in. "They don't pay attention to anybody but themselves."

"That guy on the end," Maybeth said, gesturing above and to her right, "smokes so much weed that he wouldn't notice if somebody drove a truck through the place. We call him Mr. Mellow."

"What about the woman with the kid?" Roy asked Maybeth. "I hardly ever see them."

"She's divorced," Maybeth answered, stubbing out her cigarette in a big plastic ashtray. "She works, and the kid's either at school or in day care. They don't get home until seven or so, and then they probably crash and watch TV."

"What about 1-D?" I inquired.

Both Maybeth and Roy swiveled to their left. "Oh," Maybeth said. "Mr. Rapp. I forgot about him. He's so quiet."

"He's old and crippled," Roy added. "He has to get around on a walker. I think that nurse in 1-A takes him to the store and the doctor sometimes."

"Is he deaf?" I asked.

"I don't know," Roy replied. "He never complains if we make noise."

Mr. Rapp might be deaf, but perhaps he wasn't blind. I decided to pay him a Sunday visit.

Aldo Rapp was a small, hunched man with skin weathered like an old saddle, and very sharp brown eyes. He wore a hearing aid in each ear and was dressed in a shabby dark blue suit with a frayed white shirt and a tie that exhibited a couple of stains that might have been gravy. On the gnarled finger of his right hand was a ring with the largest diamond I'd ever seen. It had to be real, since the sparkling facets indicated it hadn't come out of a Cracker Jack box.

Leaning on his walker, he regarded me with those keen brown eyes and smiled. "I'm waiting for my daughter to pick me up," he said after I'd introduced myself. "She should be here soon, though she tends to be tardy. How can a civil engineer always be tardy? You'd think she'd get in trouble."

Mr. Rapp's living room was jammed with old but solid furniture. The walls were covered with photographs of racehorses, happy people standing in winners' circles, and grimy jockeys holding the reins of handsome Thoroughbreds.

"That's me," he said, pointing to one of the pictures. "I was up on CallMeMister that day. We won the Mile out at Longacres. Would you believe I beat out Johnny Longden?"

I grinned at Mr. Rapp. "That's wonderful. How long did you ride?"

"Until I was fifty-six," he replied, pushing the walker toward a big overstuffed chair with a matching ottoman. "Have a seat, my dear. It was a wonderful career, all over the country, but mostly on the coast and fifteen years at Longacres." He held out his right hand. "Joe Gottstein gave me this ring. Do you remember him?"

I did. Gottstein had been the heart and soul of Longacres Racetrack. Both Joe and the track were gone now, but for half a century they had ruled Thoroughbred racing in the Pacific Northwest.

We chatted briefly about the old days, and much as I

hated to cut short Mr. Rapp's memories, I finally got to
the point of my visit.

"So"—Mr. Rapp twinkled, fingering his small chin—
"you want to know what I think about Mrs. Stokes's
murder."

"Or what you think about Mrs. Stokes," I put in with
a smile. "People who understand horses often understand people."

Mr. Rapp chuckled. "Let's say that Mrs. Stokes was a
fractious filly. Handsome, in her way, but she needed a
good rider. So to speak." The brown eyes twinkled some
more. "I have to admit, I'm not one to watch out the
window. I'd rather read the newspapers and watch sports
on TV. But my sight is good, very good, really. Though if
I were standing in front of the bugle, I couldn't hear the
call to the post without these." He indicated the hearing
aids as the diamond flashed on his finger.

"You're lucky," I remarked. "If I had a choice, I'd
rather be deaf than blind."

Mr. Rapp chuckled again. "Yes, what was it W. C.
Fields said when the doctor told him that if he didn't quit
drinking, he'd go deaf? I believe he insisted that what he
was drinking was much better than what he was hearing.
There's a lot of truth to that."

"Did you know Carol Stokes very well?" I inquired.

"Not really," Mr. Rapp responded. "She wasn't the
friendly sort. At least not with old coots like me. She did
have the men friends, though, including your cousin.
Ronnie, is it? He seemed like a nice soul, but what you
might call lackadaisical. No ambition, perhaps?"

"No," I said dryly. "Ronnie's not ambitious."

"One thing I do recall," Mr. Rapp went on. "It got
quite warm a few weeks ago—false spring, I call it—and I
stepped outside one evening for a breath of fresh air. This
apartment gets very close, you see. You can only open the
bedroom and bathroom windows. In any event, Mrs.

Stokes was in front of her unit with the young woman Henrietta Altdorf said was her daughter. A pretty thing, with long, lovely red-gold hair. There was a man with them, nice looking with a bald head. Like Jay Buhner, the baseball player. Do you know him?"

I nodded. I was a fan of Buhner's, the Mariners' long-time right fielder.

"It was uncanny," Mr. Rapp said. "Somehow I sensed intimacy among all three of them, as if they trusted and liked one another. I couldn't help but wonder if the bald man was the girl's father. Bloodlines tell, you see. Then he took her off for a ride on his motorcycle. It struck me then that they were like one happy family. For some reason, it made me both happy and sad."

"He may be her father," I said. "Kendra—the daughter—was born out of wedlock. I'm told that her birth father has been calling on her birth mother. Carol, that is."

"I see." Mr. Rapp grew silent. A tap on the door brought him out of his reverie. "That will be Belle," he said, struggling to get out of the chair. "You'd like Belle. She's a fine young woman. Like you."

I was touched. In fact, I had grown rather fond of Mr. Rapp in a very short time. Shuffling to the door on his walker, he paused before letting his daughter in.

"I really can't tell you anything about the night Mrs. Stokes was murdered. I didn't hear a thing. I was watching pro basketball. But," he went on as he turned the knob, "whoever killed her must have hated her very much. That wasn't Ronnie. Your cousin is like some of the horses I've ridden—they're lovers, not fighters. And they rarely finish in the money."

Chapter Ten

I CONTEMPLATED MY next move while eating a late lunch at a broiler in Ballard. It hadn't been easy to find a modest restaurant that was open on a holiday. The larger, more expensive eateries were out of the question because they'd be jammed with Easter brunch patrons. I contented myself with salad, hamburger steak smothered in mushroom gravy, and french fries. I felt like a martyr, sacrificing myself to a noble cause. Then I thought of Ronnie, lying in the jail infirmary, maybe eating thin gruel with tepid water on the side.

The broiler was crowded. I found myself at a small table surveying the clientele, which was mostly older folks who probably lived nearby. Traditionally, Ballard has been home to Seattle's Scandinavian community, but that has changed, too. I spotted a few Asian faces, two African-Americans, and a Filipino family. The city, which is made up of distinct neighborhoods, has been in a state of flux for the past two decades. Even the Norse Home, where Olive Nerstad lives, isn't in Ballard, but overlooks it.

There were two people in Carol's life that I hadn't yet met. Both were men, both were bald. I wondered if Sam Addison had come home for Easter. It would be an appropriate time for a reconciliation attempt.

The restaurant was directly across the ship canal from Magnolia. Perhaps I should cruise by Darryl Lindholm's place. There was a chance he might have gotten back from wherever he'd been when I telephoned him.

The person I wanted to talk to most was Kendra Addison. I felt that she held the key to the mystery. Not that she realized she knew it, perhaps, but it seemed possible that her reunion with Carol had somehow triggered the events that led up to the murder. If nothing else, Kendra would know more than anyone about the other people in her birth mother's life.

Except, of course, for Ronnie. He knew, but questioning him was like squeezing toothpaste from an almost empty tube. I studied the Cheez-Its that topped my green salad and wished that Vida was available for advice.

Then I pretended I was Kendra. It was hard to slip into the mind of an eighteen-year-old, fresh out of high school and full of herself. In the last year she'd faced two major life changes: high-school graduation and finding her birth mother. From what I'd seen of her, she seemed willful, confident, even arrogant. In some ways her background was similar to mine. We'd grown up in the same part of the city; we were solid middle class. But Kendra was burdened with something that I'd never had to think about. She'd been adopted, and apparently had wanted to meet her birth mother for years. Perhaps she'd harbored feelings of rejection. She may have been angry at Carol Nerstad Stokes for giving her away. A different beginning and a whole generation separated us. I couldn't assume her persona.

At Kendra's age, I'd started college and was still living at home. Ben was in the seminary, not the same one Adam was attending now in St. Paul, but north of Lake City at St. Edward's. That, too, had changed. Due to the shortage of vocations, the seminary had been closed. The last I heard, it had been turned into the Kenmore community center.

I had changed, too, of course, but sometimes I didn't know how. The visible signs of age were apparent, though there was no gray in my brown hair yet, and only a slight sagging of the jawline revealed that I was staring at fifty in the not-too-distant future. Inside was another matter. I was more cynical, more private, more independent.

That was not true. I had always been cynical, private, and independent. Maybe I was the only thing in Seattle that hadn't changed. The thought was depressing. I ate my salad and decided to call Kendra.

She wasn't home. I went out to the parking lot in the rain, but, to my annoyance, I couldn't unlock the car door. There is only one key to the Lexus, and it serves for the doors, the trunk, and the ignition. I went around to the other side to try the passenger door. That was when I realized that, once again, I was trying to get into the wrong car. This was a champagne-colored Toyota Avalon, slightly smaller, but basically the same design. The Lexus was two spaces down, on the other side of a black Ford Taurus.

Cursing myself for not paying closer attention, I headed for Green Lake. Maybe the picture of the Addisons I'd painted earlier wasn't as grim as I'd imagined. They might be seated around the mahogany dining-room table, feasting on roast duck. They wouldn't welcome my intrusion, but I was running out of time. I sensed that Alvin Sternoff needed more than alibis from bar patrons to file a motion for dismissal. If nothing else, Alvin needed to get organized.

As I looked for a parking space on Ashworth, I saw a small U-Haul truck parked in front of the Addison house. The man I recognized as Sam Addison was on the front porch, struggling with a worn blue recliner. Finding a space two doors down, I pulled into the curb, then waited for a black Taurus to pass before I got out of the car. The Taurus, which had been traveling slowly, suddenly picked up speed and tore off down the street. Impatient soul, I thought as I got out of the car, and slowly approached the Addison house. It seemed smart to wait until Sam got the chair down to the truck.

He finally made it, though he was out of breath and looking tired.

"Hi," I said in my friendliest voice. "That looks like an awful job for an Easter Sunday."

"You were expecting the rabbit to carry it?" Sam retorted with a scowl. "Maybe I should have hired some baby ducks."

"Maybe I should introduce myself," I said, keeping the smile fixed in place and holding out my hand. "I'm Emma Lord. You must be Sam Addison."

"Who do I look like? Harrison Ford?" He waved off my attempt to shake hands. "I'm all sweaty. Are you a friend of Kathy's?"

"No," I replied. "Kathy doesn't like me." Maybe the admission would ingratiate me with Kathy's estranged husband.

"She doesn't like me, either," Sam replied, taking a handkerchief out of the back pocket of his chinos and mopping his bald head. "That's why I'm moving instead of watching the NBA on TV like you're supposed to do on Easter. Hell, it's raining, too. Wouldn't you know it? What next, an earthquake?"

"April is the month for earthquakes around here," I remarked. "Where are you going?"

"Korea. Argentina. Liechtenstein. Who knows? Who cares? Not her." He jerked his head in the direction of the house, then turned back to stare at me. "Who'd you say you were? Irmgaard Something-or-Other?"

I repeated my name. Slowly. "I'm Ronnie Mallett's cousin."

"Who's he? I know a Donnie Hammer, but no Ronnie

Mallett. Damn, I should've called Donnie. He could've helped me move."

My smile had withered. "Ronnie Mallett has been charged with murdering Carol Stokes, your daughter's birth mother."

"He should've murdered her other mother," Sam asserted. "I'd have sent him a thank-you note. What do you want? Oh, hell, come inside. It's wetter than a well digger's ass out here. Kathy's gone for the day, which is why I'm here. She went to have dinner with her parents, Fang and Mrs. Fang. They roast kittens for family feasts."

The living and dining rooms looked undisturbed. Whatever Sam was taking out of the house had probably come from the basement, a rec room, a TV retreat. The faded recliner certainly didn't look like one of Kathy Addison's cherished pieces.

"Let's sit in the kitchen," Sam said. "I feel out of place in that damned sanctuary of Kathy's. Why does she buy something new every week? Does she get off on delivery trucks? Is she screwing the UPS driver?" He stopped for breath, then answered his own question. "I should be so lucky. If I ever caught her playing around, it'd be with a nineteenth century Portuguese armoire. You want a drink? Coffee? Tea? Drano?"

I declined, though Sam got some bottled water out of the fridge. We were seated across from each other at a marble-topped breakfast counter. "Twenty-four years of marriage, now this," Sam said, shaking his head. "No, not 'now this'—it's been the same way for the past six years, ever since Kathy took some freaking interior design course and turned into Martha Freaking Stewart. I make good money at Boeing, my job's safe there, but I'm not Bill Freaking Gates. She's put us in debt up to our eyeballs with her latest redecoration. What was wrong with the French Provincial stuff? What was bad about blue and white and yellow? What's good about white and white and a dash of rose? You can't walk on the rugs, you can't sit on the chairs, you can't put your feet up. I've had it. I'm out of here."

He stopped and stared at me again. "I know you. I've seen you somewhere." Sam put up a hand. "Don't tell me. I'll remember. I never forget a face. Ah—you came by the other night with a woman wearing a funny hat. She wanted to go to the zoo. Is she nuts or is she your mother?"

"Neither," I said with a smile. "She works with me on the newspaper in Alpine."

Sam's gray eyes bulged. "You're a reporter? This is an interview? Will I get sued if I say something?"

"This is personal," I said, becoming serious. "I'm trying to help Ronnie, my cousin. I'm certain he's been unjustly accused. Have you ever met him?"

"Ronnie? No. Should I? Back up, where does he fit in? Could he help me move?"

"He's in jail," I explained, "which is why I'm here. Your wife wasn't very helpful when I stopped by the other day."

Sam's hands shot up in the air, almost touching the copper kettles that hung from sturdy hooks. "Surprise! Kathy being a pain in the ass! Put that in a headline, honey!"

I managed to relate Ronnie's story—and Carol's—to Sam without further interruption. The flavored water seemed to soothe him. Or maybe he was simply worn-out.

"I'm asking if you know anything about Carol besides the fact that she's your daughter's birth mother," I said in conclusion.

A muscle tightened along Sam's jaw. "What's to know? Ever since Kendra got to be a teenager, she got this obsession with finding out why she'd been put out for adoption. The only way you can do that is to jump through about a thousand hoops and hope the birth mother cooperates."

"Did you and Kathy encourage Kendra?" I inquired.

"Well . . ." Sam rubbed at his bald head. "Let's say we didn't discourage her. Frankly, I thought she'd get over the idea by the time she was eighteen and could legally make the inquiries."

"But she didn't," I remarked.

Sam shook his head. "Kendra's very strong-minded. The last straw was when she was a senior in high school and they did some genealogy project. Kathy told her to use our ancestry, it was just an assignment, and nobody's business. Kendra refused. She wanted to know her own background. A few months back, after her birthday, she went ahead and initiated her request."

"You and Kathy didn't object?"

"I did," Sam replied. "I thought she was looking for trouble. For once, Kathy kept her mouth shut. She believed that Kendra's discovery would make her more grateful for being adopted by us."

"Did it?" I asked, though I could guess the answer.

"Not exactly," Sam replied with a wry expression. "Carol Stokes was from another world. Oh, she probably was a decent person, just unlucky. Let's face it, any young girl who gets knocked up and then has the guy run out on her is off to a bad start. Especially in a small town, which I heard is where she came from."

"Alpine," I said with a wry smile of my own. "Where I live."

"Oh." Sam looked vaguely embarrassed. "Sorry. But small towns have a reputation for narrow-mindedness."

"It's justified," I admitted. "You're right. I'm sure it was worse for Carol in Alpine, particularly twenty years ago. In fact, we're still a decade or two behind the rest of the world."

Sam gave an offhand nod. "Anyway, Kendra and Carol met right after the holidays. Kendra seemed fascinated by Carol. She was seeing life from a whole new perspective. What can I say? The sordidness of it intrigued her. Did I say sordid? That sounds bad. But so what? The meanness, the squalor, the lousy furniture I'd like better than all this expensive stuff Kathy keeps buying. Hell, maybe I'd have liked Carol better, too. She was no phony."

"How do you know?"

Sam turned slightly sheepish. "I met her once. I never told Kathy. But I was curious."

"When was that?" I asked, recalling what Roy and Maybeth had said about a bald man without a motorcycle calling on Carol the day of the murder.

Sam slammed his palms against the edge of the marble counter. "About five hours before Carol got herself strangled. Hell, I missed the *Titanic*, the *Hindenberg*, the *Lusitania*. I didn't get in the way of Lee Harvey Oswald's bullets, I didn't go to the federal building when it got bombed in Oklahoma City. But when do I show up on Carol Stokes's doorstep? Right while she's enjoying the last day of her life. Sheesh!"

"Did you tell the police?"

Sam drew back on the stool and grimaced. "Hell, no. They came by to ask if we knew Carol very well. We didn't. What was the point of mentioning my little visit? I wasn't there more than twenty minutes."

"What did you think of Carol?"

Sam shrugged. "She was okay. I mean, she didn't throw me out or pull a gun. Defensive, that's how I'd describe her. I don't think she was very happy to meet me. No brass band, no confetti, no offer of cheap wine from a box."

"Did she act afraid? Expectant? Nervous?"

Pausing, Sam finished his flavored water. I noticed that it was peach. "Not really. Just a little hostile."

"Did Kathy ever meet her?" I inquired.

"No. Kathy didn't want to have anything to do with her. She resented the time Kendra spent with Carol. In fact," he continued, with a hint of malice in his voice, "that's one of the reasons Kendra moved out and got her own apartment."

"Kendra and Kathy quarreled over Carol?"

"You bet," Sam replied, getting up and putting his empty bottle into a recycling bin marked GLASS. "Not so much because Kendra tracked her birth mother down, but because Kathy didn't like the amount of time that Kendra was spending with Carol."

"A natural resentment," I noted as Sam leaned against the counter.

"Natural for Kathy to be resentful," he said. "Resentful of me sitting on the two-thousand-dollar sofa in the living room, resentful of me balking at another five-figure bank-card statement, resentful of the fact that I've lost most of my hair. You name it, she resents it."

Since Sam hadn't sat down again, I sensed that he wanted to get back to his moving. "But you don't know anything about Ronnie and Carol?" I asked, sliding off the stool.

He shook his head. "Your cousin wasn't there when I saw Carol. If he didn't kill her, I don't know who did. I gathered that Carol ran with a rough crowd." He paused and grinned. "It takes one to know one. Believe it or not, I used to be pretty rough myself until I got off my dead butt and went to college. If I hadn't had the GI bill after 'Nam, I might have ended up hanging out in bars and bowling alleys, too."

"You were smart," I said, moving out of the kitchen.

"I was lucky," Sam said as we went through the dining room with its fine mahogany, plush carpet, custom-made drapes, and collection of imported bric-a-brac. "Or was I?" he added in an ironic tone.

"People are more important than things," I remarked, halfway through the handsomely appointed living room.

"Tell that to Kathy," said Sam.

I felt at loose ends after I got in the car. Though Sam had given me Kendra's telephone number at the last minute, I suspected that she wasn't home. Thus I found myself driving back to Ballard, across the canal, and in the direction of Darryl Lindholm's residence in Magnolia.

It turned out to be a condo, not a house, and was nestled into the side of the hill that overlooks the area known as Interbay. While Magnolia Bluff is primarily a neighborhood of conservative people and expensive homes, its east side rises out of an industrial area which includes the railroad yards and the city's roundhouse. The complex where Darryl lived was relatively new, probably built about the same time as the surrounding condos and apartments that flanked the hill.

His unit was on the ground floor, with a buzzer security system. I stood outside the wrought-iron gate, pressed the button, and waited. There was no answer. Glancing down the street, I noticed a car making a U-turn by the sharp curve at the corner. It was a black Taurus. I began to worry as I started to walk back to the Lexus.

But my concern was short-lived when I heard the roar of a motorcycle coming up the steep, winding street. Feeling like a third-rate spy, I hid behind a camellia bush and watched the rider stop in front of the garage with its wide grilled entrance. A moment later the grille rolled up and the man I presumed to be Darryl rode inside.

After almost five minutes I pressed the button again. An unsteady masculine voice asked me to identify myself.

"I'm Emma Lord, from Alpine," I said. "I'm conducting interviews with people who've moved from there to the big city. You know, twenty years after." All things considered, it wasn't exactly a lie.

"This isn't a good time," Darryl said, his voice still shaky. "Could you come back tomorrow?"

"No," I replied, "I have to be in Alpine to put out the newspaper. I'm the editor and publisher."

Maybe I impressed Darryl. In any event, I could hear him heave a big sigh. "I don't know why you're interested in me, but come on in."

I heard a buzz, then tried the gate, which swung easily. The path to the condo entrance was edged with primroses and hyacinths. Darryl Lindholm stood in the front door, a tall, strapping man dressed in blue jeans and a Sonics sweatshirt. He must have been a Mariner fan as well, since he sported the same type of blond goatee that went along with his Buhner-bald head.

"Sorry I was abrupt," he said, ushering me into a sunken living room that was plainly, if tastefully furnished. "Easter is a bad day for me."

I looked closer at my host. His eyes were red, and though his complexion was ruddy, he looked ill. "Are you okay?" I asked, genuinely concerned.

Darryl shook his head. "Not quite. I'll be better after a shot of tequila. Do you drink margaritas? I can whip some up in the blender."

It seemed wise to acquiesce to Darryl's offer. Somehow, I'd expected him to be belligerent, arrogant, even hostile.

"Sure," I said as he motioned for me to sit in one of two small leather settees that were separated by a matching ottoman. "I really appreciate you letting me see you."

"Frankly, I can use the company," Darryl said as he went behind the bar that divided the living room and kitchen. "It doesn't do any good to mope by yourself."

It dawned on me that Darryl wanted to talk. To me, to anybody. If this wasn't his lucky day, maybe it was mine.

I wondered how I could level with him and admit my real reason for being in his condo. Maybe the tequila would give me courage.

"Holidays are difficult for many people," I said. "They can bring back some unhappy memories."

"You're damned right," Darryl replied, then stopped speaking as he turned on the blender. "This is my first Easter without my family," he continued, returning to the living room with our drinks. "Christmas was even worse. I was just returning from the cemetery now. It's our wedding anniversary."

"What happened?" I inquired, tasting my drink. It was delicious, with just the right amount of salt applied to the glass's rim.

Darryl bent his head and rubbed at the back of his neck. "Is this going to be part of your story?"

I took another swallow of margarita. "Probably not. I don't necessarily want painful material."

"This is painful," he said with a big sigh. "But if you don't want to hear it—"

"I do," I interrupted. "It sounds as if you need to talk about it."

"I'm told it helps," Darryl said with a wry expression. "So far, no luck."

"What happened to your family?"

Settling himself into the matching settee, Darryl cradled his drink. "It was a year ago June. My wife, Astrid, and I were on vacation with our two boys, Jason and Damien. We were heading out of Glacier Park in the evening when the sun hit me like that!" He'd set the glass down on the ottoman and punched his right fist into his left palm. "I was blinded. I lost control of the car and we crashed into a big RV. Astrid and the boys were killed outright." His voice was shaking again. "They were only six and four."

"Dear God," I whispered. "That's horrible."

Darryl didn't speak for several moments, but stared off

toward the massive stone fireplace behind me. I knew he was reliving the moment, as he must have done a thousand times. My heart went out to him.

"I walked away," he said in an awestruck voice. "I only had a few bruises. It was incredible. It was all wrong. It should have been me."

"My parents were killed in a car accident," I said softly. "They were barely fifty. I thought my world had ended."

"It's different with kids," Darryl said. "Kids shouldn't die before their parents."

"I know." I, too, went silent.

It was Darryl who spoke first. "Just when life seems to be going along pretty good, you get screwed. I had a lousy first marriage, and was glad we didn't have kids. Then I met Astrid when I went to work for Microsoft. She was a terrific woman, smart, pretty, full of life. She quit work when we had the boys. We could afford to, because I was making good money. It was like the American dream. Until the nightmare hit."

So Darryl hadn't been divorced twice, only once, and then widowed. I was so caught up in his tragedy that I almost forgot why I had come.

"Did you keep your job?" I asked, for lack of any way to comfort him.

He nodded. "I needed the routine. Besides, it's a good job. But I sold our home in Redmond, furnishings and all. I couldn't stand being over there on the Eastside with all those memories. I moved in here . . . when? I lose track of time now and then."

"Are your parents still alive?" I asked. "I heard they moved to Mount Vernon and went into the bulb business."

"That's right," Darryl said, obviously forcing himself to get a grip on his emotions. "Dad sold the business last year and retired. They're traveling in Europe right now."

He uttered a bitter laugh. "Which is why I spent Easter at the cemetery instead of with them. But that's okay, they deserve the trip. My folks have always worked hard. Losing their grandchildren damned near destroyed them. They needed to get away."

I'd almost finished my margarita. It hadn't given me courage or much of a buzz. I hated myself for what I was about to do. It couldn't be avoided; it was the reason I'd come.

"Darryl," I said with effort, "may I ask if it helped you at all to finally meet your older child, Kendra Addison?"

Darryl recoiled in the settee. His ruddy complexion turned a dark red. "Get out!" he cried, his arms flailing. "Get out!"

I did, as fast as I could.

Getting into my car, I saw the nose of the black Taurus down at the corner. But before I could drive that far, it had turned around and disappeared.

Chapter Eleven

THE BLACK TAURUS'S ghostly appearances were upsetting. I had yet to glimpse the driver. Who would want to follow me? The first answer that came to mind was the killer. That was a very disturbing thought, though someone who killed with a drapery cord might not be otherwise armed.

Winding down the hill, I couldn't catch sight of my tail. I considered turning off onto a side street, but my recollection of Magnolia was that because of the bluff's irregular topography and some peculiar city planning, there were plenty of unexpected deadends. I didn't need to get trapped in a cul-de-sac.

I thought about going to the nearest police station, but the only one I remembered was not far from my old neighborhood and had been turned into a community center and library several years ago. Frustrated, I kept driving.

Easter Sunday was becoming dangerous, as well as depressing. My hasty retreat from Darryl Lindholm's condo had seemed like the prudent thing to do. He looked absolutely murderous, and I didn't want to tempt fate. Besides, I felt like a fool. Until I mentioned Kendra's name, Darryl had seemed like a gentle soul, mourning the loss of his wife and sons, considerate of his parents, an ordinary hardworking man who had suffered a great loss.

Then he'd changed into something menacing. Unfortunately, the revelation made me realize that he could have killed Carol Stokes in one of those lightning flashes of rage. Which meant that whoever was following me couldn't be the murderer. My mind was going around in circles.

Needing to think, I pulled the car into a parking lot in front of a neighborhood strip mall. It was after four o'clock, and unless I got hold of Kendra, I had nothing else to do for the rest of the day. As much as I enjoyed the city, it didn't make sense to while away the hours in Seattle.

With one eye on the rearview mirror watching for the Taurus, I drove back to the motel, gathered up my luggage and Vida's, and checked out. It cost me half a night's stay since noon was the regular departure time, but I figured that if I headed back to Alpine, I could work all day Monday to make sure we could meet our deadline, and return to Seattle Tuesday afternoon. Wednesday, pub day, was always slow, except for the crank calls and irate letters that followed the paper's delivery.

Before leaving the motel, I called the jail infirmary to check on Ronnie. He was doing fine, the voice on the other end said, and would be transported back to his cell on Monday. I left word that I would see him Tuesday, probably in the late afternoon.

Out in the parking lot, I scanned the cars for a black Taurus. There were two of them. Through the rain, I couldn't tell if either was occupied. Confronting the person who'd been tailing me could be dangerous. I'd already had one scare with Darryl Lindholm. I decided not to test my luck. Surely the Taurus wouldn't follow me to Alpine.

There were two routes I could take out of town. Usually, I'd cross Lake Washington on the Evergreen Point Bridge and hook onto Highway 2 at Monroe. But I could also go due north on I-5, until I hit the interchange for the

Stevens Pass Highway. On a whim, I chose the latter, if slightly longer, direction. There was a stop along the way that I felt obligated to make for Ronnie.

Peter Chan's address in Lake City wasn't far from the freeway. His house was a tidy split-level, half-brick, half-frame on a side street. The rain had stopped by the time I arrived. Two young boys were riding bikes in the driveway. The smaller boy's bike had training wheels.

A chain-link fence surrounded the yard, but I went directly to the driveway. The older boy eyed me with curiosity.

"Hi," I said, "I'm Emma. Are your mom and dad home?"

"Hi," the older boy said. "I'm Kendall. That's Schuyler. He's dopey." Kendall nodded at his brother, who'd just run his bike into the fence. "Mom's inside, making dinner. Dad's looking for the dog."

My heart sank. "Is the dog's name Budweiser?"

Kendall's handsome little face looked mystified.

"Bud? Buddy?" I suggested.

"It was," Kendall said with a show of relief. "But we call him Tubby. That's 'cause he isn't. He likes to eat all the time. Dad says he hasn't been fed much lately."

"But Buddy—I mean, Tubby—has run off?" I asked.

Schuyler had gotten off his bike and was banging it up and down on the driveway. "I want Tubby! Mr. Fields ran over Sunshine with his truck, and we got promised a new dog. Where's Tubby?"

"You'll wreck your bike, dork," Kendall said to his brother. "Dad's looking for Tubby, like I said. Stop that."

A pretty Asian woman in jeans and a loose-knit sweater came out through the open garage and eyed me warily. "Are you trying to find an address?" she asked.

I was getting tired of my usual introduction, but I rattled it off anyway. "Ronnie's worried about Buddy," I concluded. "I thought I'd see if he was okay, but I understand he's gone."

"I'm Jenny Chan," the young woman said, and held out a hand. She smelled of basil and oregano, no doubt evidence of the meal she was preparing. "The dog ran off while we were at church this morning. He must have leaped the fence."

"And your husband's still looking for him?" I remarked as the boys returned to cruising the driveway on their bikes.

Jenny gave me a wry look. "Not exactly. He looked earlier, but no luck. Pete's gone over to see his parents for a while. Frankly," she went on, lowering her voice, "I don't care if we ever find Buddy or Tubby or Blubby or whatever he's called. Our last dog just about ruined the garden. He was a serious digger."

Jenny's statement cheered me slightly. "If you do find Buddy, could you let me know?" I handed her one of my business cards. "That's a toll-free number to the newspaper in Alpine. I know my cousin will be delighted to take him back."

"Sure," Jenny said, slipping the card into the pocket of her jeans. "But I'll bet he won't be found. He may be trying to get back home, and he'll be lucky to survive in all this traffic. To be honest, he's not a very bright dog."

Like dog, like master, I thought. "Thanks, Jenny," I said, and headed down the driveway.

"Mom," Kendall called, "if Tubby doesn't come back, can we get a snake?"

I didn't hear Jenny's answer, but I could guess what it was.

As I got into the Lexus, I saw a black Taurus parked on the block down the street. It pulled out when I did, following me to the freeway. In the Woodinville suburbs, it finally disappeared. Whoever was driving must have figured that if I was leaving town, I was also leaving my inquisitive nature at the county line.

It was raining again by the time I started up Highway 2. After crossing the bridge over the Skykomish River, I drove straight up Alpine Way. The *Advocate* office and the rest of the commercial district was on my left; the mall was at my right. Under the darkening gray clouds and the shadow of Mount Baldy, the town looked bleak and insignificant. I couldn't help but kick myself for not staying on in Seattle and indulging in an expensive dinner at one of the city's finer restaurants.

Instead, I took my hunger pangs to my little log house. Usually, it welcomed me, but when I saw the lights in the windows, I knew that Amber Ramsey and Danny had returned.

Sure enough, they'd already managed to litter the living room, mostly with their unpacked luggage. Indeed, Amber had brought more back than she'd taken away. Three large cardboard cartons were stacked near the hearth and several shopping bags stood by the dining-room set.

"What's this?" I inquired, waving a hand.

Amber beamed. "My stuff. My stepmother's been cleaning out the house before they move, and she found a bunch of my old things. I decided I might as well take them now as wait until the movers come this summer."

My house has no basement. The carport's storage area is limited. There is only a small crawl space in the attic. I worked hard to pare down my possessions so that I could still fit into what is basically a four-room bungalow.

"Adam's room—your room," I quickly corrected myself, trying not to sound peevish, "is already jammed. Where will we put these bags and boxes, Amber?"

My houseguest stared at her belongings as if she'd

never seen them before. "Uh . . . your closet is pretty big, isn't it?"

"Not big enough for all this," I said.

Danny was rolling around on the floor, making gurgling noises. It occurred to me that he'd probably be crawling before the Ramseys moved out. The thought added to my frustration.

"I could sort through it and put it away in drawers," Amber said vaguely. "But I did that pretty much already. It's mostly clothes and CDs and tapes and souvenirs. You know, like from rock concerts."

"Figure it out," I said, hauling my own suitcase toward the bedroom. "It can't stay out here."

The light was flashing on my answering machine as I headed to the hall. I continued into the bedroom, set the luggage on the bed, and returned to the phone.

"Hi, Mom," said Adam's voice. "Just calling to wish you a blessed Easter. We celebrated a really intense vigil Mass last night. I was one of the acolytes. Have you got your reservations yet to come back here in June? The earlier the better, before it gets too hot and the mosquitoes chew off your fingers and toes. Talk to you soon."

Burdened with guilt, I sighed at the answering machine. I hadn't thought to call Adam from Seattle. I'd spent the most sacred weekend of the liturgical year stumbling around the city, trying to help a cousin I hadn't seen in almost thirty years. Meanwhile, my son was having deep spiritual experiences in St. Paul. What kind of a mother was I?

There was a second call. I gritted my teeth as I played the message. "Where the hell are you, Emma?" demanded my brother, Ben, in his crackling voice. "I had to hear almost two hundred confessions and say four Masses this weekend, including the big bopper here in Tuba City. Now I'm back at the rectory, drinking cheap beer and wondering if you ran off with the Easter Bunny. Call me—if you ever get home."

I hadn't thought to call Ben, either. My brother, the person who knew me best, the companion of my youth, and the comfort of my middle years. What kind of a sister was I?

I called Adam first, and as usual, it took ages for whoever answered the phone to find my poor neglected son. While I waited Amber wandered around the living room, digging into the cartons and bags. Danny started to fuss.

"Mom?" Adam's voice sounded anxious. "What happened to you?"

There is some sort of axiom that if a mother is derelict in her duty to her child, the reason must be catastrophic. Nothing short of a paralytic stroke, being held hostage by revolutionary terrorists, or having been killed in a bungee-jumping attempt could possibly deter Mom from her appointed rounds.

"I'm fine," I asserted. "I've been doing good works."

"Like?" Adam sounded incredulous.

I explained about Ronnie Mallett. Adam said he'd never heard of him.

"So what's the big deal now?" my son asked. "I mean, it's not like he was real close."

"You, my child, are studying to be a priest," I reminded him. "What about the 'When I was in prison, you visited me' quote?"

"Well . . . you're right, okay, that's cool," Adam agreed. "It just doesn't sound like you."

Danny began to squall. I caught Amber's eye and motioned for her to shush the baby. She held up a Pearl Jam T-shirt, then wandered over to Danny, who had managed to wedge himself under a chair.

"Guests still there, huh?" Adam remarked dryly. "Man, you are really turning into saintly material. Have I inspired you, Mom?"

"Stick it," I muttered. "You just never noticed before what a wonderful person I am."

"In a way," Adam said, "that's true. It's not just studying for the priesthood, though. I guess I'm getting to be a grownup."

"About time," I noted. Then, unable to keep the maternal pride out of my voice, I added, "You're turning into a top-notch person. I'd like to brag, but I don't. Much."

As Amber removed Danny from the room, Adam and I turned to the subject of my proposed trip to the Twin Cities. I had to admit I hadn't yet contacted Janet Driggers at Sky Travel to make the arrangements, but I'd try to see her on my lunch break Monday. Then we got caught up with more mundane matters. Before signing off, Adam mentioned that he'd spoken with his father earlier in the day.

"I called to give him Easter greetings," Adam said. "He sounded good." Pause. "Have you talked to him lately?"

"No," I said. "I owe him a call." It shouldn't work that way. Tom and I weren't teenagers. "I'll call him sometime this coming week."

"I think he's going out of town," Adam said. "Business, as usual."

"Business, babies, blah-blah," I said, trying to sound humorous and failing. "That's your dear old dad. Meanwhile, dear old mom waits. And waits."

"No comment."

"None needed," I responded. After more than a quarter of a century, there wasn't much left to say about Tom Cavanaugh.

Ben wasn't in at the rectory on the Navajo reservation, so I left a message. I was unpacking my suitcase when I heard the sirens. As ever, I went on the alert. Anytime an emergency vehicle takes off in Alpine, it's news. An auto accident, a domestic violence call, even a heart attack usually makes it into *The Advocate*.

I'd just put the suitcase in the closet when I heard more sirens. A decade of experience enabled me to distinguish between the wails of the various emergency vehicles. The first had belonged to one of the sheriff's squad cars. The second had been the medics. Both had headed west.

A third siren sounded, fainter and farther away. It was Milo's personal siren, the one in his Grand Cherokee. He had special-ordered it from Harvey's Hardware, and Harvey Adcock had made a mistake and ended up with a British police siren that sounds to me like a dying duck. Milo, however, professed to like it. Maybe it made him feel as if he were working for Scotland Yard.

The siren grew somewhat louder, apparently coming from the sheriff's house in the Icicle Creek development. He was also heading west. Whatever had happened must be important enough to draw Milo from his Sunday rest.

I put my shoes back on and grabbed my jacket. There was no time to phone Scott Chamoud, who might not be back from Oregon anyway. Calling to Amber that I was off on a story, I raced out to the car. Yet another siren sounded as I reached Alpine Way. The fire truck was ahead of me, rushing south, then turning left on Railroad Avenue past Old Mill Park.

It was going on eight o'clock, but not quite dark. It was easy to follow the number one engine past the community college, the ski-lodge turnoff, and onto the Burl Creek Road. A minute later the fire truck stopped, joining the squad car, the medics van, and Milo's Grand Cherokee.

We'd arrived at Cap Harquist's place, with its aging two-story house all but hidden behind a pair of huge cedars that must have prevented the sunlight from getting inside. I'd always wondered why the Harquists had let those trees block not only the sun, but their view of Burl

Creek and the mountains beyond. Perhaps the cedars were like the ramparts of a castle: not arboreal decorations, but strategic fortifications.

Cautiously, I approached the tight little knot of emergency personnel. I didn't see Milo, but Deputy Jack Mullins was talking to one of the volunteer firefighters whose face I couldn't recognize under all the official gear.

"Emma," Jack said, turning to face me. "How'd you hear about the commotion?"

"How could I not?" I replied as the red, blue, and white lights flashed eerily in the dusk. "I followed the sirens' call. What's going on?"

Jack gestured toward the house. "Milo let Ozzie and Rudy out this morning so they could go to church for Easter. Which they did. Lutheran church, that is." Jack gave me his roguish grin. He's a fellow Catholic, the type who's not above making cracks about our Protestant brethren. "Then they came home and started drinking. The next thing we know, they're prowling around outside the hospital. Stubby O'Neill is still there, you know."

I nodded. "Milo kept me informed while I was out of town."

"Oh. I didn't know you'd left," Jack said. "Our family went to the vigil Mass last night. I figured you were going this morning. Father Den's sermon sucked scissors, but everything else was great."

Dennis Kelly, our pastor, isn't famous for his homilies. A serious, middle-aged black man in an almost exclusively white parish, he's an excellent administrator and no one can criticize his handling of the liturgy itself. These days, we're lucky to have a priest at all, and downright blessed that our pastor isn't drinking himself stupid or playing games with little boys. Father Den can be dry as dust from the pulpit and elicit no carping from me.

"So what happened at the hospital?" I inquired, hearing some shouts from closer to the house.

Jack turned somber. "Stubby's daughter, Meara, came to see him this evening. The Harquist boys kidnapped her. They've got her inside and God only knows what's going on. Doc Dewey called us. He was leaving the hospital when he saw Ozzie and Rudy drive off with her about half an hour ago."

My eyes were riveted on what little I could see of the Harquist house. "That's bad. Who else is in there?"

"Ozzie, Rudy, Cap," Jack counted. "Old Lady Harquist's been dead for years. I don't know about Ozzie and Rudy's wives. The last I heard, Rudy's walked out on him and moved to Everett."

"So no women on hand to provide a softening influence," I murmured. "Why don't you and Milo and whoever else is here go in?"

"Because they're holding Meara hostage," Jack replied. "She's only fifteen. The poor kid must be scared out of her wits."

"Hostage for what? Do they want ransom money?"

Jack shook his head. "Who knows what those dingbats want? They're probably still drunk. Milo's trying to get to Cap. He figures he may have more sense than the sons." Hearing the screech of tires, Jack whirled around. "Oh, shit! Here come the O'Neills."

A beat-up SUV revealed Stubby O'Neill's two younger brothers, known as Rusty and Dusty. They flew out of the vehicle and started yelling, mostly obscenities directed at the Harquists.

Jack hurried over in an attempt to get Rusty and Dusty to simmer down. I could see why his manner was urgent. Rusty held a double-barreled shotgun and Dusty had what looked like a Smith & Wesson .38 Special revolver. I backpedaled a few steps, seeking safety behind a Douglas fir.

"Mullins!" Rusty yelled. "Move it! We don't want no trouble with you."

"Hell, no," Dusty agreed. "You're a mick, too. We want them Scandahoovians."

"Sorry, me lads," Jack responded, his right hand drifting toward his gun. "You're going to have to stay put. The sheriff has this thing under control."

I glanced toward the house. Even without his regulation Smokey the Bear hat, at six-foot-five, Milo loomed at least a couple of inches above everybody else. He was standing at the foot of the stairs that lead up to the front porch. I could hear him shouting, but couldn't make out the words. Jack's assertion that the sheriff had things under control struck me as fanciful. Especially when I saw flames at the near-side windows on the second floor.

A piercing scream tore across the night air. Everyone seemed to freeze, then Milo took off around the other side of the house. I lost sight of him, but heard him yell something to the firemen, who sprang into action. A moment later they were carrying a round blue safety net in Milo's direction. Two other firefighters were hauling hoses to the part of the house where the fire had broken out. The medics followed the safety net.

I could smell the smoke and hear the crackling as the flames licked at dry old wood. The sky, which had finally grown dark, now took on an ominous ocherous glow. Cursing myself for not remembering to bring a camera, I fumbled for the notebook in my purse and began scribbling furiously. My nerves were becoming unraveled. I doubted that I'd ever be able to decipher my disjointed handwriting.

Nearby, Rusty and Dusty were arguing with Jack, who was trying to keep the two men from charging into the house.

"Meara's in there," Dusty shouted. "Do something!"

"We're doing it," Jack replied, giving some sort of

signal to Dwight Gould, another deputy, who had assumed Milo's vacated position by the front porch.

Another scream pierced the air. It was female, I was sure of that. Thus it was probably Meara O'Neill. Pray, I commanded myself. Help her, God. Help all these idiots who've made such an ungodly mess.

The medics had rushed back to get their gurney. Jack shouted a warning as Rusty and Dusty hurtled past him. Dwight Gould whirled around, his own weapon raised. A figure came running through the front door, knocking Dwight to the ground. In the light of the fire, I recognized one of the Harquists. I could never tell Ozzie from Rudy, who were both six-footers, well over two hundred pounds, with no necks.

Milo reappeared at a run from around the corner of the house. "Halt!" he ordered, both hands on his King Cobra magnum. "Drop your weapons, everybody!"

Another figure came tearing out of the house. It was the other Harquist son, and he was also armed. As his brother and the two O'Neills hesitated, he turned, stumbled on the top step, and fired.

Milo went down.

The next female scream was mine.

"Jesus, you dumbshit!" the other Harquist shouted. "You shot the freaking sheriff!"

Despite the fact that guns were everywhere, I rushed to Milo. He was writhing on the ground, clutching at his ankle. A flood of relief swept over me. Nobody died from a leg wound.

"Are you okay?" I asked in my stupidest voice.

"No," Milo replied, exhibiting more brains than I had done. "It hurts like hell. It's my foot."

I was vaguely aware of the activity swirling around me. All of the weapons had been surrendered when Milo got hit. An argument was raging between the Harquists and the O'Neills. Smoke filled the air and I could feel water spraying out from the fire hoses. The gurney returned from the side of the house with a small, huddled figure who was sobbing softly. I heard someone yell, "Where's Cap?"

From far off came more sirens, at least two separate vehicles. Backup for the sheriff, and an ambulance, I guessed, smoothing the graying sandy hair from Milo's forehead and holding his hand. He seemed more angry than pained.

The medic van took off, with the two O'Neills hovering over their niece. Meara was about to join her father in the hospital. Doc Dewey would be called back to tend to her, and then to treat Milo. The new physician hadn't arrived in Alpine, and Doc rarely got a day of rest. Easter Sunday was no different.

Jack and Dwight were in the process of rearresting the Harquist who had shot Milo. It was, I heard someone say, Rudy.

"It was a damned accident," Rudy shouted as Sam cuffed him. "Why would I shoot Dodge?"

"Because you're an idiot," Milo yelled from his place on the ground.

Two of the firefighters who had assisted Meara in what I guessed was her jump from a second-story window were going inside, presumably to rescue Cap Harquist. The smoke was turning white, which indicated that the fire was being put out. Deputies Dustin Fong and Bill Blatt, both dressed in their civvies, came bounding out of the squad car that had pulled up across from my Lexus. The ambulance drivers had driven up just in front of them, and were already bringing a gurney for Milo.

Ozzie Harquist was yelling something after the firefighters who had gone inside. I heard several obscenities before he calmed down and walked somewhat unsteadily to the gurney where Milo was now lying under protest.

"Jeez, Sheriff, Rudy didn't mean to wing you. He fell

off the porch. This whole thing wouldn't have happened if that little bitch hadn't set fire to the place."

"Meara?" I said in surprise. "She started the fire?"

With a nervous glance at the house, Rudy nodded. "She had a cigarette lighter, and she threw it into a bunch of old newspapers. It took off like that." He tried to snap his fingers, but missed. "They better get Pa out of there. He was in the can downstairs when it started."

Milo was being wheeled away. "I'll see you at the hospital," I called after him, then turned just as Cap Harquist, struggling mightily with the firefighters, was dragged down from the front porch. His pants were around his ankles and the trapdoor of his union suit was flapping in the evening breeze.

"You haul me out of my own house? Just because of a little smoke? You sons of bitches, I'll sue you for that!"

A final glance at the Harquist homestead told me that it was probably destroyed. I should have felt sad, but instead, I figured it served them right. As I went to my car, I glimpsed Bill Blatt, using his cell phone. Bill was Vida's nephew, and her source of all things that pertained to the law. I took in the stretch of road until it curved alongside of the creek. There was no sign of Vida's big white Buick. It wasn't like her not to follow such a full symphony of sirens.

I expanded my worries to include Vida.

Chapter Twelve

MILO WENT DIRECTLY into surgery. He'd given me a feeble wave as they wheeled him down the corridor. He was so tall and the gurney so short that his head sort of lolled off the top in order to make room at the other end for his injured foot. His Smokey the Bear hat had sat on his stomach, and I hadn't known whether to laugh or cry. So I laughed, but not until he was out of sight.

I telephoned Vida from the hospital lobby, but she didn't answer. Then I remembered that she was going to Startup to have dinner at Buck Bardeen's house. It was now past ten o'clock, and while Vida didn't retire early, she usually tried to get home by nine-thirty on work nights.

I considered calling Edith Holmgren to tell her I'd retrieve the cats, but thought better of it. I preferred not leaving them with Amber while I went back to Seattle. Edith might as well enjoy the company of Rheims and Rouen for a couple of extra days.

One of the nurses informed me that Meara didn't seem to be seriously harmed, though she had a few bumps and bruises. Delicately, I asked if she'd been sexually assaulted.

"I don't think so," Debbie Murchison, RN, replied dryly. "She may have put them off."

I was mystified. "How do you mean?"

Debbie, who was young and a newcomer to Alpine, leaned close to my ear. "She's four months pregnant.

Some men don't find that a turn-on, even when they're drunk as skunks."

"But she's only fifteen," I said in astonishment.

"So? Meara O'Neill's fifteen going on thirty-five. Besides," Debbie added, "she'll be sixteen next month."

I was reminded of Carol Stokes, and wondered if Debbie's impregnator was any more gallant than Darryl Lindholm had been almost twenty years earlier. But who was I to criticize? I'd also been an unwed mother.

The surgery was supposed to last less than an hour. The bullet had gone right through Milo's foot. It didn't sound serious, though he'd be hobbled for a couple of weeks. I had started back to the waiting room when a breathless Jeannie Clay caught up with me.

"Is he all right? Will he lose his foot?" Jeannie asked, her round, pretty face looking distressed.

"He'll be fine," I reassured her. "I gather he can't walk on it for a while. That won't make him easy to live with." I winced. I didn't know if Jeannie was living with Milo or not. I preferred not to know. We had never lived together, nor did I ever want to. That had been one of the reasons for our breakup.

"Gosh," she said, her face falling even further, "that's awful. For him, I mean. We were supposed to go skiing at Sun Valley this coming weekend. I've taken Friday and Monday off, because we planned to drive to Idaho. I don't think Dr. Starr will let me change it. He and Mrs. Starr have their own plans."

"That's a shame," I lied. "I imagine this is getting to be the tail end of the ski season over there."

"Pretty much," Jeannie said, now thoughtful. "I'll have to see if Heather Bardeen can go instead."

Heather is the niece of Buck Bardeen and the daughter of Henry, who runs the ski lodge. The two young women had been best friends forever. But that didn't prevent me from thinking that Jeannie's attitude was rather callous and self-serving.

"Milo will probably need some help at home for the next few days," I said as we continued on our way to the waiting room.

"Probably," Jeannie agreed. "I'll bet his aunt Thelma will be glad to stay with him. She must get tired of that grumpy husband of hers."

It seemed incredible that Jeannie didn't consider it her duty to nurse Milo back to health. But I was a creature of another generation. The Young—in this case, anybody under thirty-five—were different. They were self-serving. And sometimes callous. It's not all their fault. They've been raised in an era of disintegrating families, which makes their sense of self-preservation much keener.

I took one look at the waiting room, saw Rusty and Dusty O'Neill, and decided I didn't want to be there. If Jeannie had come to see Milo, he didn't need me. I made a flimsy excuse and left.

I called Vida again from home. She still didn't answer.

I'd barely gotten in the door of *The Advocate* Monday morning when Ginny Erlandson handed me a phone message from Detective Tony Rojas of the Seattle Police Department. The primary on the Carol Stokes homicide case wanted to let me know that he was taking the day after Easter off, but would be in the office Tuesday.

That worked out better for me, since I wouldn't return to Seattle until that afternoon. I was hanging up my coat when Vida entered, wearing a three-tiered straw hat I'd never seen before. It was covered with fruit, and I couldn't help but think of Carmen Miranda.

"Emma!" she cried. "What are you doing here?"

I explained why I'd come back to Alpine. "At lunch we

can go over what I learned in your absence," I said. "By the way, your luggage is still in my car."

"I'm all ears," she declared, sitting down behind her desk.

"I'm sure you are," I replied with a smile. "Vida, where'd you get that hat?"

"I've had it for ages," she replied, touching a couple of mangoes. "I found it when I was packing for our trip."

"It's amazing," I said, and waited.

"I think so. Very springlike." She sounded defensive, and it made me curious.

"The feathers you wore in Seattle were a bit winter-like," I said.

Vida harrumphed. "More than just that, apparently."

"What do you mean?" I asked.

"Did you notice that disreputable man with the beard who approached me at the bus stop on Aurora?"

I said I did. "Did he ask for money?"

"No." Vida lowered her voice. "He offered it. Fifty dollars, but I had to wear the hat. Can you imagine?" She had actually gone pale.

I put a hand over my mouth to stifle a burst of laughter. "No!" I exclaimed, eyes wide. "He must have been . . . drunk." Or crazy or blind or the kinkiest man in western Washington. "What did you say?"

"I told him he ought to be ashamed of himself," Vida replied. "I can't think when I've been so insulted."

Regarding Vida with a keen eye, I wondered. Deep down, I suspected she'd been thrilled. But she made no further comment and began going through her in-basket. "Goodness, such a bunch of nonsense. There must be a dozen different recipe mailings in here, not to mention all the other unnewsworthy releases from businesses and organizations that have nothing to do with Alpine."

"I get them, too," I said, and waited some more.

"There were three weddings over the weekend," she

continued. "Diane Skylstad's bridal gown was orange. Why? I wonder. Oh," she continued, reading from the standard wedding release we provided, "her groom went to Oregon State. He wore a black tuxedo. Beaver colors, it says here." She paused while I fought my impatience. "Beverly Iverson accompanied herself on the piccolo while she came down the aisle singing 'You Are the Wind Beneath My Bings.' "

"That should be *wings*," I interrupted. "It's a typo. Vida . . ."

"The Petersen-Huff nuptials took place in a hot-air balloon at Snohomish," Vida broke in, scribbling the correction. "Talk about wind—the Petersens have enough hot air to fly an airplane. Not to mention the Huffs. The name says it all."

"Very cute," I remarked, my curiosity at the bursting point. "Vida, where have you been?"

She glanced up from the handwritten piece of paper she was perusing. "Nowhere in particular," she said, but avoided my gaze. "You wouldn't think people would get married on Easter weekend, would you?"

"Vida . . ."

"What?" Finally, she stared at me through her big glasses.

"Don't you want to know all the details about last night?"

"Last night?" The faintest and most uncharacteristic of blushes emerged on her cheeks. "Did I miss something?" I could swear I heard her groan.

"Yes," I said. "Where were you?"

"Oooh . . ." She whipped off her glasses and began to rub her eyes in that fierce fashion that always drives me nuts. "I was with Buck. We spent a very leisurely evening."

"That sounds . . . nice," I said, keeping a straight face. While Vida would use every means short of thumbscrews to elicit the most personal information from others, she is a clam when it comes to revealing details of her own private life. Unlike many nosy people I've known, there is no mutual exchange of intimate affairs. In Alpine, it's understood that my House and Home editor takes no prisoners on the battlefield of gossip.

"All right," she said, putting her glasses back on and blinking several times, "tell me what I somehow missed last night."

Scott Chamoud and Kip MacDuff arrived together, so I waited until they'd settled in with coffee and the doughnuts that I'd picked up at the Upper Crust Bakery. Ginny came in with more phone messages, and Leo showed up just after I began my account.

"Wow!" Scott exclaimed after I'd finished. "I leave town, and everything blows up."

"It's all yours now," I said, "though you'll need background from Vida on the Harquist-O'Neill feud."

"You keeping the sheriff for yourself?" Leo asked with a bland expression on his craggy face.

"No," I said with a hard stare for my ad manager. "I have to go back to Seattle tomorrow. There's no point in me staying with any of the stories just before deadline."

"You can't go back to Seattle," Leo said. "We've got lunch with Spencer Fleetwood tomorrow."

I'd forgotten. "Can we put it off until Friday?" I asked, feeling stupid.

"I'll check with Fleetwood," Leo replied, but he didn't look pleased.

Throughout this exchange, Vida had remained silent. At last she spoke, her bust thrust out, her mangoes bobbing: "It was bound to come to this. The Harquists and the O'Neills have been building toward a showdown for years."

Leo turned in his swivel chair. "Aren't family feuds kind of dated, even in Alpine? This isn't Albania, Duchess."

Vida glared at Leo. "Really, what do you know about

it? You're still a newcomer. At least the Harquists and the O'Neills take some pride in family honor. I find it rather heartwarming."

"Sicily," Leo said. "It's more like Sicilian families, having a ritual bloodbath."

"Not at all," Vida asserted. "Everyone involved is fair-complected. The O'Neills are mostly redheaded, and the Harquists are very blond. Of course Cap is bald now, but . . ."

I left Vida and Leo to their argument and retired to my cubbyhole. The workday commenced. I called the hospital to check on Milo and was put through to his room.

"I'm stuck here until tomorrow," he complained. "I argued with Doc about it, but I lost. Now I have to run this whole Harquist-O'Neill mess from here. It's damned aggravating."

Milo was never one to delegate. I sympathized, then asked how he was going to manage when he went home. Surely he'd have to stay off his foot for a few days.

"That's another thing," he said, still grumpy. "Doc wants me to keep off of it until next week. Hell, it's not that big a deal. I shot myself in the foot once when I was a kid."

"But you're going to need some help," I pointed out. "I talked to Jeannie last night at the hospital, and it sounded as if she's going out of town for a few days." I couldn't resist putting the needle into Milo.

"Right," the sheriff responded. "You have to give seven days' notice at the place where we had our reservations. The deadline passed last Saturday. Janet Driggers tried to wheedle an exception, but no luck. They're sticklers in Sun Valley."

So Milo was making excuses for his youthful sweetheart. "Goodness," I said, "you wouldn't want to be out two or three hundred dollars just because you got shot in the line of duty."

"What does that crack mean?" Milo snapped.

I was silently chortling. "Get well, cowboy. I'll bring you a tuna casserole when you get home." Milo hated tuna casserole. I hung up, still chortling.

Vida and I ate at the Venison Inn, where she listened in relative silence to my adventures the previous day in Seattle.

"I'm actually relieved that I didn't have to go to those seedy bars," she admitted. "However, I can't help but wonder if things might have gone more smoothly with Darryl Lindholm had I been there."

I bristled a bit. "How? You couldn't have avoided mentioning Kendra."

"Perhaps you should have inquired about Carol first," Vida said, taking a bite from her Reuben sandwich.

"Why?" I shot back. "I was trying to add a positive note to what was otherwise an extremely negative conversation. Mr. Rapp said that Darryl, Carol, and Kendra looked happy together, like a family. I thought that mentioning Kendra would make him feel better."

"Apparently not," Vida murmured, looking faintly smug. "Oh, well. I'll call on him tomorrow."

"You're going with me?" I said. "What about the paper?"

"I told you, I already have my section well in hand," Vida said calmly. "All I need now are some 'Scene Around Town' items," she added, referring to her gossip column. "I could use some of the information from the encounter last night at Cap Harquist's—if you could make it amusing."

"It didn't seem amusing at the time," I retorted. "Besides, I don't think that would be in very good taste."

"Oh—it could be," Vida said airily. "You know— 'Half-clad but doughty Cap Harquist protesting removal from family homestead built in thirty-three.' 'Forty years later Sheriff Dodge gets shot in other foot. Was he waiting for the other bullet to drop?' 'Meara O'Neill uses old copies of *Advocate* to start fire.' That sort of thing."

"Those are not funny," I asserted. "And you know better."

Vida shrugged. "Then give me something I really can use."

"I haven't been here much the past few days," I said, then brightened. "How about 'Darryl Lindholm, formerly of Alpine, now working for Microsoft in Redmond'?"

"You know I'm not one to use 'formerly of Alpine' items," Vida said, frowning. "I like to keep things local."

"I know," I agreed, "but what if somebody who's known him since he left comes up with something interesting. Something recent, maybe."

Vida sprinkled extra salt and pepper on her potato salad. "Hmm. That's possible. But it's rather unfortunate that his name would appear in the same issue with his ex-girlfriend's murder, don't you think?"

She was right. "It probably wouldn't do any good anyway," I allowed. "Darryl cut his ties with Alpine a long time ago."

"But did he do it willingly? I wonder," Vida mused.

I looked up from my hot pastrami and rye. "As in?"

"It seems to me that his parents moved from here not long after he graduated from high school," Vida explained. "He was two, maybe three years older than Carol, and already enrolled at Pacific Lutheran in Tacoma. Carol went off to have the baby in Seattle—where she lived with Olive and Burt Nerstad. It wasn't long before the Lindholms sold their house on First Hill and moved to Mount Vernon."

"You're suggesting that Darryl was coerced out of marrying Carol?"

Vida nodded. "Perhaps. This is all coming back to me. Darryl was quite bright. I believe he'd won a scholarship to PLU. The Lindholms were fairly well-off, however. Mr. Lindholm had been a superintendent at the old Tye

Lumber Company before it closed. Darryl's mother came from Sultan, where her parents owned a great deal of property north of the town. The Lindholms had enough money to buy that bulb company in the Skagit Valley. They certainly didn't want to see their son marry too soon or beneath him."

"His first marriage failed," I remarked.

"Probably because it wasn't to Carol," Vida said. "Perhaps he really loved her. Perhaps he didn't mind what she'd become."

"Perhaps," I noted dryly, "he blamed himself for that."

"Perhaps," Vida said with an ironic smile. "He certainly must have blamed himself for the accident that killed his second wife and their two boys."

"I'm afraid so," I said. "All right, we'll leave at noon tomorrow for Seattle. I had the motel reserve a room for Tuesday night."

Amber seemed relieved that I was going away again. Obviously, she enjoyed the freedom to pig up the place. In her favor, she'd actually fixed dinner: overdone rib steaks, a can of string beans, and baked potatoes. I'd been trying to teach her how to cook. It was an uphill battle.

I'd tried to see Milo on my way home from work, but he was conducting a staff meeting in his room, so I left. Scott had learned earlier in the day that Cap Harquist had been hospitalized for smoke inhalation, but was already released. Rudy Harquist was back in jail, charged with unlawful discharge of a firearm. Apparently, even Milo wasn't sure that the shooting hadn't been an accident. Meara O'Neill was also out of the hospital. The Harquists wanted to charge her with arson, but our new prosecutor, Rosemary Bourgette, was probably going to nail both Rudy and Ozzie for kidnapping. The two O'Neills, who had carry permits, had been brought in on unlawful brandishing of a firearm. I'd written the first part of Scott's story myself. It was a big one, and I didn't mind giving him credit, but I'd have to go over his part with a fine-tooth comb. The whole mess was fraught with libel possibilities. Assuming, of course, that any of the feuding instigators could read.

About an hour after I'd cleared away the dinner things, I urged Amber to clean up the living room with its usual obstacle course of toys, tabloids, and wearing apparel, both large and small. The phone rang while she was still staring at the litter.

"What's this about Cousin Ronnie?" Ben demanded, the crackle in his voice more apparent than ever. "I haven't thought about him in thirty years."

I'd briefly mentioned in my message that I'd been trying to help get Ronnie out of jail. Since Danny was yelling his head off because he didn't want to surrender a big plastic toy that looked like an octopus wearing bells, I scampered into my bedroom.

"You're a good kid," Ben said after I'd given him the details. "Now I feel guilty for not being there to help him, too." He paused and lowered his voice. Some of the crackling lost its snap. "You aren't on some kind of family-connection search, are you?"

"Of course not," I replied, still able to hear the leather-lunged Danny. "Ronnie contacted me. Why would you ask such a question?"

This time the pause was longer. "I haven't mentioned this before, Sluggly," he said, using his childhood nick-name for me, "but I've felt a little guilty ever since Adam went into the seminary."

Amber was calling my name. She sounded desperate. "Hang on, Ben," I interrupted, removing the cordless phone from my ear and rushing into the living room.

Amber was trying to loosen Danny's grip from a box of fireplace matches that had somehow fallen off the mantel. He'd pried the lid open and was trying to stick one of the matches into his mouth. His anxious mother was hampered from rescuing him because—or so I gathered from her incoherent yips—she'd sat down in my new recliner and the footrest part had gone up instead of down. She was stuck in the chair.

I snatched the matches away from Danny, put them out of harm's way, and gave the footrest a terrific yank. It came down. I shot Amber a look that said, "If you'd been picking up all this junk, you wouldn't have gotten stuck in the damned chair, you lazy little twerp."

"As you were saying?" I said to Ben with a sigh. "About guilt?"

"Right," my brother responded. "Let's face it, I was very pleased when Adam told me he wanted to become a priest. He said I'd been his inspiration. Naturally, I was flattered, not so much on a personal level, but that the idea of my own vocation and the way I was handling it had influenced him. It's hard to explain."

"You don't want to brag," I said dryly. "Never mind, go on."

"Well—" He stopped to clear his throat. In the living room, Danny was crying again. "You know Adam's track record better than I do when it comes to choosing careers. Over time, he's wanted to be everything from an anthropologist to a circus clown."

"He was only twelve when he got that idea," I put in.

"But you know what I mean," Ben continued. "He was off in every direction. I figured that maybe the vocation thing was just another wild hair."

"I guess not," I said. "He's been in the seminary long enough now to know if being a priest is what he really wants."

"I agree." Ben had grown very serious, almost formal. I could picture him counseling someone with a crisis in faith or a broken marriage. "And that's what makes me feel guilty. I've robbed you of your earthly immortality. Robbed myself, too, in a way."

A terrible crash resounded from the living room. I didn't want to interrupt Ben again, not when he was in such a solemn mood, so I ducked out of the bedroom to see what new horror had occurred.

Danny had pulled the lace cloth off the dining-room table, and with it, a potted azalea I'd bought at Alpine Gardens the previous week. He was screaming his head off. Amber was nowhere in sight.

I started running to the child, tripped over the plastic octopus, and fell flat on my face. The toy's little bells played a cheery tune. It should have been a dirge.

"So," Ben went on, "when you told me about Ronnie, I began to feel guilty all over again. I sense that you want grandchildren after all, and somehow, it's my fault you don't have them to jiggle on your knee."

It was my knee that hurt most. Amber appeared from the kitchen with a broom and a dustpan. I struggled to sit up. Danny began eating dirt from the potted azalea.

"Shut up," I said to Ben. "Don't ever mention the word *grandchildren* to me again."

Ronnie had a smaller bandage on his ear when I visited him Tuesday afternoon in jail. The first thing he asked about was Budweiser.

I lied. "He's fine," I said, relating how I'd gone to Pete and Jenny Chan's house. "The little boys are darling. Their own dog had been run over, so they're taking good care of Buddy."

It was the wrong thing to say. "They'll get attached," Ronnie said, bowing his head. "They'll want to keep him."

"No, they'd prefer a snake," I said, finally telling the truth.

"You sure they didn't eat him?" Ronnie looked suspicious.

"Of course not," I retorted. "I think they were having lasagna for dinner."

"Hunh." The idea of Asian-Americans eating Italian food seemed to stump Ronnie. I felt like telling him that back in Alpine, Deputy Dustin Fong's favorite foods were chimichangas and quesadillas.

Instead, I asked Ronnie about Darryl Lindholm.

"You mean Kendra's real dad?" Ronnie's eyes shifted away from me. "Yeah, I met him once before he tried to buy me off. He acted like a big shot."

"Did he?" I remarked. "He's had kind of a terrible life."

"Right," Ronnie said sarcastically. "He works for Microsoft. I'll bet he's loaded."

"I'm not talking about money," I said, sounding testy. Ronnie's value system seemed to be skewed along with the rest of him. "His wife and children were killed in a car accident last year."

Ronnie blinked twice. "No kidding. That's rough." The words didn't sound very sincere.

"How did you happen to meet him the first time?" I asked. Interviewing Ronnie was like questioning a two-year-old. My patience was ebbing. I'd had better luck getting Danny Ramsey to spit out most of the dirt from my potted plant.

"This Darryl character was with Carol one night about a month ago when I came home from work. I got bad vibes off that dude."

"They were talking, I assume?"

"Yeah. Really talkin'. Like serious. Like maybe I should go sit out in the parking lot in my 4X4 and play fetch with Buddy."

"Did Carol ask you to leave?" I inquired.

Ronnie shook his head. "Nope. I went and changed and got a beer and by that time Darryl was takin' off. I guess he wanted to see Kendra, but she wasn't around."

"Is that the only time you met him until you talked to him at the Satellite Room?"

"Right." Again, Ronnie wasn't looking at me. He gave a single nod. "He pissed me off. He just struck me all wrong, that's all. Him and his big freakin' bike. Who needs it?"

"Did Carol ever talk about Darryl Lindholm?" I asked.

"Nope." The answer came too fast, especially for Ronnie.

"Not regarding Kendra?"

"Oh—maybe she said something about . . . I forget." He stopped, then wagged a finger. "I know—'too little and too late.' I suppose she meant his showin' up."

"Do you know if he met Kendra?"

"Nope." This time the denial struck me as genuine. But I knew better. Mr. Rapp had told me so.

"Did you ever meet Sam or Kathy Addison?"

"Who're they?"

"Kendra's adoptive parents."

"Nope."

I'd run out of questions for Ronnie. "Look," I said, glancing at my watch, "I've got a two-thirty appointment with Detective Rojas. I want to find out why the homicide investigation was so sloppy. From what I've learned so far, the police did a poor job. They arrested you because you were the obvious suspect. There's no evidence against you, really. Maybeth Swafford's statement is worthless."

"Maybeth?" Ronnie showed a spark of interest. "Whaddaya mean?"

I explained about the mistake in time, the probability

of at least one and maybe two other visitors arriving before Carol was killed. "The police took her evidence
verbatim," I said. Then, seeing Ronnie's blank stare, I
elaborated. "That is, they didn't dig enough to realize she
was wrong. Or perhaps Maybeth was lying to make you
look bad."

"Maybeth wouldn't do that," Ronnie said. "We broke
up, but she was cool about it."

Men. If a discarded woman didn't ram a shish-kebab
skewer through them, everything was just fine. I'd not
only run out of questions, I'd run out of patience.

But Ronnie had one last question for me. "Why don't
you get Buddy from those kids and take him with you?
Then I'd know he's okay."

I'd already stood up. "I'll see," I fibbed.

Then, feeling a tug of guilt for the simplicity of my
cousin, I walked away.

I almost collided with Vida. "I've been given permission to see Ronnie, too," she said, radiating triumph. "His
aunt, you see. So concerned. So loving. So near death's
door."

I was surprised, though I shouldn't have been.

But not as surprised as Ronnie would be.

I definitely felt sorry for him now.

Chapter Thirteen

MAYBE MY SYMPATHY had been misplaced. After fifteen minutes Vida emerged with the swallows on her silk cloche wobbling up and down.

"My!" she exclaimed. "Your cousin is a bit dense. All I could get out of him was that he didn't do it, and he can't think who did, unless it was Darryl Lindholm."

As we waited for the elevator, I frowned at Vida. "Ronnie didn't tell me that. Did he have a reason other than bad vibes?"

"He thought Darryl wanted revenge," Vida replied.

"For what?"

We stepped into the elevator, which was crowded with police personnel, office workers, and at least two obvious perps. Vida stared straight ahead and whispered through taut lips:

"Betrayal."

"With whom?"

"Ronnie."

"Huh?" We'd reached the floor that would lead us to the detectives' offices. "That's nuts," I declared as we exited the elevator.

"Of course," Vida replied at her normal decibel level. "But it raises a pertinent question. Why did Darryl try to buy Ronnie off?"

"I never got the chance to ask Darryl before he threw me out," I said as we approached the main desk. "It might indicate that he was serious about getting back with Carol."

Vida nodded. "But in that case why would Darryl kill her? And was her murder really premeditated?"

I shot her a curious glance before giving my name to a ruddy-cheeked blond behind the wide desk. We were directed to go down the hall and turn to our right.

"What do you mean?" I asked as we passed a couple of men in plain clothes who had cop written all over them.

"Who might be carrying around a length of drapery cord? In a pocket, a purse, a shopping bag."

I made a face at Vida. "When was the last time you stuffed a drapery cord in your handbag?"

"February fourth," Vida responded. "My mother's birthday. I took it to the cemetery to tie up a big chrysanthemum I was putting on her grave. As you recall, we'd had so much wind last winter. I didn't want the pot blowing over, so I tied it to my parents' tombstone."

I laughed so hard that a white-coated woman who was passing by stopped to stare. Thinking she might be the prison psychiatrist, I sobered up fast. But Vida had an answer for everything. I hoped Tony Rojas would have some answers for me, too. A petite, pretty Filipino woman pointed the detective out to me. He was sitting at the second desk on the left, a telephone cradled between his shoulder and his ear.

Rojas gestured for us to get another chair so that we could both sit down beside his desk. Even seated, I could tell he was a big, shambling man with a drooping black mustache and electric-brown eyes.

"Sorry," he said in a deep voice as he put the phone down. "You miss a day, and it feels like you have to make up for two. Now, which of you is Ms. Lord?"

I put out my hand, which was enfolded in a paw about the size of a grizzly bear's. His grip was gentle, however.

"I'm Emma, Ronnie Mallett's cousin," I said. "This is my associate, Vida Runkel."

Vida arched an eyebrow at the word *associate*, but merely smiled as she, too, shook Rojas's hand. "A pleasure, Mr. Rojas. Are you related to the Rojases who own a chicken farm near Sultan?"

The detective confessed that he wasn't, no doubt a major disappointment to Vida.

Not wanting to waste time, I stated my concerns about Ronnie's incarceration and my doubts about his guilt. Then I zeroed in on Maybeth Swafford's confused statement and the alibis that I'd gotten on Ronnie's behalf from the two bars on Greenwood Avenue.

Tony Rojas listened in silence, though his expression remained unchanged. When I'd finished, he picked up a ballpoint pen and began doodling on a notepad. Any optimism I possessed faded when I saw that he was drawing small nooses.

"I understand why you're upset," Rojas said in his calm, deep voice. "It's always hard for family members to accept that one of their own can commit a violent act. But," he added with an ironic little smile, "it happens all the time. The worst part is that the violence is usually directed at another family member."

"What about the alibis?" I asked. "Honey, the bartender at the Satellite Room, seemed very sure about the time. I understand you never questioned her. She said that Ronnie was there with another man."

A flicker of interest showed in Rojas's dark eyes. "Did Ronnie tell you who he was?"

I shifted in the uncomfortable metal chair. "Yes. It was Darryl Lindholm." Wanting to get Rojas's reaction, I didn't elaborate.

This time the blank expression on his face indicated ignorance, not reserve. But he said nothing, which turned out to be a mistake.

"What did Darryl have to say for himself when you interviewed him?" Vida demanded, fists on hips.

Rojas, who had been ignoring Vida, must have taken her silence for shyness, which made me question his perceptiveness. "I beg your pardon, Ms. Punkel?"

"It's *Runkel* . . . *Mrs.* Runkel," Vida burst out, causing heads to turn in the squad room. "See here, young man, it seems to me that you've conducted a most cursory—I might even say sloppy—investigation. My nephew Billy is a deputy sheriff, and if I ever thought he'd been so slapdash, I'd certainly take him to task. Now, it's about time you reopened this case and did your homework. Otherwise, Emma and I shall be forced to write an exposé in *The Alpine Advocate* and send copies to the wire services. I suspect you and your superiors wouldn't like that."

Tony Rojas looked as if he didn't like Vida very much, either. "You're out of line," he declared, tossing his ballpoint pen aside. "We conducted this investigation by the book. Ronnie Mallett couldn't provide an alibi for himself, he'd been drinking, and he'd obviously been in a fight. So had Carol Stokes. They'd been heard quarreling, and she was found strangled a couple of hours later. We turned up no other suspects, found no one to alibi Mallett, and frankly, he didn't protest his innocence very convincingly. In my book, that's an open-and-shut case."

"He doesn't do anything convincingly," I put in. "Furthermore, his public defender is inexperienced. I understand that you're overworked and underpaid, but who isn't? All I'm asking is that you check out the woman named Terri from Freddy's Bar, and Honey, the bartender at the Satellite Room. Oh, and Maybeth Swafford. She has an ax to grind with Ronnie, and may have lied about when he left the apartment."

Rojas's electric gaze was chilling. "That's all, huh? What do you suggest I do about the drive-by last night in Rainier Valley and the ax murder in Belltown? Or the shooting that left three people dead, including two little kids, on Beacon Hill? Get over yourself, Ms. Lord. If my partner and I can squeeze ten minutes out of the end of our shift, we might do some checking. Otherwise, it's all up to a jury."

I sensed that Vida was about to unleash another diatribe. But I didn't want to leave empty-handed. Before she could speak, I leaned across her and held out a beseeching hand to the detective.

"Tell me this much," I said, humbling myself. "Have you considered—even briefly—anyone else as a suspect in this case?"

"No," Rojas said bluntly. "Why should we?"

"Because," I replied, trying to look intimidating and aware that with my short chin and pug nose, the attempt usually made me look like a grumpy Pekingese, "there are several of them. What would you say if I told you that Darryl Lindholm had a very good reason to strangle Carol Stokes?"

Rojas looked as if he were trying to control a smile, no doubt of derision. "I'd say, 'Who the hell is Darryl Lindholm?' "

"That," I said, standing up and trying to muster some dignity, "is exactly what I figured."

Somewhat to my surprise, Vida didn't have a last word. She also stomped out of the squad room, ignoring the stares and a couple of titters from Rojas's fellow detectives.

"Buffoons," she muttered as we headed for the elevator. Then she turned to me with a curious expression. "Why Darryl Lindholm?"

"Because it suddenly occurred to me that Ronnie

might be right," I replied. "Darryl may have had a motive for killing Carol. What if she didn't want him horning in on her relationship with Kendra?"

"I thought Mr. Rapp told you that the three of them looked happy," Vida remarked as the elevator arrived.

This time we were the only occupants except for a helmeted messenger. "He did say that," I replied. "But maybe he misread the scene. Or, just because they weren't all trying to kill each other, he mistook cordiality for intimacy."

The sun was trying to come out when we left the municipal complex. I'd agreed to meet Alvin Sternoff at his condo in Belltown. He was working at home because, as he'd explained, it was quieter, and he had a lot of catching up to do.

"I don't have so many interruptions here," he elaborated as Vida and I were ushered into his first-floor condo not far from Seattle Center and our motel. The apartment building had been converted some ten years earlier. If the rooms had been small to begin with, the ones occupied by Alvin seemed claustrophobic. Like his office, there were legal tomes, files, briefs, and other job-related items piled around the living room. I decided that in another six months Alvin would have to tunnel his way to reach the computer.

Even though my memory needed no jogging, I'd made notes of the particulars I wanted Alvin to check. Maybe if I read them off, he'd take me more seriously.

"Alibis, huh?" Alvin scratched his head. "They're a funny thing. You get somebody—say this Terri person—on the stand, and she swears she saw Ronnie in the bar at eight-thirty. Then the prosecutor calls a witness—let's say a roommate—who testifies that Terri didn't leave home until a quarter to nine. Or Honey, the bartender. They go after her to see if she's working off the bar clock—it's always set ahead because of closing time, you know—or her watch. And if it was a Friday, wouldn't she be too busy to notice much of anything?" Alvin shook his head. "Alibis are tough to prove, easy to disprove."

"That's not the point, Alvin," I said, thinking that he was the perfect attorney for Ronnie. Both seemed to prefer accepting defeat to risking victory.

"I'm thinking about an insanity plea," Alvin said. "I'd like to get Ronnie evaluated by a psychiatrist."

See if you can get a two-for-one examination, I thought. You're both nuts.

"I don't see the point," I said. "He didn't do it."

Alvin gave me a pitying look. "But we can't prove it."

"Yes, we can." If I'd had a piece of drapery cord, I might have used it on Alvin. "Just pay attention and—"

Alvin held up his hands. "Look, Ms. Lord, Mrs. Runkel, I'm not trying to upset you. Ronnie's been charged with Carol's murder. He's going to make a poor impression on the witness stand. Even if I put him in an Armani suit, he'd still look like a loser. All this alibi stuff is worthless."

Vida, who had been remarkably silent, leaned forward, the swallows in her hat looking as if they were about to dive-bomb Alvin's desk. "See here, what about reasonable doubt? Isn't that all you have to do to get the jury to bring in a not-guilty verdict?"

"Yes, but—"

"Well, then? What's so difficult?"

Alvin threw his hands up in the air. "The reasonable doubt. Where is it? What is it? I don't have one."

"What about the witnesses? The alibi?" Vida demanded.

"I already told you, they're flimsy," Alvin responded in a weary voice. "Hey, I don't want to lose my first homicide case."

"Hold on," I said. "Do you honestly believe Ronnie killed Carol?"

Alvin's boyish face became miserable. "I don't know."

"That," I said, rising from the chair, "is an easy out. For you."

Vida and I left.

Kendra had mentioned that she worked at a QFC grocery store, a big chain with outlets in almost every Seattle neighborhood. From the time frame she'd given me about the night of the murder and judging from the location of her family home, I guessed that she was probably employed at one of three locations: on Forty-fifth Street near her parents' house, off Roosevelt Way south of her apartment, or possibly the store in Ballard, a block from where I'd had lunch on Easter Sunday.

The closest of the three was on Forty-fifth. Vida and I arrived there just after four o'clock. In my youth, the store had been Food Giant, a mecca for the working-class residents of Wallingford, Fremont, and Green Lake. But again, change had swept away another landmark. A younger generation had moved in, with many of the new-comers connected to the University of Washington, a mile and a half away. The shelves and bins of the Forty-fifth Street QFC catered to health-conscious, organic-only, natural-food lovers.

The front-end manager had never heard of Kendra Addison. Vida was shaking her head at the organic arti-chokes when I spotted Kathy Addison entering the store.

"Well, well," Vida murmured. "Don't tell me she buys beans in bulk."

"She's all yours," I said, ducking back into the produce section. "Kathy and I don't get along."

Vida marched up to the front and grabbed a grocery cart just as Kathy wheeled away toward the deli depart-ment. I followed at a discreet distance, seemingly ab-sorbed in a soda-pop display.

Conversation was initiated by Vida in front of fruit

salads. Kathy seemed amiable. I wondered what spiel
Vida was giving her as they headed for fish and meat.

Fifteen minutes later Vida was going through the express lane, having purchased toothpaste, bunion pads,
and two cans of Ajax.

"I had to get something," she announced when I met her
out at the car. "Otherwise, she'd have been suspicious."

"She wasn't?" I asked.

"Heavens, no. I started out by mentioning how hard it
is to cook for one person. Especially when your husband
is no longer with you and your daughters have moved
out." Vida simpered a bit as we started off into heavy
traffic on Forty-fifth.

"Kathy fell for that?"

"It's true," Vida asserted. "In a way. Kathy told me she
knew exactly what I meant, then I said that in my case, it
was even more difficult because my granddaughter was
adopted, and I'd never been sure if she felt accepted by
me. I blamed myself, of course, for being inadequate.
Kathy said it wasn't my fault, it was one of the problems
of adoption. An adopted child should be grateful for
having been placed in a loving family."

"Did she admit she had an adopted daughter?" I
asked, turning off onto Meridian Avenue to avoid the
crosstown traffic.

"Yes," Vida responded. "She bragged about how she
and her husband had treated Kendra—yes, she mentioned her by name—as if she were their own. Now, how
do you do that when she's not? You love a child because
you're the parent. You shouldn't pretend, as if there's
shame in adoption."

"What else did she say?" I asked, stopping at the
Fiftieth Street light. The old Good Shepherd Home still
stood on the block to my left, but it was no longer a refuge
for wayward girls; now it was a community center. Another change. Ben couldn't threaten me anymore with

being sent there to get thumped by the nuns and eat un-salted potato soup.

"Kathy mentioned what a lovely home they'd provided for Kendra," Vida said, "with every advantage. The main advantage seemed to be Kathy herself. She sacrificed everything for Kendra, including her career."

"Which was?" I inquired.

"An interior decorator," Vida replied, "which explains the house you described. Unfortunately, she got off on a tangent regarding color schemes and fabrics and such. I finally lost her in feminine hygiene."

"She didn't seem angry with Kendra for moving out?"

"No. She insisted that young people should try their wings." Vida paused, her head swiveling. "Where are we going?"

"To the QFC on Roosevelt," I answered.

"Good," said Vida. "That's the one where Kendra works. Kathy told me that, too."

I shot Vida an admiring glance. "It's too bad we can't figure out a way to arrange another chat between you and Kathy."

"But we can," Vida replied as we passed the entrance to I-5 and kept heading east. "She gave me her phone number."

My admiration soared. "How did you manage that?"

"I humbled myself and asked for her advice," Vida replied complacently. "I told her that my granddaughter was a teenager, such a difficult age, and I was afraid that since her parents had moved her to another city and a different school, she might be tempted to drop out in her senior year. Kathy said that although that had never been a problem with Kendra, she—Kathy, of course—could certainly counsel me on how I might help my granddaughter and her parents weather the storm."

I had to wait to turn left on Fifteenth Avenue, since Roosevelt is one way in this part of its north-south direction. While I waited for traffic to clear in the opposite lane, I glanced in the rearview mirror. There was no sign of the black Ford Taurus. Happily, I hadn't noticed anyone following us since our return to Seattle.

"Let's hope Kendra and Kathy don't compare notes about mature women who wear exotic hats," I said as we headed for the Roosevelt business district.

"Exotic?" Vida echoed, smoothing her swallows. "It's called flair. Besides, they're both too self-absorbed to pay much attention to someone else."

At twenty minutes after five on a Tuesday afternoon, the store was busy. I spotted Kendra right away, helping load bags for a middle-aged woman with a long gray ponytail.

"Kendra said she got off at five-thirty, at least she did on the night of the murder," I said in an undertone to Vida as we hid ourselves in the flower section. "Let's see if she quits work then. We can grab her before she goes to change."

The plan struck Vida as sensible. We admired the flowers, browsed the paperback books, and gazed at the magazines. Kendra made five trips to the parking lot and, after the last one, nodded to one of the checkers. She started toward the back of the store; we were right on her heels.

"Are you free for dinner?" I asked, a mere two feet behind her.

Startled, Kendra stopped so abruptly that I bumped into her. "Oh! You scared me," she gasped, a hand to her breast. "What do you want now?"

Kendra's scowl didn't make me feel optimistic. Fortunately, Vida intervened. "My dear," she said, placing a kindly hand on the girl's arm, "we've come to the conclusion that you may hold the key to this entire mystery. May we treat you to supper so that you can enlighten us?"

"I don't know what you're talking about," Kendra retorted, pulling her arm away. "You two give me the creeps."

"Canlis?" Vida said, mentioning the city's most revered restaurant.

"Canlis?" Kendra's eyes seemed to pop out of her head. "Are you kidding?"

"Of course not," Vida replied. "Do you have your car with you?"

"Yes, but . . ." Kendra's hand fluttered over her QFC apron. "I'm not dressed for Canlis. I mean, I've got my other clothes here, but they're jeans and a sweatshirt."

"We'll make a six-thirty reservation and meet you there," I said. "How's that?"

Kendra gulped. "Fine. Cool. I'll see you there." She hurried off down the aisle.

"Canlis?" I said to Vida as we headed out of the store. "Why not fly her down to San Francisco and eat at the Fairmont Hotel?"

Vida was grimacing. "I'm sorry. It was the first thing that popped into my head. I'm not familiar with Seattle's finer restaurants. Canlis has been around forever."

It had, for almost half a century, having survived all sorts of rumors, mostly unfounded, about its prices, its exclusivity, and its most famous regular, the Teamsters' Dave Beck. But because it retained an exalted reputation, I stopped at a pay phone to see if we could get a reservation. For all I knew, Canlis had been taken over for the evening by Bill Gates.

We were in luck, unless I considered the limit on my credit card. We could get in at six, which meant we'd have to wait for Kendra. Vida and I drove back to Aurora, then went south over the bridge. The restaurant is located just at the south end, which meant taking the Queen Anne Hill turnoff and making a loop under the bridge and coming back onto Aurora just a few feet from the entrance to the valet parking lot.

The Lexus fit in nicely with the Cadillacs, BMWs, Mercedeses, and other cars of quality. I felt slightly dowdy in my black slacks and red sweater—even though it was cashmere, courtesy of a Nordstrom after-Christmas sale. Vida's swallow-covered hat would give her cachet just about anywhere, including Buckingham Palace.

I hadn't been in Canlis for thirty years. My ex-fiancé, a Boeing engineer, and I had gone there to celebrate our engagement. I remembered almost nothing about the evening except that I'd had to lend Don twenty bucks to cover the bill and tip.

To my amazement, Vida ordered a Tom Collins from our lovely, kimono-clad Japanese waitress. "I don't want to seem like a cheapskate," she said, with a lift of her chin.

I grinned at her. "I know, but that's probably a ten-dollar gesture."

"What?" Vida stared at me. "I thought five would be excessive."

"It would be," I agreed, "in Alpine."

"Am I paying for the view?" she asked, leaning back to gaze out over Lake Union and the University of Washington. If it hadn't been a cloudy evening, we could have seen the Cascades in the distance.

"Not really," I said as the waitress brought our cocktails. I'd splurged, too, and gotten a Rob Roy. "You're paying for the quality of the food, the excellent service, and the right to say you dined at Canlis. Try that on Mary Lou Hinshaw Blatt."

A slight smile curved on Vida's lips. "So I shall. It's as good a reason as any to speak to her again. She may be my sister-in-law, but Mary Lou is an idiot."

Kendra arrived looking wide-eyed and well groomed. She wore a short black dress with white piping around the neckline and patent-leather high heels.

"It's my high-school graduation dress," she explained, twisting and turning in every direction after she'd been seated. "Are all these people rich?" she asked, taking in the half-filled dining area.

"Either that, or they're on an expense account," I said, noting that Kendra seemed to have forgotten that Vida and I gave her the creeps.

The black dress must have added a couple of years to her appearance, because the waitress asked if she, too, would like something to drink before dinner. Kendra, however, demurred.

"I don't want to get busted in a place like this," she confided after the waitress had left.

"The salad is separate," Vida hissed from behind her menu. "Everything is separate. Goodness!"

We ordered salads anyway, then Vida began her quest for information. "Kendra," she said, making a face after every sip of her Tom Collins, "we want you to go back in time, to the night of Carol's murder. I know this is difficult, but it's terribly important."

"I already told you about that," Kendra protested. "There's nothing more to say."

"Yes, there is," Vida responded. "You've no idea how important your recollections and observations are to this murder case. Sit back, relax, and close your eyes. You're a very smart young woman, and I know you want to make sure that the person who actually killed your birth mother is punished. Now, see if you can remember what you saw in Carol's apartment when you found her body."

Kendra frowned, seemed uncertain, then shrugged. "Okay, I'll try. But I doubt I'll think of anything I haven't mentioned before."

We waited in silence while Kendra sat with her eyes shut and her head thrown back. If any of the other diners noticed, they did so discreetly. After almost a full minute Kendra spoke.

"My mother's purse is on the floor. Some of the stuff had spilled out." She paused to take a deep breath. "A lipstick, a pen, a mascara wand. I put everything back and set the purse on the end table by the sofa." Kendra opened her eyes. "I suppose I shouldn't have done that. The police asked if I'd touched anything. I said not really, but I had. It didn't seem important."

"It probably wasn't," I said. "You're doing beautifully. What else?"

Kendra closed her eyes again. "The phone. It was off the hook." Her eyes flew open. "I did forget that. But I remember now. I had to click it several times to get a dial tone to call the police."

Vida and I exchanged curious looks. "You didn't tell the investigating officers?" Vida asked, keeping any reproach out of her voice.

Kendra shook her head. "No. I didn't even think about it until now. What does it mean?"

Our salads arrived, three Caesars that had to be tossed at our table. It took a few minutes. Vida squirmed impatiently in her chair.

"It might mean that Carol—your mother—was trying to call for help," I said. "If she'd actually dialed 911, the call would have registered the number and the location. The police would have come at once. They didn't, so it appears that she never got through. If, in fact, that's what happened."

Kendra gave me a helpless look. "I hope not. I'd hate to think she was just a second away from getting help." Her eyes started to glisten.

Vida put a hand on the girl's arm. "Don't fuss. Even if she'd gotten through, it would have been too late. The killer was already on the attack."

Kendra nodded slowly, then brushed at her eyes with her napkin. "Shall I try again?"

"Not now," Vida said, her voice at its most kindly. "Eat your salad. I'm sure it's delicious."

It was. Vida began questioning Kendra about the cleanup process. "You were responsible for most of that, I understand?"

Kendra made a face. "Yes, even though I didn't want to do it. But there wasn't anybody else. Ronnie was already in jail. Mr. Chan insisted it wasn't up to him."

"So you did your duty," Vida remarked. "Most admirable. Do you recall anything you saw or found that seemed odd?"

"Like what?" Kendra asked. "My mother—my birth mother—wasn't much of a housekeeper. My adoptive mother is way at the opposite end of the scale." She sounded as if she didn't approve of either extreme.

Vida paused in the process of demolishing her Caesar and sat back in the chair, fists on hips. "You might have seen things that didn't seem to belong. Items that wouldn't or shouldn't have been in Carol's apartment. Or notes she'd written to herself, telephone numbers, anything of that sort."

"I had to go through the mail," Kendra said. "It was just bills and the usual junk. She had a bunch of phone numbers stuck to the refrigerator, but I think they were mostly friends." She stopped suddenly and put a hand to her mouth. "There was something that should have been there that wasn't. It made me mad, that's why I remember it."

"What?" I asked, eager.

"My picture," Kendra said. "The one from my graduation. My mother had it pasted on the refrigerator. It was gone. Why would anyone take it down?"

Chapter Fourteen

VIDA AND I grappled with the disappearance of Kendra's graduation picture. Was it taken as a souvenir? Torn down out of spite? Or had Carol herself put it away?

"When was the last time you saw it on the refrigerator?" I inquired of Kendra.

She looked blank. "I don't know. I gave it to my mother about a month after we were reunited. Right around New Year's, I guess. It was in one of those cardboard frames, but she took it out after a while because she said Ronnie's dog had knocked it down off the end table a couple of times. Buddy couldn't get at it on the fridge."

"So it might not have been there just before the murder?" I asked.

Kendra regarded me with a quizzical expression. "You mean, my mother put it someplace else? I don't think so. I'd have found it when I was going through her things."

The removal of the picture sounded like an angry gesture. Who would have that reaction? Almost anyone who hated Carol enough to kill her, I thought. Yet I felt it was a more personal statement regarding Carol and her relationship with Kendra. The Addisons. Darryl. Even Kendra herself, though her grief seemed real.

"Can you think of anything else that was missing, unusual, out of place?" Vida asked.

The arrival of our entrées interrupted Kendra's recollections. We'd all ordered steak, with a baked potato as big as Rhode Island on the side. Even Vida seemed impressed.

"Unusual, like weird stuff, right?" Kendra said after the waitress had glided away.

"Sort of," I said. "Things that don't fit."

This time Kendra didn't bother to close her eyes. Instead, she began cutting her filet. "I remember finding an acrylic nail. Chartreuse. It was next to the wall, by the front door."

My eyes widened. "Had it been broken off?"

Kendra shook her head. "It was a whole nail. Like for this finger." She held up her pinkie.

"Did your mother wear acrylic nails?" Vida asked.

"No," Kendra replied. "She said they were too expensive and too much trouble."

"Maybeth, then," Vida murmured. "Did she often call on Carol?"

"Not when I was around," Kendra said after she'd finished chewing a bite of steak. "Wow, this is really good. No, my mother and Maybeth didn't get along. They fought over Ronnie, which I thought was really stupid. Why would anybody fight over him?" She glanced at me and winced. "Sorry. But he's kind of a dork, isn't he?"

"Kind of," I admitted.

"He gave me the creeps," Kendra said.

I suppressed a smile. Maybe if Ronnie had taken Kendra to Canlis, she would have gotten over her aversion. "Anything besides the nail?" I prodded.

Kendra giggled. "Now you've got me thinking about all the junk I threw out. A hundred used Kleenexes. Tons of tabloids and magazines. Old newspapers. Even—ugh—a couple of used condoms. It took me several days. I gave everything else to the Salvation Army. What else could I do?" She'd stopped giggling and was holding up her hands in a helpless gesture.

"That's it?" I remarked, feeling disappointed.

Kendra remained looking helpless. "Honest, it was just . . . junk. Empty envelopes, cigarette packages, used hairspray cans, ticket stubs, broken CD cases, old batteries—really, I'm sorry."

"That's perfectly all right," Vida soothed. "Enjoy your meal. It's quite tasty."

Kendra, who had loaded her baked potato with everything except the orchid that stood in a handsome marble vase, suddenly put her fork down. "One thing—it was a torn piece of cloth, like from a woman's suit." She made a circle with her thumb and index finger. "Blue and green with flecks of gold. It was like it had been torn off something. I remember it because my mother didn't wear suits. Neither did any of the women she hung out with. They were all pretty casual."

"Where was it?" I asked.

"Under one of the living-room chairs," Kendra replied. "I wondered if Buddy had taken a bite out of someone."

"Where was Buddy that night?" Vida asked.

Kendra paused. "I don't know. I never saw him. Or heard him, either. If he'd been tied up outside, he would have barked his head off."

We were silent for a few moments, savoring our food and the atmosphere. Finally, I asked her about Darryl Lindholm.

Kendra had only met him once, apparently the time that Mr. Rapp had seen them outside of the apartment. "He seemed okay. I had trouble taking in that he was my real father. All those years I wondered mostly about my real mother. Somehow, a dad didn't seem part of the equation."

"How did your real mother treat him?" Vida inquired.

"Nice," Kendra responded, a faraway look in her eyes. Though the clouds had lifted, dusk was falling over the city, and lights were coming on, from the University district to Capitol Hill. In the distance, the Cascade Mountains were outlined against the darkening sky. Small points of light glittered in the foothills of suburbia, and Lake Washington lay quiet behind Husky Stadium. Much closer, I could see the university's sprawl, the ever-present construction cranes towering high over the campus, like exclamation points. The single spire of Blessed Sacrament Church, the lighted dome of Holy Names Academy, the bulk of St. Mark's Episcopal Cathedral were all old, endearing sights. Thankfully, some things had not changed.

Kendra, however, was focused on something else, perhaps an impossible dream. "I got the idea—this sounds crazy—that maybe they could get back together. Maybe that's what I wanted, for selfish reasons." She shook herself and gazed at Vida and me. "Does that sound silly?"

"Certainly not," Vida said. "The family unit. Blood tugs at you." She glanced at me, then looked back at Kendra. "It's quite natural. Nor does it reflect on your adoptive parents. It's just there."

Kendra's smile was one of relief. "That's it. It was always there. Gosh, I don't know why I thought you two were creepy. This," she went on with a wave of her fork to take in her surroundings as well as us, "is nice. I feel better, just for talking to you. I wish I could be more help. Especially if Ronnie really didn't kill my mother."

"He didn't," I said quietly. Then, to alter the mood, which I feared might grow maudlin, I suggested dessert.

The rest of the meal was spent talking about Kendra's plans, how she wanted to work for a year before going to college, whether she would major in social work or biology, if she should let Gavin Odell move in with her or be completely independent for a while. I didn't really envy her open, uncharted future, though I found her enthusiasm contagious. She seemed like a nice, normal, bright young woman.

And never once did I give Sam and Kathy Addison credit for making her that way.

Since Vida always carried cash and disdained credit cards, we divided the rather astronomical bill between us. I put the whole thing on my Visa, and she gave me her half in bills. It was only eight-thirty when we left Canlis and Kendra. Vida decided she should contact Kathy.

"Desperation," she explained in the parking lot. "I've called my daughter long distance, and she's having a crisis with Sara Lee."

"Sara Lee?" Though Vida had granddaughters, none of them bore that name. "How'd you come up with that?"

"I was in frozen delicacies at the time," she replied. "It was all I could think of. Anyway, shall I?"

"If Sam's moved out, then Kathy will probably be home alone," I replied. Kendra had only mentioned her adoptive parents in passing, but had alluded to the fact that they were having marital problems, some of which she blamed on herself for leaving home.

"Dial her for me," Vida said, pointing to my handbag.

I jumped through the required hoops on the cell phone, then handed it to Vida. There was no answer.

"Drat," Vida said, surrendering the phone to me. "Where do you think Kathy is?"

"Anywhere," I said. "Maybe she takes night classes in interior decorating. Maybe she's visiting her family. Maybe she has friends."

"Most annoying," Vida said, tapping her fingernails on the dashboard. "What do we do now?"

"How about Mr. Chan?" I suggested. "I'm curious about Budweiser."

"Hasn't he run away? What will Mr. Chan be able to tell you?"

"I don't know," I admitted. "That's what I'll have to find out."

I still had Mr. Chan's phone number and address in my purse. He lived out in Crown Hill, a neighborhood north of Ballard and adjoining the Greenwood district. After a brief discussion, we decided to go directly to his home instead of calling first. I finally pulled out of the Canlis parking lot and onto Aurora. It was a risky move, because Aurora is such a busy avenue, but I waited until there was no sign of oncoming traffic for at least two blocks.

Behind me, on the verge between the street and the parking lot, the lights of another car went on. I gripped the steering wheel hard and glanced quickly at Vida.

"I hate to say it, but I think we're being followed. A car just pulled out behind us."

"Really?" Vida was agog as she strained to look out the rear window. "It's a dark car. I think the driver is the only person in it, but I can't be sure. My, my! I've never been followed before. This is quite thrilling. Who can it be?"

"I told you," I said, not in tune with Vida's excitement, "when it happened to me Sunday, I thought it might be the killer, trying to figure out what I was up to."

Vida was still looking behind us. "The killer! Now, wouldn't that be something? Should we stop to let whoever it is go by so we can see?"

"The windows are tinted," I said. "Can you make out the license plate?"

"No," Vida said with regret. "Only that it's a Washington plate. Why don't you slow down so I can get a better look?"

But there's no dawdling on busy Aurora with its forty-mile-an-hour speed limit.

"What shall we do?" Vida asked after I'd explained the predicament.

"Lose whoever it is," I replied. "Besides, I could be wrong. It may be a coincidence."

Apparently, it wasn't. The car kept to our route, though sometimes falling a vehicle or two behind. I drove due north to Eighty-fifth, not only the logical turn for Crown Hill, but also for Carol's apartment building. I pulled into the lot and turned off the lights. No one approached. The Ford Taurus, which I'd managed to identify at a stoplight even though it was one car back, was undoubtedly waiting a block or so away.

Vida and I sat there for almost five minutes. Finally, without turning the lights back on, I edged out through the alley that led to the side street. The Lexus crept along for a full block. Luckily, there was no other traffic. I put the lights back on and tore off in the direction of Crown Hill.

"Did we lose our pest?" I asked Vida.

"I don't see anyone," she replied, craning her neck.

"Good." I noticed that I was doing fifty-five and eased up on the accelerator. I didn't need to get picked up for speeding and land in jail with Ronnie.

The senior Chans lived in a well-tended two-story house on a side street that overlooked Puget Sound. Being a landlord served Mr. Chan well. I suspected that he owned several small apartment houses around the city. Over the years real estate had been a means for many Asian immigrants to prosper.

Mr. Chan came to the door. He was small, almost bald, and was wearing a sweatshirt that said, RENO—THE BIGGEST LITTLE CITY IN THE WORLD.

We identified ourselves, but received only an indifferent stare from Mr. Chan. I elaborated. Carol's murder, Ronnie's arrest, Budweiser's whereabouts—nothing seemed to pique his interest.

"I manage," he finally said when I'd run out of steam

and was considering lighting a fire to get his attention. "I take monies."

"Now see here," Vida said, elbowing me out of the way, "you must know the people who rent from you. The people with the monies. You took Ronnie Mallett's dog away and gave it to your grandchildren. They're charming little boys, but they said that the dog had . . ."

Vida rattled on. Mr. Chan remained unmoved. I was about to give up when a small, plump woman whose black hair was streaked with silver came into the entry hall. She appeared so swiftly and so silently that I was certain she had been listening around the side of the open door that apparently led into the living room.

"Beat it," she said to Mr. Chan. "Go watch stupid baseball. I manage this."

Without any change of expression, Mr. Chan disappeared from the entry hall.

"I Mrs. Chan," the woman said with a frown. "Mr. Chan never talk when watching baseball. Break concentration, he say. Lose track of count. You want stupid dog?"

"Is the dog here?" I asked, a faint hope surfacing.

Mrs. Chan shook her head, then glanced at Vida. "You right. Dog run away from grandsons. Not back yet. I talk to son just one hour ago. Grandsons very sad."

The faint hope was extinguished. "Where did Mr. Chan find the dog the night of the murder?"

Mrs. Chan's frown grew deeper. "Didn't find dog then. Didn't know about murder until next day. Dog was at apartment-house door, howling. Police give dog to Mr. Chan. Dog dig up peonies." Her small plump hand gestured toward the front yard. "Give dog to grandsons."

I nodded. "So he's not come back," I murmured. "Thank you, Mrs. Chan." I started to turn away.

Vida, however, wasn't finished. "Peonies are difficult to grow. I have to dig mine up every year and replant them. We have such cold winters in Alpine. Dahlias have to be taken up, too, right at the end of September. Often, they're still blooming. It seems a shame."

Something sparked in Mrs. Chan's dark eyes. "Alpine no good for gardens. Too much snow, frost, cold. We live first on farm, at Sultan. Not so cold as Alpine."

"Sultan!" Vida beamed at Mrs. Chan. "Why, we must have been practically neighbors. Did you know the Carnabys or the Johnsons—the Elmer Johnsons—or the . . ."

I backed off as Vida and Mrs. Chan reviewed their mutual acquaintances. In a deft conversational move, Vida returned to the apartment house and Carol's murder.

"So much harder to make friends in the city," she said, shaking her head. "Of course you and Mr. Chan have the apartment complexes, but people tend to come and go. Did you ever meet Carol Stokes? She was from Alpine, you know."

"She was?" Mrs. Chan seemed intrigued. "I meet her only twice. She your friend?"

Vida caught the dubious note in Mrs. Chan's voice. "No, I barely knew her. But she'd had a hard life. What was your impression?"

Mrs. Chan frowned some more. "Not good. Bad manners. I tell Mr. Chan, make her beat it. Not good tenant. But Mr. Chan softhearted. He let her stay. Big mistake. Mr. Chan spend too much time watching baseball."

Vida nodded solemnly. "Sports often take priority in some men's lives."

Mrs. Chan also nodded. "Not woman's. We smarter than men."

"Exactly." This time Vida's smile practically reached her ears. "I hope Carol and her boyfriend didn't do much damage to the unit."

Mrs. Chan sniffed. "They do plenty bad things. Dog ruin rug, tear drapes, chew furniture. People burn holes, spill, break toilet. Always, Mr. Chan must fix. Damage deposit not enough. We keep."

"I should think so," Vida said, no longer smiling, but oozing sympathy. "Managing an apartment house is very demanding work."

With a solemn nod, Mrs. Chan agreed. "People next door just as bad. Men trade units, men trade women. Much drink. Many fights. Neighbors complain. Not sorry to see 1-B people go."

On that self-serving note, Vida and I made our farewells.

"Take me to the Addisons," Vida commanded as if I were a chauffeur. "I must pay a call on Kathy."

"How are you going to explain a ten o'clock visit?" I inquired, checking the rearview mirror just in case the Taurus had found us.

"I told you," Vida replied. "I already set the stage. Kathy virtually invited me to stop in. She should be home by now."

It could be helpful for Vida to have an extended conversation with Kathy Addison. It certainly wouldn't hurt, as long as I stayed in the shadows.

There was an alley in back of the house on Ashworth. I dropped Vida off in front but pulled around out back. I'd keep the Lexus hidden by the Addison garage for twenty minutes. Then I'd start circling the block until Vida showed up at the corner. She would pretend to have walked down the street to her imaginary car.

The single-car garage was shut and a Cyclone fence enclosed the property. There was just enough room by the garbage cans and recycling baskets so that anyone coming through the alley could get past me. Nobody did, however, so I sat there in the dark, trying to see into the backyard. There were several trees, possibly a lilac and a couple of ornamental cherries. I assumed that the flower beds in back were as well maintained as the ones in front.

The lights in the rear of the house were faint, which meant that Vida and Kathy must be in the living room. I debated whether to risk peeking in the Dumpster and the garbage cans. If memory served, on this side of the Ship Canal the recycling pickup was every week. Cautiously, I stepped out of the car, then peered into the trio of baskets. The one for paper products was full, with newspapers on top. I dug deeper. There were some hunting-and-fishing magazines, no doubt discarded by Sam Addison before he moved out. Another basket held a few glass jars and one empty wine bottle. The third, presumably for aluminum, was empty.

Just as I straightened up, something brushed against my legs. I jumped, struck one of the baskets with my foot, and stifled a cry. A tabby cat stared up at me, its golden eyes glowing in the dark. Reaching down to stroke its fur, I noticed a piece of paper sticking out from under the basket I'd knocked out of place. Gently, I tugged the paper free.

It was an envelope with a handwritten address. The tabby cat circled my legs, then wandered off to the garbage cans. The writing on the envelope was somewhat blurred by damp, but I could see that it was addressed merely to *Addison*. The printed return sticker, which featured tiny red hearts, was more legible. It read *Maybeth Swafford,* with the apartment address off Greenwood.

The envelope was empty. Tucking it into my jacket pocket, I got back into the car and checked my watch: five minutes to go. The cat had disappeared, leaving the alley eerily quiet.

Just as I was about to drive off, a car entered the alley from behind me. All I could see was headlights, moving slowly toward my car. Could it be the Taurus? Should I wait to find out? Or should I launch the Lexus like a bottle rocket?

I did neither. The other car stopped two doors down and turned in to a garage. Letting out a big breath of relief, I started the engine and crept away.

Somewhat to my surprise, Vida was waiting for me on the first pass. "Did she throw you out?" I asked.

"Certainly not," Vida said, adjusting her hat, where the birds seemed to droop in exhaustion. I didn't much blame them. It had been a very long day. "I just got here," she went on. "We had a pleasant visit until Kathy was interrupted by a phone call she had to take in private."

I was taken aback. "So you left?"

"I really had no choice, but," she added with a sly glance, "I may have heard enough."

"Such as?" I braked at the arterial before heading onto Green Lake Way.

"She took the call in the living room," Vida explained, swerving around to look behind us. I was sure she hoped we were being followed again, but the side street was empty. "Kathy seemed rather astonished," she continued, giving up and facing front. "There was a long pause on her end, and then she said in a rather strained voice, and I quote, 'Excuse me, Darryl. I'm just saying goodbye to a visitor.' "

"Darryl?" My foot slipped off the brake and we almost collided with a fast-moving sports car. "As in Darryl Lindholm?"

"I think it's likely. Kathy seemed puzzled at first, then agitated. That was when she turned her back to me and finally got a word in edgewise with Darryl. Then she put her hand over the receiver, looked at me to apologize, and said goodbye. Kathy had turned quite pale."

"Darryl, huh?" I mused, finally getting an opportunity to enter traffic on the busy street. "Why would he call Kathy Addison?"

"It must have to do with Kendra," Vida said.

I thought about that for a minute or so, then told Vida

to reach into my pocket. Somewhat clumsily, she retrieved the empty envelope.

"My, my!" she exclaimed. "Where did you get this?"

I told her how I'd spotted it by the recycling baskets. "It must have fallen out when the recycling gang threw the stuff into their Dumpster. The envelope ended up under the basket. Can you read the postmark?"

"Not in the semidark," Vida admitted. "Should I?" She gestured to the overhead light.

"Go ahead." We had crossed the Aurora Bridge and were heading for our motel by Seattle Center. "I can manage."

"It's either March fifteenth or eighteenth," Vida said. "Let me think—the fifteenth was Billy Blatt's birthday, which was a Sunday. Do they postmark on Sundays in Seattle? They don't in Alpine."

I didn't know. "Either way, it was before the murder. Now, why would Maybeth Swafford write to the Addisons?"

"It wasn't good news," Vida responded, after a momentary lull. "What do you do when you get an ordinary letter or note? You answer it, if necessary, and then discard the whole thing. I suspect that Kathy—or Sam—ripped up the letter, then threw out the envelope later."

"Maybe," I allowed. "But that doesn't tell us much about what was in it."

"Perhaps Maybeth was getting even with Carol by telling the Addisons that her birth mother wasn't fit company for Kendra," Vida suggested.

"That's possible," I said, pulling off Aurora at the sign for the center. "But maybe it was more self-serving than that."

"Such as what?" Vida asked.

I turned as we stopped for a red light. "How about blackmail?"

"To what purpose?" Vida asked.

"I don't know," I admitted, easing the car into a parking stall. The motel was beginning to feel like home in some weird, impersonal kind of way.

I waited until we were inside the room to get the details of the visit with Kathy. Vida removed her hat and coat, plopped down on the bed, and tipped her head to one side.

"I'm not sure I learned much except for some family history," Vida said. "Kathy and Sam met at the University of Washington. She was from Seattle, but he grew up in Port Orchard. Sam was in engineering school, and Kathy was a domestic-sciences major. I believe they used to call it home economics. Anyway, they didn't meet in the classroom but at a sorority-fraternity party. Sam was a year older, but it took him an extra year or two to finish the engineering program. They married a few months after he finished school."

"You're right," I put in. "So far, no help."

"It gets marginally better," Vida said without enthusiasm. "Sam got a job with a security alarm company. Kathy worked at Frederick & Nelson in the home-furnishings department. She hoped to move up into interior decorating, but she got pregnant. They decided to buy a small house in the Fremont district. They'd just gotten the loan approved when Kathy miscarried, but they went ahead with the move anyway. It's not uncommon, of course, for first pregnancies to end in a miscarriage."

"True," I allowed. Mine hadn't, thank God.

"Less than a year later Kathy had another miscarriage, then a third," Vida continued. "Sam had gotten on with Boeing by then and was making decent money. They felt that if Kathy quit her job, she'd have a better chance of carrying a baby to term. Kathy agreed, but she thought the house in Fremont was bad luck. That's when they bought their present home by Green Lake."

"*Her* present home," I remarked. "I wonder where Sam is staying."

Vida shrugged before taking up her tale. "The next pregnancy also ended in a miscarriage. The Addisons went to a specialist, who told them that she could never carry a baby to term, though Kathy didn't explain the medical reasons, and I never pry. Anyway, that's when they decided to adopt."

I'd sat down in one of the motel room's two wooden chairs. "How did they go about it?"

"Privately," Vida responded, then made an impatient gesture. "I should have asked Olive when we called on her. The Nerstads used the family OB-GYN who was treating Carol after she moved from Alpine. A Dr. Mc-Farland in Ballard. He retired some years ago, however. In fact, Kathy thought he'd died recently."

"So everything was on the up-and-up?" I asked.

"It seems that way," Vida said. "Private adoptions are expensive, but highly respectable. Both young Doc Dewey and old Doc Dewey have done them over the years."

"What else did Kathy say?"

Vida made a face. "Not much. She'd gone on at length about the sorrow and disappointment and frustration of miscarrying four times. Then, after the Addisons got Kendra—the name means knowledge and understanding, which may or may not fit her—Kathy expressed great joy. Endlessly. She'd just begun to discuss Kendra's move into the apartment—in a rather defensive manner, as you might guess—when the phone rang."

"Kathy didn't talk about Carol?" Frankly, I was disappointed in Vida.

Apparently, she sensed my reaction. Drawing herself up on the bed, Vida scowled. "There wasn't time. You might know I was going in that direction."

I smiled weakly. "Yes, of course." I got out of the chair and began pacing around the small room. "The problem is, we seem to be going off in all directions and not getting anywhere."

Vida was very solemn. "We cannot fail."

I gave her a droll look. "Yes, we can."

I was beginning to think we already had.

Chapter Fifteen

YEARS AGO I'D read in a classic murder mystery that no so-called clue could be overlooked. Every piece of evidence, no matter how small, had to fit in order to solve the puzzle. It made sense at the time, because the author had plotted the story so craftily that by the last page, everything had come together in perfect, homicidal harmony.

But that was fiction, and I was living in reality. While Vida was in the shower I made a list of our meager shards of evidence before we headed to the nearby Denny's for breakfast.

"Very sensible," Vida said after we'd checked out of the motel and given our orders at the restaurant. "What's number one?"

"The drapery cord," I said, studying my notebook. "We still don't know where it came from."

"Most mystifying," Vida allowed as a rather shabby-looking middle-aged man in the next booth asked if we had extra sugar. I handed him a half-dozen packets before Vida continued: "The cord was introduced, perhaps solely for the purpose of strangling Carol."

"Possibly," I said, moving on to the second item. "Kendra's missing graduation picture. Who took it off the fridge?"

"That indicates a definite relationship between Kendra and whoever did it," Vida noted. "Which could mean the Addisons or Darryl."

I frowned. Were they the only ones who might have strong feelings toward Kendra? Or more precisely, toward the relationship between Kendra and Carol? I omitted Maybeth. She didn't strike me as a frustrated Mama Wannabe who'd resent Carol's reunion with her daughter. Roy was out, too. I couldn't picture him as wanting much of anything except to keep the beer cans rolling and get laid on a regular basis.

The shabby man asked if we had extra cream, so I passed on a couple of tiny containers before moving on to the broken acrylic nail. "Maybeth, maybe," I said. "But when? Carol was a lousy housekeeper. It might have been there forever."

"I don't know much about false nails," Vida admitted. "If one comes off, could you reapply it?"

Unable to answer the question, I asked Vida if she meant that Maybeth could have lost it without noticing while she was strangling Carol.

"Something like that," Vida replied. "Carol and Maybeth might not fight over Kendra, but they'd certainly quarrel over men. Have you listed the piece of fabric? Women's suiting material, that's what Kendra said."

I checked off the cloth scrap. "Again, we have to take Carol's poor housekeeping into account. Who knows when it got on the floor?"

"That's so," Vida said, "but this is intriguing. A professional woman calls on Carol, a woman who would wear a suit. Why?"

"I can't begin to guess," I said. "What does she do when she gets there, start shredding her clothes?"

Vida sighed. "That's the problem. We have so little to go on with any of this."

The shabby man had gotten up from his booth and was shuffling off toward the exit. I glanced at the table to see if he'd used up the extra sugar and cream. There were no signs of empty containers or packets; only several empty plates, a mug, and a glass remained. The man must have been hoarding the extras.

"We're missing somebody, maybe even the woman in the wool suit," I said, flipping the pen onto the table. "That's where we're at a disadvantage. If the police hadn't been so quick to arrest Ronnie, other suspects might have surfaced."

Vida, however, shook her head. "We'd have heard something by now. Not everyone believed that Ronnie killed Carol. Look at Henrietta Altdorf. And Mr. Rapp."

"True," I admitted, "but still . . ." I sighed. "Okay, we'll drop it for now. It's too bad that Mr. Stokes moved to California or wherever."

"The circle *is* rather small," Vida acknowledged. "Let's go back to our clues."

I shot her an ironic glance. "Both of them? Okay, there's the phone call last night to Kathy Addison from— we presume—Darryl Lindholm. What was that about? Is Darryl trying to get some sort of legal right to Kendra? She's eighteen, it doesn't matter."

Vida opened her mouth to say something, shut it, and pressed her fingertips together. "That may be the point," she said. "At eighteen, parents are no longer legally obligated to support their children. What if—now, this is a big if, mind you—Kathy and perhaps Sam were so angry about Kendra's moving out that they decided to stop helping her financially?"

"And Darryl wants to leap into the breach because his other children are dead?" I considered the idea. "That's possible. What else would he do with his money? He's all alone now."

"That's a plausible idea," Vida asserted. "Make a note."

A commotion at the door distracted us. A young man in a shirt and tie had collared the shabby man and was pulling him back inside the restaurant.

"Dine and dash," I said to Vida. "He must have tried to leave without paying."

The young man gave the errant customer a good shake. Sugar packets, cream and syrup containers, butter pats, and pieces of silverware tumbled onto the floor.

"Really," Vida said in disgust, "I haven't seen anything like this in Alpine since Arthur Trews tried to leave the Venison Inn without paying. Arthur had the money, of course, but he was so forgetful in his later years. That was the same day he'd shown up at Harvey's Hardware not wearing any pants."

Another man, about the same age as the would-be dasher, approached the door. He had his bill and his wallet in his hand. The discussion was brief. Apparently the third man was offering to pay for the shabby man's meal. The younger man, who I assumed was the manager, agreed. The little drama concluded with the two customers exiting together.

"Very generous," Vida said in approval. "Still, such tawdry little scenes must be played out all over the city. Tsk, tsk."

I didn't contradict Vida, because I knew she was right. Instead, I asked her to explain the envelope from Maybeth to the Addisons.

"I can't," she confessed. "We already made those conjectures. I've nothing new to add."

I glanced over at the serving area, where what looked like our orders were being placed under heat lamps. "Let me call *The Advocate* before we get served," I said, digging for the cell phone in my capacious—and cluttered—handbag. "I want to make sure everything went off all right by deadline."

Since it was barely eight o'clock, I wasn't surprised to find that only Ginny Erlandson was at work. In her accurate, if phlegmatic way, she informed me that there had been no big problems. Nor had there been further developments in the O'Neill-Harquist matter, except that everyone involved was threatening to sue everyone else.

"All systems are go," I informed Vida as our breakfasts arrived, "and the rest is status quo. Where were we?"

"I believe," she said dryly, "we'd finished studying our clues. I suggest we now discuss the suspects themselves and their possible whereabouts the night of the murder."

"Okay," I agreed, drizzling syrup on my pancakes. "We don't know where Kathy and Sam Addison were, but even if they're estranged, I'd guess they'd alibi each other."

"Probably," Vida said, diving into her eggs, sausage, hash browns, and toast. "Maybeth was home, Roy wasn't. Now, if he's living with her, where did he go that night? Do we know?"

I tried to remember. "Playing poker? A night out with the boys? It might be true. Let's leave Roy hanging. Figuratively speaking, of course."

"And Maybeth as well," Vida put in.

"Which leaves Darryl," I continued, "who we know was in the vicinity because he met Ronnie at the Satellite Room."

"Darryl's arrival at the apartment house would have been noted," Vida said, daintily sipping her orange juice. "He has a motorcycle."

"He probably has a car, too," I said.

Vida, however, shook her head. "He managed to kill his entire family while driving a car. It's quite likely that he has only a motorcycle. They can be even more dangerous. Darryl may have a death wish."

I thought that was stretching it, but not by much. "Okay, so maybe we can rule out Darryl, but only because he wouldn't have been offering Ronnie money to leave Carol. By ten-thirty that night, if Darryl had been the killer, he would have known that Carol was already dead."

"Unless he wanted to establish that sort of alibi," Vida said. "It would be very clever. Let's say he'd set up the meeting with Ronnie, but went first to see Carol. He told her what he planned to do. Or perhaps he asked her to marry him then. She refused his proposal. Darryl strangled Carol in a fit of rejection, but realized he must still keep his rendezvous with Ronnie."

I grinned at Vida. "If you ever kill someone, I swear you'll get away with it. You have a very cunning mind."

Vida shrugged. "Not at all. I consider myself extremely straightforward. But I'm trying to think like a murderer."

"And doing it very well," I insisted. "But that doesn't explain the lack of motorcycle noise at the apartment complex."

"He could have parked down the street and walked," Vida argued.

"No. If your theory is correct, then he wouldn't have known he'd be rejected by Carol. It wouldn't matter if anyone heard him approach. He didn't know that the encounter would lead to violence."

Vida grimaced, not an easy thing to do considering that she'd just forked in a massive load of hash browns. "Do motorcyclists travel with drapery cord wrapped around the handlebars?" she inquired.

"Good point," I admitted. "We're back to that stupid murder weapon."

Vida nibbled sausage, then spoke again. "We're leaving Kendra out."

I winced. "I hate to put her in. She seems to have been genuinely fond of her birth mother."

"Yes, yes," Vida said a bit impatiently. "But how much of that was rebellion? She's still a teenager. What if her relationship with Carol was a fraud, to get back at Sam and Kathy? And by the way, what was the issue that sent Sam

Addison flying out of the house after over twenty years of marriage?"

"Money," I said. "Kathy's extravagant expenditures for the house."

Vida gave me her gimlet eye. "Do you believe that?"

I thought about it. "No," I confessed. "It may have been the last straw, but it wasn't the real reason. Maybe Sam and Kathy had stuck together for Kendra's sake. Then, when she moved out, he split. I suspect it was a cumulative situation that festered over many years. That's usually what happens when couples with long marriages separate. Some event finally spurs them to break up. Usually, it's when the children are grown. They've stayed together for the sake of the kids."

Vida's expression was wry. "Spoken like a true single woman. Even if you've never married, you have at least observed."

"Thanks, Vida," I said sarcastically. "But you know I'm right."

She gave a nod. "Which brings us to the Addisons themselves. Why would either of them kill Carol?"

"Because she'd created a wedge between Kendra and her adoptive parents? Because they hated her for the attention Kendra was giving Carol? Because Sam had a perverse lust for Carol and felt guilty? Because Kathy is menopausal and had a hot flash that went awry?"

Vida sprinkled more salt and pepper on her fried eggs. "That's the trouble. It's so difficult to get inside other people's minds. We can't know for certain what demons are driving them."

"I think we know Darryl's," I said. "He's racked with guilt and still in mourning. He was trying to create another family for himself."

"Yes," Vida said thoughtfully, "out of what he'd started in the first place with Carol. That makes sense. Not having seen Darryl since he was a teenager, I can't judge how the years have changed him. I'll rectify that this afternoon."

"Darryl works at Microsoft," I pointed out. "It's Wednesday. He won't be home until evening, and by then, we'll be headed back to Alpine."

"Hmm." Vida rested her chin on her fist. "I could call him tonight after I get home, but that's not as good as a firsthand impression. Tell me exactly what you thought of Darryl."

Darryl's angry expulsion of me from his condo had colored my assessment. I ran the tape backward in my brain and reflected on his manner when I'd first met him. He'd been suffering then, after his visit to the cemetery. He'd needed someone to talk to, a grieving man with a heavy heart.

I expressed those thoughts to Vida. "I liked him. He seemed like a straight-arrow type. Responsible, reliable. He's got a good job, and even if he lost his real home, the condo is very nice and didn't come cheap."

"In other words," Vida said dryly, "not Carol's type anymore."

"No. But he does have an explosive temper and I would guess that he's living on the edge. That makes him unpredictable, not to mention altering his good judgment."

"Grasping at the past," Vida murmured. "Understandable. But dangerous."

I couldn't dispute Vida's opinion. Still, I didn't want Darryl to be the killer. "We're at loose ends," I announced. "Maybeth, Roy, Darryl—they're all at work. Henrietta Altdorf may be, too. We've run out of interviewees. What do we do next except visit Ronnie?"

"Henrietta," Vida said in a musing tone. "We have only her word for it that she was at work that night, correct?"

"Surely the police questioned her about that," I said.

"But took her at her word," Vida noted. "As we did."

"Surely you can't suspect Henrietta?" I said, flabbergasted. "What kind of motive could she possibly have?"

Vida shrugged as she chewed the last of her sausage. "A quarrel between her and Carol over the noise and carryings-on? Henrietta works long hours. She needs her sleep. And she's no spring chicken."

"That's not much of a motive," I remarked.

Vida's expression grew enigmatic. "Hidden agendas. Dark secrets. Forbidden passions."

I made a face at my House and Home editor. "You're off base on this one," I said. "Henrietta is a very straight-arrow kind of person."

"You just said the same thing about Darryl," Vida pointed out.

So I had. We were still going in circles. As we left the restaurant, the shabby man was standing by the driveway into the parking lot. We had no choice but to go right by him.

"Got any spare change?" he mumbled.

Reacting to the Good Samaritan's example in the restaurant, I reached into my wallet and handed the man two one-dollar bills. He mumbled his thanks as I started to move on.

Vida, however, was not so easily gulled. "See here," she admonished, "you look like a healthy specimen. Why don't you have a job?"

The man, who must have been asked that question before, just stared past Vida.

"The economy is quite good," she went on, "so I don't understand why you aren't employed. Do you drink?"

The man kept staring, his watery gaze fixed on Aurora's busy traffic.

"Really!" Vida huffed. "You ought to be ashamed of yourself." She stomped away in her splayfooted manner.

"You should have saved your breath," I remarked after we'd gotten into the Lexus. "He doesn't want to

work. And he probably couldn't hold a job. I suspect he
has mental problems."

We reached the driveway just in time to see the object
of Vida's disdain get into the backseat of a Yellow Cab
and drive away.

Our immediate destination was the jail to check on
Ronnie. Vida, however, was warring with herself about
seeing my cousin again.

"He's quite useless in terms of information," she said
as we passed the old site of Frederick & Nelson, which
had been transformed into Nordstrom's flagship store. It
was one change I deeply regretted. In its heyday, F&N
had been on a merchandising pedestal all by itself, a full-
fledged department store that sold everything from English lawn mowers to the latest Paris fashions.

"I know Ronnie isn't very helpful," I admitted. "I'm
only going to see him because I feel an obligation. I'd really
rather not come back down here over the weekend."

"We may have to," Vida said, and I knew it was true.
"If I could figure out some way to get Ronnie to stay with
the pertinent facts. If," she added with a big sigh, "he'd
just divulge some facts in the first place. It's rather like he
can't grasp reality, isn't it? What has made him hide from
facing up to life?"

I swiveled around to look at Vida. Fortunately, we
were at a stoplight in the middle of Fifth Avenue. "That's
it. Ronnie's hiding. He's hiding in jail." I paused as the
light turned green and also to organize my thoughts. "He
finds the world a scary place. Serving time doesn't seem
to bother him much. Now, why would anyone feel that
way?"

"Because life has become unbearable," Vida suggested. "Because it always was." It was her turn to twist
around in the seat and look at me. "You mentioned that

his parents live in Arizona. Why not call them? After all, you *are* their niece."

I wondered why I hadn't done it earlier. But Ronnie's vague references to his mother and father had suggested that he'd virtually lost touch with them.

"I will," I said. "Maybe I should do it before we see him. We're early for visiting hours, so we have some time to kill."

Much of that time was taken up finding a parking place that wouldn't bankrupt me. I had to park the car deep in the bowels of a garage two blocks away from the county-city complex, which meant that the cell phone probably wouldn't work. Thus, I ended up using a pay phone in the building's lobby.

It took Directory Assistance several minutes to search for Gary Mallett in what I assumed was the greater Phoenix area. He was finally located in Apache Junction, apparently a suburb.

It was only when I heard Uncle Gary's whiskey baritone that I realized I didn't know how to begin the conversation. Would he remember his niece from Seattle? Did he know that his son was in jail? Would he care?

"*Who?*" he rasped into the phone.

"Emma Lord," I repeated, grimacing at Vida, who was leaning on the stall of the next booth. "Your wife's niece. From Seattle. Martha and Ray's daughter."

"Ray? He's been dead for years. Plane crash or some damned thing. You got the wrong number."

I gritted my teeth. Uncle Gary sounded as if he were already in the bag at ten A.M. "Let me speak to Marlene," I said, investing my voice with what I hoped was authority.

"Marlene?"

Good grief, the man was drunk *and* deaf. What a combination. And, as I recalled, he was stupid, too. "Your wife. Mrs. Mallett."

Uncle Gary turned away from the phone, his words

muffled. I assumed he was calling for Aunt Marlene. After what seemed like an interminable wait, a husky voice reached my ear.

"Who's this?" demanded my aunt.

Marlene Lord Mallet had always been on the heavy side. I pictured her weighing about three hundred pounds, wearing a muumuu, with flip-flop sandals. "It's Emma, your niece," I said. "Ray's daughter. You remember Ben and me?"

"Of course I do," Aunt Marlene retorted. "What do you want? If you're stranded, we can't get you. Gary don't drive no more. His legs got too bad."

Hoisting those cases of Old Snootful will do that, I thought nastily. "No, I'm in Seattle. When was the last time you spoke with Ronnie?"

"That little shit?" Aunt Marlene, all warmth and charm, paused. "A couple of years ago, maybe. I forget. Why do you want to know?"

It didn't seem like a good idea to tell Aunt Marlene that her son was in jail on a homicide charge. Obviously, her opinion of Ronnie wasn't very high.

I fabricated. "I'm doing a family retrospective, and I'd like to—"

"A what?" Aunt Marlene cut in. "You're expecting? How old are you anyway?"

"It's like a family tree," I said, wishing my patience wasn't on such a short leash, "only with old pictures and souvenirs. Tell me about what it was like raising Ronnie and his sisters."

Aunt Marlene snorted. "Are you kidding? It was like hell. Isn't that what raising kids is all about? Say," she said, lowering her voice, which had grown suspicious, "what are you doing? Is this for some book?"

"No, it's a family album," I said. "Just for me and for Ben." I left Adam out. As far as I knew, my aunt and uncle weren't aware of my son's existence.

"You sure?" Still the wary note. "I thought you was going to be a writer."

"I were," I felt like saying, "but grammar don't run in the family." How could this woman have been my father's sister? They were like day and night, light and dark, a handsome stag and a big fat cow.

"I work on a newspaper," I said, "but this has nothing to do with my job. It's strictly personal. I wanted to include you and Uncle Gary and your children. What can you tell me about them?"

It took my aunt a few moments to round up her thoughts, which I assumed were scattered around the floor like so many loose marbles. "Lucy's in Dallas. This third husband works in some factory there. They got five kids between them. Or maybe six, I forget. Leah got the one boy, must be in high school by now. I forget his name. I ain't heard if her divorce is final, but that was a while back. She's up north, Montana. One of those towns that begins with a *B*."

Butte? Billings? Bozeman? It didn't matter. I barely remembered the Mallett girls, except as a pair of pale, nondescript entities who spent a lot of time pointing at people and talking to each other from behind their hands.

"And Ronnie?"

"Ronnie's up north, too, still in Seattle, I think. We ain't much at writing letters and it costs too much to call. Say, how're you affording all this?"

"I've saved up a bit," I lied, wishing Vida wasn't leaning so close that it must look as if we were both wearing the same ostrich-plumed hat. "Tell me, Aunt Marlene, does it make you at all sad to have your children so far away?"

"Ha!" My aunt started to laugh, then choked, and began coughing. "Sorry. Cigarette smoke went down the wrong way. What was that? Sad? Hell, no. Me and Gary always wanted some peace and quiet. You don't get none of that when you're raising three kids. Oh, the girls weren't so bad, but Ronnie was a pistol. Always into something. He drove me and Gary nuts. I can't tell you how many times Gary had to get out the old strap. With the girls, it was different. All Gary had to do was show it to 'em."

Good old Uncle Gary, I thought, my heart sinking. Poor Ronnie. No wonder he was scared stiff of what blow life would bring him next. No wonder he lived with a woman who beat him up. No wonder he didn't mind that Bubba was treating his head like a cantaloupe. At least there were guards to finally call off the bully; at least there was medical attention.

"School of Hard Knocks, huh?" I said feebly.

"You bet. How else can you bring 'em up proper?"

If she didn't know by now, there was no point in telling her. Anyway, it was too late. The damage had been done. And no wonder Ronnie didn't care if he was found guilty—he always was, in his parents' bloodshot eyes. I suspected he'd been framed before, many times, by his silly sisters.

"Thanks, Aunt Marlene," I said. "This has been very helpful." It had, in a pathetic, tragic way.

"Sure. Say hello to Bob when you see him." She hung up before I did.

"Bob," I echoed dumbly. "I think she meant Ben. Not that it matters."

Vida had caught most of the conversation at the other end. As we walked the two blocks to the jail, she agreed with my assessment. "An occasional swat on the bottom until a certain age," she said. "That's permissible in my opinion. Why, I've even been tempted to give Roger one—but not since he got older."

Forty lashes wouldn't deter Vida's evil grandson. If

ever a child had needed a good paddling somewhere along the line, it was Roger. But the poor kid had been coddled and pampered by both parents and grand-parents. It was he who wielded the whip in the Runkel family.

"You're upset," Vida remarked with sympathy. "You never guessed that Ronnie was abused?"

"I hardly ever saw him," I replied. "Three, four times, maybe. He was so much younger, and Uncle Gary and Aunt Marlene didn't live close by."

Vida held on to her hat as the wind blew up from Elliott Bay. "Such a shame when families don't stay close."

"It happens," I said tersely. "Uncle Gary worked for the state, though I don't know exactly what he did. The Mallets aren't all that old, middle sixties, I think. He must have taken early retirement."

"Disability, I'll wager," Vida said as we entered the building that housed the jail. "How long have they been in Arizona?"

"I don't know that, either," I admitted in a miserable voice that surprised me. "And I can't figure out how my father and his sister could have been so different."

"That's not surprising," Vida said as we headed for the elevator. "My husband and his brothers were all very different. Drink, that's what can happen. Ernest never took more than a glass of wine. But the rest of them . . ." She glanced at me and rolled her eyes.

Maybe that was the answer. Gary Mallett had changed Marlene Lord. I didn't remember either of them as ever being young. Mainly, I remembered Ronnie, hopping around in that sack at the rare family picnic. He had lost that race, too.

"My mother's brothers are good people," I said, going on the defensive. "They live in Texas and Colorado now, but I keep in touch with them and my cousins." I paused, aware that I was exaggerating. "Well, at least at Christmas. We exchange cards and letters. But I'm not ashamed of that side of the family."

"Your mother's side," Vida murmured as we got into the elevator. "Then who all was at the family picnic on your father's side?"

"There were other cousins," I said. "My father's aunts and uncles and cousins. But we were never close. People died, they married, they moved away. The picnic was the last time I ever saw most of them."

"Sad," Vida intoned. "So sad. No wonder you—" She bit off the words and I eyed her with curiosity.

But Vida shook her head. "Nothing. Here we are," she added, striding out of the elevator.

Somewhat to my surprise, Vida had decided not to see Ronnie. Her mind had been made up by my conversation with Uncle Gary and Aunt Marlene.

"This is strictly family business," she asserted in uncharacteristic fashion. "I can't possibly insert myself into this matter."

As Ronnie entered on his side of the table, I noticed that not only was his bandage smaller, but he also seemed to have shrunk. In fact, the pale blue walls of the visiting area appeared as if they were encroaching on him, destined to squeeze out whatever life was left in Ronnie Mallet.

His first question was about Budweiser. I related my visit with Mrs. Chan and how her husband had found the dog at the door to the apartment the morning after the murder. It was *some* news, if not the bad news that Buddy was still missing.

"Good ol' Buddy," Ronnie said with the hint of a smile. "He never goes far. I wonder how he got loose?"

"I don't know," I said, then stared at my cousin. "You had him tied up?"

Ronnie nodded. "Out back. He never liked that, but I

was kinda bushed that night. I didn't feel like takin' him for his usual run."

According to Maybeth, Buddy had stopped barking after the fight between Ronnie and Carol was over. "Did you let Buddy loose after you left the apartment to go drinking?"

"Naw." Ronnie's expression was rueful. "I was mad, so I just took off. Anyways, I don't like lettin' him run. There's too much traffic on Greenwood. He might get hit. And I sure couldn't let him into the apartment with Carol. She'd have kicked him out, just to get even with me."

"What started the fight, Ronnie?"

"I thought I told you," he said with a frown. "Carol wanted me to pitch in more."

"With money?" I asked, aware of a painful reunion next to us, apparently between mother and son. Both were crying.

"Money 'n' other stuff," Ronnie said, now mumbling. "You know, stuff around the apartment."

"You didn't want to contribute more?"

"I was already payin' most of the rent," Ronnie said, his voice now helpless. "She bought most of the groceries, but I gave her money for them, too. I did lots of stuff around the apartment, like takin' out garbage and doin' dishes. And so what? She always said I did it all wrong."

"You loved her despite all that?" My voice had grown very soft.

Ronnie shut his eyes. "Yeah, I guess. She could be real sweet when she wanted to."

"But she hit you, didn't she, Ronnie?"

He lowered his gaze. "Sometimes."

"Did you hit back?"

"No." He paused, still avoiding my gaze. "I'd push her sometimes. You know, to keep her from whalin' on me."

"Why did you put up with that kind of treatment?"

"Well . . . maybe I deserved it."

"Maybe you didn't," I said.

The pale blue eyes flickered up at me, then turned away. "I'm a screwup."

"Who said so?"

Ronnie raised his eyes again, this time with a befuddled expression. "Everybody. I always screw up."

"Nobody screws up all the time, Ronnie. And everybody screws up some of the time."

"Not like me." Ronnie gave an impotent little shrug.

Sadly, I shook my head. I could sit here arguing for a week with Ronnie and not be able to convince him he wasn't a loser. It hadn't taken a homicide to put Ronnie where he was now. The steel bars and high walls weren't his real prison. For thirty-five years he had let his parents, his sisters, his so-called friends and girlfriends tell him he was worthless.

"God, Ronnie," I said, feeling as powerless as he was, "I wish I could make you believe otherwise. What if I told you I thought you were a good-hearted, decent human being?"

Ronnie chuckled. "I guess I'd wonder why you said that."

I guess I wondered why I'd tried.

The mother and son next to us were still crying.

Chapter Sixteen

"SUCH A CRUEL pattern." Vida sighed after I'd described my visit with Ronnie. "When it comes to grown men and women, I understand—and it's usually the man, of course—that it's a matter of manipulation. The pattern is established from the onset, with the abuser not keeping a date or showing up three hours late, and then apologizing in such a humble, extravagant way that the other person actually feels even luckier in love. It grows from there, like a cancer, with other, more vicious kinds of abuse, but always the penitence and the promises. I know, I've seen it."

"It has something to do with domination when it comes to men," I said as we reached the parking garage to claim the Lexus. "I suspect that Carol—and Maybeth and some of his other girlfriends—had some sort of sexual hold over Ronnie."

Vida eyed me from under the ostrich plumes. "If you're going to start talking about whips and leather, I'm not getting into the car with you. Really, Emma, sometimes you shock me."

I didn't, of course. On the other hand, I had to stifle a sudden image of Vida in long black boots, silver studs, and a corset that—

"I'm talking about psychology," I said, interrupting myself lest I become overwhelmed with mirth. "Anyway, it has more to do with control and self-esteem. Of which my cousin has none. Where do we go from here?" I asked, slipping into the driver's seat.

"I don't know," Vida admitted. "If only there was a way I could meet Darryl."

"I can't think of any," I said, "unless you get Bill Gates's permission to tackle him at work."

"Do you think I might?" Vida asked as we wound our way out of the garage.

I told Vida I knew next to nothing about the work culture at Microsoft, except that it involved long hours and complete dedication. "Not a kind of drop-in environment," I added.

"Drat." Vida was silent until after we'd paid an exorbitant parking fee and were going down Sixth Avenue. As we passed the Sheraton Hotel, she suddenly said, "Roy."

"Roy Sprague?" I said. "He's probably at work, too. And what could he tell us that Maybeth hasn't already?"

"His version may be different from hers," Vida pointed out. "I realize he wasn't at the apartment house— supposedly—when Carol was killed, but that doesn't mean he hasn't got some sort of information we haven't yet heard. Where does he work?"

"I don't know. I don't think we asked." I kept driving north, past the Westin Hotel and the Sixth Avenue Motor Inn.

"Maybeth," Vida said. "We must find out about that letter to the Addisons. Where does she work?"

Once again, I had to confess ignorance. "I think it was a hair salon, but I forget the name."

"Hmm," Vida murmured. "Very well. Let's have one final chat with Henrietta Altdorf before we leave town. She should be able to tell us where these people are employed. I sensed that she was a knowledgeable sort of woman."

In other words, snoopy, like Vida. "We're grasping at straws," I said. "Besides, I'll bet Henrietta's on duty at the hospital by now. She's had several days off."

Undeterred, Vida insisted that I use the cell phone to call Henrietta. I pulled off into a parking space across from the old *Seattle Post-Intelligencer* building, now home to Group Health Cooperative, one of the country's first HMOs. After getting Henrietta's number from Directory Assistance, I was surprised when she answered on the first ring.

"Well, isn't this nice?" Henrietta exclaimed. "I could use some company. I don't have to go back to work until tomorrow. Stop by and I'll make sandwiches for lunch, if you give me half an hour or so to run down to Safeway and back."

I accepted the offer. "By the way, Henrietta, do you know where Maybeth and Roy work?"

"Sure," she replied. "Maybeth works at a beauty salon out by Sears. Shear Beauty, I think it's called. Roy has a job installing appliances." She paused. "Drat, I can't remember which one. It's been around a long time, though."

Vida was pleased with the luncheon invitation. "What did I tell you? Henrietta is a very helpful sort of person."

I smiled at Vida, then decided to check for messages on the cell phone. There was only one, and it was from Ed Bronsky.

"Where are you, Emma?" Ed demanded in a vexed tone. "I've been trying to call you off and on for days. Leo said you'd gone back to Seattle. Are you sure you're still running *The Advocate*? Anyway, I gave Scott my big story yesterday just before deadline. The series is set for summer, two years from now. Oh, I know it seems like a long way off, but I guess it takes a while to draw all those cartoon figures. And guess what? They're going to use my face on Chester White, the hero pig."

"They could have used Ed's entire body," I said,

passing the phone to Vida so that she could listen to my former ad manager's long-winded message.

"Honestly," she said after I'd told her how to switch the phone off, "wouldn't you think Ed would be embarrassed?"

"Nothing embarrasses Ed," I responded as we headed north on Aurora. "As long as he's getting attention, you could tar and feather him and shoot him out of a cannon."

"So true," Vida agreed. "So depressing. Is Shirley going to be Mrs. Chester White?"

"I suppose." I was less concerned with the casting of *Mr. Ed*—or was it now *Mr. White*?—than with how many inches of copy Ed had conned out of poor, unsuspecting Scott. My newest staff member wasn't used to dealing with Ed.

The Shear Beauty Salon was tucked into a strip mall a couple of blocks from the Sears store between Aurora and Greenwood. Vida and I sat out in the parking lot for a few minutes, debating how we should handle Maybeth while she was on the job.

"It's almost eleven-thirty," Vida said, checking her wristwatch. "She may have a break coming up. I don't think we should both go in. Shall I?"

"Only if you bring her out to the car," I admonished. "I don't want to miss anything."

"Of course," Vida said, getting out of the Lexus. "I wouldn't dream of hogging the conversation."

Vida wasn't gone more than three minutes before she stalked back into the parking lot. "Maybeth goes to lunch at one. She didn't act very accommodating."

I frowned at my watch. "We're supposed to be at Henrietta's a little after twelve. This is going to be a tight squeeze. At least it won't take us long to get to the apartment, but we'll be early."

"No harm in that," Vida said. "Perhaps I could meet Mr. Rapp."

That wasn't the worst idea Vida had ever had, so we drove away toward Greenwood. To my surprise, Mr. Rapp was leaning on his walker outside of Henrietta's unit.

"Miss Lord," he said in surprise when Vida and I came around from the parking area out back. "I didn't expect to see you again."

I introduced Vida, then noticed that Mr. Rapp's brown, nutlike face wore a worried expression. "Is something wrong?" I asked.

Mr. Rapp put his full weight on the walker and frowned. "I'm not sure. Henrietta very kindly asked if I'd like to go to the store with her. That was over half an hour ago. I waited and waited, but she never came to fetch me. Did you notice her car out back? It's light blue, one of those Japanese models."

"I saw a blue car," Vida put in. "A smallish sedan. It was the only one in the lot. Would that be it?"

"Probably," Mr. Rapp replied, looking more worried by the second. "No one else in the building has one like it." He held the walker with one hand and reached into his pocket with the other. "I have a key to Henrietta's. She has one to mine, in case I fall . . . or something. Do you think I should . . . ?" He extracted a small silver ring with a horse's head charm.

I winced. The drapes were drawn in Henrietta's apartment, and despite the traffic out on Greenwood, a strange quiet seemed to have settled around the small apartment house. "Maybe you should," I said, trying to hide my sudden alarm. "Henrietta might have had some kind of accident. I take it she doesn't respond to your knock?"

Mr. Rapp shook his head. His hands were shaking, too. He shoved the key ring at me. "You do it, please. I'm afraid I feel a bit queer."

I was feeling queer, too. To make matters worse, I've never had a knack for unlocking doors. After almost ten years I still have trouble getting into my own house, especially when I'm tired or frazzled.

"Oh, here," Vida snapped, seizing the key chain, "let me do it." With a deft motion, she tripped the lock and opened the door.

The sun had come out just a few minutes earlier. It was directly overhead and sent shafts of golden light into the unit's living room. Specks of dust stirred in the air, but Henrietta Altdorf wasn't moving. She was facedown on the floor, with a patch of dark red matting her hair and neck. At her side lay one of the bowling trophies I had seen on my earlier visit.

"Don't come in," I cried as Mr. Rapp began his laborious entrance into the living room.

It was too late. Mr. Rapp had already gained the threshold and could see Henrietta's still form between Vida and me. He shuddered, let out a terrible little cry, and crumpled to the floor. The walker fell to one side.

"Oh, my!" Vida gasped, rushing to Mr. Rapp. "We must call a doctor. And the police."

Stunned and confused, I gazed helplessly around the room in an effort to find Henrietta's telephone. Finally, I spotted it on a side table next to the recliner. With trembling fingers, I dialed 911. In an anguished voice, I relayed the urgent need for both the medics and the police.

Mr. Rapp, however, was coming around. Vida had propped him up against the door frame and was chafing his hands.

"Water," she said. "Get a glass of water. And put the teakettle on. I must have some hot tea. This is terrible, terrible. Henrietta seemed like such a nice woman."

It seemed to take forever to find a glass, but I finally got one out of the last cupboard I searched. The teakettle was on the stove, so I switched on the burner. Then I raced into the living room and handed the glass of water to Vida, who proffered it to Mr. Rapp.

"Is she . . . ?" he whispered.

Despite my revulsion, I was trying to find a pulse. As I'd feared, there was none. "Yes, I'm afraid so," I said in an unnatural voice. I put a hand over my face, but remained down on one knee beside Henrietta's body. The least I could do was say a prayer. It was also the only thing I could do. What was worse, the terrible feeling crept over me that if it hadn't been for my well-intentioned meddling, Henrietta might still be alive.

After determining that Mr. Rapp hadn't broken anything, Vida and I managed to settle him on the sofa. As the distant wail of sirens sounded, I smelled something hot. Rushing into the kitchen, I saw smoke coming out from under the teakettle. Apparently it had been empty when I'd turned it on. Feeling like an idiot, I yanked it off the stove and put it in the sink. The medics arrived just after I made sure the kettle hadn't been ruined.

The male-and-female team checked first to make sure that Henrietta Altdorf was beyond help. Then they examined Mr. Rapp. They were still gently probing when the police and firefighters arrived a couple of minutes later.

The patrol officers were also evidence of equal opportunity employment. A black male named Isaacs and an Asian female named—oddly—O'Brien surveyed the carnage with unfathomable expressions.

"You touch anything?" Isaacs asked after he'd made a call on his cell phone.

I nodded. "The stove. A glass. The teakettle." The apartment still smelled as if an arsonist had been let loose. "Oh—and the phone. But not the body or the alleged weapon."

The hint of a smile touched Isaacs's broad face. "You found the deceased?"

"We all did," Vida put in. I noticed that her eyes were moist, and realized that Vida had never come upon a corpse before. "Mr. Rapp had a key. We thought Henrietta had had an accident. She was supposed to take him to the grocery store and then meet us for lunch."

"Let's sit at the kitchen table," O'Brien suggested in a brisk voice. She was younger than her partner, and might have been pretty if she'd worn makeup. "Mr. Rapp—is that his name?" She saw us nod. "He can stay where he is for now."

Officer O'Brien was thorough. After checking IDs, taking down our addresses and occupations, she sought out the most recent details first—our time of arrival, our reason for being at the murder scene, if we'd seen or heard anything, and finally, how we knew the victim.

Vida started to answer, but for once, I interrupted, and with a question of my own. "Are you aware that another murder took place next door about three weeks ago?"

O'Brien nodded slowly. "It wasn't on our shift, but we know about it."

"My cousin Ronnie Mallett was accused of the crime," I said, going on to describe how I'd gotten involved. "My colleague"—I gestured at Vida—"and I have been doing some investigating of our own because we don't believe Ronnie's guilty. I think Ms. Altdorf's murder proves our point."

O'Brien made no comment. Isaacs had now joined us, but didn't sit down. "You say you only met the victim a few days ago?" he asked.

"Yes," Vida replied, jumping in before I could say anything. "This past weekend. I might point out—since Carol Stokes's murder wasn't on your shift—that Henrietta wasn't home at the time of the slaying. She told us she'd been working that night at the hospital."

Both Isaacs and O'Brien remained impassive. I assumed they understood her point, which was that if there was a connection between the two killings, it wasn't because Henrietta had been an eyewitness. At least not as far as we knew.

"Are you planning to leave town soon?" O'Brien asked.

"Yes," Vida answered. "We're returning to Alpine later this afternoon. I must say, the city is a very violent place. I can't imagine living here. I'd never feel safe."

The remark didn't go down well. Isaacs scowled and O'Brien's eyes hardened. At least they owned a couple of expressions besides those of department-store dummies.

"You'll have to make a statement at the station," Isaacs said. "Do you know where the north precinct is?"

I did. It wasn't far from the Greenwood district, and just west of the Northgate shopping center.

"Can we do that now?" I asked.

"We'll go with you," O'Brien said. I thought she seemed pleased by the idea. Maybe she was fantasizing about shackling Vida to a tree while we waited. "The detectives are on their way, along with the ME and the photographer. Do you know if the victim had any family?"

"A son, in Puyallup," Vida replied. "His name might not be Altdorf. I believe Henrietta had been married more than once. You might try her address book. There's also a wife and grandchildren."

Isaacs gave an abrupt nod just as the teakettle finally sang. It struck an odd note, a painfully happy death knell burbling Henrietta's demise.

"What about Mr. Rapp?" I asked. "Does he have to come, too?"

O'Brien glanced out into the living room, where Mr. Rapp was still talking to the medics. "Yes. He reached the scene first, didn't he?"

"We all discovered the body at the same time," Vida said. "Surely he can be left at home. He's quite old and frail."

"We won't use a rubber hose on him," O'Brien said,

though there was no humor in her tone. "Hey, Dave,"
she said to her partner, "here come the 'tecs."

Tony Rojas and a burly fair-haired man in his late forties lumbered into the apartment. They were trailed by a
young woman with photographic equipment and a much
older man who carried a black satchel.

"Your turn," Rojas called to the officers. "You missed
the first one." He seemed inappropriately cheerful.

"Just when we were going to lunch, too," Isaacs shot
back. "You owe us, Tony. Why not send for a pizza?"

"Oh!" Vida looked furious. "Can you imagine?" she
said to me in her usual stage whisper. "Would Milo act
like this? He has more sense."

The police contingent ignored us and went about their
business. I made tea, but wasn't allowed to enter the
living room to offer Mr. Rapp a cup. Since the apartment
was getting crowded, the firefighters stepped outside.
Maybe, I thought as my nerves steadied and my temper
frayed, they were going for a smoke.

Tony Rojas frowned when he finally saw me. "I know
you. What's your name?" he demanded. "You some sort
of ambulance chaser?"

"Emma Lord," I replied. "We met at your office. Are
you going to arrest Ronnie Mallet for this murder, too?"

Rojas turned his back on me and went into the living
room. O'Brien and Issacs joined the rest of the police
contingent. There were more ribbings and chuckles. Vida
looked fit to spit.

"This is dreadful," she said. "How can they make
jokes when poor Henrietta is lying there dead?"

"It's how they survive," I said. "Would you want their
job? They have to put distance between themselves and
the cruelty they encounter every day." It was true of jour-
nalists, too, which is why many reporters are considered
hard-bitten and cynical.

Given Vida's career as House and Home editor, she

couldn't quite empathize. "Callous, that's what I call it," she declared.

The kitchen was growing warm, oppressive. At last the detectives, the ME, and the photographer finished their tasks. Rojas returned to the kitchen.

"Okay, Emma Lord, how come you happened to show up just as another body hit the deck?"

Since Rojas was looming over me, I stood up. I'm a boss, I know how to use intimidating body language. I rarely do it, of course, because it wouldn't work with my small staff. Especially with Vida. She looms when she's sitting down.

"You may have given up trying to find Carol Stokes's real killer," I said, "but I haven't. If you ask me, whoever it was has struck again." I jerked one hand in the direction of the living room, where ambulance attendants were removing the body even as we spoke.

"You didn't answer my question," Rojas said, unfazed. He still loomed, being a good eight inches taller. "How did you end up with another corpse?"

"I was trying to explain that," I said, keeping my voice even. "I've been conducting my own investigation. Henrietta Altdorf had been very helpful, and we were meeting her here for lunch. I talked to her on the phone about eleven o'clock. She was fine, and heading for the grocery store with her neighbor, Aldo Rapp." I nodded in the direction of the living room, where Mr. Rapp was now talking to Isaacs and O'Brien. "We got here early and found Mr. Rapp at the door. Ms. Altdorf hadn't come to get him yet and he was worried."

"How'd you get in?" Rojas asked.

"Mr. Rapp has a key. He and Ms. Altdorf each had a key to the other's apartment. I gather they sort of looked out for each other."

Rojas glanced into the living room. Maybe he was assessing Mr. Rapp in terms of his fitness as a murderer.

The poor old guy didn't look like he could pick up a golf ball, let alone a bowling trophy.

"Did Mr. Rapp hear anything, see anything?" Rojas asked.

"Not that he mentioned," I replied. "Anyway, he's quite deaf."

Vida had also risen. "Could we move along now? It's almost two."

"I can tell time," Rojas retorted.

In her big plumed hat, Vida actually stood taller than Tony Rojas. "Need I point out," she said at her most caustic, "that you might consider how these two murders in adjoining apartments could be linked."

Rojas shot Vida a baleful look, turned on his heel, and stalked out of the kitchen.

"Really!" she exclaimed. "The man has no manners. Why, if I thought my nephew Billy ever treated a witness so disrespectfully, I'd—"

"Vida," I interrupted, "don't make things worse. Do you want to get locked up for impeding an investigation?"

"*Impeding?*" Vida cried, her voice carrying not only into the living room, but possibly all the way to the Satellite Room down the street. "We're solving it for them." She yanked off her hat, sat back down, removed her glasses, and began punishing her eyes. "Oooh! I hate the city! It makes me cross!"

Fifteen minutes later Mr. Rapp was able to return to his apartment, where Vida insisted he call his daughter to let her know what was going on. We were then directed to head for the north precinct to write up our statements. Apparently Mr. Rapp had been allowed to give his verbally.

Vida and I saw him to the door of his unit. "Promise you'll phone your daughter right away?" she said to Mr. Rapp. "And you might consider checking in with your doctor. You've had a very nasty fright."

"I'm feeling better," Mr. Rapp said, though I noticed that his hands still trembled slightly on the walker. "I hate to bother people. Dr. Fitzgerald still makes house calls, but I wouldn't want him to come until he's seen his patients at the clinic."

Vida's eyes grew wide. "A doctor who makes house calls? In the city? He must be very old-fashioned."

Mr. Rapp smiled feebly. "He is. Dr. Fitzgerald should have retired years ago, but he still sees his longtime patients. Such a wonderful man. Henrietta recommended him when my doctor died. She worked for an obstetrician at the same clinic before she took the job at the hospital."

"Remarkable," Vida murmured as we walked to the car. "Even young Doc Dewey has had to give up making house calls. My, my."

The statements turned out to be a cut-and-dried affair. Rojas and his partner didn't accompany us, and Isaacs and O'Brien apparently returned to their regular patrol duties. We were out of the precinct station by two-thirty, heading back to the Shear Beauty Salon.

This time, we both went inside to see Maybeth Swafford. She was cutting an elderly Vietnamese woman's hair and refused even to look at us until she'd finished.

"I don't like being stood up," she declared in a low, angry voice after her client had headed up front to pay the bill. "Especially when I'm doing you a favor. What do you want? Make it quick."

"I think we'd better speak privately," Vida said, looking solemn.

"Why? I don't have any secrets around here." Maybeth swung a hand in the direction of the three other hairdressers who were plying their trade along the mirrored wall.

"Trust me," Vida urged. "We have shocking news."

Maybeth looked taken aback. "About what?" Her belligerence faded.

Vida gestured toward the rear of the salon. "Is there a room back here where we could speak? It won't take long."

Maybeth sighed. "Yeah, the coffee room. Come on."

The coffee room was small, windowless, and dirty. Maybeth sat down at the Formica-covered table. We sat opposite her, where used paper cups, empty snack-food bags, and soda-pop cans cluttered the scarred surface.

"What's shocking?" Maybeth asked.

Vida cleared her throat. "Henrietta Altdorf has been murdered."

Maybeth's stare was incredulous. "No shit!" she exclaimed.

Before Vida could reprimand her for her language, before I could explain, Maybeth slid off the chair and collapsed in a dead faint.

Chapter Seventeen

A WATERCOOLER STOOD at the far end of the room under a calendar with the theme of World Wrestling Federation Hunks. I filled a paper cup from the cooler and dumped it over Maybeth's head. It probably wasn't Red Cross–approved first aid, but Maybeth twitched, sputtered, and flailed her arms.

"Jesus!" she gasped. It had taken her at least a couple of minutes to become oriented and coherent. "What *is* this? A serial killer?"

"Probably not," I said. "Here, let me help you back into the chair." Putting one arm around her waist and the other under her armpits, I managed to hoist her into a sitting position. "Do you have any idea who might be killing your fellow tenants?"

Maybeth, who had started to tremble, shook her head. "No. God. No."

Vida, who had remained seated, shoved some of the debris out of the way and leaned across the table. "Come, come, Maybeth," she said, not unkindly, "you must have some idea why Carol *and* Henrietta were murdered. It can't possibly be a coincidence or the work of a madman."

Maybeth didn't reply. She sat there staring at the battered Formica, looking as if she might cry. We waited at least a full minute, but Maybeth remained silent.

"How about this?" I finally said. "Has anybody moved

out of the building in the last few months? A disgruntled tenant, let's say?"

Slowly, Maybeth shook her head. "No," she said at last. "Everybody there, even the college kids, have been renting for at least a year."

"A stalker?" Vida suggested.

Again, Maybeth shook her head. "Not that I ever heard of. We found a homeless guy passed out by the Dumpster, but that was months ago."

"Were Carol and Henrietta close?" I asked. "I mean, closer than just neighbors?"

Maybeth frowned at me. "What do you mean by that? Something kinky?"

"No," I replied. "I mean, did they share confidences?"

"Not that I ever knew," Maybeth said, drawing herself up in the chair. "Jeez, I could use a drink. I wonder if Annabelle would let me go home? I only got two more clients today."

"But there must be a connection," I insisted.

Maybeth, however, didn't answer. Instead, she got up on wobbly legs and left the coffee room.

"The police will question her," Vida murmured. "No doubt they'll interview everyone in the building."

"I don't think anybody was around, except Mr. Rapp," I noted. "Wasn't Henrietta's the only car in the parking lot?"

"You're right," Vida agreed, getting up from the table. "I certainly hope those detectives do a more thorough job this time. They ought to be ashamed of themselves."

We went out into the salon, where Maybeth was talking to a hawk-faced woman at the front desk. Presumably it was Annabelle, and she was the boss or the owner or maybe both. Annabelle, however, didn't seem very sympathetic.

Maybeth saw us and made a face. "I have to stay until four," she said. "You'd better go."

We didn't have much choice. Annabelle was glaring at us with beady black eyes. I apologized to Maybeth for bearing bad news, then we exited the Shear Beauty Salon.

"We should head home," Vida said, but the words weren't convincing.

"What can we do if we stay in Seattle?" I asked, and then suddenly remembered what I *could* do. "Alvin," I said, getting behind the wheel. "He should know about this. Maybe he can get Ronnie out of jail."

I dialed the young attorney's number. He answered on the third ring, sounding frazzled. The news of a second murder didn't seem to cheer him.

"Gosh, I don't know . . . I mean, like I'd have to file a motion and . . . maybe I can get around to it tomorrow. What's tomorrow, anyway? I can't find my calendar."

"It's Thursday," I said, never knowing whether to feel sorry for Alvin or charge into his office and give him a swift kick. "Come on, Alvin, do you still believe your client is guilty?"

"Well . . . no, I don't know if I was ever . . . I mean, it's my first criminal case and . . . Tell you what, I'll go see Ronnie tomorrow morning. No, it'll have to be tomorrow afternoon. I've got . . . hey, who was this other woman anyway?"

I explained. Alvin left me with a vague promise that he'd do what he could. When he could. If he could.

"I have to let Ronnie know," I said. It was an afterthought, and I felt guilty. Ronnie always seemed to be an afterthought. "I hate to say it, but I think we should go back to the jail."

Vida nodded. "That's fine. Perhaps Ronnie knows something about Henrietta that we don't. Did you ever inquire?"

"No. I never thought of Henrietta as playing any part in this," I said, steering the Lexus back onto Greenwood.

"Obviously, I was wrong. There's some connection. But what could it be?"

Vida didn't answer right away. When she did, I noted an odd expression on her face. "Someone said something this afternoon—but for the life of me, I can't recall exactly what it was. Still, I know that it gave me an idea at the time."

There was no point in prodding Vida; eventually, she'd retrieve the thought without prompting. Meanwhile she berated both of us for not using the opportunity to search Henrietta's personal possessions.

"We had plenty of time," she asserted, "waiting for those detective fools to finish making jokes and get down to business."

"You know better, Vida," I said. "They would have yanked our chain if we'd started shaking down the place."

"We'd have been more subtle. A trip to the bathroom. A side trip to the bedroom. Really," she went on, her annoyance building, "what were we thinking of? There were probably things right there in the kitchen that might have proved helpful."

"Like a slip of paper stuck to the refrigerator with a Mickey Mouse magnet that said, 'The killer is . . .'?" I made a face. "I agree, Henrietta knew something dangerous, but I'm not sure it was the killer's identity."

"Why do you say that?" Vida asked, suddenly tense. "Do you know what you mean?"

To be honest, I didn't. It was one of those utterances that slips out, with no rationale behind it. "Hunh. I guess I meant that Henrietta knew something that was dangerous to the murderer. Maybe something she didn't even realize she knew."

"Exactly," Vida said. "Now what on earth could it be?"

"Something she'd overheard earlier, before Carol was killed?" I speculated, negotiating my way through the steady build of the city's early commute. "A quarrel, a visitor, a misdirected piece of mail." I slapped my hand on the steering wheel. "Damn! We never had a chance to ask Maybeth about that envelope addressed to the Addisons."

"Please don't swear," Vida said primly. "Maybeth should be home from work by the time we've seen Ronnie."

Our departure from Seattle was creeping ever later. Maybe that was just as well. If we left earlier, we'd hit the full commute, no matter which route we took. The two-hour drive wasn't that difficult in good weather. I was, however, uneasy about leaving Amber and Danny alone for too long. One of these days I feared that I'd come home and find my little log house burned to the ground.

Then a brilliant idea struck me. "When Ronnie gets out of jail," I said excitedly, "*if* he does, of course, I'm going to introduce him to Amber. They're a perfect match. What do you think?"

Vida looked skeptical. "Isn't he a bit old for her?"

"Ten years, more or less," I replied. "Anyway, do you really consider Ronnie that much older emotionally?"

"No," Vida said, not yet getting caught up in my enthusiasm. "Really, Emma, I never knew you to be a matchmaker."

"It's not matchmaking; it's self-defense," I countered. "They might do each other some good. Ronnie would have to grow up and act responsibly. Amber would move out of my house. I think it's brilliant."

"You're dreaming," Vida said.

Maybe I was. But at the moment it sounded good.

As I sat across from Ronnie for the second time that day, he listened to the news of Henrietta's murder with confusion rather than shock.

"That nurse next door?" he said, wrinkling his nose. "I don't get it."

"Henrietta must have known Carol better than I realized," I said. "Can you think of anything Carol might have confided in Henrietta that would have put her life in danger?"

Ronnie didn't bother to reflect. "Nope."

"Come on, Ronnie," I urged. "This is important. Did they talk to each other sometimes?"

"Nope." He reached up to adjust his bandage. "My ear still hurts. I need some painkillers."

An idea occurred to me. "Did Henrietta ever give you or Carol painkillers?"

"Huh?" Ronnie rubbed at his upper lip. "Yeah, maybe a coupla times. I hit my head on a ladder on the truck once. That nurse said she had something to help. I forget what she gave me, but it worked. Then another time Carol dropped a case of smoked tuna on her foot at the seafood place where she worked. Carol got some of those pills, too."

"Is that all?" I asked.

"Far as I remember," Ronnie replied. "How's Buddy?"

"Fine." I'd forgotten about Buddy. For all I knew, he was decorating the grillwork on somebody's car. "You're sure? Henrietta didn't drop in often?"

Ronnie shook his head. "Nope. Never, far as I remember. I went to her place to get them pills."

Apparently, Ronnie hadn't yet drawn any conclusions about Henrietta's murder. "Do you realize that there's a good chance you may be able to get out of here soon?" I asked.

"Huh?" Ronnie looked blank. "How come?"

"Because," I said patiently, "the police will figure out that there must be a connection between two murders that occurred next door to each other. Since you were in jail when the last one happened, you couldn't have done it. Thus they'll realize you probably didn't kill Carol, either."

"I didn't," Ronnie said simply.

"I know that," I said, still patient. "But it would help a

lot if you could remember more about Henrietta and Carol."

"Carol didn't like Henrietta," Ronnie said after a long pause. "She said she was a busybody. One time—I forgot till now—Carol went over there to borrow a lightbulb. It was a month or so ago. She was gone for quite a while, and I thought maybe she'd run to the store instead. Anyways, when Carol came back, she was all wrought up. I asked her how come, but she wouldn't say. She just got mad at me and . . ." He ducked his head.

I could guess the rest. Carol had taken her anger and distress out on poor Ronnie. It's a wonder he hadn't asked Henrietta for more painkillers.

"Did Carol say what got her so upset?" I inquired.

Ronnie shook his head again. "Not really. But I think she got riled up over something Henrietta said about Kendra."

"Kendra?"

"Yeah. I never seen Carol so pissed off. She was almost cryin'. She called Henrietta a big fat old liar."

I was surprised by the incident, amazed that Ronnie could have forgotten about it until I prodded him. But Carol must have thrown many a temper tantrum. Maybe Ronnie only recalled them in relationship to his own wounds.

"Do you," I asked slowly, "remember anything at all that Henrietta said to Carol about Kendra? Any phrase, any words?"

This time Ronnie put some effort into his response. "It was hard to catch, what with Carol carryin' on so. But maybe it was something like . . . I don't recall exactly . . . but like 'There's no way Kendra could be your daughter.' "

I frowned at Ronnie. "Do you know why Henrietta said that?"

"Nope." Ronnie fished out a cigarette from behind his undamaged ear. "Can I go back now?"

"Sure," I said, and tried to smile.

He seemed relieved as he stood up and signaled to the guard. Maybe he felt safer in prison. At least nobody there pretended to love him.

Chapter Eighteen

"WHAT ON EARTH could Henrietta have meant?" Vida demanded as we once again headed north. I'd driven up and down Aurora so often lately that I swore I recognized some of the hookers. Vida had already been scanning the cars behind us to see if she could spot the Taurus. She'd seen two of them since we'd left downtown, but both had disappeared along the way.

"It could mean a couple of things," I said. "That Carol wasn't fit to be anybody's mother. Or that Henrietta didn't believe Kendra was Carol's daughter."

"Now, why would she think that?" Vida remarked. "This is very puzzling."

"That's so," I agreed as we found ourselves in stop-and-go traffic, "but I felt I was lucky to get anything at all out of Ronnie. It took some doing, believe me. At first, all he could talk about was painkillers that Henrietta had given them. I suppose she got the pills through the hospital."

"Oh!" Vida snapped her fingers. "That's it! I remember now what was said earlier. It was Mr. Rapp, talking about his doctor. He told us that Henrietta had recommended him because she'd worked with him—a Dr. Fitzgerald, wasn't it?—at the same clinic where she'd worked for the OB-GYN."

"That's right," I said, not sure of Vida's point. "So what?"

"Really," Vida huffed, "you're being rather dim. OB-GYNs handle adoptions. What if this doctor Henrietta worked for was the one who found a baby for the Addisons?"

I considered the idea. "It's possible. Olive Nerstad might know. He was her doctor, right?"

"Kathy Addison said his name was McFarland," Vida said. "I believe he died not long ago. But it would be easy to check to see if a Henrietta Altdorf had worked for him at the clinic around the time of the adoption."

"It would," I said dryly, "if it weren't after five. I'll bet the clinic staff has gone home for the day."

"Tell me again how to use your cell phone," Vida commanded, reaching into my handbag. "I'm going to call right now."

I gave her the simple directions. Then, while waiting for yet another interminable stoplight, I watched her face fall.

"The answering service," she said, switching the phone off without bothering to speak to whoever was taking the clinic's calls. "Drat."

An idea occurred to me. Years ago in Portland, I'd had a friend who worked as a nurse for a dermatologist. The office staff automatically switched incoming calls over at five, whether they were still there or not.

"Try the backline," I said. "Dial the same number, but go up one digit on the last one. You might be able to get through."

Vida looked at me as if I'd just turned water into wine. "Very clever," she said, clicking away on the phone. "Ah!" She rocked back and forth in the passenger seat. "Yes, I'm calling for Dr. Fitzgerald. Is he in?"

Vida stopped rocking. "Oh." Her face fell again. "I see. Tell me, is there anyone in the clinic who worked there twenty years ago?" Pause. "Really. Yes, people do tend to come and go these days. Thank you."

"Well?" I asked, feeling as if Vida's disappointment was contagious.

"Only Dr. Fitzgerald has been there that long," she said, "and he's left for the day. I suppose we could call him at home. He makes house calls, after all."

"Maybe he's seeing Mr. Rapp," I suggested. "We might kill two birds with one stone at the apartment house."

"An excellent idea," Vida responded, brightening. "Goodness, all these cars! However do people put up with this traffic? I'd go quite mad."

"So would I. It's been a long time since I've had to fight freeways and bridges," I said. "That's one thing I don't miss about the city."

"I wouldn't miss any of it," Vida declared as we finally reached the left-hand turn for Greenwood Avenue. "It's a dismal place. Most depressing, not to mention dangerous."

Arguing was pointless. Alpine was bedeviled by family feuds, gossip, backbiting, an economy that still hadn't been completely resuscitated by the advent of Skykomish Community College, and intermittent violence, which seemed all the more painful because it involved people you knew. But Vida would never admit that small towns, particularly hers, could be anything but utopia.

So instead of contradicting her, I merely mentioned my exclusion from the local bridge club. "You'd think they would have gotten over it by now," I said. "It's been five months. They certainly found out that I didn't kill Crystal Bird."

The allusion was to the homicide of Amber Ramsey's mother, who had attacked me in her scurrilous self-published newsletter. Briefly, everyone in town—except maybe Vida herself—considered me the prime suspect.

"But they thought you *might* have killed her," Vida said. "Now they're embarrassed."

"That's supposed to make me feel better?" I shot back.

My former bridge partners weren't, for the most part, stupid women. To be fair, I understood that only a minority of them had insisted on my expulsion. The point was that these few, these callow, these easily prejudiced members of a narrow-minded clique had prevailed. I liked to think it wouldn't have been that way in the city.

"They'll come 'round," Vida said easily. "You'll see."

I uttered nothing more than a snort. We were back at the apartment house, where two unmarked city cars were pulled up out front, blocking the driveway.

"Forensics people," I said, forgetting about the bridge club. "We'll have to find a place on the street."

We finally did, but had to leave the Lexus a block and a half away. There was no crime-scene tape posted yet on Henrietta's unit and the door was closed. Vida buzzed the button at 1-C. We waited for Maybeth to answer.

Roy Sprague, looking disconcerted, opened the door. "It's you," he said with all the enthusiasm of a person welcoming the Grim Reaper. On second thought, maybe that's who he expected.

"Is Maybeth home?" Vida asked in her most chipper voice.

"She's lying down," Roy replied, nodding in the direction of the bedroom. "She's whipped. What's going on around here? We're moving out. This place has one of them curses on it."

"Do you suppose," Vida wheedled, tipping her head to one side and trying to look coy, "we might come in for just a minute? We found Henrietta's body, you know."

"Oh." If Roy had known, he'd either forgotten or not made the connection. The offhand remark served as our password, however. "Well . . . yeah, sure, come on. Want a beer?"

"No, thank you," Vida responded just as I said that it sounded like a great idea.

Vida glared at me while Roy went to the fridge. "You're driving," she murmured. "Is this wise?"

"One beer a drunkard does not make," I said. "What's more, I'd like a beer right now."

"You don't drink beer," Vida countered.

"I don't, at least not very often. Should I have asked for a Singapore Sling?"

"A what?" Vida said, puzzled.

Roy came back into the living room and handed me a bottle of Henry Weinhard's pale ale, which was a bit tonier than I'd expected. "Maybeth called me at work, so I took off early," he said. "She got home before I did, but wouldn't come in by herself. Hell, I never seen her so scared. This whole thing's really got her down."

"She took it hard," I said. "She passed out when we told her about Henrietta."

Pulling on his beer, Roy nodded. "That's why we're leaving. Tomorrow. I don't care what that Mr. Chan says. This place ain't safe."

I offered Roy my most pleading expression. "Do you think we could ask her one quick question?"

Roy looked skeptical. "About what?"

"About a letter she wrote a while back, to Kendra Addison's parents."

Roy tipped his head back and scratched under his chin. "You mean the blonde babe who hung out with Carol? Jeez, I don't know why she'd write a letter to them. Maybeth's no letter writer. You sure?"

I produced the dirty envelope from my handbag and pointed to the return address. "Are you sure you don't know anything about this?"

"Hell, no," Roy said emphatically. "Weird." He stood up, clutching his beer bottle by the neck. "Let me see if Maybeth's awake."

She was. Much to Vida's displeasure, only I was

allowed to go into the bedroom. I figured that was because I drank beer and Vida didn't. It made me one of the gang.

Maybeth was cowering under a quilt, looking terrified. "What is it?" she asked hoarsely.

The only place to sit was on the double bed. I still had the envelope in my hand. "What was in this?" I inquired calmly.

Maybeth, who had started to sit up, fell back against the pillow. "Jesus! Where'd you get that?"

"At the Addison house," I replied, still calm. "Why did you write to them? Was it about Carol? Or Kendra?"

Maybeth rolled over, buried her face in the pillow, and began shrieking. Roy came charging into the room.

"What's going on?" He grabbed me by the shoulder. "What did you do to her? Get the hell out!"

I was yanked off the bed and shoved in the direction of the door. Tripping over my own feet, I fell flat on my face. Vida jumped up from her chair and rushed to my side. Roy was somewhere behind me, fussing over Maybeth.

"Emma!" Vida cried. "What's this? Are you all right?"

Both knees hurt, as did one of my elbows. "I'm okay," I gasped, struggling to get up.

Carefully, Vida pulled me to my feet. Maybeth was still shrieking and Roy was trying to calm her.

"Get the hell out!" Roy shouted at us as he gave Maybeth a little shake. "Get out before I throw you out!"

Vida had turned mulish, but I steered her toward the front door. "Come on," I said, limping a bit. "Give it up. We lost that round."

"Oooh . . ." Vida swiveled this way and that, heard Roy yell at us again, and finally followed me outside. "I hate to let a bully tell me what to do," she said angrily.

"I've been thrown out of better places lately," I muttered. "Like Darryl's condo in Magnolia."

"Yes," Vida began, then stopped as Tony Rojas came out from 1-A, Henrietta's unit.

"You again?" he said, obviously not pleased.

Vida's arm shot out in the direction of 1-C. "Have you interrogated the occupants in this apartment?"

"Why do you ask?" There was a weary note in Rojas's voice.

"Ms. Swafford knows more than she's letting on," Vida retorted, jerking away the envelope I'd managed to hold on to despite my tumble. "Here, ask her about this. It was sent to the adoptive parents of Carol Stokes's daughter."

Rojas eyed the envelope dubiously. "So? Maybe the Swafford woman knows the Addisons."

"She doesn't." Vida actually stamped her foot. "That is, not in a social context. I'm quite certain this has something to do with Carol's murder. Maybeth Swafford is absolutely terrified. I'm sure she believes she'll be the next victim."

"Really." Rojas put the envelope in his inside pocket. Apparently, he didn't think it was serious evidence or he would have been more careful. "Where'd you get this anyway?"

I explained.

Rojas slapped his hand against his forehead. "Christ! Who *are* you? Hanging out in alleys and going through the garbage—aren't you two a little old for Nancy Drew?"

"I told you," I said between clenched teeth, "I'm trying to help clear my cousin of a murder charge. What's so weird about that?"

Rojas sighed. "Ever hear of private detectives? That's what most people do when they want a secondary investigation. All this amateur sleuthing crap can get you into big trouble."

I feigned contrition, which wasn't too difficult since

my knees hurt like hell and I felt sorry for myself. "You're right, but somebody had to help Ronnie. He's pretty much alone in the world. Are you going to talk to Maybeth and her boyfriend?"

Rojas glanced at the door to 1-C. "I stopped by there about an hour ago, but nobody answered." He paused, perhaps trying to figure out if I was a serious menace or just a bumbling idiot. "Yeah, I'll talk to them."

"You better hurry," Vida put in. "They're moving out. That's how frightened Maybeth is."

"Hunh." Rojas glanced at 1-C again. "Okay, if it makes you feel any better, I'll go talk to them now."

We stood on the walkway while the detective buzzed Maybeth and Roy. Nothing happened. Rojas buzzed again. Still nothing. Then he hammered on the door and shouted, "Police!"

From where we were standing, I couldn't hear what was being said from inside the apartment. Rojas could, though, because he was leaning down, listening through the door.

"If that's the way you want it," he said at last, "that's the way we'll do it." Rojas started back down the walk. "The guy in there says no dice unless we come back with a warrant."

"Why," Vida demanded, "don't you arrest him for withholding evidence?"

Rojas laughed and tapped his suit jacket where the envelope reposed. "On this? Not a prayer. Still, I want to ask them some questions, even though I don't think they were around today when the murder occurred."

"They weren't," I said, then added, "that I know of."

Rojas gave single nod. "Okay. Now run along. And stay out of trouble. We're handling this just fine."

I didn't ask him why Ronnie was still in jail.

*   *   *

I'd turned to leave when Vida let out a sudden yelp. "Oh! I forgot my asthma medicine!" She caught Rojas by the sleeve. "Do you mind? I believe I left it in Henrietta's bathroom."

Rojas grimaced. "What does it look like?"

"It's blue," she said. "No, it's green. Or did the doctor give me the maroon one this time? My, my—I'm not sure."

"*What* is it?" Rojas asked, impatience showing on his face. "Pills? A bottle?"

"No," Vida responded vaguely. "It's one of those . . . oh, you must know what I mean." She made some indecipherable gestures with her hands. "It's a whatchamacallit."

I watched the little scene with amusement, knowing that Vida didn't have asthma and therefore didn't have any asthma medicine. Finally, Rojas relented.

"I'll have to go in with you," he said, then held up a hand to me. "Stay put. This can't take long. I've got personnel working inside."

I nodded assent, then heard a diffident Vida ask if she might use the bathroom while she was there. "So awkward," she remarked. "So embarrassing to have to ask."

Less than five minutes later Vida emerged, looking a trifle smug.

"Well?" I said. "Are you still wheezing?"

"I'd be chortling if I thought I'd found anything worthwhile," she said, the smugness gone. "All I could manage was to slip from the bathroom to the bedroom and snatch an address book and a photo album."

"You couldn't fit a metal box or a file folder into your purse," I said with a smile. "You were lucky to have gotten what you did. I'd have thought the police would have confiscated the address book."

"Not yet," Vida said as we reached the Lexus.

Just in case Rojas might have discovered the missing

items, I moved the car around the corner. Vida was flipping through the address book first.

"Drat," she said. "This is an old book. These phone numbers still have prefixes with letters, like *LA* and *SU*. The police must have taken Henrietta's more recent one."

"What about the album?" I asked.

"It's fairly full, unlike Carol's," she said, "though of course there may have been others we never got to see at her apartment. Henrietta was more organized. These first pictures seem to go way back. Many of them are tourist sites, just like the ones on her walls. Victoria, Mount Rainier, the Olympics, the ocean. Here's a nice-looking young man on a horse. Perhaps that's one of her husbands. Henrietta must have taken most of these, since she's not in them. Ah! Here's a group shot of nurses, no doubt a graduating class. They wore uniforms then. How nice."

"Doc Dewey still has his nurses wear uniforms," I pointed out.

"No caps, though," Vida said. "No smart navy-blue capes with red lining. Such a shame, all this casual . . . What's this?"

"Where?" I leaned over to look. In between photos of Grouse Mountain and Grand Coulee Dam was a picture of Kendra Addison. "I'll be darned," I said. "How did that get in here?"

Vida didn't answer right away. "It's not Kendra," she finally said through stiff lips. "See here, she's wearing what we used to call Capri pants and her hair is much more stylized. Bouffant, really."

Jarred, I sat up straight. "Then who is it?" I wasn't sure I wanted to know the answer.

Vida, however, didn't say anything. She continued to page through the album. "Here," she said, still sounding tense, "could this be Henrietta?"

It was a picture of a young woman with a baby. She was pretty, with short red-gold hair and a plumpish figure. "It might be," I said. "Take another look at that nurses' graduation picture."

We spotted Henrietta Altdorf in the second row. She was thinner and younger than in the picture with the baby. But she definitely looked like the girl in the Capri pants—which meant that she bore a startling resemblance to Kendra Addison.

Vida announced that we had to track down Dr. Fitzgerald. We drove up Greenwood to Holman Road and found a service station with a telephone directory that hadn't been stolen or torn to shreds. Dr. Philip Fitzgerald's clinic was just off Market Street in Ballard; his residence was out in North Beach, about a ten-minute drive from where we were now parked.

"I'll call first," I said.

"Let me," Vida urged. "I'm more in his age group."

I wasn't sure what that had to do with interviewing Dr. Fitzgerald, but it seemed to work. Vida returned from the pay phone looking pleased with herself.

"He remembered Olive Nerstad." She beamed. "Such a kindly sounding man. He'd love to see us."

That was probably an overstatement, but we drove off under a spring sky that was beginning to cloud over. The Fitzgerald house, a well-kept Colonial with twin sets of pillars along the full front porch, was at the bottom of a hill, with a view of Puget Sound.

The doctor met us at the door. He looked about seventy and was wearing a black cardigan over a pale blue shirt and gray flannel slacks.

"Come in, ladies," he said, almost sounding as if he were indeed glad to see us. "We were very sorry to hear about poor Henrietta. I saw her not long ago, when Mr. Rapp had a fall in his kitchen."

"It's a terrible thing," Vida murmured. "She seemed like a very fine woman."

"She was, as I recall," Dr. Fitzgerald said, leading us down a hallway carpeted with an Oriental runner. "A good nurse. Of course it's been twenty years since we worked together." He paused at an open door. "My wife put the teakettle on. I hope you approve."

"Certainly," Vida said with her toothy smile. "Hot tea is always an excellent idea."

The doctor shoved his wire-rimmed spectacles up on his nose and led us into his comfortable study. The shelves were lined with medical tomes on one side, fiction and mostly travel books on the other.

"We live in violent times," Dr. Fitzgerald said in a heavy voice. "Do sit. Myra will be along shortly with the tea."

"As I explained on the phone," Vida began, "Emma and I met Henrietta while researching the earlier murder of Carol Nerstad Stokes. Our newspaper, *The Alpine Advocate*, is planning a special section on what happens when young people move to the city. Rarely is it anything good, and Carol is a case in point."

I tried not to roll my eyes. *Our* newspaper? The worst part was that Vida might not be lying. Maybe she really did plan to do such a piece. I foresaw trouble brewing back at *The Advocate*.

"I didn't know this Carol person," Dr. Fitzgerald put in, "though I was aware of her death. Mr. Rapp told me about it."

Vida nodded. "Such a sweet little man."

We were interrupted by the arrival of Myra Fitzgerald, bearing a very large silver tray. Fortunately, she was a stalwart-looking woman with iron-gray hair and a jutting jaw. The doctor introduced us, and Myra put on a sympathetic face.

"Honestly, you never know who's next, do you?" she

said, setting cups on saucers and pouring tea. "I baked today. One of our neighbors was attacked just down the street a while ago. Sugar cookies and some lemon bars. We had a break-in here just a year ago. I get in this mood every so often, for no reason, to bake up a storm. My sister-in-law's cousin was mugged over by the Ballard Locks last October. Does anyone take lemon?"

We accepted both tea and cookies. I discovered I was starving; we hadn't yet had dinner, and it was almost seven-thirty.

"I don't think you ever met Henrietta when she worked at the clinic," Dr. Fitzgerald said to his wife.

Myra shook her head. "No, I was too busy with my guild work in those days. Now it's grandchildren. Are you sure you don't need lemon?"

"Henrietta actually worked for Dr. McFarland, didn't she?" Vida asked, after assuring our hostess that lemon was superfluous.

Dr. Fitzgerald looked grave. "Yes, that's so. He was an OB-GYN. We had other doctors in the clinic besides myself back then, an internist and two general practitioners. I was one of the GPs. Now there are eight of us, but the rest are all specialists. That's how it goes in medicine these days. No one wants to be a jack-of-all-trades."

"It's the money," Myra put in. "Specialists can charge more. Of course medical care in this country is going downhill. It's a disgrace. Say, I've got a loaf of pumpkin bread in the freezer. Should I thaw it out?"

We thanked Myra, but declined. "Dr. McFarland handled adoptions," I said. "Do you remember anything about the baby that a Mr. and Mrs. Addison got through the clinic while Henrietta was working there?"

Again, Dr. Fitzgerald pushed his glasses up on his nose. "Not particularly. Henrietta only worked at the clinic for about three years. I borrowed her a few times when my own nurse was ill or on vacation, but I really didn't know her all that well. I don't recall the Addisons. They may have gone to the other GP."

"There was something peculiar about Henrietta," Myra said. "What was it, Phil? Didn't she leave under a cloud?"

Dr. Fitzgerald frowned. "There *was* something odd about that. Of course, Dr. McFarland could be ... difficult."

"Yes," I said, "Henrietta mentioned something like that."

"She did?" Dr. Fitzgerald looked startled.

As usual, Vida was quicker on the uptake than I was. "Shocking, really. But I suppose one shouldn't be surprised."

I had no idea what she was talking about. I guessed that she didn't, either. Vida was on a fishing trip that went beyond Henrietta's complaints about Dr. Fitzgerald's tightfisted ways, including his refusal to provide medical insurance.

"It's not an uncommon problem in the medical profession," Dr. Fitzgerald said with a sigh. "So much pressure, so much stress—and the drugs are readily available. Luckily, Barney—Dr. McFarland—went through treatment not long after Henrietta left. He stayed clean for the rest of his life, as far as I know."

The account had taken an unexpected turn, one that I couldn't see helped us much as far as Carol Stokes and Henrietta Altdorf were concerned.

"I always wondered," Myra remarked, "if Henrietta wasn't blackmailing him. Maybe that was why I felt she left under a cloud. What do you really think, Phil?" She paused and waved a lemon bar. "Do you think these are too tart? I should have used more sugar, but you know what recipes are these days. Does anybody kitchen-test anymore?"

"Dubious," said Vida, who regularly complained that many of the recipes she received through the mail had to be inedible.

"Blackmail?" Dr. Fitzgerald was looking bemused. "Myra, sometimes you have a very wicked mind. I shouldn't think blackmail was involved, though. Dr. McFarland's habit was no secret at the clinic. His patients, of course, were another matter. Still . . . "

"You've always been poor at bringing home office gossip," Myra said in reproach. "All that doctor-patient confidentiality." She turned to Vida and me. "Don't you think he could at least confide in his wife?"

"I should hope so," Vida said, no doubt having in mind the thumbscrews she regularly applied to her niece Marje Blatt, who worked for Doc Dewey.

"Now I *am* curious," Myra declared. "Really, I haven't had a decent source of information since Gail Morris retired ten years ago. Whatever happened to Gail, anyway? Here," she added, passing the cookie plate. "Have some more. Next time I'm making snickerdoodles."

"I don't think Gail went anywhere." Dr. Fitzgerald chuckled. "She came into some money, as you may recall, and bought one of the first condos by the Ballard Locks. She kept working for another fifteen years, but still retired early."

"I should have kept in touch," Myra said with a shake of her head. "But that's when the grandchildren started coming. I think I'll bake chocolate-chip cookies when they come for the weekend."

Vida was making for the door in what I thought was a rather hasty fashion. "So lovely," she murmured. "So gracious of you to invite us. It's been a genuine pleasure."

I suppose I looked as surprised as the Fitzgeralds. "Must you go so soon?" Myra asked. "I was thinking about fixing ice-cream sundaes."

"It's a long drive to Alpine," Vida said. "We both have

to work tomorrow. Lovely cookies, delicious lemon bars, excellent tea. Goodbye now."

I had no choice but to make my own hurried farewell and follow Vida out the door.

"What got into you?" I asked, settling behind the wheel.

"Gail Morris," Vida replied, rapidly paging through Henrietta's old address book. "I did my arithmetic. Gail must have bought her condo at least twenty-five years ago. Henrietta ought to have her number in here. Ah! It's an SU prefix. What did that stand for?"

"Sunset," I replied. "It was mainly for Ballard."

Vida read off the address. It was another ten-minute drive. "We haven't eaten," I protested, "and you're right, it's getting late. Are you sure you want to do this?"

"We ate cookies," Vida retorted. "And yes, I feel we're getting somewhere. The Fitzgeralds weren't a complete washout."

This time I made the phone call. Gail Morris sounded intrigued by my explanation. But she was about to leave for the evening.

"What can I tell you about Henrietta?" she inquired. "Lord, I hadn't thought about her in ages. I can't believe she was murdered. I saw it on the news this evening."

"It's complicated," I said, wishing the cell phone wasn't trying to break up on me. We were parked off Twenty-fourth Avenue by Larsen's Bakery in Ballard. "Basically, I'm curious about why she quit the clinic. She told me it was a matter of money and benefits."

Gail laughed. "I guess you could say that. Lord, this isn't funny, is it? I mean, the poor woman is dead. Maybe I shouldn't say anything."

"It might help find her killer," I said. "In fact, if you know anything about her, you ought to inform the police."

"Ohh . . . I'm leaving for Europe tomorrow," Gail said. "I've always wanted to see the tulips in Holland. I

ɔn't want to get mixed up in this, but if I tell you and
ɔu feel it's pertinent, you can pass it along to the police,
ght?"

"Of course."

"Okay." Gail sighed, a sound that ended in a squawk
ven out by my phone. "Henrietta left because she was
regnant. Forty years old, unmarried at the time, re-
ɪsing an abortion because she'd been an OB-GYN
ɪrse, and many of them simply don't believe in it.
hey've spent their careers making sure babies arrive
ive. But you'd think she'd have known better than to
ɛt knocked up at her age, especially being a nurse."

I gave Vida, who was doing her best to listen in, a
ride-eyed stare. "What happened to the baby?" I asked.

"She'd already raised one kid, and didn't want to start
ver at forty-odd, particularly not on her own," Gail
ɛplied. "What else could she do? She had Dr. McFarland
ut the baby out for adoption."

Chapter Nineteen

WE HAD MORE to chew on than our dinner when w
stopped to eat at a Coco's Restaurant not far from the en
trance ramp to I-5. Unfortunately, Gail Morris hadn
worked for Dr. McFarland, but she was certain that he'
handled the adoption of Henrietta's baby. Henrietta
meanwhile, had tried to keep her condition a secre
She'd been more embarrassed than ashamed, and ha
quit the clinic in her fifth month. Gail thought the bab
was a girl, but once Henrietta left, they sort of lost touch

"I was in the middle of a divorce at the time," Gail ha
explained. "Being a buddy was something I couldn
handle. If I hadn't inherited some money, I don't knov
how I'd have raised my own two kids."

She'd never heard who had adopted Henrietta's baby
Gail didn't pay much attention to the OB-GYN side o
the clinic. She had enough to do working for Dr. Gregory
one of the other GPs. And no, she didn't recall any pa
tients named Addison.

"Is it too much to guess that Kendra was Henrietta'
child?" I ventured as our entrées arrived.

Vida looked up from her gravy-covered pork sand
wich. "Certainly not. It makes perfect—if unfortunate—
sense. But what happened to Carol's baby?"

"As you know," I said, "I asked Gail. She thought i
had been a stillborn, but she wasn't sure. Again, she wa
all caught up with her own problems back then."

"And Dr. McFarland's nurse moved away," Vida said oughtfully. "I suppose she wanted to get out of the y."

"Gail thought she'd gone to L.A.," I said dryly. nyway, she got married, and Gail didn't know her hus-nd's name. I don't think asking for 'Joan' would get us ry far with Los Angeles Directory Assistance."

"No, of course not," Vida said, still thoughtful. "This rtainly casts a different light on Carol's murder. Not to ention Henrietta's."

"We're stuck for now," I said, glancing at my watch, hich showed that it was after nine. "As it is, we won't t home until after eleven."

"We can't go home," Vida declared, her jaw set. We're going to have to spend the night again."

"Vida," I began, "that's impossible. I've missed two ys of work in the past week. I can't spend any more time this right now. We can come back over the weekend. ott is too inexperienced to put out the paper by himself, d Leo's got his hands full with the advertising."

"Then go," Vida said. "I'll stay."

"What about your section? Who's going to do House d Home?"

"I told you. It's virtually complete," she responded, oking dogged. "Besides, I've got plenty of filler and ndouts."

"That's not what your readers expect," I pointed out. You, of all people—"

Vida waved a hand. "You're forgetting Maybeth. Do u want to see her dead, too?"

"I don't know what Maybeth has to do with all this, ankly," I said. "She wrote a letter to the Addisons. A olish letter, I suspect. Now she's gone off the deep d."

"You don't know what that letter said," Vida argued. t may not have been foolish. But Maybeth is a fool for

not telling us—or the police. What we need to do now
talk with Sam Addison. And Darryl, too. How mu
would a taxicab cost to go from here to Magnolia?"

We were clear out at the county line, well beyond t
city limits. "It'd be cheaper to buy a car," I said, th
threw down my napkin. "Okay, you win. But we're n
spending the night. We'll go see Darryl—or at least yo
will. Meanwhile I'll call Kendra to get her father's pho
number and address."

Kendra was at her apartment. She actually seeme
pleased to hear from me. Since she didn't express any r
action to Henrietta's murder, I assumed she didn't kno
about it. I decided not to tell her. Not yet. The poor g
had troubles of her own, some of which she had yet
discover.

Sam Addison was living in the basement of a frien
house near Seattle Pacific University. Since SPU is locate
at the bottom of Queen Anne Hill, he was only a few mi
utes away from Darryl Lindholm's condo in Magnolia.

"I'll drop you off at Darryl's," I told Vida, "and the
go see Sam Addison. But I won't drive off until I kno
Darryl will let you in."

"He'll be surprised, but polite," Vida said blithe
"After all, I did know him when he was a boy."

Vida knew everyone in Alpine when they were boy
girls, puppies, or piglets. Feeling about ready to dr
from weariness, I took the freeway back into town, e
ited at Fiftieth Street, crossed over into Ballard one mo
time, waited for the bridge over the ship canal to go u
and then down again, zipped by the commercial fishir
fleet at the wharf, wound around the ramp to Magnoli
and finally reached Darryl's condo.

"Good luck," I said. "Just don't get him riled or I'll
picking your spare parts up from the curb."

"Nonsense," Vida said, and got out of the car.

Sure enough, Darryl let her in. I waited a few minutes to see if he'd give her the bum's rush, but nothing happened. With lingering misgivings, I drove the short distance to the address Kendra had given me for her other father. Not that either of them was her real father, I thought, at least the way things were unfolding.

The older house where Sam had moved was on a steep side street, three stories of eclectic renovation. There was a light on in the daylight basement, though the upper stories lay in darkness.

There was also a black Ford Taurus parked outside.

When I'd first seen Sam Addison what seemed like eons ago, he'd been driving a Honda. Of course there were hundreds of black Tauruses in the city; there was no reason to think that this was the one that had been following me.

Still, I hesitated. Sam Addison could have two cars. The people who lived in the rest of the house or next door or down the street might own a Taurus. After several minutes of procrastinating I steeled myself, got out of the car, and walked to the basement door.

There was no bell. I knocked and waited. No one responded. I knocked again, harder. Through the mottled glass in the door's window, I could see a large form approach. The door opened slowly, revealing a disheveled Sam Addison.

"Emma!" he cried. "Oh, my God!"

A car screeched behind me. I turned quickly to see a Yellow Cab with a turbaned driver behind the wheel. A passenger burst out of the backseat. It was Vida.

"Wait, Emma, don't go in! The killer is in there!"

Shunning his fare, the frightened cabdriver tore off down the street just as Sam Addison yanked me across the threshold and slammed the door. I could hear Vida yelling outside.

Sam's new digs had probably been a rec room. The furnishings were sparse and makeshift. It was a far cry from the beautifully decorated house on Ashworth. As Vida pounded on the door, I stared at Sam. There was a terrible gleam in his eyes and his mouth drooped at the corners. He looked as if he'd gone mad.

"Emma," he repeated, his voice now low and jagged. "You shouldn't have come here."

"I guess not," I said, swallowing hard.

Vida was screaming for somebody to open the door. I started to turn, but Sam caught me by the shoulder.

"No," he said with a frightening calm. "No more. I can't take any more. It's over."

I'd never figured Sam Addison for the killer. Maybe I could reason with him or at least stall until Vida got help. But as I tried to conjure up the right words, Kathy Addison entered through a door at the rear of the room.

"God!" she cried. "Not you! Why can't you leave me alone?" She dove at me, her hands outstretched, her fingers like talons.

Sam had released me. I ducked to one side, trying to elude Kathy. The blow that Sam sent flying struck me on the jaw. I could still hear Vida yelling as I crashed to the bare floor.

I must have been unconscious for only a few seconds. When I came to, Kathy was lying sprawled on an old tweed couch and Vida was looming over me.

"You didn't exactly miss," she was saying to Sam, "but you missed Kathy the first time. Sit down, Sam. We really ought to call the police and perhaps an ambulance."

Sam was leaning against the wall, his hands clenched on top of his bald spot. "I had to stop her," he mumbled. "She might have killed Emma."

Kathy wasn't coming around. After Vida helped me to a chair, she checked for the unconscious woman's pulse.

"She's alive," Vida said, picking up the phone from an apple crate that served as an end table. "When you hit her, she fell in such a way that she struck her head on this." She pointed to the apple crate's sharp, rough corner.

Sam slowly came over to where I was sitting. "I'm sorry, I didn't mean to knock you out, Emma. That's me all over. If Hitler and Mother Teresa were in the same room, I'd have coldcocked her instead of him."

Frankly, I was still wary of Sam. "I got in the way," I mumbled, my jaw feeling stiff. "It's okay. But I don't understand what's going on."

Vida had completed her call to 911. "I learned the truth from Darryl Lindholm," she said, sitting on the arm of the couch, "so I raced over here as soon as I could."

Sam had knelt down next to Kathy. "Did Darryl get a phone call last night, too?" he asked of Vida.

"Yes." Vida nodded. "And so, I assume, did Kathy."

"It wasn't the first one, I gather," Sam said dully. "Not for Kathy, anyway." Gently, he stroked his wife's motionless hand.

I wasn't following any of this. Maybe Sam had made scrambled eggs of my brain. "What phone calls?" I demanded, wishing my jaw moved more easily.

"From Henrietta," Vida said. "Calling Kathy, Sam, and Darryl to make threats and trouble over Kendra. Henrietta had gone 'round the bend, poor thing. Which," she added sadly, "is why Kathy killed her."

I could hear the sirens coming closer. Sam sat on the floor, his hands hanging slack between his knees.

"I'd never heard of this Altdorf woman before last night," he said. "She called out of the blue, and told me she was Kendra's real mother. I thought it was a crank and tried to hang up on her. But then she started talking about Dr. McFarland and a dead baby and how she had a right to be Kendra's real mother. It turned out that Kathy had gotten a call, too, even before last night, but she kept it to herself. Hell, when it's bad news, she usually rents a billboard."

"Henrietta also phoned Darryl," Vida said. "Poor man, he's a mess. I hated to leave him."

"Henrietta was telling the truth," I said to Sam. "Her child was substituted for the baby you and Kathy were supposed to get. You helped pay for Carol's medical care while she was pregnant, didn't you?"

"Yes," Sam replied, his voice still toneless. "We paid for her care and then for the baby. Kendra didn't come cheap. Nothing at our house was ever cheap."

The sirens were getting closer. Kathy still wasn't moving. "It was a horrible coincidence," I said. "Henrietta lived next door to Carol, and when Kendra showed up, she—Henrietta—recognized her right away. Kendra was the spitting image of Henrietta when she was young. I saw Carol's picture," I went on as the sirens stopped and Vida went to the door. "She and Kendra didn't look much alike. Kendra didn't look like Darryl Lindholm, either. He was the man who got Carol pregnant. I don't know for sure, but I'm guessing that Kendra's birth father was your wife's doctor at the clinic where Henrietta worked. McFarland's dead, too, so we may never know."

The emergency personnel filed into the basement. I half expected to recognize them, but I didn't. My sojourn in Seattle, even my brief return to Alpine, seemed to be filled with sirens and ambulances and efficient people in uniformed garb.

Vida and I got out of the way while Sam explained what had happened. The medics weren't particularly sympathetic, but didn't waste time berating him. All attention was focused on Kathy. Meanwhile the firefighters and police arrived. Hushed words were exchanged, glances thrown at Sam, at least one sent my way. I was probably being pegged as the Other Woman. They had it all wrong. The other woman was Henrietta, and she was dead.

The medics removed Kathy; the patrol officers stayed. Vida and I identified ourselves as concerned friends from out of town. They regarded us with suspicion, but didn't order us to stay put.

To my surprise, Vida insisted that we follow the ambulance to Harborview Hospital. "Sam's riding with Kathy. We should be there to see him through this. They may arrest him for assault."

"What about me?" I objected. "My jaw may be broken. Between Sam and Roy shoving and socking me around, I could use some sympathy, too."

"You can get an ice bag at the hospital," Vida said blithely as she got into the car. "Come, come, let's go. We don't want to lose sight of the ambulance."

"We already have," I announced in my perverse manner. The street was now empty of emergency vehicles, though curious neighbors milled about on the sidewalk. To further pique Vida, I didn't let on that I knew exactly where the ambulance was heading. "So you figured everything out during a five-minute chat with Darryl. I'd applaud, but I might dislocate my shoulder."

"Don't be snide," Vida retorted. "You're just angry because you couldn't see the forest for the trees. Will you please get going?"

"What did Darryl tell you?" I demanded, taking my time to start the car.

"Another blow for the poor man," Vida sighed. "Darryl never knew that Carol's baby—his baby—died until Henrietta called him last night. Carol didn't know it at the time, either. It wasn't a stillbirth. There were severe breathing complications. The baby—a boy, actually—died the day after Carol got out of the hospital. She was never informed. In fact, she had asked that she not be told anything about the baby, including its sex, so that she couldn't form any sort of attachment. Then Henrietta became obsessed, wanting Kendra all to herself. And to think I thought she was a nice woman!"

"You were wrong." My voice was tinged with spite. Still it was rare for Vida to be mistaken in her judgment of others; usually, she tended to be overly critical.

"I can guess why the fake nail was in Carol's apartment," Vida said.

"So can I. Maybeth lost it when she confronted Carol with what she'd heard through the wall when Henrietta and Carol had it out. That's why Maybeth wrote to the Addisons. She wanted to get back at Carol for stealing her boyfriend."

We were cruising along Fifteenth, past the driving range that had been built over an old garbage dump. Maybe some changes *were* for the better. "You've figured out the fabric scrap, I'm sure."

"What?" Vida seemed rattled.

"The so-called women's suiting that Kendra found," I said, at my most patronizing. "After all, you *are* the House and Home editor."

"Well, naturally . . . I suppose . . ."

"An upholstery sample," I crowed, "that Kathy dropped after she got the tell-all letter from Maybeth and came to see Carol to find out if any of it was true."

"Yes, well, certainly," Vida said, still flustered. "Are you sure we're going the right way?"

"Positive," I replied. We'd reached the turnoff to lower Queen Anne. I cut up through the west side of the hill, heading for Mercer, the crosstown street that would eventually take us to Harborview.

"You knew that Kathy was following us in the Taurus," Vida remarked, her aplomb restored.

"I do now," I said. "I mean, when I saw the Taurus parked in front of Sam's, I thought it belonged to him. I never saw the car that was parked in the Addison garage when I was in the alley waiting for you. The door was pulled down."

"Such a silly stunt," Vida remarked as we drove past the opera house and the home of Pacific Northwest Ballet. "Kathy might have known we wouldn't be scared off so easily."

"She wasn't trying to scare us," I said, turning onto Fifth Avenue and driving past the Space Needle and under the Monorail. "Kathy was desperate to know what we were up to. She may have thought we'd found out something she didn't know."

"Nonsense," Vida shot back. "If anything other than frightening us, she wanted us out of the way at the apartment house. Just about every time she followed us, we were headed in that direction. Thus she couldn't go there to have a showdown with Henrietta. We were thwarting her."

"Make up your mind," I said, turning on Denny Way to head for Capitol Hill. Thousands of darkened apartment and condo windows stared blindly out over the city. I felt a pang. I belonged there, not in a burg like Alpine, where I could count the multiple-dwelling complexes on two hands.

"Does it matter which is right?" Vida replied, bristling. "Like Henrietta, Kathy had become unhinged."

"Let's hope she's not also dead," I put in, "because only she can tell us what happened with Henrietta."

"She'll be fine," Vida responded, still testy. "A slight concussion, that's all. You'll see."

"Vida, do you always have to be *right*?"

"It's better than always being wrong," she snapped.

"Are you saying *I'm* always wrong?"

"No, of course not. But you can be very pigheaded."

"*I* can be pigheaded? And *you're* not?"

"I try to keep an open mind."

"Vida . . ."

We had reached our destination. Harborview Hospital sits on the edge of what is known as Pill Hill, overlooking downtown and Elliott Bay. It looked like a fortress in the dark, a citadel to ward off death, with a special wing to keep the mental cases away from the rest of us who refused to admit that we were crazy, too.

I pulled up at the main entrance and waited for Vida to get out of the car.

"Aren't you going to park?" she asked. "I saw a sign that said the lot was on the other side of the hospital."

"I'm not staying," I said, glancing at my watch, which indicated it was almost ten-thirty. "I'll pick you up in an hour or so. In fact, let's say midnight." Vida should have given Sam Addison all the comfort he could stand by then.

"Where are you going?" Vida demanded, half out of the Lexus.

"Never mind," I said. "By the way, I assume you know who killed Carol."

Vida leaned down to stare through the passenger window. "What?"

"Never mind," I said, and drove away. In the rearview mirror, I could see Vida shaking a fist. No doubt she was dying of curiosity, for several reasons.

She should have known where I was headed, however. There was only one place I could go, that I should go: I drove to the freeway and Kendra's apartment in the north end of the city.

Despite the late hour, there was a light on in Kendra's unit. Maybe she was with Gavin Odell and didn't want to be disturbed. But I had to disturb her, upset her, too. And all I could wonder as I climbed the wooden stairs was, Why me, Lord?

However, it appeared that Kendra was alone. She was wearing a short chenille bathrobe and the TV was on. A half-empty glass of milk sat on an end table and a bag of pretzels was on the floor next to the sofa.

I asked Kendra if she had any liquor on hand. We were both going to need it before we finished the evening's business.

Naturally, Kendra looked alarmed. "There's some wine," she said. "Gavin bought it. What is it? You look awful, Ms. Lord."

"Call me Emma. Call me Awful." I followed her into the kitchen. Kendra might have wine, but she didn't have wineglasses. I watched while she poured Merlot into two juice tumblers.

"Can you be candid with me?" I asked as we sat down in the living room.

Kendra clicked the remote to turn off the set, then stared at me. "About what?"

"About your feelings for your parents—all of them."

Kendra started to answer, then shut her mouth and shook her head. "No deal. I want to know what's happened first. Is it Mom?"

"Kathy, your adoptive mother?"

"Right." Kendra's voice was tight and there was fear in her eyes.

"She may have committed a crime," I said. "Your father—Sam—had to hit her. She's at the hospital."

Kendra had taken a gulp of wine, which caused her to make a face. "*Dad* hit *Mom*? That doesn't sound like him. What do you mean, she committed a crime?"

"She may have killed Henrietta Altdorf, the nurse who lived next door to Carol."

"*What?*" Kendra was stunned. She had to set the glass down on the end table because her hands were shaking.

"Henrietta was murdered late this morning. Did you know her?"

Kendra folded her hands in her lap. She was wearing a brave face, perhaps telling herself that I was nuts. "That older lady who was always butting in?" she said. "Yeah, I met her a couple of times. She gushed over me. I hate gush. God, is this real?"

I was seated in a big white chair across from Kendra's place on the sofa. I leaned forward, wishing I dared sit next to her and put an arm around her shoulders.

"Henrietta probably was your real mother, your birth mother. Carol Stokes's baby died a few days after he was born."

The brave look collapsed, sinking somewhere inside Kendra's lacerated heart. "No! That's a lie! My mother told me I was her daughter! My mom and dad knew she was! You're crazy!"

I shook my head. "Ask your dad. Both your dads. Of course," I continued slowly, "neither of them is your birth father. He was probably your adoptive mother's OB-GYN at the clinic that handled your adoption. That's where Henrietta was a nurse before you were born."

Tears had welled up in Kendra's eyes. "I don't get it," she said, sounding frantic. "Why did everybody lie to me?"

"They didn't know," I said. "Kathy Addison wanted a daughter, isn't that right?"

The tears were falling, but Kendra nodded. "She . . . always said . . . girls were easier . . . to raise."

"I'll admit, I don't know what would have happened if Carol Stokes had given birth to a healthy boy. But she didn't, and about the same time Henrietta had a girl. She and Dr. McFarland made the switch. I don't know if it was illegal, but there could have been problems. The Addisons had paid most of Carol's medical expenses. Dr. McFarland may have been in a bind. Not only did he probably get a nurse in his clinic pregnant, but he was a drug abuser, so he may not have been in his sane and sober mind. At any rate, the substitution was made and the adoption papers were filed with the court. Dr. McFarland had to lie. I suspect he was under tremendous pressure from Henrietta and he caved. Also, he knew how desperately your mother wanted a child after all her miscarriages. Carol's baby died after she left the hospital. She didn't know the truth, neither did your adoptive parents. You can't blame them. They didn't lie, because they never knew."

Wiping at her eyes, Kendra remained silent for a long time. I guessed that she was trying to sift through everything I'd told her. I wouldn't have blamed the poor girl if it took her a week.

"But the crime . . . ? The murder? Did I hear wrong?" she finally asked in an anguished voice.

"I don't think so," I said, wishing it were otherwise. "It seems that after Carol's death, Henrietta became obsessed. She'd seen how much you liked Carol; she wanted you to like her in the same way, as your mother. She had a son, but he rarely visited her. I suspect she'd grown lonely and bitter. You can imagine her shock when she saw you next door." I opened the photo album that I'd brought in from the car. "Look," I said, pointing to the picture of the young and pretty Henrietta, "isn't she your spitting image?"

"Oh, my God!" Kendra recoiled from the album and put her hands over her face.

"Anyway," I continued, retrieving the album, which had fallen next to the pretzels, "she began making phone calls to Darryl Lindholm, to your adoptive father, to your adoptive mother. Did she call you?"

Kendra dropped her hands. Her face was blotchy and wet with tears. "No. Why?"

"Then she must have gotten your father's number from your mother," I said.

"He has a listing," Kendra replied. "He just got a phone yesterday."

"Bad timing," I murmured. "Henrietta told all of them the truth about your birth. She may have made demands.

Money, perhaps, or simply that she be acknowledged. It sounds as if your adoptive mother went off the deep end. She'd already suffered through having you form an attachment with Carol. Now Carol was gone, but another woman had claimed you as her own. I think your mother snapped and went out to see Henrietta this morning. I also think she'd called on Carol earlier, after receiving a letter from Maybeth Swafford. Maybeth overheard Henrietta and Carol arguing about which one of them was your mother."

Kendra shuddered. "A month ago," she said, her voice dragging. "It was right after I moved out. Mom was so upset about me leaving—she thought I was too young to be on my own. I came back to the house to get some more of my stuff one afternoon just after the mail delivery. Mom was white as a sheet. I asked her what was wrong—she said that the store had made a mistake on the bill for the new drapes and that Dad would be furious if he thought she'd actually spent that much. It sounded typical, the way they fought over the house all the time, so I didn't think anything about it."

I nodded. "It was probably Maybeth's letter, which sent her rushing off to see Carol. I don't know how Carol would have handled the situation. Maybe she didn't believe what Henrietta had told her about your birth. I suspect that both Kathy and Carol would have been into denial. They may even have formed some sort of bond."

"Mom never mentioned it," Kendra said dully.

"The visit to Henrietta turned out differently," I said, speaking softly. "Either Kathy called on Henrietta more than once, or she was working at the hospital on earlier attempts. But today, everything went wrong. Henrietta must have rebuffed her, or maybe she was insulting, angry, unmoved by your mother's pleas. Whatever the cause, your mother—your adoptive mother—hit her with a bowling trophy and killed her. It may even have been

elf-defense. We'll have to wait and see when Kathy re-
ains consciousness."

Kendra was slumped against the back of the sofa.
'This is a nightmare," she said in a hoarse voice.

"I know. Your adoptive mother's at a difficult age.
ome women have terrible emotional problems during
nenopause."

Again, Kendra was silent for some time. "So she killed
Carol, too? I can't believe it. I can't believe any of it."

I shook my head. "You don't have to believe all of it. I
lon't think Kathy killed Carol."

Kendra stared at me. "Then who did?"

"Henrietta," I said, then added, "I know, because of
he dog."

Chapter Twenty

BUDWEISER HAD PLAYED his role in the murder of Carol
Stokes. While both Henrietta and Maybeth had complained about the dog, Henrietta had been the most vehement. Perhaps too vehement, because she'd made an
effort to soften her stance on Buddy by mentioning that
she thought it was cute when Ronnie had put a funny
hat on the dog. The remark had struck a false note at
the time.

Ronnie had tied Buddy up outside before he left for the
bars on the night of Carol's murder. Apparently, the police had never checked Henrietta's alibi, but I was certain
that at some point she'd left the hospital. A sixteen-hour
shift is unusual, though Henrietta mentioned something
about a nurse who didn't show up. Still, it was only a
twenty-minute round-trip from there to the apartment
building. Carol, who must have been in a foul mood after
the fight with Ronnie, may have telephoned Henrietta at
work to have it out with her. Arriving at the apartment,
Henrietta would have heard Buddy barking. The dog
drove her crazy, so she cut him loose.

"I have a feeling he was tied up with an old drapery
cord that Ronnie had taken from the Dumpster out
back," I told Kendra. "Henrietta brought it with her into
Carol's apartment. The women quarreled. Carol may
have been tough and capable of beating up on men who
didn't feel it was right to fight back, but Henrietta was a

g, strong woman. She strangled Carol, and then re-
rned to the hospital."

"Crazy," Kendra said in a small voice. "They're
crazy. And why? It's my fault. They were all fighting
er me."

"Not you, specifically," I said. "They were fighting for
e right to be a mother. The maternal instinct is very
rong, sometimes overpowering. Look at nature—a
oness or a bear or any kind of female animal will do
erything she can to protect her young."

"They weren't protecting me," Kendra protested.
They were ruining my life."

"Yes," I agreed. "I didn't say that mothers—or would-be
others—are always right. Sometimes it's the concept of
otherhood. It can be thought of as endowing a woman
ith an automatic halo. Even the very real sacrifices are
ade not so much for the child as for the martyrdom the
other achieves. Being a mom is not just about giving—
s about giving up and letting go."

Perhaps the little homily was aimed at me as much as it
as at Kendra.

"I haven't heard so much guesswork since the junior-
gh spelling bee," Vida declared the next morning on
e way back to Alpine. Our quarrel was forgotten. We
oth knew that we'd been under a terrible strain. I could
ever stay mad at Vida and, fortunately, she could never
ay mad at me. "Still," she went on, "all we can do is
uess what really happened. With Henrietta dead, there's
ot much proof, especially about Carol's murder."

"Enough to spring Ronnie, I hope." After spending the
ight at Kendra's apartment, I'd visited him that morning
efore we left Seattle. As usual, he'd been vague and un-
ertain. "At least," I said as we approached I-5, "he re-
embered that the rope he used to tie up Buddy *might*
ave been a drapery cord."

Vida rearranged herself in the passenger seat. She
ended up going home with Sam to the house on As
worth and sleeping on a handsome but uncomfortab
bed in the spare room. "Sam admitted he'd gone to s
Carol the night of the murder rather than that afte
noon," Vida said, readjusting the seat belt over her bus
"He'd been afraid that he'd be considered a suspect if
confessed he'd been there so close to the time she w
killed. Sam thought that it was Carol instead of Maybe
and Henrietta who was upsetting Kathy so badly. He ar
Carol got into an argument, of course, which is wh
Maybeth overheard."

"So Maybeth never heard Henrietta quarreling wi
Carol before the murder," I mused. "I suppose the T
was on too loud."

Vida lifted one wide shoulder in what I took for agre
ment. "After strangling Carol, Henrietta took Kendra
graduation picture off the refrigerator. Of course she'
want that. It's such a milestone in a child's life."

"And one which no parent can do without," I noted.

"Someone at the hospital surely will remember if He
rietta disappeared for half an hour or more," Vida sai
"Particularly if she got a phone call from Carol that se
her racing off."

"I hope Kathy comes out of that coma," I remarke
as some idiot cut me off in the right-hand lane of th
freeway.

"Poor Sam." Vida sighed. "Poor Kathy. Maybe it w
self-defense. Henrietta had killed before. And Darryl—
only hope that his work can help mend him. He's su
fered more than anyone."

"Except for the people who are dead," I remarke
"Kendra's had no picnic, either."

"She's young, resilient, and has some sense," Vid
replied. "At least I think she does. I'd like to think th
Maybeth will tell us what she knew now that her life's n

onger threatened. But if she was blackmailing Henrietta
or the Addisons or even Carol, she'll be afraid of the
police."

I glanced in the rearview mirror, not to see if we were
being followed, but as a symbolic farewell to the city behind us.

Vida must have read my thoughts. "I feel safer already," she declared. "This has been a terrible few days.
Typical, I suppose. So much violence."

I said nothing.

"And such an incredible coincidence," Vida went on.
"Imagine, Henrietta living next door to Carol Stokes. I
find that almost hard to believe."

"Vida," I said with a small smile, "we have coinci-
dences like that all the time in Alpine."

"That's because it's so small," she said. "Thank
goodness."

"But a city like Seattle isn't so much different in some
ways," I said. "It's really a bunch of clearly identifiable
neighborhoods tied together. Henrietta Altdorf probably
worked and lived all her life in the Ballard-Greenwood
area. She'd know all sorts of people from way back, almost like you do in Alpine. Her circle would be quite
small. Believe me, it happens all the time. I've even heard
of neighbors who lived next door to each other for years
and then found out by chance they were second cousins."

"They should have known that to begin with," Vida
asserted. "You see? Families become estranged in the
city."

Again, I didn't argue that point specifically. "Families
are strange."

Vida harrumphed, but remained silent for several minutes. We were approaching Everett and the turnoff to
Highway 2 and Stevens Pass. As I guided the car around
the big curve that led over the rich farmland of Snohomish County, Vida uttered another, bigger sigh.

"I can see the mountains," she said. "Soon we'll be in Monroe. It won't be long then. We'll be home. Emma, don't *ever* invite me to go to Seattle again."

I hadn't invited Vida; she'd invited herself. And though she'd never admit it, I knew darned well that she'd had the time of her life.

We went straight to the office. To my relief and astonishment, everything seemed to be under control. We had even added another staff member, if not someone exactly new, and only temporarily: Scott had called on Carla Steinmetz Talliaferro to help out in our absence.

"I've got plenty of time this week," Carla said. "My parents were jealous because Ryan's folks spent Easter with us, so they insisted on having the baby stay with them in Bellevue for a couple of days. The college paper is still in the works. These kids are really slow."

Carla had never been all that fast, and when she was, carelessness reigned. But I enthused anyway. "That's terrific, Carla," I said, wondering what havoc she had wreaked since returning to *The Advocate*. "Would you like to get paid in free baby-sitting?"

"Cool," Carla replied. "Ryan and I were talking about going out to dinner this weekend. Omar will be back with us by then. How's Saturday?"

I said Saturday was fine, though I planned on making a day trip to Seattle—alone—to check in with Ronnie. "I should be back by five," I told Carla.

The latest *Advocate* was on my desk. Above the fold, everything looked good. Glancing below the fold, I winced at the bold black headline:

MR. ED IS NOW A PIG

Oh, well, I thought, Mr. Ed had always been a pig. It wasn't exactly front-page news.

* * *

Because there was quite a bit of catching up to do, I was late getting home that evening. It was after seven when I trudged through the side door and realized that not only was the house dark, it was empty.

There were no toys on the floor, no TV blaring from the bedroom, no sign of Amber Ramsey and her baby. Worried, I looked everywhere for a note. Finally, I checked the front porch. It would be just like Amber to forget that I often came straight into the kitchen from the carport, especially when I was carrying items like luggage.

Sure enough, there was a note attached to the screen door.

Dear Emma, Amber had written in an awkward hand, *My dad closed the deal on the McNamara house last weekend. I forgot to tell you about it when you were here a couple of days ago. He was able to move right in, so I did, too. He bought some new furniture and the rest will come from Oregon when the family moves in later. Thanks for all your help. You've been just like a mother to Danny and me. Love, Amber.*

I thought I'd been a bitch. Well, maybe not all the time. By comparison with Amber's oddball mother and indifferent stepmother, I guess I wasn't so awful after all.

Ironically, the house felt empty, even lonely. I didn't recall that it had seemed that way before Amber and Danny moved in, certainly not since Adam had gone away to college. Bemused, I wandered from room to room, ostensibly looking for any items Amber might have forgotten. In reality, I was in search of comfort. Even the cats were gone, receiving their creature comforts from Mrs. Holmgren across the street.

The phone rang. I hurried from Amber and Danny's old room to answer it.

"Sluggly, what's up?" demanded my brother, Ben. "Where the hell have you been? Still trying to bake a cake that can hold a file? I've tasted some of your cakes, and nobody would ever notice. Why don't you try using flour instead of library paste?"

"Shut up, Stench," I shot back. "I'm exhausted and I don't need any crap from you."

Ben just laughed. Funny man, I thought grimly. Hilarious brother. Zany priest. I wanted to kick his butt.

"Ronnie didn't do it," I said, still irked. "So ha-ha on you because I found out who did."

"Wow, I'm impressed," Ben said sarcastically. "Tell me all about it."

I did, because I knew that deep down, Ben *was* impressed. He was just faint with praise. I always figured that was because he didn't want to puff me up and encourage me to vanity and other forms of sinfulness. Or maybe it was just because he was my rotten brother.

"Amazing," he finally said when I'd summed things up as succinctly as I could. "You and Vida. What a team. Tell me, how many different hats did she wear, and were any of them used as a defensive weapon?"

"I feel like I've been away off and on for weeks," I said, having wandered into the kitchen with the gypsy phone to make a hefty drink. "I still have to go back this weekend to see if Ronnie's really getting out. Honestly, Ben, I don't understand how he and his parents could be so different from the rest of us. Do you remember Uncle Gary and Aunt Marlene very well?"

"Sort of," Ben said. "They were always loud and often drunk. Sometimes I feel remiss, though. I mean, they're living in the same state as I am, and yet I've never made an effort to visit them. Of course they're at the other end of Arizona. I guess that's my excuse."

"Don't beat yourself up," I said. "You've got a full plate as it is. I'd just like to know how our dad and his sister could have turned out so totally unalike. They sure ruined Ronnie, and probably their two daughters. I suppose it was Uncle Gary's influence on Aunt Marlene."

"That's a big part of it," Ben said. "Aunt Marlene must have felt she had to live her husband's lifestyle. And of course you've got to remember that she was adopted."

"*Adopted?*" I shrieked. "I not only don't remember it, I didn't even know it. Are you kidding me?"

"No," Ben said calmly. "You really didn't know? That's weird."

"Are you sure?" I demanded, still aghast. "Where did you ever hear such a thing?"

There was a long pause. Finally, Ben spoke. "Well," he began, and I could picture him scratching his crinkled chestnut hair, "I think Dad told me when we were having one of our heart-to-heart talks before I went into the seminary. I honestly can't remember why he told me. Maybe it had something to do with charity, and how his parents had taken pity on a family they knew who couldn't afford to raise another child during the Depression. Anyway, Grandma and Grandpa took Aunt Marlene off the neighbors' hands and adopted her. I guess they'd always wanted another baby, but had had no luck."

"I'll be damned," I said, a little breathless. "Then Ronnie isn't really family after all."

Another pause, much briefer than before. "Oh, yes he is, Sluggly. We're all family, and you damned well better not forget it."

The journey, if that is what it was, had begun in memory, of a small boy tied to Ben in a sack race. Now that small boy was a grown man, seated across from me in a coffee shop several blocks away from the county-city complex where he'd been wrongfully imprisoned. Ronnie Mallett had finally won something, though I feared that his freedom could still be his undoing. Hopefully, the experience had changed him. But I was probably wrong.

"I'm pickin' up Buddy this afternoon," Ronnie said with a shy grin. "Mr. Chan is lettin' me keep the apartment. Maybeth said Buddy showed up two days ago, all hungry and lookin' kinda bad. He'll be okay, doncha think?"

"He'll be fine," I assured Ronnie. "I'm so glad Alvin got you out of jail. How do you feel?"

There was still a small bandage on Ronnie's ear. He looked pale and drawn, but otherwise he seemed all right. At least for a guy who was terrified of facing the real world.

"I'm okay," Ronnie said. "I still can't believe that that nurse killed Carol. And then Kendra's mom killed the nurse. That seems just plain wacko to me."

Kathy Addison had come out of her coma on Thursday. She had admitted striking the fatal blow to Henrietta's skull, but insisted that the victim had threatened to kill her first. It seemed that Kathy was right: a butcher knife had been found under Henrietta's body. Vida and I had never seen it, because we didn't see the corpse being taken away.

Maybe the Addisons would somehow heal themselves and be a family with Kendra again. She *was* their daughter. Some birth mothers must discard their children, for various reasons. The burden of raising them, with whatever motives, falls on the adoptive parents. We are complicated creatures, and rarely are any of our actions pure.

"Roy's takin' care of Buddy right now," Ronnie said, finishing his hamburger. "Roy's okay. Maybeth don't like Buddy, but she'd never hurt him. Can you drop me off at the apartment?"

"Of course," I said. "Do you think you'll get your old job back?"

"I hope so," Ronnie said with feeling. "Mr. Lang's a

good guy. Maybe I gave him a lot of shit. I'll try harder this time."

"That's a good idea," I said, and picked up the tab.

The last time I saw Ronnie he was running to meet Buddy outside of the apartment house in Greenwood. He embraced the dog, then stood up to wave at me.

"Hey—keep in touch, okay?" he called.

I leaned out of the car window. "I will, Ronnie. I promise."

Ronnie nodded, then picked up something and threw it about twenty feet away. Buddy ran after the object and brought it back to Ronnie. Man and dog embraced again.

I drove away, wanting to remember Ronnie as happy. After a mile or so, I realized that Ronnie *was* happy, in his own strange way. For him, happiness was a simple thing—a dog fetching a stick. For others, like me, it was more complicated. I shouldn't judge the Ronnies of this world. We were all different.

And, as Ben had reminded me, we were all the same.

Family.

MARY DAHEIM AND
EMMA LORD

MARY: **Welcome back to the Big City, Emma. You grew up here in Seattle, but you've lived in Alpine for almost ten years. I've lived in small towns twice in my life, and frankly, I had trouble adjusting. How do you manage?**

EMMA: It's attitude, Mary. When I made the decision to buy *The Alpine Advocate,* I knew it would be a long-term investment of my life, maybe even a permanent one. That made it easier for me—I knew I was going to stick around. The other thing that helped was being the local newspaper's editor and publisher. I automatically became part of everyone's life. I had an identity. But don't get me wrong—since I wasn't born in Alpine, I'll always be something of a stranger. And, yes, I definitely miss the cultural and sports activities of a big city. Weekend high school football and the St. Mildred's Christmas pageant just don't do it for me. And while they got rid of Loggerama, I don't think I can stand another year of Ed Bronsky as the Winter Solstice Parade's grand marshal. Ed should never ever wear anything diaphanous.

MARY: **I don't really want to think about that. Let's talk career paths. Like you, I always thought I had printer's ink in my veins and started out in newspapers. Then I**

discovered you had to walk a lot, so I went into P.R. What made you hang in there?

EMMA: For one thing, Mary, I don't have flat feet like you do. Maybe the real difference is that I do have printer's ink my veins. Keeping the public informed, having the power to wield some influence (though it be rather small) through my editorials, and meeting deadlines all keep me alive. There's an enormous satisfaction to producing a paper every week. You can see what you've done. You can share it with the community. You feel as if your job has some meaning in a nutty world where personal achievement is hard to find.

MARY: You also have a knack for sleuthing. How did you develop this, or is it a gift?

EMMA: Journalism is all about sleuthing. It's tracking down graft in the union pension fund, it's figuring out the rationale of timberland swaps, and sometimes it's as simple—and important—as making sure you've identified the right John Smith in an article about sexual perversion. I once made a horrendous mistake in *The Oregonian*. There were two Alan Barkers in the news. Alan L. Barker had won a prestigious poetry prize. Alan R. Barker had been arraigned for indecent exposure at Jantzen Beach. I got them mixed up, and there was all hell to pay. What made it even worse was that at the trial the Barker exhibitionist quoted Tennyson's "Some civic manhood against the crowd." The jury was bewildered.

MARY: **Speaking of sleuthing, don't you feel that the murder rate is rather high for a town the size of Alpine?**

EMMA: You mean since I arrived? I have to admit, sometimes I feel like a one-woman crime wave. But, in fact, the murder rate has risen in smaller communities over the past few years. People are increasingly transient, communication is so much faster, and while small town residents didn't used to feel the same pressures as city dwellers, that's changing quite rapidly. Also, historically, Alpine has been a lumber town. It's a rough, dangerous way to make a living. Life and death in the woods goes back five or six generations. Violence is no stranger here.

MARY: **Let's get personal, Emma. Do you ever see yourself married to Tom Cavanaugh? Or do you ever see yourself married, period?**

EMMA: That's a toughie. I've thought and thought about it, and I can't come up with a straight answer. I love Tom. I've tried not to, but you can't simply tell love to go away. I realize that maybe it's not a healthy attitude. There are practical considerations, too. I can't quite envision Tom living in Alpine. On the other hand, I can't imagine giving up *The Advocate*. Maybe what I'm really saying is that I've put my career between us, though that sounds horrid to me. I mean, newspapers are a dying breed. Ten years from now, there may be no *Advocate*. In fact, there's a radio station starting up in town. How will that affect us? Again, I don't have any cut-and-dried answers.

MARY: **What will you do if Vida Runkel, your House and Home editor, ever retires?**

EMMA: I can't even think about that! An *Advocate* without Vida would be like Alpine with no mountains. But I don't think she ever will—she's strong as a horse, and she couldn't bear not to be involved with the paper. If printer's ink runs through my veins, curiosity runs through Vida's. I'm not sure she needs a rationale to snoop, but as long as she's on the staff, she has an excuse.

MARY: **One last question—do you think that you and Milo Dodge can ever be real friends again?**

EMMA: I hope so. I actually love Milo, but not necessarily in a romantic way. I suppose I've always felt he's rather limited as a person. That's not fair—who isn't limited? But now that I see him in a new relationship, I must admit I feel jealous. Maybe *annoyed* is a better word. Or perhaps I worry about him. He's kind of vulnerable, and I don't want to see him hurt. I already did that to him, and he doesn't deserve another unappreciative woman. I do wonder, if there had never been a Tom Cavanaugh, would there have been an Emma Dodge? But that's speculation, one of the things I am good at.

MARY: **Well, keep your spirits up, Emma. And thank you for the insights.**

EMMA: I'm the one who should be thanking you.

*Don't miss any of the
Emma Lord mysteries:*

THE ALPINE ADVOCATE
The first Emma Lord novel

THE ALPINE BETRAYAL
THE ALPINE CHRISTMAS
THE ALPINE DECOY
THE ALPINE ESCAPE
THE ALPINE FURY
THE ALPINE GAMBLE
THE ALPINE HERO
THE ALPINE ICON
THE ALPINE JOURNEY
THE ALPINE KINDRED
THE ALPINE LEGACY
THE ALPINE MENACE

by

Mary Daheim

**Published by Ballantine Books
Available at your local bookstore**